Kate Noble is a national bestselling, RITA-nominated author of historical romance, including the acclaimed Blue Raven serie She has also written television for NBC and FOX, as well s the Emmy award-winning hit YouTube series *The Lizzi Bennet Diaries*. Kate lives in Los Angeles.

Keep up to date with Kate via www.katenoble.com, by follov ng her on Twitter: @NobleRorick or visiting her on Facel ok: www.facebook.com/katenoblewriter.

Praise or Kate Noble:

'Kate oble brings the delicate elements of Regency England brillia ly alive with her prose' *USA Today*

'An ex aordinary and unique romance worth savoring' *Smart Bitche Trashy Books*

'The s ry's prologue literally gave me goose bumps – goose bump hat never went away throughout the whole book. This is the ind of deep, touching read that romance fans search for' *R nantic Times*

')espit being a delight and thoroughly winning, the book i 300 ages of confirmation to what I'd suspected and now ow: he Regency belongs to Kate Noble, and it's in very, v g d hands' *All About Romance*

' en were alive and writing novels today, the result e something exactly like *Follow My Lead*, a wickedly d superbly satisfying romance' *Chicago Tribune*

' d captivating ... an outstanding and memorable *eekly* (starred review)

historical' *The Lusty Literate*

'Clever and gr

By Kate Noble

Winner Takes All Series
The Game And The Governess
The Lie And The Lady
The Dare And The Doctor

The Dare and the Doctor

KATE NOBLE

headline
ETERNAL

Published by arrangement with Pocket Books,
a division of Simon & Schuster, Inc.

First published in Great Britain in 2016
by HEADLINE ETERNAL
An imprint of HEADLINE PUBLISHING GROUP

1

Cataloguing in Publication Data is available from the British Library

ISBN 978 1 4722 2345 6

Offset in 12.21/14.10 pt Granjon LT Std by Jouve (UK)

Printed and bound in Great Britain by CPI Group (UK) Ltd, Croydon, CR0 4YY

Headline's policy is to use papers that are natural, renewable and recyclable
products and made from wood grown in well-managed forests and other
controlled sources. The logging and manufacturing processes are expected
to conform to the environmental regulations of the country of origin.

HEADLINE PUBLISHING GROUP
An Hachette UK Company
Carmelite House
50 Victoria Embankment
London EC4Y 0DZ

www.headlineeternal.com
www.headline.co.uk
www.hachette.co.uk

For my brother-in-law Andy, who, much like Rhys, is weird. And happy. And weirdly happy.

For my sister, a doctor who always has an answer when I ask, "Let's say I want to grievously injure someone . . ."

And for my friend Margaret—when I borrowed your name for a secondary character, neither you nor I ever thought I would be writing love scenes using it. So . . . that happened.

 ACKNOWLEDGMENTS

I am so grateful to everyone who helped me with this book. Thank you to my mother-in-law, Suzanne, for loving Margaret and Rhys so much she flat out convinced me they needed their own book. Thanks to my writing pals, the Shamers, who soothed and petted and caffeinated me through the long, hard process of writing the first draft. Annelise Robey is, as always, a fantastic career guide, and Abby Zidle is the most understanding editor I could hope for. And thanks go to my son, for providing daily inspiration. But the biggest thanks of all is, as always, reserved for my husband, who is endlessly supportive, even when this means he has to wait for me to finish typing before we can watch *Game of Thrones*.

1

To Dr. Gray—

Thank you very much for the pamphlet you sent on the scrub bushes of the African wilds. I am spurred to adjust my experiments to see if any of our Lincolnshire plants could be pressed to grow their roots that long out of thirst. It must be quite solitary to be a shrubbery in the desert. Have you been to Africa and witnessed them for yourself?

I am afraid not much has shifted in my world since your visit ended a few weeks ago. My father's gout is much better. Leticia—now Mrs. Turner—has settled into the mill house, and Mrs. Turner—or Helen, as I have been told to call her—is such a frequent guest at Bluestone Manor that Father has given her a room of her very own, for when she plays cribbage with him far too late.

Reading that back, I suppose a great deal has changed. Although it does not feel as if it has. It feels as if things are as they ever were, or ever were meant to be.

Oh, I nearly forgot! Something amazing has happened—the roses have gone to a third full flower this season! Lovely to have fresh blooms so late in the

*year. I think I have perfected the manure-to-lime ratio
in my fertilizing formula.*

Sincerely,
Miss Margaret Babcock

To Miss Babcock—
*I hate to disappoint you, but I have not been to
Africa. The farthest south I have been is the middle
of France, and as it was the middle of the war, I was
happy to go no further. The pamphlet comes from
another academic correspondent of mine who has been
to Africa and wrote it to present to the Horticultural
Society of London. I attended the lecture and thought
you might find it interesting as well.*

*It is good to hear about your father's gout—it was
a particularly troublesome case and gave me a devil of
a time—and that Leticia and Mr. Turner have settled
in. John has long been a friend of mine and he deserves
his happiness. But I understand what you mean about
how while everything has changed, it feels as though
nothing has. It is like when you theorize the outcome
of an experiment, and you are proven correct. Such as
when my brother comes to visit, I can easily theorize
he will ask me for money. And I will be proven correct.
Something has changed, but the result is exactly as you
knew it would be. So really, everything is the same.*

*That is excellent to hear about the third flowering. The
Horticultural Society of London has managed to shift the
color of some blooms by what minerals they put into
the soil. I wonder if you could do that with your roses.*

Yours, etc.,
Dr. Rhys Gray

Dear Dr. Gray—
I feel at times my inquiries are so numerous it is easier to address them in the form of a list.

1. *I am not disappointed you have not been to Africa. Rather, I find myself relieved you came back from the war.*

2. *"Another" academic correspondent? Does that mean I am an academic correspondent too?*

3. *I was not aware you had a brother.*

4. *The flowers that you mention that changed color based on their soil could not, I think, have been roses. They sound like hydrangeas. Depending on what food is in the soil, they can be pink or blue or white or some mixture of the above. I have never successfully changed the color of roses.*

In other news, I have taken initiative and begun the construction of a new greenhouse! This one an arid environment, as opposed to a damp one. (Yes, I was inspired by the African pamphlet.) I thought to ask Father about it, but then was advised by Leticia and Helen that, as my father tends to question expenditures, I should simply order the construction and tell him about it after.
He has yet to notice.

Sincerely,
Miss Margaret Babcock

Dear Miss Margaret—
A list should be answered in kind.

1. *Thank you most heartily. I too am glad I came back from war. It relieved me of my desire to travel, and I find myself happier and more at home in my laboratory than anywhere else.*

2. *Of course we are academic correspondents. You know more about plants than anyone else I know, and I like to know people who like to know things.*

3. *I have a brother. I actually have three. And three sisters. I'm the second of seven. But the brother in question is Daniel, and I am his elder by almost a decade. For some reason, he thinks that means I am a stodgy bore. I, in turn, think he is heedless and troublesome, but I am assured by my mother and general resemblance that we are indeed related.*

   Also, I have to admit to a little familial affection. A very little.

4. *Yes, hydrangeas! I had completely forgotten the name. To my uneducated eye, they looked fluffy. I equate fluffy with roses. I'm sorry to hear rose color is not as mutable, but if anyone can do it, I imagine it would be you.*

Mrs. Turner and Mrs. Turner both give excellent advice. I presume that your father will notice when you have African tumbleweeds growing on the east lawn?

Yours, etc.,
Rhys Gray

Rhys—

Happy Christmas! Thank you for the gift you sent with your last letter—where on earth did you find an African shrub in England?

Your gift is this stray bit of gossip from Leticia that she and John might be coming to London for a few days in the New Year to sign some papers with the bank— John has the opportunity to buy another mill to add to his growing empire. I know how you hate surprises, so should he turn up in your lab in Greenwich mid-January with a furrowed brow and an intention to disrupt your work, you'll be prepared.

Did I tell you that Miss Goodhue finally succeeded in talking me into going to the public ball in Claxby? She caught me in a sentimental mood, and she begged me to come along, saying that having a friend there would make her so much more comfortable.

So I went, and had a . . . not overly bad time. I danced with four separate gentlemen.

I was taller than all of them.

Is there a remedy for extremes in height? Slouching? Any shrinking formulas that you men of medicine have been devising?

Until such a time, I think it best if I continue spending my winter trying to graft roses. I make my own fun.

Yours, etc.—
Margaret

Dear Margaret—

Here is the leading prescription for dealing with issues of height:

—*shoulders back*

—*head high*

—*wear the tallest shoes you can find*

—*reach things on the top shelves for those poor*
   souls who are not blessed with length

*In other news, John wrote me himself and said he
and Leticia would be down here in a few weeks. We'll
see if he actually tears himself away from his mills
to make the journey. He spent so long in London,
I wonder that he would ever want to come back.
Although it does have its charms—in Greenwich I'm
just far enough away to make me wistful for it, which
is easily remedied with a few days' visit.*

*Although if you were ever to venture south, I would
make certain to become wistful for London over the
exact dates you would be there. What powers would it
take to remove you from your beloved greenhouse?*

*I admit, as winter has settled over the land, the
quiet and the cold make me enjoy the coziness of
my laboratory more and more. Holidays and their
attendant obligations have passed. This is the time for
work, for lectures and letters to write. People even seem
to have left off injuring themselves or contracting rare
illnesses, thus I have been given the freedom to putter.
I too make my own fun.*

*You might be one of the only people of my
acquaintance who knows what I mean.*

Affectionately—
Rhys

Dear Rhys—

It's spring! It's spring, it's spring, it's spring! Things have finally begun to bloom again, and my happiness abounds. Of course, I keep all that inside. It wouldn't do for anyone to see me smiling—it would no doubt cause paroxysms of shock. But thank goodness the spring has finally come and my work can begin in earnest again.

In your last letter (or was it the one before?— I swear you are so prolific in your communication that I'm receiving two a week now. Not that I'm complaining) you mentioned that your most recent lecture at the maritime hospital was on the benefit of binding a wound in a braided pattern—and I admit, I tried it on the stem of a juniper bush that had sustained injury from overenthusiastic pruning. But the branch in question remained quite healthy! Perhaps next time you can extend your lectures to flora as well as fauna.

If I attempt to graft roses again, I will use your wrapping technique. Right now, however, I am far too excited about my experiments with rose hybridization to dabble in grafting. I hybridized my mother's China rose with an English variety, and find myself in awe of the results—I've included a detailed breakdown of my hybridizing technique and my observed results, so you tell me: dare I hope the resulting shrubs will bloom all summer long?

In other news, it's been very dull here since Miss Goodhue went to London—I hope you received the rhododendron I sent with her. It's been dull here in general . . . which is not something I ever thought I would say. Usually, I enjoy the quiet. Plants don't really thrive on loud noises and chaos, you know. But for some reason, I just feel a little anxious, as if I've been still for so long that I wonder if I can move when I need to. But I know that's silly. I do things. Things outside of the greenhouse, even. I take tea with Leticia and I go into Helmsley on market days and I've been to three public balls this winter (I have yet to dance with a man taller than myself. I'm certain they exist, they just don't care to dance), but I still feel this strange sense of "what if."

Perhaps what I need is what you have—the ability to go visit excitement for a few days, and come home to work and silence, content.

I know this is a silly feeling that shall pass. I cannot imagine that I could ever be comfortable out of Helmsley and my greenhouse. But still . . . the strange notion exists.

I cannot tell you how delightful it is to have a friend who understands these things.

As always, yours—
Margaret

My dear Margaret—

Of course. I'm always here to listen to silly notions and strange feelings. After all, what are friends for?

Rhys

2

Dear Margaret—

Do you recall in my last letter I told you of a visiting lecturer coming to Greenwich? It was a Sir Kingsley, who spoke very eloquently on botany. I was so certain that you and he would be of like minds, I took the liberty of telling him about your latest experiment. He was so astounded by the progress you have made in hybridizing your rose that he said you should come to London and present it to them—did I mention Sir K—— is a member of the Horticultural Society of London?

Please don't be angry with me or think I violated a confidence. I know you prefer your greenhouse in Lincolnshire. But if you are so inclined to come to London, Margaret . . . know I will do everything in my power to make the trip worthwhile.

*A*t the age of twenty, Miss Margaret Babcock had discovered a few fundamental truths about herself.

She knew herself to be overly tall.

She knew she was most at home in her greenhouse.

She knew she was—as her mother had once termed it—a bit of a late bloomer.

When her mother had first said it, it made no sense to Margaret. She wasn't a cherry tree that exploded in white and pink in the spring. She didn't sprout or flower. She was a girl. A tall girl, true. She grew, would continue to do so until she stopped, and then would be an adult.

But then she started to notice something odd. Yes, she kept growing up, up, up . . . but the other girls in town were growing *out*. Becoming rounded like petals and their skin turning white and pink in patterns that seemed to force attention from the young men toward them. They would slide their gaze to the side like they knew something Margaret didn't, laughing lightly at a joke Margaret couldn't understand.

And Margaret just kept getting taller.

It was only when she was sixteen or so that the upward trend slowed. And she waited patiently for the outward trend to begin. And waited. And waited.

"Like I said, you're just a late bloomer," her mother had said as they repotted a ficus. "You'll catch up."

"But I'm already taller than everyone! Shouldn't they be catching up to me?"

"Margaret," her mother said, smiling. "You don't have to be in such a rush. I like you very much just as you are."

As impatient as Margaret was, she knew her mother was right. She tended to be. So she went back to humming and planting and wondering when her mind and body and everything would change, and she would be let in on the secret that all the other girls seemed to know.

And change did come. But not how anyone had pictured it. Because that winter, Margaret's mother fell ill. And the chill just wouldn't leave her.

They buried her mother in the spring, in the family plot in the back corner of the garden. Margaret planted roses beside her headstone. It was the only time she had ever seen her father cry. And suddenly, Margaret didn't want anything to change anymore.

She stayed in her greenhouse. She worked with her plants. Making things grow was what she and her mother always did.

It was strange, but watching her fruit trees and violets and roses move through their seasons was a kind of consistency. It was a pattern that could be predicted. And controlled.

But even with her head down, she noticed that as much as she wanted things to stay the same, everything around her was changing. First, her father decided to remarry and brought Leticia Churzy into their lives. She was a countess, and beautiful, and she made Margaret realize that her old skirts had become too short and that just because she blushed when she thought of certain members of the opposite sex, it didn't mean she was meant to marry them.

Just like Leticia was not meant to marry Margaret's father, as it turned out.

And then Dr. Rhys Gray came to stay with the Babcocks at Bluestone Manor for a few weeks.

A friend of Mr. Turner's, the local miller, he'd come for a visit and ended up tending to Margaret's father's gout-riddled foot.

And Margaret discovered what it was like to have a friend.

Oh, she'd become friends with Leticia—eventually—and Miss Goodhue, the schoolteacher in Helmsley, who for some unknown reason seemed happy for Margaret's companionship. But with Rhys, Margaret learned what it was to build a friendship out of shared interests and mutual understanding.

Every time she received a letter from him, her heart leapt a little as she broke the wax *G* that sealed the pages, a thrill of "yes!" running through her veins.

So when the butler brought Rhys's latest letter into the greenhouse, that same joy lifted the corners of her mouth as she used a relatively clean garden spade to break the seal.

She stared at the letter in her hands, reading it for the seventh time in as many minutes. Then she folded it up and tossed it onto her workbench.

Then snatched it up again and reread it once more, her eyes flitting to certain phrases automatically, confirming for the eighth time that they were indeed real.

. . . *your latest experiment* . . .

. . . *Horticultural Society* . . .

. . . *come to London, Margaret* . . .

"Margaret, here you are, we've been waiting for you for—*achoo!*—for tea," Leticia Churzy—now Leticia Turner—said as she poked her head around the greenhouse door.

Margaret hurriedly put the letter into the pocket of her apron.

"I'll be there in a few minutes, Leticia," she said, turning her attention back to little vines she had been potting in individual containers. "I just need to finish this."

"Well, of course your . . . green peas? They simply cannot wait," Leticia said with a slightly sardonic smile.

"No, they cannot," Margaret retorted. Rare was the

person who understood that while plants seemed unmoving and patient, in truth timing was everything. Leticia, for all her good qualities, was not one of those people. "I'm testing a new formula for my fertilizer—there's a different amount of fish guts in the soil of each of these pots. If I plant them all at different times it adds another variable to the experiment and ruins everything."

Leticia turned green around the gills at the mention of fish guts, but still came forward. "Well, you're almost done. I can keep you company while you . . . fertilize."

Margaret's mouth tipped up at the corners. "And you can make sure I don't lose track of time and make it in time for tea, correct?"

"I admit to having ulterior motives. It doesn't mean I don't enjoy your—*achoo!*—company." She gulped again. "Oh heavens, that smells."

"You must, if you're willing to brave your sensitivity to flowers to be in here," Margaret replied, smiling.

Margaret first met Leticia a year ago in this very greenhouse, and the encounter had been dramatically different. Margaret had been deeply angry to find *anyone* in her greenhouse, let alone someone professing to be her soon-to-be stepmother.

It was the first time she was forced to realize that the world had kept turning since her mother's death. That it had continued to turn for her father, Sir Barty. She had been an angry, lost girl who lashed out with her tongue and her recalcitrant nature.

Over those weeks that Leticia had been engaged to Sir Barty, Margaret had been convinced that not only was Leticia changing everything at Bluestone, she was actively trying to change Margaret. Her too-short dresses were out-of-date—made for girls in their youth, not a young woman. That she should present herself for dinner with the family. That she should take tea with the ladies in the town. That she should be a *part* of things—and Margaret had *hated* it.

It wasn't until Leticia had a pair of trousers made for Margaret to work in—the trousers she was currently wearing—that Margaret realized she wasn't trying to change her. Not in fundamentals. Just that Leticia had been trying to find her way to being her friend.

Things got much better after that. Margaret could almost be sad that Leticia had not ended up her stepmother. Almost. But seeing how happy Leticia was as the wife of Mr. Turner, and that her father had found a happy companion in Helen, Mr. Turner's widowed mother, Margaret felt everything was as it should be.

Except . . .

When the five of them sat down to meals—Leticia and Mr. Turner were often guests—it was cozy and happy, but Margaret couldn't help feeling like there was still a chair empty, next to hers.

She wondered who was meant to fill it. For a time she thought it was her mother, but now . . . she wondered if it was something else.

Maybe it wasn't that there was a chair empty, but instead that the table was too full. Maybe, she thought, there was somewhere else she was supposed to be.

Absentmindedly, she reached inside her pocket and felt for the paper—that didn't seem to be there.

"What's this?" Leticia asked, stooping to pick up the folded letter down by Margaret's feet. Drat it all, in her rush to hide the letter, she must have missed her pocket.

"Nothing," Margaret said quickly, reaching for it. Leticia, to her credit, handed it over immediately. "Just a letter. From Dr. Gray."

Leticia's look became concerned. "Is it your father's

gout again? Helen says she's encouraged him to stay away from rich sauces, but Mrs. Dillon says Cook has caught him more than once in the larder."

"No, it has nothing to do with Father," Margaret answered. And seeing Leticia's completely not-interested look of interest, she knew she had to explain. "We've been corresponding."

"Corresponding?" Leticia's eyebrow went up to the ceiling. "You've been corresponding with a man?"

"No . . . not like that. It's an academic correspondence." Oh blast, she was blushing. She once thought that if a man made her blush it meant they were meant to be together forever. But now she knew it to be an inconclusive theory, because almost *any* awkwardness made her blush. And explaining her letters with Rhys was definitely awkward.

"Academic?" Leticia repeated. "He asks about your work and such?"

"Yes," she replied. "He sent me a pamphlet on African scrub bushes once that inspired me to have the arid greenhouse built. And . . ."

Leticia blinked, waiting. "And . . ."

"And . . . well, I don't know what to do, because . . ." Margaret bit her lip, and then made a decision. "Read this, please." She held out the letter.

Leticia gingerly took the paper from her. She unfolded it, and kept her expression stoically neutral as she read.

It was a short missive, from Rhys. Sometimes he could fill up both sides of the page with writing if he had a particularly interesting experiment he wished to explain. But Leticia was done reading before Margaret could so much as plant another pea pod.

"Well, this is something, isn't it?" Leticia said, smiling. "What a marvelous opportunity."

"What is?"

"To go to London, of course. And show the Horticultural Society your . . . flowers."

"It's not just flowers, Leticia," Margaret replied impatiently. "They are hybridized reblooming roses! And there's no way I can take them to London."

She flung her hand out toward the small, meticulously cultivated rose plant that sat in its pot on the stand near the north-facing windows. Its blooms were delicate and white, and it was perhaps the most important plant in the entire greenhouse.

It was her mother's China rose. She had been quite the rosarian, and when a cultivator brought seeds back from the Far East, her father had purchased them (at an alarming price, he was always sure to mention) for her mother's birthday several years ago.

Only one of the seeds took, and grew into the potted shrubbery that sat on Margaret's windowsill that day. The China rose was not hardy like the English and European varieties, but it bloomed continually through the summer and into the fall. It had begun to flower just last month—pretty little white things with wide petals. But Margaret knew all those blooms came at a cost, and if she took the plant outside, for even a day, she risked it withering into nothing.

But she had great hopes for the children of the China rose.

They were planted in the earth right outside the north windows, where—as Margaret liked to think—the China rose could keep an eye on them. They had sprouted into tangled stems and thorns, and now the newest set of flowers was beginning to bud. She'd mated the China rose to stockier English rose varieties. For the past three years, she'd tried—and failed—to produce a rose that would bloom and be able to live outside of a conservatory . . . but this year, she might have done it.

The light pink blossoms on the bramble didn't look like much, not yet. But they had survived a late frost last month. And there were more and more buds sprouting every day.

A rose that bloomed all summer long. And could survive outside in the English climate.

She shouldn't be surprised that the Horticultural Society was interested.

"Why can you not take them to London?" Leticia asked cautiously. "It seems Dr. Gray thinks it quite the accomplishment."

"But . . . what if they don't survive the journey? They would have to be uprooted and balled. Balled, Leticia! And what if they don't have the right kind of soil or fertilizer in London? What if it's—"

"Margaret," Leticia said in that tone she'd used so often last year when she was trying to impress her stepmother wisdom on her. "There are flowers in London, so there is plenty of fertilizer and soil, I assume. And you out of anyone can keep a plant alive for a short trek south. Of all the things for you to worry about, I would not think your talent with plants would be one of them." Leticia eyed her. "So I wonder what it is about London that really concerns you."

"I . . . well, for heaven's sake, can you imagine me in London?" Margaret said, her cheeks blazing hot as she tugged on the end of her long blond braid that fell over her shoulder. "It's one thing to go to public balls in Claxby, but in London everything is so very fine, I would stick out like a . . . like a weed in a hothouse. What on earth would I do there?"

Leticia took a step forward and gently brought Margaret's hand down from worrying her braid to shreds. "Goodness, is that all?" she said, a wry smile twisting the corner of her mouth.

Margaret shot her a look of disdain for the entire three seconds she could maintain it.

"First of all, of course I can imagine you in London. I don't think you give yourself enough credit. You are a young lady of excellent family. You have been stepping out of your shell. And when you are not in your work clothes, you present yourself very well. Not like—"

Leticia stopped herself before finishing that sentence, but it was too late.

"Not like last year?" Margaret replied dryly.

As difficult as it might be to acknowledge, Margaret's dress sense had shifted for the better in the past year. Though Leticia might have wanted to hold her down and force her into petticoats of the appropriate length immediately upon their meeting, it had happened much more gradually than that.

And it happened because of her mother.

Ever since Margaret had been made aware of her late-bloomer status, she found herself a little hesitant to try anything new. To even go out into Helmsley, lest she be marked as a curiosity. But her mother knew her better and knew the one thing that would coax Margaret into the world.

She would lean down and whisper three magic words into Margaret's ear.

I dare you.

Margaret was not the kind of person to respond to something as childish as a dare. Normally she was the exact opposite. But there was something about the way her mother leaned over and met Margaret's stare with a twinkle in her eye. Then she would nudge a hair further by asking, "What's the worst that could happen?"

And Margaret knew there would be nothing to fear.

It had been years since she had heard those words. And with no one to whisper them to her, she had retreated into herself, into her greenhouse, where it was safe and everything was within her control.

But then, after Leticia's wedding to Mr. Turner, and when Helen came to sit at their dining table with such frequency, Margaret had begun to wonder if there weren't some things she had missed out on.

It started when she wandered by Mrs. Robertson's dress shop. There was a gown in the window, in a violent shade of apricot. Something about it spoke to Margaret, and had her looking down at her old faded gown that she had let the hem out of three times. She was used to clinging to the safety of that old gown. But then she caught sight of something in the window—it looked like her mother. And the twinkle in her eyes said "I dare you."

It took her a few seconds to realize that it was not her mother, but her own reflection. But the twinkle was still there. *What's the worst that could happen?*

The worst that could happen was that the apricot shade of the gown would make her look strangely ill. And that was it. She didn't buy the gown. But since she was in the store, Mrs. Robertson convinced her to look at a different material in a similar cut. And then another. And then Leticia showed up—no doubt alerted to the situation by Mrs. Robertson's shopgirl—and helped her choose another few.

Then that Sunday, Miss Goodhue, the sister of the vicar's wife, asked if she was considering going to the assembly that next week in a town over. And she caught a look at her reflection in the church window, and the twinkle in her eyes.

Then Molly, the little laundry maid who'd become Leticia's lady's maid, asked if she could practice putting up Margaret's hair, seeing as she was going to apply as a lady's maid for another local family, as it was not likely a miller's wife could afford the luxury.

There was no way Margaret could say no.

And so her long hair—usually worn in a braid down her back—was pinned up. And she went to a dance. And she sometimes took tea in Helmsley with Miss Goodhue. And she spent every Sunday after church with Leticia and Mr. Turner at the mill. And her life began to open up by just a crack.

It was terrifying.

But it was also not terrifying. All the fear she had piled onto being pointed out as something freakish and unbloomed turned out to be nothing. And as she became more comfortable in the role, she became more confident in it.

But London was still an entirely different animal.

"And as for your second question," Leticia continued, drawing Margaret's thoughts back to the present, "what would you do in London?" She smiled in that feline way she had, as if she were four steps ahead of you in the dance. "I imagine you would do whatever you wanted."

"Whatever I wanted?" Margaret asked.

"Of course. You would not be going to town for a season. Just to speak to these Horticultural Society gentlemen. So you would not need bear the social rigmarole, if you didn't wish to. But you don't need to be dancing across the *ton* to go to the opera or a play, if that was of interest. Or the gardens of Vauxhall."

Margaret's head popped up at that. The Vauxhall Pleasure Gardens certainly would be something interesting to do . . . if she had to go to London, that is.

"And if you *did* find that you wanted to attend a party or two, I'm certain we could introduce you to the right people, and you would be more than welcome at any social event."

Well, that thought killed off a bit of Margaret's enthusiasm . . . but not all of it.

"And of course, Dr. Gray will be there," Leticia said nonchalantly. She glanced back down at the letter from Rhys she still held in her hand. "From the tone of this letter, he is quite eager to make your stay a memorable one."

"Perhaps . . . perhaps a dance or two would not be so bad," Margaret mused. After all, she had been to the balls in Claxby, and they were admittedly on the right side of enjoyable. And if she could dance with Rhys, someone she knew—and had verification he was at least her height, if not a half inch or so taller—she would not disgrace herself or her father.

"Yes, you might even enjoy yourself," Leticia said, smiling. "And I imagine Rhys would enjoy himself too."

"I hope so," Margaret replied, her eyes falling to her pea pods again, so she did not notice the mischievous look in Leticia's eyes for some moments.

But then she did see it.

"No, Leticia," she said.

"No, what?" Leticia replied. "I said nothing."

"You didn't have to say anything. I can see it in your face."

"What do you think you see?"

"I think I see someone trying to conjure up a romance between two people who are merely . . . academic correspondents!"

Leticia gave her a look of supreme skepticism. "Admittedly, my experience with academic correspondence is virtually nil, but this does not sound like writing to a dusty old chemist or astronomer. He's writing to a vital young woman. Who harbored a bit of a crush on him at one point, no?"

Margaret felt her cheeks go hot. Yes, when she first met Rhys, he had caused her to blush. But ever since then, her thoughts of him were far more cerebral—or rather, far less girlish—so she decided it was just a passing fancy.

"That was a year ago; I was a full year younger. And it was of very short duration. He's been in Greenwich and I here—and we are much better as friends than otherwise."

"Friends?" Leticia's eyebrow went up. "Not academic correspondents?"

"Friends *and* academic correspondents," Margaret replied. "But here's another problem we haven't considered. If I go to London, what will I do about Father? He'll crow and rail about the expense, and having to travel . . ."

"You leave your father to me—or rather to Helen and me—and I know she will be absolutely delighted that you have been invited to town by an eligible gentleman."

"For the last time, Rhys—Dr. Gray—is my friend. That's all."

"Just friends?"

"Leticia . . ."

"All right, all right," she replied, holding up her hands in a gesture of peace. When she did, the letter slipped out of her grasp and tumbled into one of the little pots for the peas—which was freshly filled with fertilizer.

"Oh hell!" Margaret cried as she dove for the note, fishing it out. "Please don't let it be ruined."

"You're awfully worried about a letter from 'just a friend,' " Leticia said wryly.

Margaret flushed again, but this time she kept her eyes down on the pots in front of her and managed to do something she never thought possible.

She told the littlest white lie.

"You assume I'm worried about the letter, when I could just as easily be worried about my pea pods."

3

Dear Rhys—

You once wondered what it would take to get me out of my greenhouse. Well, you hit upon it: I will be coming to London in a fortnight's time.

I am as surprised as you. You have Leticia to thank for convincing me—and for convincing my father. Although he did not take as much persuasion as I expected. I had some odd notion of the entire affair throwing him into spasms—and it did, at first. But he was quickly reminded (by me) that I'm not going down to partake in the delights of the season, and he would not need to buy the full new wardrobe that comes with it. Then he was positively delighted to discover that Leticia had her husband write to his friend Lord Ashby—a friend of yours as well—and they happily agreed to host us while we are there. I am told the gardens at his London house are suitable for my needs.

And yes, I said "we." Leticia and Mr. Turner will be escorting me, as Mr. Turner is _finally_ going to speak with the banks about acquiring that new mill. Helen *will be staying with my father—to assuage him in his loneliness, she explained.*

Reading back the previous sentence made me realize you might think it contains sarcasm—and it might have, had not my father taken me aside after dinner tonight and asked me if I had everything I needed for the journey and was all right traveling so far. He said he would come down with me if I wanted.

I suppose that's his way of saying he'll miss me.

I know I will miss him as well, but I'll be home before he really notices I'm gone—considering he still has yet to notice the second greenhouse.

So, barring any change of plans or large felled trees across the road, we will be on Lord Ashby's doorstep on the ninth. I dare to hope to see you shortly thereafter. The nervous feeling in the pit of my stomach would calm upon seeing a friendly face, I'm sure.

Your friend—
Margaret

*I*t was not an exaggeration to say that Dr. Rhys Gray was elated to receive Margaret Babcock's latest letter. A letter from Lincolnshire always made him smile, but this time he knew its importance and rushed to open it—and as soon as he had, he hurried over to Ned's house first thing and confirmed the good news.

"Yes, John wrote that he and Leticia are coming down," Ned answered, blinking in surprise. "But what are you doing here? You never come to town without giving me warning."

"Rhys, how lovely to see you!" The light voice floated down from the staircase, followed quickly by a gentle but firm, "No, don't grab that! No touch."

"Good afternoon, Phoebe. Good afternoon, little Rhys." Rhys smiled at the six-month-old child wiggling in his mother's arms.

"His name's not Rhys," Ned said sardonically. "It's Edward."

"It's Edward John Rhys Granville, and I choose to ignore the first two names." Rhys smiled as Phoebe snickered. "Besides, don't you think he looks more like a Rhys than an Eddie?"

"Over my dead body," Ned said darkly, but then laughed and kissed the top of his boy's head. "But you still haven't told me what you're doing here—is it the royal duke again? Or the Earl of Liverpool this time?"

"Don't be ridiculous, darling," Phoebe said. "He's here because of our impending guests."

"Yes, John and Leticia," Ned said. "I just told him. But—"

"Not John and Leticia," Phoebe replied. "Miss Babcock."

"Who's Miss Babcock?" Ned said, turning to Rhys.

"Good lord, did we read the same letter?" Phoebe rolled her eyes. "Miss Babcock is the young lady they are bringing with them. She's quite the horticulturalist, and she's coming down to present a shrubbery of some kind to the Horticultural Society."

"Oh yes!" Ned cried. "Now I remember. But what does that have to do with Rhys?"

"Because Rhys is the one who contacted the society on her behalf."

"Rhys is also the one who is standing right here," he interjected, rolling his eyes. "Miss Babcock and I have been corresponding since last year—"

"You have?" Phoebe's eyebrow went up.

"On topics of academic interest, yes. I keep up a number of correspondences like that. Ned can confirm."

Ned shrugged. "It's true. If you want to know something random and obscure, chances are Rhys is in correspondence with someone who will have the answer."

"Anyway," Phoebe replied, "we are to host Miss Babcock as well as John and Leticia, and Rhys is here to . . . well, I'm not entirely certain why. Only that it has more to do with Miss Babcock than with John."

"Yes, well . . . it has to do with them both, actually," Rhys said, feeling oddly flustered. "I wanted to invite myself over to dinner when they arrived. Welcome them to town, as it were. Heaven knows it will be difficult, traveling from Greenwich every day, but—"

"Of course we'll have your room ready for you, Rhys, don't doubt it," Ned said, his attention taken by the baby's sudden fascination with pulling his father's ear.

"Excellent," Rhys said upon receiving the invitation he had been angling for. "I'm much obliged. And I should mention, Miss Babcock will need a place to work with her plants."

"We have the conservatory off the garden; we never really go in there . . . it's a bit of a mess, I hate to say," Ned said. "Our old gardener had been here before even my uncle took on the earldom—when he retired a year ago, we never really replaced him. But as long as Miss Babcock doesn't mind . . ."

"Ned, forget the conservatory. He can't stay here!" Phoebe said. "Not if we are chaperoning Miss Babcock!"

"Wait—we're chaperoning her now? I thought we were just hosting them—"

"That's what hosting means, when it's a young girl of marriageable age."

"Er—not to quibble, but Miss Babcock and I have stayed

under the same roof before," Rhys offered, confused. "At her home in Lincolnshire I was a guest of her father—"

"That was in Lincolnshire," Phoebe said with a kind of pity for the thick male mind. "This is London, which eats gossip and breathes scandal. And her father is not going to be here to protect her. It's up to us."

"Protecting her from Rhys?" Ned asked. "Why on earth would we need to protect her from Rhys?"

"My thoughts precisely," Rhys added.

Phoebe sent her husband a pointed look. And as Ned remained his usual oblivious self, Rhys was the only one who caught it.

"I assure you, there is no need for such strict adherence to the rules," Rhys said. "I have no such intentions toward Miss Babcock, nor she me."

"Really?" Phoebe asked, her eyebrow skyward. "Have you asked her as much?"

"I don't need to ask her—we're friends, for heaven's sake," he replied.

"It sounds more like you are protecting Rhys from Miss Babcock than the reverse," Ned replied dryly.

"I'm protecting everyone," Phoebe said. "And you are invited to dinner and tea and even breakfast every single day our guests are here, but you shall have to put up elsewhere. On that score, my foot is down."

"And a delightfully dainty foot it is," Ned added, then turned to Rhys. "I apologize, my friend, but I must defer to the lady of the house."

"You have become much wiser since you married."

"It's earned wisdom." Ned nudged his wife's side. She nudged him back, interrupting the baby from gumming his mother's shoulder, causing a short wail.

"Come along my darling," Phoebe said to the baby. "Let's go find a nice toy to chew on, not mama's pretty dress."

Once Phoebe left, Ned turned to Rhys.

"I'm sorry about that, but I have a feeling she'll be proved right," he said, shaking his head.

"I understand. I think it ridiculous, but I understand," Rhys acknowledged.

"But where will you put up? It's the full swing of the season. I have to think the Carlyle is fully booked—"

"No matter," Rhys replied. "I suppose I'll have to put up at my house."

"Of course there's the British Hotel in Jermyn Street— wait, what do you mean, 'your house'?"

"Well, my family's house in town," Rhys said, rubbing his chin. "Come to think of it, it's just a few streets over— practically around the corner."

"You've had a house in town this entire time?" Ned asked, incredulous. "I've been putting you up for years!"

"It's been empty for ages," Rhys replied. "My family doesn't come to town anymore. And for me to open it up for just a day or two here and there is preposterous. Wasteful, even."

"So I get to bear your expenses? Do you know how much you eat?"

Rhys just grinned at Ned and slapped him on the back. "No, but keep a tally when I come over for dinner tonight; I'm deeply curious."

"You're leaving?" Ned asked. "Where are you going now?"

"Your guests will be here in less than a week, by my calculations, and I have a house to open up. It's a great deal of work. I imagine that come this evening I will be exceptionally famished."

So it was that Rhys went two streets over into Berkeley Square and found himself on the front steps of the London residence of the family Gray. It was the first time he had been there in years. And for the first time in years, he was actually not ill at ease to be so.

No, what was making his stomach so unsettled was why Lady Ashby had felt the need to banish him here.

It was the most laughable thing—the idea that he and Margaret Babcock would be anything other than friends. Good friends, but friends still. When they first met, a year ago in Lincolnshire, Margaret had been such a shy thing, more than happy to hole up in the greenhouse and keep to herself. As Rhys also liked keeping to himself, they naturally gravitated toward each other. And they very happily kept to themselves side by side, working in Margaret's greenhouse, or writing notes. The companionable silence was exactly that—companionable.

And while there might have been a moment or two when he'd suspected Margaret might have felt more than her demeanor let on, he'd never encouraged it. She was sweet and kind, and perhaps a time or two he had caught sight of her in a sunbeam, looking prettier than he suspected she knew . . .

But he had at least a decade on the girl! Such a notion was absurd. And obviously, any sentiment on her side must have passed, for her letters never hinted at any such feelings. Instead, they talked intensely of flowers and what he was lecturing on.

So the fact that Phoebe had put her foot down before she had even seen him and Margaret together was preposterous. And showed a distinct lack of trust, he thought, miffed.

But then again . . . Phoebe Granville was one of the most levelheaded people of his acquaintance—she'd have to be, to steady such a rocky ship as Ned. So if she said that society would frown upon them both staying with the Earl of Ashby, then that would almost certainly be the case.

And it would not be fair to Margaret for her first trip to London to be edged with gossip and whispers.

No, he thought as he knocked on the door of his family's townhouse, that would not be fair at all.

He waited. And waited.

Someone should be there. The townhouse had a housekeeper and butler who stayed with the property, even though it had been unoccupied by the family for some time.

Gingerly he tested the doorknob. And felt his blood run cold when he discovered it was unlocked.

"Hello?" he called as he ducked his head in. He searched his memory for the name of the old family retainer who had been keeping the townhouse during its dormancy. "Mrs. . . . er, Watson?"

There was no answer from Mrs. Watson. And as Rhys made his way through the foyer, he began to worry that something terrible had occurred to the poor woman.

The entire house was in disarray. The furniture that hadn't been touched in years had the covers thrown back, everything set at odd angles. One chair in the hall was overturned, a vase broken on the floor . . . a candlestick on the floor with red wax spilled across the black-and-white tiles—a grisly effect, even for a doctor used to carnage.

And as he peeked into the drawing room, he could see the remains of a fire smoking in the grate.

"Mrs. Watson?" he tried again as he picked up the candlestick. Good enough weight for a weapon, if necessary. "It's Dr. Gray . . . and I have a weapon. And a number of friends just outside the door. Friends . . . from my army days."

Hell, it could be true. Ned was only a few blocks away. And while he may not have been engaged in active combat, Rhys had been as close to the front lines as any solider and he knew how to fight.

A long, large couch had been pulled in front of the fire, the white cloth that had covered it for the past eight years askew, and as he leaned over the back and looked down, he saw it was covering something.

Or someone.

His entire body tensed. He held the candlestick aloft.

"Mrs. Watson?" Rhys said one last time before he whipped the cover back.

"Goddamn it to hell, why is there so much light?" came the pained cry from the young man curling into a ball on the sofa. A young man with sandy-colored hair and green eyes similar to his own.

"Daniel?" Rhys said. "What the hell are you doing here?"

"Rhys?" his little brother croaked out, a bloodshot eye peeking through fingers. "Can you shut the curtains? I've a splitting head."

"The curtains aren't even open," Rhys replied. "You're sitting in a darkened room with a sheet over your head."

"And you're holding a candlestick and interrogating me like I'm an intruder!"

Rhys looked up and noticed that yes, he was still holding the candlestick aloft. He swiftly lowered it, placed it on the floor.

"You are practically an intruder. What on earth are you doing here?"

"This is my house," Daniel said, shooting him a look as he forced himself to sit up. "Our house."

"Yes, but you're supposed to be at Cambridge."

"Not at all—was sent down."

"Bloody hell," Rhys groaned, coming around the couch to face his brother. "What did you do now?"

"Nothing, and that was the problem," Daniel replied, flashing him a grin . . . then cringing. "Most schools seem to expect effort and work from the matriculating."

"So you came to London?" Rhys said as he pushed the couch into its proper place. "And what . . . decided to destroy the house?"

"What? No!" Daniel cried. He looked up, and for the first time seemed to notice the carnage that surrounded him. "Oh, that."

"Yes, that."

"I met up with a friend—you know Haverford? He's down from Cambridge too, although for doing too much up there, not too little. Last night he introduced me to some of his mates, we went to a club, and then another place . . ." He patted his pockets, searching for something. "I remember playing faro. I remember losing at faro."

"You're lucky they dragged you home, else you would have lost the shirt off your back too." Rhys patted Daniel on the shoulder. The movement might not have been an intelligent one, as the jostling caused Daniel to turn a rather green shade.

"Oh hell," Rhys grumbled as he jumped to his feet, looking for the bell pull, and of course, not finding it. "You need some water. Mrs. Watson!"

"Don't yell," Daniel moaned. "Yelling makes it worse."

"Where is Mrs. Watson?" Rhys said. "And . . . what's the butler's name? Darrow?"

Daniel, his pallor slowly returning to just pale instead of verdant, blinked a few times. "What day is it, Sunday? If it's Sunday I imagine Mrs. Watson went to church and then has her half day off. If it's not Sunday, then I've been drunk longer than I thought."

"It's Sunday."

"Well, I suppose that's a blessing, then."

That at least would explain why the place had not yet been cleaned. Although if Rhys had Mrs. Watson's command, he would force Daniel into scraping up his own spilled wax. That might make him appreciate the advantages of studying up at Cambridge.

But that was something his mother would never hear of. Not for one of her "darling" children.

Rhys had had the good fortune to never be darling.

The thought of his mother made him want to shove his head in his hands.

"I've going to have to drag you home to Somerset, aren't I?" Rhys said. "Mother will be absolutely livid when she finds out you've been sent down."

Daniel let out a scoff of laughter.

"She will," Rhys replied, adamant. "And more to the point, she'll be livid with me. Not you."

"Rhys, don't you know?" Daniel said through his laughter.

Bewildered, Rhys just shook his head.

"Why do you think I'm here? Mama said if I was to be down from Cambridge I might as well keep going down and open up the house for us."

Something settled over Rhys's body. Something cold, and something very, very sharp. Like the feeling he used to have when he stepped out of his medical tent on the battlefield.

"Us."

"Yes. We're all coming to town. Mama, Delilah, Jubilee, Benji . . . even Eloisa. She's been visiting from Scotland for however long. Said she'd rather come to London than go back to McTiernan." Daniel rolled his shoulders back, his color returning to his cheeks. It seemed that youth was the best weapon against the effects of drink, and he was feeling much more steady. "Darrow should be off at the hiring hall, getting a full new staff."

"But Mother doesn't come to town," Rhys said, his jaw tight. "Not since Father."

"According to Mama, that will soon be in the past."

That cold sensation that had been running over Rhys's body soon found its way to his chest, and held there. Waiting.

Waiting for what he knew was coming.

"Why?" he asked.

"Because Sylvia Morton is out of mourning," Daniel said, a half-cocked grin on his face. "And she's coming to London for the rest of the season."

Rhys sank onto the couch. Suddenly he was the one feeling rather green.

"It's time, Rhys," his brother said, rising to his feet. "Time for you to do as you promised and finally get married."

4

I simply do not understand why we have to go so very slowly," Leticia grumbled, for the fourth time in as many hours. "This carriage is very well sprung."

"I'm sorry," Margaret said, also for the fourth time in as many hours. "But the rose plants are at a very delicate stage. I simply cannot have them overly jostled."

"Then let them be—*achoo!*—not overly jostled in the servants' carriage. They can arrive after we do."

"Leticia, the plants are the reason we are going. They come first."

Leticia sniffled, but put up no further argument. To be fair to her traveling companion, it had been a very trying morning. They had left Helmsley early, for what should have been an easy two-day journey. But being cooped up in a carriage with four recently dug-up rose plants and Margaret's mother's potted China rose had not been kind to her nose and eyes, both of which were red and running. Margaret felt briefly guilty, but she was not about to let her hybrid roses and their parent out of her sight on the journey. She needed to be on hand if they started to look a little dry or fallen. She had to make certain they still received sunshine and nourishment. A sharp turn here or a rut on the road there, and the plants could fall over and do irreparable damage to themselves.

Traveling hundreds of miles south was very precarious for something that usually stayed rooted in the ground.

"Why do we have a second carriage at all?" Margaret said. "We are only staying a few weeks, and my trunk would fit up on the back of the carriage."

"Yes, the trunk you packed would," Leticia agreed. "But the other trunks I had Molly pack, and Molly herself, would not fit."

Margaret rolled her eyes. When Leticia had seen what Margaret meant to pack, she had shot one look to Helen, and then very kindly but very firmly told Molly to go pack a full wardrobe for London. Molly had nodded quickly, and then rushed off to find another, much larger trunk.

Why on earth would she need more than three day dresses, one evening gown in case they went out, and her work clothes? And poor Molly! Why should she be forced to come on the journey? Perhaps she might want her hair done properly for when she met with Sir Kingsley from the Horticultural Society, but other than that it would be a very dull few weeks for a lady's maid whose mistress was adamantly *not* partaking in the season. No one would notice her dress or hair, because no one would be noticing *her*.

But on this matter, she decided it was best to stay silent. Leticia had set forth her decree, and had Helen on her side. And for her part, Molly did not seem at all beleaguered to be making the journey—in fact, she practically skipped when she heard the news.

Margaret had learned over the past year that it was sometimes easier to let Leticia do as she determined and just follow along in her wake. At least she was able to have her roses in the carriage with her. On that point Margaret had been adamant, and Leticia had been forced to give ground.

"*Achoo!*"

Although it was currently a rather miserable ground.

"Margaret, dearest, I'm afraid I—*achoo!*—cannot endure—*achoo!*"

"Driver, pull over!" Margaret said, rapping on the ceiling of the carriage, and they came to an easy stop.

Leticia flung open the door of the carriage, only to be met by her husband, John Turner, riding alongside on horseback. "What is it? What's wrong?" he asked, perplexed.

"Nothing, we just needed a little air," Margaret replied, as a violently sneezing Leticia practically ran out of the carriage—right into a cow pasture.

Which was something Leticia only noticed once her foot stepped into something decidedly squishy.

"Oh, excellent," Leticia said once she stopped sneezing. "From the frying pan into the fire."

"On the bright side, you're not sneezing," her husband said, coming down from his horse.

"Yes," Margaret added as she disembarked, then reached into the carriage. "Thankfully we were right by a cow pasture that has already been mostly grazed."

"And very recently too," Leticia grumbled, and rolled her shoulders back. "When the second carriage comes by, I'll get a new set of stockings and shoes out of my trunk."

"Er . . . the second carriage is past us, love," John replied. "I told them to go on, and arrange for us to luncheon at the next posting house—it's about ten miles or so along. We were going so slowly—"

"Margaret, what are you doing?" Leticia said.

"If we are going to stop, I'd like the rose plants to get

some proper sun. It's the perfect time of day," she said as she hauled her rose plants out, one by one.

"But there's a posting house only ten miles—" John began.

"A posting house full of dirt and people and horses? Goodness, no. Imagine if something happened to them!" Margaret said. "Cook made me some cheese sandwiches before we left, if you'd like one."

John looked to his wife. "The plants come first."

Leticia sighed. "Or, I suppose we could stop here. In a cow pasture. On the side of the road. Well, this is quite the auspicious beginning to our trip to London. Imagine what else will be in store!"

And so Margaret and Leticia and John Turner all arrived in London after some of the most anxious, sneeze-inducing travel anyone had ever experienced. A journey that should have been an easy two days of travel was stretched to three to accommodate the slow pace of the carriage and the necessary midday stop to allow Leticia a chance to breathe and the roses full sun. The only bright side to this delay was that by the time they arrived on the front steps of the Earl of Ashby's Grosvenor address, the luggage carriage had been there for several hours, and they were unpacked and settled before they even set foot into the house.

"John!" Lord Ashby cried as he came bounding down the large marble staircase in the foyer of the house. John bent to a bow, but was stopped and caught up in his friend's bear hug.

"Ned," John said, his voice little more than a squeak. "Good to see you. I'd like to breathe now."

But Lord Ashby didn't let him go for some moments. Finally, a soft voice behind him said, "Darling, if you want your friends to stay with us and not in the hospital, you might want to let Mr. Turner go now."

"Hm? Oh, yes. Sorry," Lord Ashby said, releasing his friend, but grinning without any of the remorse he just expressed.

"My lady," John said, turning to the lovely woman with pale blond hair and sparkling eyes who could only be Lady Ashby. "An absolute pleasure to see you again."

He bowed over Lady Ashby's hand, and she laughed as her husband broke in with, "Enough of that! Get a beautiful woman of your own."

"Funnily enough, I did." And John turned to offer his hand to Leticia, pulling her forward.

For the first time, Leticia looked a little nervous. She had started becoming agitated once they hit the city limits. And while her sneezing calmed down once they were in the city atmosphere—and Margaret had obligingly covered the plants lightly with a linen to ease them into the change of air—her anxiety rose sharply.

And now, as she stood face-to-face with the Earl of Ashby and his wife, she took two deep breaths, rolled her shoulders back again, and stepped forward.

Even Margaret, who was often accused of not paying attention to human interactions, knew why—because Leticia had not seen Lord Ashby nor his wife since two summers ago, when Leticia had been Lady Churzy, the widow of an Austrian count, and Lady Ashby has been nobody but Miss Phoebe Baker, a governess in Leticia's sister's household.

Margaret didn't know all the details, but she knew that Lord Ashby had switched places with his secretary, John Turner, each pretending to be the other for a fortnight as they visited a small town called Hollyhock. Some kind of wager, apparently. And while there, Lord Ashby met Miss Baker, and Leticia met John.

Since Lord Ashby really was Lord Ashby, he was able to marry Miss Baker without any delay, but the scandal of a countess falling for a commoner like John Turner was something that had sent Leticia running. It had taken a very long time for John to overcome the lie he had told and to win Leticia back.

And now they all stood in the foyer of Lord Ashby's home, staring at one another.

There was an awkwardness more acute than Margaret had ever felt. And Margaret was well acquainted with awkwardness.

"My lady," Leticia said, dipping to a curtsy. "You are looking very well."

"As are you, my—I mean, Mrs. Turner," Lady Ashby said, a fine blush spreading over her face.

And then they stood there.

For seemingly ever.

"Er, I realize this is all very strange," Margaret said after far too long. "But I need to get the roses out of the carriage, so perhaps . . . ?"

Everyone seemed to break out of their strained silence with utter relief. "Oh, of course! Margaret, allow us to introduce you to our hosts, Lord and Lady Ashby."

"Ned, Phoebe," said John, "this is Margaret Babcock."

Margaret stepped forward—or rather, was pulled into the fray by a visibly relieved Leticia—and gave her own bow. A rather neat one too, she thought, happy to know she had not disgraced herself first thing upon meeting new people.

"Miss Babcock," Lady Ashby said, coming forward to take her hand. "Welcome to London. We are so happy that you have all come—and that you have made it in good time for dinner. I will have a note sent over to Rhys at once."

"Rhys?" Margaret said, her voice strangely warbly. "Er, I mean, Dr. Gray? He's coming in from Greenwich?"

"No, he's right around the corner, at his own home!"

Lady Ashby said with a sly look to Leticia. "He's been here since he received your letter saying you're coming. And he said he wished to be notified at once upon your arrival."

Leticia's eyebrow went up as she sent a similar look back to Lady Ashby. "Wonderful. We'll have just enough time to clean up and get settled before he arrives."

"No . . . I mean, I'm not ready," Margaret said, a strange nervousness shooting over her skin. "I . . . I have to get the roses settled before I get settled."

"Of course," Lady Ashby said. "In fact, we can set dinner back a half hour easily."

"We can?" Margaret asked. "Lady Ashby, I would not want to—"

"Nonsense, we keep town hours here," Lord Ashby chimed in. "People, roses, everyone will be happily ensconced in no time. Chalmers!" he called out, and a short but very straight-backed butler appeared out of nowhere. "Show Miss Margaret to the conservatory, and have footmen fetch her plants—"

"Very carefully!"

"Very carefully—and bring them there."

Chalmers nodded, and with a snap of his fingers, footmen whooshed in from another room and a few whispered words later, disappeared again, presumably out to the carriage.

Then Chalmers bowed, murmuring, "This way, miss," and led her down a long hallway.

It all happened so quickly Margaret could barely hear Lady Ashby as she moved down the hall.

"I was under the impression Miss Babcock would have been more excited to see Rhys."

"She is," Leticia said. "More excited than she even knows."

"I think . . ." Lady Ashby said thoughtfully, "that you should call me Phoebe."

"Leticia. I think you and I are going to work very well together."

Margaret wanted to scoff. But she couldn't because she was in a new place, and didn't really know where she was going, and didn't want to get off on the wrong foot. But honestly, even for someone as generally obtuse as she knew herself to be, she could tell what Leticia and Lady Ashby—Phoebe—were thinking.

And beyond being utterly preposterous, their presumption was starting to become a bit annoying. She knew exactly her level of excitement at seeing Rhys, thank you very much!

After all, she hadn't thought about Rhys at all during the journey down. She was too worried about her roses—which was as it should be. Let flights of fancy be left to her maid, Molly. And when her mind did wander for a moment or two, Rhys did not cause any excitement or nervousness to be launched upon her person. Rather, she felt relieved to know he would be there. An easy comfort, not a blush-inducing, nerve-racking sensation. That's what they wanted from her—that's what they wanted her to feel. But honestly, she didn't.

Except . . .

Well, except when she was told Rhys would be here for dinner, what on earth was that strange queasiness?

Nothing, she decided as she followed Chalmers around the corner and through a door into the conservatory. Nothing but concern for her roses.

And once she got them positioned properly in the soil and watered and fed, she would be able to turn her attention to—

"What on earth is this?"

Margaret's jaw dropped as she stepped through the French doors and into the light-filled room that was the conservatory. But light was the only thing that filled it.

"It's the conservatory, miss," Chalmers said with a deep, gravelly tone.

There were no workbenches. No pots for replanting. No plants! If one didn't count the withered palm in one corner by an unused settee and a Madonna lily in a glazed Chinese bowl that had lost most of its petals.

"Lord Ashby and his predecessor never had much use for this space. And Lady Ashby's concentration has been elsewhere—the nursery and upstairs rooms."

"How on earth am I supposed to work in here?" she said, her voice echoing off the walls.

She should have brought her own spades and trowels. Hell, she should have brought her own watering can!

For a brief moment she was completely overcome with despair. This was absolutely terrible. The entire trip to London would prove worthless if she could not work with her plants while she was here. Why, she would be a laughingstock!

And while she might not care too much about how she was perceived by society, she cared very much how the Horticultural Society saw her. How Rhys saw her.

Rhys. That strange nervousness filled her stomach again, for the second time in five minutes.

He had vouched for her. He had sung her praises to men of learning. If he thought she had not been truthful about her work in her letters . . .

She would never receive another letter from him.

And that would be just horrible.

Then the moment of panic slipped away as one clear thought came to the front of her mind.

What would her mother say about this situation?

Look at the positive, her mother's voice rang in her ear.

There is no positive, she almost snorted.

Come now. I dare you. She felt a small smile play over her face. *What's the worst that could happen?*

All right, then. The positive. She took a deep breath and looked around with new eyes.

Well. The room was of good size, at least. It had excellent light, thanks to the east- and south-facing windows that lined two sides. There was another pair of French doors out into the garden, so she could open them up for fresh air as often as necessary.

It wasn't so bad. The things that couldn't be changed were exactly what she needed. And the things that could be changed . . .

"Miss, if you tell me what is needed, I will have the gardener provide it for you. And if there is something he does not have, it will be procured." Chalmers spoke in the soothing manner of a lifelong servant.

Margaret gave a small laugh. "There's a gardener, and the potted palm looks like that?"

Chalmers could only sigh and shrug. "He's relatively new to the trade, I'm afraid. Until a few weeks ago, Frederick was a footman. I don't think he knows that the plants inside the house fall under his purview as well."

Margaret took a deep breath and peered out one of the large windows to the small garden behind the townhouse.

At least this "gardener" was not a complete idiot. The lawn was healthy and well trimmed. The cherry tree that shaded the grass was in full fruit, and the crown imperials planted along the garden wall were tall and strong . . . if placed badly to receive appropriate sun.

Although it would be the perfect place for some rose bushes.

Margaret flung open the doors that led from the conservatory to the gardens. "Mr. Chalmers," she said, "if you would be so good as to grab that potted palm."

"Miss?"

"First thing, we are going to move it outside. So it will be under the gardener's purview and might actually get some water and food every now and again."

While he did so, Margaret went over to the Madonna lily. This one she would repot herself—in a vessel with some drainage, she decided, shaking her head.

Chalmers coughed. "Miss Babcock, what do you require?"

She needed her trousers, or at least an apron.

She needed trowels. Pots, troughs. Water, preferably on hand, although she doubted there was a well in the back garden of a London townhouse. She needed worktables, a clock. Paper to make charts of the sunlight and how it moved through the room.

She needed seeds and cuttings, and to move the crown imperials to make way for her roses.

It was time to get to work. Dinner, she was afraid, would have to be pushed back more than a half hour.

"I need dirt," she said, rolling up her sleeves. "Lots of dirt."

5

$\mathcal{D}$inner was planned for seven. Rhys was ready to walk the six and a half minutes over to Ned's house by ten minutes past six. He did not adhere to the town's blasé attitude toward appointments. At times it seemed like he and the Almack's patronesses were the only ones in London who had possession of a clock.

Hence one of the many reasons he enjoyed living in Greenwich.

But nor did he want to be too early. He knew it would be utterly unseemly if he were to disturb his friends before they were ready to receive him, especially after long days of travel.

So if he were to walk around the block twice, surely he wouldn't be *egregiously* early.

"Where are you going?" his brother's voice came from behind him. Rhys turned away from the front door. Daniel was on the main staircase, yawning.

"Did you just wake up?" Rhys asked.

"No, I woke up around noon," Daniel replied. "Then I was bored so I decided to go back to sleep."

"You could read, study . . . bathe," Rhys replied, eyeing his brother's rumpled form.

But Daniel just waved his hand dismissively. "I'll have a bath before I go out later. Haverford's got a friend at the opera—said they'd introduce us to the opera dancers."

"Then a bath is an absolute must. Before and after."

"Want to come along? You're due for some fun." Daniel grinned.

"Catching the clap is not my idea of fun, but you go along. I'm having dinner with Ashby and some friends."

"Are you sure?" his brother offered again. "It's the last night before we have to be upstanding citizens. Mama arrives in the morning."

"I am aware," Rhys grumbled. And it was the last thing he wanted to think about. Darrow and Mrs. Watson had welcomed him with open arms and a visible relief. They had been madly running around the house, preparing it for the rest of the Grays to descend. Rhys had been the person they turned to for answers, for expenses, for direction.

Daniel slept through most of it.

"I will be back after dinner. Not too late," he said, this time opening the front door and not letting anything, not even the footman he saw crossing the street heading toward their steps, stop him.

"I'll be back exceptionally late," Daniel called out as the door closed on him.

The moment he stepped outside, all idea of walking around the block twice to kill time flew away, and Rhys felt like he could breathe again. Not only that, he let his pace quicken.

It wasn't that he did not love his family—he did, rather dearly—it was just that . . . he could not be comfortable with them. Ever since his father had left . . . he ground his teeth thinking about it. See, they weren't even here yet, and already he was on edge.

But now he was finally going to where he was able to be comfortable again. In the bosom of his friends and their warm—and sane—families. And of course, Margaret would be there too.

At that thought, his feet moved faster than ever.

Not that he was excited—oh no. At least, not beyond the bounds of what was completely normal for seeing a good friend after a year.

He was on Ned's doorstep before he knew it and stepped through the door before Chalmers even had a chance to open it all the way.

"Hello, Chalmers—I know I'm a touch early, but I didn't think anyone would mind."

"Sir, did you not—"

"Rhys? Oh blast, Phoebe will have my head." Ned's voice came from the open door to his study. His head came around the door. "Didn't you get our note?"

"No," Rhys said, only slightly guilty when remembering the footman wearing Ned's livery that he'd passed on his way out the door. "I'm afraid I didn't."

"Dinner's delayed, my good man. There's apparently a bit of a hullabaloo in the conservatory."

"Is everything all right?" he asked, immediately alert.

"Relax, it's not an emergency—not a medical one, anyway," Ned said, ushering Rhys into the study and pouring him a drink from the sideboard. "Miss Babcock felt it necessary to see her plants settled, and the conservatory was sadly lacking in equipment."

"I told you she would need a place to work," Rhys said, his brow coming down. "Did you not—"

"Darling, Leticia is lying down, a sudden headache."

Phoebe rounded the door and almost bumped into Rhys. "Oh! Goodness—Rhys, did you not get our note?"

"Apparently not," Ned said.

"Phoebe, is Leticia quite well?" Rhys said, his eyes flying to the stairs. "Should I . . ."

"No, no," Phoebe said, leaning up to kiss his cheek by way of greeting. "She's just overly tired. The travel finally caught up with her, and apparently spending three days in close quarters with Miss Babcock's plants wreaked havoc. A quick lie-down before we eat will have her to rights. John is with her."

"Yes," Ned said. "I'm sure a quick lie-down will have them both to rights," and he added an "*Oof!*" as his wife kicked him in the shin.

"So, dinner is delayed, then?" Rhys asked. "Should I come back later?"

"No! You're here now, so perhaps you can talk some sense into Miss Babcock," Ned grumbled.

"Ned . . ." his wife said with warning.

"But I'm hungry . . ." Ned pouted, and earned a pitying smile from Phoebe.

"It's completely our fault," Phoebe said. "We didn't think about what Miss Babcock would need—we thought she would be happy to arrange the room tomorrow."

"Well, no wonder," Rhys said. "Her entire purpose in being here is to present her plants to the Horticultural Society. Phoebe, what would it have been like if the nursery was not done when you gave birth to little Rhys?"

"I would have been frantic," Phoebe said, and, turning to her husband, added, "And more to the point, dearest, you would have too."

Ned looked a little ashamed, but before he could say more than a "Well, I suppose—" the lady in question appeared in the doorway.

"Lord Ashby, do you have any horse manu— Oh."

Margaret Babcock came bursting through the door with all the subtlety of a battering ram. And Rhys had to reach out and steady her before she rammed into him.

He caught her arms, and was immediately nose to smudged nose with her.

"Rhys!" she said, her soft blue eyes lighting up.

"Margaret," he replied, conscious of a grin coming over his features. "How wonderful to see you!"

And it was. Wonderful. Although, not in the sense that it was full of wonder. He was not completely undone at the sight of his young friend. Rather, he was slowly aware that there was a nice warm sensation from his hand being on her arm. A very pleasant sense of comfort.

They stood that way for a few moments. And it was Margaret who remembered herself first, blinking and looking away before taking a step back, putting the appropriate amount of space between them.

"Rhys—I mean Dr. Gray. I apologize, I'm . . ." A hand flew to her reddening cheek. "I'm such a mess."

"You are?" he said, glancing down at her outfit. She was still in a traveling dress, but someone had given her an apron to throw over it, so the dirt and muck that seemed to be caked up to her elbows and across her knees was somewhat contained. There were smudges of earth across both cheeks, and yes, even on her nose. Her long blond hair was coming out of her braid, sticking out from her head like she had been electrified.

Pretty much like every other time he had seen her working in her greenhouse.

"I suppose you are," he added with a shrug. "But no matter, I've seen you dirt covered before."

"Yes, but . . ." She blushed again.

"But perhaps not in London?" Phoebe offered.

Rhys whipped his head around. Goodness, he'd almost forgotten they had an audience. And the way they were looking at him, they were overly invested in the show.

At least, Phoebe was. Ned was distracted by the gurgles from his stomach.

"Pardon me," Ned said. "My stomach is making itself known."

"I'm so sorry, Lord Ashby. I would not have you delay dinner any further," Margaret said.

"Oh good!" Ned cried. "Are you ready to eat, then?"

"No, but please, eat without me. I can scrounge something later."

Ned threw up his hands while Phoebe threw a look to Rhys.

"Margaret," Rhys said with a smile. "There will be no scrounging. Not on such an occasion."

"But I have so much to do . . . and the gardener barely knows where the trowels are kept."

"The boy is new, and I had no notion things were in such a state," Phoebe said, her cheeks turning pink. "I am mortified."

"Oh no!" Margaret said, herself turning pink. "I do not mean to mortify you. I just . . . Oh bollocks, I'm making such a hash of it, aren't I?"

"Possibly, but your language is spot-on," Ned said, laughing. Which only had the unfortunate effect of making Margaret blush harder.

"I'm sorry, I'll just . . . I'll clean up. We can have dinner now," Margaret said, folding her arms over her apron, doing her damnedest to hide.

"No," Rhys said.

"No?" Ned whined.

"No—I find that I'm not hungry just yet, and must work up my appetite. Margaret, what's left to do in the conservatory?"

"I . . . I need to move some of the furniture around a bit. But I can ask Chalmers if there is someone who can help—"

"Nonsense. Chalmers and the others are busy preparing for dinner, I am sure. Show me what needs to be done and we will do it," Rhys said, taking off his coat and rolling up his sleeves before Margaret could protest or Ned could complain.

Then, with a hand at Margaret's back, a light push had them heading for the study's door. Rhys called over his shoulder, "We'll have it done in half the time together. A third of it, if Ned would let his head rule him as much as his stomach."

"Oh hang it, I'll be right behind—" Ned said, only to be interrupted by his wife.

"Ned would be absolute bollocks at it, to use Miss Babcock's term," Phoebe said. "But you two have fun! And we will see you at dinner—sooner, rather than later."

"I'm so glad you're here," Margaret whispered as they made their way down the hall. "I knew I was going to make a muck of something. I'd only hoped to keep my true self hidden for a few days, and let them think I was normal."

"You made a muck of nothing. And do me one favor for the rest of your trip," he said, pulling her to a gentle stop, forcing her eyes to meet his in the dim light of the hall. "Don't ever keep your true self hidden. It would be devastating, if to no one other than myself and your plants."

And as her face split into a smile, and a soft laugh escaped her lips, that warm, easy feeling spread across Rhys's chest again. A simple happiness, and he realized it was because he was, for the first time in a week, where he wanted to be.

DINNER WAS SERVED forty-five minutes after Rhys's arrival. A touch later than Ned would have liked, but his wife had Cook bring up a plate of cold cheeses to appease his stomach and he was much happier after that.

Rhys and Margaret made good time with moving the furniture, and then, after a lengthy debate, decided that the actual planting of the rose shrubberies would be best done in the morning, as they would have the full day to take root and not be subject to the potential of frost.

The fact that it was the middle of June meant little to Margaret on this score. However, it did mean that she was able to run upstairs and wash the dirt off before throwing on a new dress. And once Molly had held her down and forced a brush through her long hair and rebraided it simply, Leticia deemed her presentable enough for dinner.

Thankfully, dinner was a delightful affair. The difficulties and delays were quickly forgotten, as old friends laughed over old stories and showed their new spouses and academic correspondents just what they were like when they were rowdy young men stuck in a muddy field camp on the Continent.

"I did not! I absolutely did not lose that bet!" Ned had cried, his stomach now full of both roast bird and wine. "Stuart Thorndike was the one who lost and had to run into that stream with only his boots on."

"Yes, Thorndike was the one who lost," John said. "But for the life of me I still don't know why you followed suit."

"Because Thorndike was our fellow soldier," Ned said blithely. "Where he goes, we should follow."

"You followed him right into a fever that had you both bedridden and annoying me for three days," Rhys added.

"And that was when you taught me all the names for the bones of the human body. See, I know how to find a silver lining to every cloud."

"And what use had knowing all the names for the bones of the human body ever been to an earl?" John asked.

"It's come in more handy than you might think," Phoebe said, sipping her wine.

A brief pause filled the air before the entire room burst into laughter.

And while Margaret didn't quite know why everyone found that funny, she was having such a marvelous time that laughing along seemed like the only thing to do.

"So, Margaret," Rhys said, turning to her from his seat at her left. "While we are waiting for Sir Kingsley to name the day and time of his visit, what would you like to do?"

"I think I should like to start some cuttings. And there's a ficus in the garden that needs reviving—"

"I think Dr. Gray means, what would you like to do in London?" Leticia said from Margaret's other side.

"These are all things I would be doing while in London," Margaret replied, confused. And then, as everyone burst out in laughter again, Margaret blushed with realization. "You mean, what London things would I like to do?"

"Yes, dear. Like the opera. Or Astley's Amphitheater," Leticia supplied.

"There's the Davenport Ball!" Phoebe added. "We have just been invited, and I'm certain the Davenports will extend the invitation to our guests."

"Oh . . ." Margaret said, uncertain. "I suppose that would be nice—"

"There's also Vauxhall Gardens," Leticia interrupted.

"Vauxhall," Margaret replied immediately.

"Yes, the gardens are a delight, and must be seen," Phoebe said, nodding. "Especially at night."

"Can we go now?" Margaret asked. "After dinner?"

"It's far too late to plan an outing for tonight," Leticia said, shaking her head. "But what about tomorrow? Dr. Gray?"

"Hm?" Rhys looked past Margaret to Leticia.

"Are you available tomorrow evening to come with us to Vauxhall?"

"Oh. Yes, of course," he replied. "Nothing would delight me more."

"Famous!" Phoebe cried. "Ned will get a box for supper, and we'll all go. What a merry party we'll be, won't we, darling?"

"Brilliant," Ned said as he took another bite of roast. "Marvelous."

THE FOLLOWING MORNING, Margaret was dressed in her work trousers and up for breakfast with the sun and had her entire day planned out in her head before she'd sat down at the table. It would go thusly:

—She would consume her kippers and eggs at a leisurely pace, because apparently no one in London was awake before ten and she had oodles of time at her disposal.

—She might even peruse the paper! She didn't care much for the gossip pages, but if there were any articles about the Corn Laws, she tended to find those interesting.

—Continue work in the conservatory, and take Frederick, the young gardener, in hand and teach him how to properly aerate a root ball. The boy badly wanted training.

—Finally plant the hybrid roses, and pray for a temperate next few weeks.

—Give the Madonna lily a little attention—for all its wilted posture, it was full of pollen and ready for fertilization. Then the ficus. Then the palm. Then gather up the rest of the plants in the house and save them from their inevitable bad endings.

—Luncheon, assuming the rest of the house was awake.

—Begin some cuttings to be planted in the hedgerow. The best thank-you she could possibly give Lord and Lady Ashby was a thriving garden. Of that, she knew both her mother and Leticia would approve.

—Find horse manure and fish heads, and begin making fertilizer compound.

—About this time, Molly would force her inside to change for their evening at Vauxhall.

—Vauxhall with Rhys . . . And everyone else, of course.

But almost as soon as she had thrown on her apron and shown Frederick the appropriate way to dig up crown imperial bulbs, her well-laid-out plan was utterly thwarted.

"Margaret, what on earth are you doing?" Leticia said as she came through the conservatory doors to the garden.

"Planting my roses," Margaret answered. It was possible Leticia couldn't see Margaret's actions, what with her eyes already watering.

"For heaven's sake, there's no time for that! Phoebe has made us an appointment with her dressmaker."

Margaret almost rolled her eyes. "I have dresses, Leticia. You made me pack a dozen of them."

"Yes, but we would be remiss if we did not at least go and see that the dresses you have are in the current style."

"They were made six months ago!"

"Yes, and perhaps they are appropriate for winters in Lincolnshire, but what if the fashion is now for short sleeves? How would you get on at Vauxhall tonight?"

"I imagine I would survive being warmer than everyone else," Margaret grumbled, thankful that only Frederick snorted with laughter.

She shot him a look. "Shouldn't you be collecting those fish heads from Cook right about now?"

Frederick turned a dull red, and with the posture of a child chastised by his favorite teacher, slunk off to the kitchens in search of fish heads.

"My dear," Leticia said as she approached, in a soft and concerned voice that told Margaret she was about to be subject to levels of persuasion unseen since the late King George was persuaded to give up the American colonies. "I had thought you might enjoy going. This is an opportunity to become a bit more comfortable in town, before you officially go out tonight."

"I'm not 'officially' coming out, or . . . going out. I thought Vauxhall was just Vauxhall."

"It is! But still, you will be seen. Of course, if you don't want to . . ." Leticia shrugged.

All Margaret had to do was look at her friend's expression of adamant weariness to realize she had no hope of following the rest of her plans for the day.

"I have to get these roses planted," she said. "We can go when I'm finished."

"Excellent!" Leticia's face lit up immediately. "But be finished and ready to leave in an hour's time. This will be ever so much fun!"

It turned out to be no one's idea of fun. Oh, it wasn't bad, per se, and once Margaret even found herself wondering if a moss-green dress would do with her complexion. Also, it was discovered that shorter, fatter sleeves were the fashion, but since Margaret was so tall, it was also decided they made her look like a tree. Therefore, between the dressmaker and Leticia, they chose a gown with short, tight sleeves and a wrapped bodice that gave her a more generous figure than her parents had thought to.

But while Leticia was conferring with the dressmaker, and Margaret mentally composed a list of what she needed to get done *tomorrow*, the little bell at the door jingled. Two ladies entered, wearing bonnets overladen with fruit.

They browsed the neatly stacked bolts of fabric as they chatted, waiting for the dressmaker to become available, when one of the two—the one with lemons on her head— suddenly gasped. She whispered something to the one wearing cherries.

". . . the woman . . . Lady Churzy."

". . . Churzy, but you don't mean . . ."

". . . total scandal. Now married to a merchant or some such thing, back to her station . . ."

Then they realized they had an audience. While Leticia had stilled when she heard their words, she kept her face toward the dressmaker, ostensibly continuing her conversation. Margaret, meanwhile, could not help but stare openly at them.

Lemon Hat turned a mottled shade and grabbed her friend by the arm, then pulled her out the door. Just like that, the door jingled again, and they were gone.

"Leticia," Margaret asked carefully, as the suddenly stiff

dressmaker put forward the bill for the gown they'd ordered. "Are you all right?"

"Absolutely delightful," she said, turning a smile toward Margaret—who did her best to not notice that Leticia appeared a little ill. "That was nothing worth worrying about."

But it seemed like it was something worth worrying about—because that evening, as Margaret made her way down the stairs to meet everyone, it was to find that Leticia was not to join them.

Margaret was not wearing the new gown they had just purchased—that one needed several inches added to the hem, among other adjustments. Instead she was wearing a light green gown she had worn to the dances in Claxby, and if her sleeves were a shade too long, no doubt her height would make up for it.

She fully expected to be the last one down the stairs—the way Molly had been poring over every strand of her hair had Margaret eyeing the mantel clock in her bedroom more than once. Instead, she only found John, Rhys, and Lord Ashby. And oddly, only Lord Ashby and Rhys were dressed to go out.

"I'm afraid my wife is feeling a little under the weather," John said to Ned and Rhys. "I think it only prudent I stay with her."

"Do you need to avail yourself of my services?" Rhys asked, concerned.

"Perhaps later," John said, a shadow clouding his eyes. "Right now I think she just wants to be waited on by me."

"And I'm afraid that I cannot attend either," Phoebe said, her voice coming from behind Margaret on the stairs. "Little Edward is a bit fussy. Nanny is having no luck with him, so I must stay."

"Then I suppose I must stay as well," Ned replied with a confused look down at his evening kit.

"Perhaps it would be best if we rescheduled—" Rhys said, but Phoebe cut him off.

"No!" she said, with enough force to move every pair of eyes to her. "Erm, I mean, Ned, you went to the trouble of booking the box, and Miss Babcock is so looking forward to it."

Margaret chanced a glance at Rhys. She had been looking forward to it, although with a strange feeling of . . . unknowing. Usually she would want to know everything about Vauxhall Gardens before she went there, and be able to point out things she had learned. But nowhere did "reading about Vauxhall" make it onto her list of things to do today. For some reason, this outing had a sense of discovery about it.

And that, she realized as her eyes met Rhys's, was what she had looked forward to.

But she had manners, and occasionally the foresight of when to employ them.

"It's quite all right, Lady Ashby," she murmured. "I'm sure we can go another time."

"*No*," Phoebe said again, with even more force. "Ned, there's no reason for you to stay. You three should go to Vauxhall. Besides," she said in an offhand manner, "there can be no doubt that Rhys and Miss Babcock are well chaperoned with you present."

"I don't believe I require a chaperone," Rhys drawled, but was met with Lady Ashby's dangerous look.

"Have a marvelous time," she smiled at everyone brightly. "Ned, a word before you go?"

As Lord Ashby trotted up the steps, conferring with his wife, Margaret and Rhys were left alone together.

"This will certainly be an adventure," Rhys said. "Two recluses and an earl morose over his wife not being there navigating the darkened winding pathways of London's most famous pleasure gardens. We'll need a map and a guide to find our way out."

She studied his face. "Why are you so sad?" she asked, forcing his eyes up to hers.

"You think I'm sad?"

"You tried to make a joke, but the smile didn't quite reach your eyes. And your voice . . ."

"I'm sorry," he said, sighing out a long breath. "I've had a bit of a day."

"Why?"

"My family has decided to come to town," he replied.

"Oh . . ." she said. "All of them?"

"Not Father, of course—nor Francis, my elder brother." He shrugged. "But everyone else. They arrived this morning."

"I see," she said, not really seeing anything. He'd alluded to certain feelings about his family in his letters, but she thought he felt about them the way she felt about hers. Often exasperated, somewhat bewildered, but ultimately loving. And vice versa.

She never suspected anything that would have put that look in his eyes.

"But I'm not sad," he said, his green eyes returning to their normal clear brightness. "Not now, at least. I'm endlessly happy to be with you, and not my family."

She blushed, and an awkward silence descended for three full seconds.

"Can we talk about something else?" Rhys asked. "How was your day? Did the roses make it into the ground?"

"Yes, but I was pulled away to go dress shopping before I could crush any fish heads for my fertilizer."

He bit back a laugh.

"I wasn't joking."

"I know. That's what makes it all the more delightful," Rhys replied. "And you look lovely, by the way."

"Oh, this is not the new dress. This is one of my dresses from home and I am assured that the sleeves are all wrong."

He guffawed. Then his expression grew serious. "Margaret, you look lovely. You know that, don't you?"

Margaret stood, rooted to the spot. She could feel her toes inside of her slippers, pressing into the floor, the same way she could the very furthest tips of her fingers. There was something about the way Rhys looked at her and the words that floated between them that made every inch of Margaret's body aware of something she had never even suspected.

Tonight was important. The gardens. Dr. Gray. Everything before tonight would be before. Everything after would be after.

"Now, what do you think?" he asked. "Will we be able to give our erstwhile chaperon the slip and have a lovely evening strolling the garden grounds?"

She felt a small smile play about her face. She was certain that a sparkle had affixed itself to the corner of her eye. And in the distance of her mind, she heard a whisper.

I dare you.

"Are we ready?" Lord Ashby's voice boomed as he galloped back down the steps. "Shall we be off to Vauxhall?"

Margaret spared one last twinkling glance at Rhys.

"Yes," she said. "We shall."

6

"One used to have to take a ferry across the river to go to Vauxhall," Rhys said as the carriage made its way across the Thames. Margaret turned back from the window, the sunset framing her head like a halo. Unfortunately, moving as quickly as she did meant her eyes did not have time to adjust properly, because as she did her nose collided with his chin.

"Oh!" she cried, recoiling, her hands going to her nose. "I'm sorry!"

"No, I'm sorry!" Rhys replied. "Are you all right? Let me see."

His medical training had him moving his hands to her face before he realized what he was doing might be improper ... if it was anyone other than Margaret, of course. And he was anyone other than a doctor.

Gingerly he touched the bridge of her nose, and she flinched.

"Did that hurt?"

"No," she replied softly. "Not really."

"It doesn't look broken," he said, keeping his eyes on her nose. "Just a surprise, I suspect."

"A surprise for you too, I don't wonder," she said, and he realized he'd begun to rub his chin absentmindedly.

"I'm fine," he said, grinning. "But we missed the rest of the sunset."

Her head whipped back to the window. The carriage had clattered beyond the bridge, hiding the sunset behind buildings.

"Well, that's a pity." She sighed. "At least there will be another one tomorrow. Although not over the river. Too bad we can't take a ferry anymore and enjoy it."

"I agree completely. I enjoy a good boat ride. In fact, it's how I get here from Greenwich."

"Really? By boat?"

"A nice little yacht. It's a few hours' trip. Far more pleasant to cruise than it is rocking about in a closed carriage."

"That sounds delightful." Margaret sighed wistfully.

"It's horrid," Ned said.

Rhys had almost forgotten his friend was there, playing the strident watchman of Margaret Babcock's virtue. Although he was more like the drowsy chaperon, having pulled his top hat low over his eyes and sitting there in sullen silence as they drove along.

"It is not horrid," Rhys assured.

"It is when the river smells like a sewer," Ned grumbled.

"For heaven's sake, it smelled *slightly* fishy the one time you deigned to visit me six years ago," Rhys replied. "The truth is you hate boats."

"People were meant to be on land." Ned lifted the brim of his hat just enough to peek out one eye. "Miss Babcock agrees with me, don't you, Miss Babcock?"

"I'm afraid I cannot," she said, turning red at being put on the spot. "I have a feeling I'd like sailing. Although I've never been. But I'm not one to rule it out because of lack of experience."

Rhys inwardly cheered, while Ned outwardly harrumphed. "Brilliant. Marvelous. First my wife says I have to babysit you two and not be with my actual baby, and of course you both gang up against me. Why oh why can't I be where I want to be?"

"Complain all you like," Rhys said. "I'm exactly where I wish to be."

And he was. If he couldn't be up the river at Greenwich, it felt damn good to be in a close carriage with friends on his way to an enjoyable evening, leaving his troubles behind him.

His troubles, which took the form of two brothers, three sisters, a nephew, a mother, and a dog older than dirt, all of whom had arrived on the doorstep of Berkeley Square just after breakfast.

"Rhys, my love!" Lady Constance Gray had cried as she burst through the door, practically knocking the stoic Mrs. Watson over in her determination to get to her second eldest son. "I'm so glad! When Daniel wrote to say you were already here my heart nearly burst. But of course you would be, I told him. Rhys has always been the best of my children and knows exactly what to do."

His mother had attacked him with fluttering embraces, pulling him to her overruffled bosom.

"Of course Rhys is the best of your children," the sharp voice came from behind his mother's ruffles. "The rest of us merely try to keep our heads up in his wake."

His sister Eloisa swanned into the foyer, looking every inch the fashionable *ton* lady. Which, considering she lived in Scotland, seemed somewhat incongruent.

"Eloisa," Rhys said, accepting her light embrace. "I see you've been shopping."

"This old thing?" She ran her hand over the bold blue pelisse and smart, sleek hat. "Heavens no—I will be spending my husband's money on Bond Street starting tomorrow."

"I take it Lachlan isn't joining us?" he replied.

Eloisa's expression became hard. "Lachlan can go sit on a caber, for all he cares about me. About us."

"What about Pa?" said the redheaded urchin in short pants as he ran up and clung to Eloisa's leg, ruining her perfect London image.

"Nothing, sweetheart," Eloisa said, painting a smile on her face. "Shall we go find your room? Won't that be fun?"

But the boy didn't move at his mother's prompting. Instead he sucked on his finger and stared at the stranger in the room.

"Never mind him, darling. That's just Uncle Rhys," Eloisa said as she picked up her son and floated past him to the staircase. "Barely worth notice."

"You're my uncle?" the boy asked.

"Yes," Rhys replied, curt.

"How come I dinna know you?" The boy had a disconcerting Scottish accent, which made his mother's nose wrinkle.

"Because you live up in Scotland, and I live down here."

The boy seemed to contemplate that for longer than Eloisa had patience.

"Rory, come along. Uncle Rhys will be here when we get back . . . one hopes."

"Now, where is Daniel?" his mother had asked, drawing attention back to her—where she preferred it. "Still in bed, I suspect."

"Still out from the night before," Rhys replied, and watched his mother blanch. Then, true to form, she swallowed it.

"Oh well, he'll be home soon no doubt. Young men do such things."

"I never did."

"Daniel takes after his father." She shrugged. "And me. Why let petty things like the sun and time rule us?"

Rhys sighed, knowing full well that there was no answer he could give that would turn his mother into . . . more of a mother. Lady Constance Gray may have borne seven children, but to Rhys's memory, that was the extent of her parenting.

"Rhys!" someone squealed as she navigated a growing maze of trunks being placed in the foyer by footman after footman. A warm body slammed against his in an enthusiastic hug.

"Delilah?" Rhys had to ask. Granted, it had been almost a year since he had last been home to his family's estate in Suffolk, but he did not remember his little sister being this . . . not little. The last time he had seen Delilah, she had not yet worn her hair up. Nor had she worn gowns that were cut in a way that showed body parts to an advantage that made brothers squeamish.

"Please tell me you are talking some sense into Mama!" the dark-haired Delilah cried after having thrown herself against her brother. She looked up at him with big wet eyes and a pout so perfect he was certain it had to have been practiced in the mirror. "She says I cannot come out even though I *am* eighteen and we *are* in London and it just makes the most sense of anything."

"Good lord, girl, you know you cannot come out yet!" his mother snapped. "Not until this business with the Mortons is cleared up. Then you can make your debut with no stain upon you, and you'll have them all eating out of your hand, just like Eloisa did."

However, patience was not Delilah's strongest virtue.

"But, Mama," Delilah whined prettily. "Just one ball? I'm an excellent dancer—or would be if I ever got to dance with someone other than Benji."

As if at the sound of his name, a gangly twelve-year-old Benjamin came whizzing through the room.

"Hullo, Rhys!" he said as he raced past, taking the stairs two at once. "G'bye, Rhys! C'mon, Gus."

And an ancient, snarling, three-legged mutt ceased snarling at Rhys and, limping up the stairs, followed his young master.

"Don't mind him," came his youngest sister's voice. Jubilee Gray stood next to him, appearing like a ghost. And as pale as one too. To be expected of course, considering the inaptly named girl's propensity to lock herself in her room either writing or reading poetry. She had a sheaf of papers under one arm and her spectacles sliding down her nose. Of all his siblings, Jubilee was the most like him—practical and unruffled by his family's general chaos.

Unfortunately, she tended to get lost in their wake because of it. Half the time he was convinced his mother plain forgot the girl was there.

"Don't mind either of them, actually. Benji has a bee in his bonnet to see if his window faces the street—the better with which to drop puddings on people, I imagine." She sighed in her flat monotone as Rhys buffeted her shoulder. "And Gus hates anyone who doesn't have a ready supply of puddings."

"I am aware of Gus's predilections," Rhys replied. "But Benji's are new. Getting into trouble these days, is he?"

"You know us Grays. It's encouraged."

"Now, Rhys." His mother, who had been giving detailed and incomprehensible orders to Mrs. Watson, came back over. "I— Oh, Jubilee, there you are. You might want to step aside, the footmen are going to be bringing the bathing tub in."

"Bathing tub?" Rhys asked as Jubilee ghosted away again to parts unknown. "This house has bathing tubs."

"I know, but if memory serves, they are ever so small. I like a little room to relax, so I had the one brought over from Suffolk. Now, what do you think about the drawing room for my portrait?"

"Your portrait?" A cold sense of dread swelled in Rhys's stomach. "You don't mean the, ah, *nude* portrait?"

"Of course, darling," she said breathily. "I was quite the artist's muse, you know. He went mad with grief when your father saw it and fell madly for me . . ."

Rhys refrained from rolling his eyes. He knew this story all to well (although he was not certain how much he trusted his mother's version, considering the date on the picture was after his parents' marriage). And he was familiar with the portrait in question. God knows he'd seen it far too often than was healthy for a growing boy.

"You cannot hang that in the drawing room—where people come to call."

"Don't be such a prude, darling," she scoffed. "You're a doctor, you should know something of human anatomy."

"Mother, as a doctor I've seen more nudity than you would care to imagine," Rhys drawled. "But you still cannot hang the portrait where we receive guests."

"Fine." His mother fluttered a gauzy handkerchief in his direction. "I will have it hung in the bathroom, so I *and I alone* can enjoy it while I bathe."

He nodded briefly, and as his mother smiled, he had the funny feeling she had gotten exactly what she wanted: leave to hang her portrait anywhere else.

As trunks and bags and boxes were trooped through the

house, Rhys had again refrained from rolling his eyes. In less than three minutes, his entire family had descended and turned the order and quiet of the townhouse on Berkeley Square into the center of a whirlwind. He loved his family immensely, but sometimes he wondered if they had any notion of just how much noise they made.

It was why he liked Greenwich. Away from the cacophony. It had been why he'd liked school. Hell, it was why he had joined the army—for some peace and quiet.

"Rhys, as I was saying, it's so wonderful you're here. Now, I was going to send out cards this afternoon, and we already have an invitation to the Ketterings' for tonight. I had to force it out of Lady Kettering, but she's my cousin and cannot cut us as easily as all that so—"

His heart began to stutter, knowing what was coming— he had to nip it in the bud.

"Tonight I have plans, Mother," Rhys interrupted.

His mother looked him in the face for the first time since she arrived. She opened and closed her mouth like a fish.

"But . . . no, you certainly do not. Your family has just arrived in town. After a very long absence. You are needed by their side."

"It cannot be helped," he replied sternly. "I am having dinner out with Lord Ashby and his guests."

"Lord Ashby," his mother repeated, musing. "At least it's an earl you're throwing us over for."

"I'm not throwing anyone over. And he's my old friend, Mother, not a social ladder to climb."

"Well, if he's your old friend, then he'll understand if you have to cancel."

Rhys was about to equivocate. He was about to say "that may be" or "perhaps he would," but he knew his mother would jump on that as her opening and he would find himself dancing in the Ketterings' ballroom before nightfall.

"No, Mother. We have a box reserved at Vauxhall, the plans cannot be adjusted. My apologies."

Lady Gray's face turned an unbecoming mottled shade.

"After all we've been through . . . Rhys! I'm *assured* the Mortons will be there. Finally our troubles are almost over, and you just sit in your laboratory in Greenwich and poke at poor, ill people while your family wastes away! Now is the time for you to—"

"*No*, Mother. Tomorrow will be the time for that conversation," he replied, so sharply his mother shut her mouth immediately. "And a conversation it will be. We need to come to an understanding about the next few weeks. And about the Mortons in particular."

His mother must have seen the look on his face, because instead of arguing, she simply shrugged her beruffled shoulder. "Very well, Rhys. It seems you have taken to being the eldest in your father's and brother's absence."

He stepped away before he found himself drawn in by his mother's verbal traps. In fact, he stepped out of the house completely, breathing a sigh of relief as he did so.

He wanted just one more day. One more day where he didn't have to worry about the trouble his family would get up to. One more day where he didn't have to face the Mortons, and what they—and his mother—had demanded of him.

Under normal circumstances, he would have just gone over to Ned's and hidden there, safely ensconced in his friend's library and with his kitchen's larder at his disposal.

But it didn't feel right somehow. Oh, he would have been welcome, he knew. But, with Margaret there, trying to settle herself . . . he could only be in the way.

Also, they had made a plan for that evening. And

knowing women—at least in the vaguely familiar way that a man with three sisters knew women—Phoebe and Leticia would wish to prepare for it. And Margaret would get roped into that too.

So instead he wandered the streets. He thought about going to the club—after all, what were clubs for if not to escape one's family? But then he remembered his membership had likely lapsed, as he had not been there in years, ever since Ned talked him into joining. They never had any of the scientific periodicals in stock, and sitting silent in a smoke-and-aristocrat-filled room never really appealed.

But there was one place that had the scientific periodicals always in stock, and he turned toward Pall Mall East and the Royal College of Physicians, where his membership was quite up-to-date.

But as he tried to lose himself in a copy of the *College Pharmacopoeia,* written in Latin, his mind kept traitorously turning back to the crowded Gray house on Berkeley Square, and what his family's presence meant.

It's time, Rhys. His brother's voice echoed in his head. *Time for you to do as you promised and finally get married.*

It wouldn't leave his brain. Only when he started reading an article about herbal remedies and the healing power of plants did he find a subject that would remove all thoughts of his parents and siblings.

He was able to lose himself long enough that when he looked up, the light was fading, and he had just enough time to duck home and sneak up to his room to change for his evening out.

He felt certain that his mother would try to waylay him. But oddly, he managed to make it out of the house and to Ned's with no delay.

Now, here he was, finally relaxed, happy, and himself in the company of his friends. The carriage rumbled to a halt and Margaret, who had been staring out the window, trying to find a last glimpse of the sunset between buildings, turned back to him, anticipation lighting her eyes.

"We're here," Ned said, stretching and pushing his hat back on his head.

The carriage bounced as the driver hopped off his seat and trundled down to open the door. Ned stepped out first, followed by Rhys, who turned back to take Margaret's hand.

And looking at her face as she saw the Vauxhall Pleasure Gardens for the first time, Rhys felt a strange sensation lance through him, erasing any of his family troubles from his mind and crystallizing in one single thought.

There truly was no place he would rather be.

MARGARET MIGHT HAVE been in London only two days, but from what she could tell, the Vauxhall Pleasure Gardens were *the* place to be on an overwarm summer night in London. Just far enough away from the city that it qualified as having fresh air, and enough entertainments to keep those who had seen everything enthralled. And it wasn't only the jaded elite who took part in its delights. Since the price of admission was only a shilling—three of which Lord Ashby handed to the porter at the large wrought-iron gates—even merchants and shop workers could have an evening out and take some gentle exercise.

And it was the most polished, manicured place Margaret had ever seen.

"Oh my," she breathed as they entered the main drive, called the Grand Walk.

"Impressive, no?" Rhys said, watching her closely.

"Very," she replied, not taking her eyes off the tall trees that lined the Grand Walk, heading up to the rotunda. The branches swayed in the dying light, inky against the pink sky. Lamplighters walked on stilts, lighting the newfangled gas lamps that made the main walks and rotundas as bright as day. "Oh, I'm so glad," she said. "I was so worried when Lord Ashby said we would go to the gardens at night. I thought I would not get to see everything."

Rhys laughed. She turned to him and realized he had been studying her carefully.

"You might be the only person who comes to Vauxhall Gardens to see the gardens." A smile played across his face.

"Ah . . . what do other people come to see?" she asked.

"Music!" Lord Ashby cried, piping up from behind them. "And dancing, and tightrope walkers and fire eaters—Vauxhall has to keep up with the competition. Ranelagh Gardens is more fashionable, other gardens are easier to reach . . . but Vauxhall is Vauxhall, dark walks and all."

"Dark walks?" Margaret asked. "Those sound interesting. Do they have night-blooming plants and such?"

For some reason, Rhys sent his friend a hard look.

"Yes, erm, never mind those," Ned said, blushing under Rhys's stare. "Can't see any plants there in any case. My goodness, I'm hungry! Is anyone else famished?"

They made their way to one of the two main rotundas featuring boxes around an open area, which acted as sort of a stage. In the center was a string quartet, and merry couples danced in circles, high and low, aristocrat and plebian.

A porter approached them, and learning Lord Ashby's name, ushered them to a box in the center of the loop.

"I always forget that when I go out with you, Ned, I am part of the entertainment," Rhys said.

"Part and parcel with the earldom," he said, shrugging. "Phoebe is still getting used to it."

Margaret's brow came down. "So, not only do people

come to Vauxhall to see music and tightrope walkers, they come here to see you."

"And others of our ilk," Lord Ashby said. "But don't worry, you're perfectly safe."

"I shouldn't think I wasn't safe," Margaret replied, biting her lip. "I worry more about doing something to embarrass you."

"Oh, don't worry about that," he said. "Goodness knows I'm enough of an embarrassment to the title—or at least that's what my uncle would say if he were alive. Oh, lamb!"

And Margaret was left to contemplate his meaning as he turned his attention to the food. The first course had arrived with amazing speed. No sooner was their wine poured than roast lamb was placed before them, with potatoes and leeks and long green beans.

Margaret stared at the plate before her, her mind seemingly elsewhere. And Rhys thought he could guess where.

He leaned in close to her, his voice pitched low. "Ignore Ned. He's just miserable because Phoebe isn't here. Please don't worry about your behavior. You are above reproach."

She glanced at him, a little hesitant. Completely unable to ascertain his meaning, she decided instead to respond squarely with comfortable self-deprecation. "I assure you I'm not. Leticia and Helen have made a sport out of reproaching me. Half the time I'm tempted to use the wrong fork just to watch their faces."

"Well, use the wrong fork here, and no one will say a word."

"Even though we are part of the entertainment?"

"We are less so than Ned would have you believe. Most people here are too wrapped up in each other to notice the Earl of Ashby and his wrong-fork-using guest." Rhys smiled. "I promise."

Dinner proceeded quite smoothly after that. Lamb was

followed by fish, followed by pork, followed by pies and then trifle. Wine flowed, and while the night grew darker and the lamplight brighter, the crowd grew rowdier and the music livelier.

But all the while Margaret's mind was occupied by two separate but equal thoughts—what did Rhys's attentions mean, and where on earth was the garden part of Vauxhall Gardens?

"What is it?" Rhys asked, leaning over to whisper in her ear.

"Nothing," she replied immediately.

"Come now, you're fidgeting with the tablecloth and have been turning your head around like an owl for the last ten minutes."

"Nothing. Just . . ." She took a deep breath. "How long do the lamps stay lit?"

"How long . . . ? All night, I expect."

"I just don't want to miss anything. I suppose we could come back in the daylight sometime . . ."

"Ah, I understand," Rhys said, throwing his napkin onto the tablecloth and rising. He held out his hand to Margaret. "Let's not keep you from the garden's earthly delights any longer."

As she hesitantly took his hand, Ned looked up from the dancing, a glower set across his face. "Wait, where are you two going?"

"Miss Babcock came to Vauxhall to view the gardens. And so we are going to do just that."

"But they haven't brought out the port yet."

"Why don't you drink your port, and then you can catch up with us," Rhys said. Then, pointedly, "We'll be fine."

Lord Ashby, Margaret knew, was faced with a dilemma. On the one hand, his wife had placed him in charge of her safety and honor, and that included her reputation. On the other hand, Margaret heard Phoebe whisper in her husband's ear to not stay *too* close to Rhys and Margaret, for reasons that only made Margaret more nervous. And yet again on the other hand, there was port to finish off the meal.

It was two to one in favor of staying, and so Lord Ashby sat, grinned like a man who had come to a satisfactory conclusion, and took a fork to the last few bites of his trifle.

Rhys moved Margaret's hand to his arm and led her out of the noise and jubilee of the rotunda.

"Where are we going?" she asked.

"If I recall correctly, the Spring Gardens are this way." He steered her farther up the Grand Walk.

They moved leisurely—a bit too leisurely for Margaret's taste. But everyone who strolled around them kept to that same pace, so Margaret sighed and settled her long legs into a shortened stride.

Finally they came to a T in the path, and while everyone else took the well-lit side, she began to lean toward the other.

"No," Rhys said, coming to an abrupt, if gentle, halt. "We should keep with everyone else."

"Why? Perhaps this is a shortcut," she reasoned. "Indeed, it's more in the direction you indicated."

"True, but . . ." He hesitated. "Better not to venture onto one of the dark walks. Leticia and Phoebe would have my head."

Margaret turned around, eyed the path again. "Why?" she asked. "What's down there?"

It was dark, yes, with shady trees canopying the footpath, but for goodness' sake, it wasn't pitch-black. The moon was full and lines of light cut across the ground.

Rhys took a deep breath. "Vauxhall isn't just famous for its gardens," he said.

"Considering the lack of garden so far, that much is obvious."

"Since anyone can gain admission, that includes less savory elements. Footpads and prostitutes use the dark, unlit walks to ply their trade. It's no place for a young lady."

"Indeed?" she asked, more curious than ever. "I would think it would be more dangerous for you than for me."

One clinical eyebrow went up.

"I don't have to worry about being approached by prostitutes," she said. "Therefore I only have half the worry you do."

He chuckled at that, which had her chuckling too.

"Well, then keep me safe and let's follow the rest of the crowd."

"It does beg the question," Margaret said as they moved down the well-lit path with the rest of the gardens' patrons, "why Vauxhall is so popular if it is so dangerous."

"Perhaps it is not *so* dangerous. Perhaps it is popular because it is just dangerous enough." At her look he continued. "People enjoy a little jeopardy in their entertainment. A bit of a thrill."

Margaret thought that over. "Of course. How else to explain the baffling existence of fire-eaters?"

They had come to a second rotunda, this one with acrobats and circus performers as its entertainment, using the distant strains of the music from the first rotunda to set their feats to a tempo. There were jugglers, a trained large cat in a cage, tightrope walkers high above the ground, and yes, even a fire-eater.

"Gracious," Rhys said.

"Yes," she mused. "Imagine the damage to the poor man's throat."

Rhys stood stock-still for a moment, and then threw his head back in laughter.

Margaret looked at him like he was losing his mind. "Now what did I do?"

"Nothing," Rhys replied. "Simply spoke words that hadn't yet made it to my lips."

He smiled at her wide. And for the first time all evening—hell, for the first time since she had come to London—Margaret realized she was completely at ease. Why couldn't it always be so? Why couldn't she and Rhys just have their own bubble, where they didn't have to listen to people who questioned their friendship? Why did she have to spend all night wondering about his intentions and making herself nervous?

And why could she not simply be left to enjoy the company of a person of so much the same mind as she that just his laughing made her laugh, and vice versa? That she said what he thought before the words could make it to his lips, as he said?

At that thought, her gaze slid down to his mouth. It was open slightly, ticked up at the corners. And for some reason she could not take her eyes off it.

Off him.

Something was . . . stirring. Something warm, and anticipatory. And for the briefest second, she understood why people liked fire-eaters and coming to a place with dark walks. There was danger in them, yes. But there was also possibility.

I dare you.

The little voice echoed in her head. As she stood there, in the lamplight, it was all she could hear. Not the people walking by. Not the ones who would no doubt see . . . all she had to do was lean in . . .

But then, just as it seemed like Rhys was leaning toward her, about to let her in on some secret, he suddenly shook his head and jerked back.

"We should . . . keep moving," he said, and deliberately put a foot of space between them.

After some minutes, he cleared his throat. "Miss Babcock—Margaret," he said. "I'm afraid we need to have a conversation. I don't know what your expectations have been about this trip to London, but I . . . that is, I have no expectations of you."

"You mean you did not expect me?" she asked, confused. "But we arranged it, via our letters."

"Yes! No—I mean," Rhys said, stumbling both literally and figuratively as they approached the entrance of the Spring Gardens. "What I mean to say is that I don't want you to have any expectations of me."

"But I do."

His head came up and he sought her face in the sudden dark.

"I expect you to help me meet with Sir Kingsley from the Horticultural Society."

"Well, yes, of course I'll do that."

"Thank goodness, because that's the entire reason I'm here."

"But is that the only reason you're here?" Rhys said, his voice gentle, as if she were one of his patients.

"What other reason could I have?" she asked.

Rhys took another deep breath. It did little to dispel the awkwardness in his voice. "I want to ascertain that you don't have any, er, *romantic* reasons for coming to London."

"*Romantic* reasons?" Margaret repeated. Then blinked. "With you."

"Well . . . yes."

"No."

"No?"

"No, I did not come to London with romantic intentions toward you," she answered with complete honesty.

The fact that thirty seconds ago she couldn't tear her eyes away from his lips was neither here nor there. "What on earth ever gave you that idea? What, did you think I was going to throw myself at your feet and beg you to make love to me?"

He closed his eyes. "Actually . . ."

She rocked back on her heels. "You . . . you thought I was going to—" she said, her hands coming to her cheeks.

"Well . . . no?" Rhys said. "But then you . . . you blushed a moment ago when I mentioned my lips. And you went shopping for a gown this afternoon—"

The cheeks under her hand began to flame.

"Leticia dragged me out to that. I am fully convinced that the dresses I have are perfectly adequate to be in London for a few weeks, but she said otherwise—"

"And given what my friends have been saying," Rhys continued, "I was beginning to be afraid that you had gotten the wrong idea from my letters."

Margaret looked at him like he had grown an extra head. "Unless your idea was for me to come for a pleasant visit, experience London, and show my roses, then I would have gotten the wrong idea." She stopped for a moment. "But to be honest—ever since *you* told me that I looked lovely this evening, I was afraid that *you* might think that—"

"No!" Rhys hastened to assure. "Although you do look lovely. But I am capable of recognizing loveliness without feeling a need to act on it."

"I would hope so. So . . . you're not . . ."

"No," he replied. "And you are not . . ."

"No. Not at all."

"Thank God," he said, sagging against a tall shrubbery. "What a relief."

"I know exactly how you feel," she said, laughing. And

then suddenly she couldn't stop laughing. And neither could he.

"We have been quite the fools, haven't we?"

"How could we help it?" she replied. "I was beginning to think I was going mad. I kept telling Leticia that there was nothing between us. We were merely friendly, academic correspondents."

"I can only imagine how that went."

"Leticia kept giving me looks and asking pointed questions, and then when I met Lady Ashby and she gave me the same sort of looks, I thought I was *supposed* to have expectations . . . Heavens, it even made me nervous to see you for the first time yesterday, which is the most ridiculous thing I could possibly imagine!"

"My God, exactly! They've been doing it to you too? I've been fielding dropped hints like they were cannonballs from Ned and John. Did you know Phoebe said I could not stay at their home, even though it is our custom?"

"Why ever not?" Margaret cried.

"Some stupid thing about propriety."

Her scoff included a snort, which made Rhys grin. "As if my honor could ever be in danger from you. For heaven's sake, you're harmless."

"Thank you!" Rhys replied. Then, his brow coming down . . . "I think. But, I'm glad we had this talk." An unfathomable look crossed his face. "Because I would not want to toy with your affections. Knowing where we stand—it's for the best."

"Yes," she replied, wondering at him. "Of course."

"Come on—" he said, shaking off whatever had darkened his mind. "Let's show you some of this garden you came to see."

The Spring Gardens of Vauxhall were something else entirely. No acrobats, no musicians and dancing. The fireworks remained in the distance. Here, spring bloomed eternal, with flowering bulbs forced out of season, jasmine vines climbing walls, and an atmosphere dedicated to the beauty of growing things.

"I just wish I could see it in daylight." Margaret sighed. "Those day lilies over there—why have day lilies in a garden that only opens for supper?"

"We'll come back sometime right as they open, see the whole thing before the sun goes down and be deeply unfashionable doing so."

Margaret was about to give her ready consent when a voice came from the other side of a vine-covered wall.

"Rhys? Is that you?" Lord Ashby said. He sounded very far away.

"Ned?"

"Rhys! I thought I heard you—I got turned around looking for you. Any idea how I get through this wall?" Then, "Ow! It's prickly!"

Rhys shook his head. "Stay there, we'll find you."

They looked at the wall—and as far as Margaret could tell, it was a solid mass of vines, no exits or entrances in sight.

"You go left, I'll go right. We'll shout when we find the way in." Seeing his face, she offered. "I'll be fine. Never out of sight."

Rhys hesitated a moment. Then, upon hearing a crash and another "Ow!" from beyond the wall, he threw up his hands. "If you find an opening, I'll be a shout away."

She nodded and they set out in their opposing directions.

She walked the entire length of the wall before finding a person-sized gap. "Rhys!" she called out. But there was no answer. There was no Rhys. Indeed, there was no one, as far as her eyes could see in the torchlight.

He must have found another way in, she thought, and was looking for Lord Ashby. And that left her there. Alone. Which, as best Margaret could gather from the various lessons on propriety people had tried to fix in her brain over the years, was not ideal.

A young lady standing on a path alone was as bad—if not more so—as a young lady walking a path, correct? Even if that path was darkened. With that thought in mind, she knew that the option of going through the opening was equally as safe and/or dangerous as standing right where she was.

Come now, a voice in her head said. *What's the worst that could happen?*

Surely she could find Rhys and Lord Ashby. All she had to do was walk in the general direction that Lord Ashby's voice had come from, and keep in mind her way back.

Which was easier said than done. It was dark, yes, but the full moon gave enough light to mark her way. And while the trees hung low here, she was never one to be cowed by plants. But that confidence was where things began to go wrong. As she took a sharp corner, the entrance to the dark walks disappeared behind her, and suddenly she was not entirely certain of the way back.

She walked for about another minute or so before she happened on other people—two young ladies and a young man.

"Thank goodness," she breathed. "Excuse me, but have any of you seen either one or two gentlemen? One is quite tall with sandy hair, the other—"

"Never mind that," said the youth. "Gimme your purse."

"Why?" Margaret's head came up.

"Because I asked nicely."

"Miss, please . . ." the older of the two young ladies said, her voice shaking as her eyes never left the form of their robber.

Yes. Their robber. It seemed she was meeting one of the famed dangers of the dark walks.

But in truth, he did not seem that dangerous. He was very young, with the thin length of a male barely in his teens. His voice broke when he spoke—and it also slightly slurred, as if one too many tipples were had in an attempt to up one's courage. He had his hands in his pockets, so she could not see a weapon. His clothes were fraying around the edges, but they weren't threadbare. He wasn't starving and desperate for money.

But the two young ladies who were pale with fear didn't know that.

"And I refused nicely," she answered the boy.

"I got a knife," the youth said. "So next time, I won't be askin' nicely."

"Really?" Margaret asked. "Where? I cannot see it."

"I . . . er. It's dark. But it's right here." The youth raised his hand (which notably did not hold a blade of any sort) and unconsciously scratched at his neck.

"It's not that dark," she replied.

"All right, I may not have a knife, but I don't need one," the boy argued. "I can bring pain into your life without it."

"Really?" Margaret asked again. "How?"

And once again, the boy seemed flummoxed.

"By . . . attacking you. With my . . . my fists an' such. Ladies are softer, an' canna defend themselves."

"Ladies who are six inches taller than you can defend themselves," Margaret pointed out.

A snort came from behind her. The girl who still wore her hair in braids was giggling, and the young lady was trying to shush her.

"Hey now, there's no call for that!" their would-be robber said, again scratching at his neck.

Margaret cocked her head to one side. "Were you hiding in those bushes over there?"

"Who cares where I was hiding—right now I'm in front of you, taking your purses!" he said weakly.

"Are you aware that the vine growing on those bushes is poisonous?" Margaret asked.

"It is?" the boy squeaked, his hand coming down from his neck.

"It is?" the young lady asked, taking a curious step forward.

"I'm afraid you are going to have the most horrid rash," Margaret said, sucking in her breath.

In the distance, Margaret heard rapid footfalls.

"Margaret!"

Relief flooded through her. "Rhys!" she called out. "Over here!"

Rhys came around the corner, Lord Ashby right behind him. His eyes searched the dark for her. When he found her, his shoulders relaxed . . . but only until he saw the company she was currently keeping.

"Rhys, thank goodness you're here," Margaret said. "This young man is going to have the most awful rash imaginable. Itching, red welts . . . do you have a salve you could rec— Oh, he's gone."

At the sight of the broad-shouldered pair who were obviously gentlemen, the youth had scampered away. The rustling in the bushes told them which way he'd gone.

"No!" Margaret called out into the dark. "Not that way! At the very least avoid vines with leaves shaped like stars!"

"That was," the breathless voice of the young lady made Margaret turn around, "the bravest thing I think I've ever seen."

The young lady was smiling up at Margaret with a perfect look of vulnerable gratitude. She seemed to be about Margaret's age—if not her height. Her perfect features and proportions made Margaret feel like a plain, gangly Amazon. Which was not an abnormal feeling. The young lady's golden curls bounced in the moonlight as she shook her head. "I don't know what Alice and I would have done if you had not come along."

"We would have gotten our purses stolen and Papa would have lost his temper," the younger Alice piped up. She must have been about twelve or so, judging by the freckles across the bridge of her nose. "More so because we got lost."

"Yes, we were on the main path with everyone but got turned around at an odd corner," the young lady added with a tremulous smile.

"I believe I went around the same corner," Margaret said, smiling.

"So did I," piped up Lord Ashby. "But all's well that ends well, right, ladies?"

Miraculously, Margaret then remembered her manners and dipped to a curtsy. "I'm Margaret. Margaret Babcock. And this is Lord Ashby." As that gentleman bowed, she turned to the oddly silent and still tense Rhys, "And this is—"

"Cor, it's Rhys!" Alice piped up.

"Alice, don't say *cor*," her companion admonished.

"Yes," Rhys croaked after a moment. "How fortuitous to see you again, Miss Alice." He gave a stiff bow. "And you, Miss Morton."

The elder girl, Miss Morton, blushed with a prettiness that was only enhanced by the moonlight as she made a curtsy more graceful than should have been possible for anyone who was being robbed thirty seconds before. "Dr. Gray. A pleasure."

"Oh, you know each other?" Margaret asked, pleased. She was certain she had made some kind of social faux pas in simply forgetting to introduce herself until now, but if Rhys was friends with them, she could perhaps be excused for being a bit casual.

Alice snorted in reply. And then she said the words that made Margaret's stomach pitch as if she was stuck in a runaway carriage, without any way to reach the reins.

She didn't know words could do that.

"Of course they know each other. Sylvia's going to marry Dr. Gray."

7

I feel I owe you an explanation."

Margaret looked up at Rhys, her face completely open and utterly unreadable.

The ride home from Vauxhall had been alarmingly silent. Especially considering the carriage contained Ned. But perhaps for once in his life, Ned had the good sense to realize that his contribution to the conversation could only cause trouble. Or perhaps he could think of nothing to say.

After the meeting with Sylvia Morton and her sister, Alice, Rhys escorted everyone out to the main path. There, he led the Morton girls back to their father, whom they found at the second rotunda, his attention having been captured by the acrobats, such that he'd hardly noticed his darling daughters had gone on walking without him.

Mr. Morton greeted Rhys like a hero. Or perhaps like a prodigal son.

"Dr. Gray! Of course you're the one who rescues my girls when they find themselves in trouble. Very naughty of Alice to go walking off without me."

Mr. Morton was a very large, very gruff man. He was

thick chested in a way that spoke to a lifetime of hard work, and thick bellied in a way that spoke to a fondness of indulgence. Rhys had never minded Mr. Morton, but his roughness had always offended Rhys's father on a personal level. As if something so unrefined couldn't possibly exist right next to Gray Manor.

In fact, Morton's limp and cane were remnants of the discord between himself and Rhys's father.

"Oy, I did not—" Alice piped up.

"Alice, don't say *oy*," her sister Sylvia admonished gently. Then she turned to her father. "But it was not Dr. Gray who saved us. It was Miss Babcock."

Rhys pivoted around as all attention turned to Margaret, who was silent as the grave behind them.

"She called the robber's bluff and made him scamper off, itching from a phantom rash," Sylvia said, a laugh in her voice. "It was the most marvelous thing I've ever seen."

"Well, Miss Babcock, then!" Mr. Morton cried, grabbing Margaret's hand and shaking it and her with vigor. "Much obliged to you, much obliged! Can I convince you all to join us at our box?"

Miraculously it was Ned who had stepped in and had the ability to put off Morton with grace. "I'm afraid we cannot. Miss Babcock was just saying how tired she was, and I know my wife will have my head if we exhaust our guest."

And with that, they excused themselves, with promises to meet soon, compliments to Lady Gray, etc. And then they walked quickly to the gates, to the carriage, and drove off.

And Rhys had not said a single word. Neither had Margaret. And as noted, neither had Ned.

Until, that is, they arrived in the warmth and safety of the Ashby townhouse sitting room.

"Yes, you bloody well do owe us an explanation!" Ned exclaimed.

Obviously, he had reached the limits of his silence.

"You are to be *married*? To a girl none of us have ever heard of?" Ned said, pacing about the room. "Unless you told John . . . Oh hell, did you tell John and not me? That's not fair!"

"I didn't tell John either," Rhys said, answering the one question that he felt he could at the moment. Of course, that tack only brought about new ones.

"Where did you meet the girl? How long have you been betrothed?"

"I'm not betrothed. Not technically . . ."

"What on earth does 'not technically' mean?" Ned said, his voice becoming as blustery as the color of his cheeks.

And all the while, Margaret Babcock sat on the settee. Quiet. Watching.

Waiting.

Luckily—or unluckily, depending on how cowardly Rhys was feeling at the moment—Ned's outbursts had the effect of reminding them that they were not alone in the house.

"What on earth . . . ?" Phoebe said as she came through the door of the sitting room, drawn by her husband's voice. "Ned, darling? The baby is asleep. What is going on?"

"What is going on is that tonight we met Rhys's fiancée!"

Phoebe's gaze went directly to Margaret, whose expression did not shift. Being a dispassionate observer was an excellent trait in a scientist, Rhys thought. It was a disconcerting one in a friend.

Especially one he knew had a depth of feeling that would shock those who did not have the privilege of receiving her letters.

But while he was unable to ascertain what was going on

in Margaret's mind, Phoebe Granville, Countess of Ashby, was an open book.

"This is the first I'm hearing of it," Ned was ranting. "My best friend, forgetting to mention that he's engaged—although not technically he says—and here you had been worried that Rhys was going to make love to Margaret—"

"Ned," Phoebe said, her eyes shooting to Rhys. He could only pray she understood what he silently begged of her. "Come away with me. John is in the study with Leticia—she's feeling better enough to take a cup of weak tea."

"Oh good, John will have something to say about this too, I've no doubt."

"*Ned.*" His wife's tone finally had the earl breaking out of his verbalized stream of consciousness and glancing her way. "Come. Rhys will inform us when and what he wishes. But for now we have other guests."

"Other guests? But Joh—" It seemed that it was at this moment that Ned finally got a good look at his wife's face. Because he immediately closed his mouth and followed her out the door without another word.

Phoebe closed the door behind them, sending Rhys a pointed look as she did so. As if he needed it. No, he knew he had completely bungled the entire evening. And there was only one way to make it right.

But damned if he didn't have a clue where to start.

"It's all right," Margaret said before the silence could envelop them any further. "You don't owe me anything."

"But I do," Rhys replied quickly. Although, when he thought about it later, lying on his bed, stuck in sleeplessness, he would not be able to tell you *why* he felt he owed Margaret Babcock an explanation. He just knew that he did.

"I owe everyone an explanation," he said, covering his feelings. "You saw Ned, he's completely unable to comprehend it. And I don't blame him. Being somewhat betrothed is not something one neglects to tell his best of friends."

"Why did you?" she asked, calmly. "Neglect to tell them, that is."

Rhys sighed, his eyes going over to where embers still glowed in the hearth. "Would you believe I forgot?"

"Possibly," she replied candidly.

His head came up.

"You are a dedicated physician," she said. "Your work is consuming, and I know what that can be like. Little things tend to slip out of one's mind."

Idly, he reached out and took the poker, stoking the fire. "I do not believe anyone would qualify a fiancée as a 'little thing.'"

She gave a shrug of agreement. She could have asked so many questions then. She could have made gentle but leading inquiries, asking how he had met Sylvia Morton, why they were to marry, if he loved the girl—queries that would have him giving a stilted explanation of the entire affair. Instead, she just waited.

And gave him the time he needed to breathe and to tell his story.

"My father is the eighth Lord Gray," he began, turning to her. "My great-many-times-over grandfather was a courtier to Queen Elizabeth, given a title for helping to defeat the Spanish Armada. Family history is something no Gray is ever allowed to forget, no matter how scandalous. It is what makes us . . . better than. At least, according to my father."

"Better than what?" Margaret asked, blinking.

"Better than anyone. Anyone who *isn't* a Gray. Anyone who tries to lift themselves into higher circles. Anyone who might wish to call us out on our nonsense. And Thomas Morton—Sylvia's father—is all three."

Again she waited, with infinite patience for him to continue. He sat down beside her on the settee and stared into the fireplace, now crackling with low flame.

"Thomas Morton is a man of low birth—but he's brilliant in business. He worked in a slaughterhouse, saving up enough pennies to eventually buy the place from the owner, who was aged and thought of him like the son he never had. Then he promptly razed the slaughterhouse and began digging in the land the building had sat upon. Lo and behold he was sitting on a coal mine, with one of the richest veins in the north. He used that good fortune to buy up all the surrounding land and expand his coal mine into a small empire.

"Thomas Morton then managed to marry extremely well—an aristocratic young lady who could gain him entrée into society. He built her a beautiful house in Suffolk . . . which happens to sit right next to Gray Manor."

"I see," Margaret said. "So you are neighbors."

"A fact that irritated my father more than it had any right to," Rhys said wryly. "And my father is a man of . . . high spirits."

"High spirits?" Margaret repeated. "I suppose he's like my father, always blustering and laughing and enjoying company?"

"Yes," Rhys replied. "But also no. Your father has no meanness in him. If the Mortons moved into your neighborhood, he would have been the first to have them over for dinner. But my father . . . he enjoys being the center of attention, enjoys what he thinks of as his due. And if he finds you offensive in some manner, you will be dealt with."

Rhys's father, Lord Bellamy Gray, was larger than life. Rumor had it when he met with King George III as a youth, he'd wagered the man a crown that he could run faster than he—it was only after he won that he had the audacity to demand the crown on the king's head, and not the coin in his pocket.

It was stories like that that peppered his youth. Everyone Rhys met would exclaim that his father was the most mischievous, interesting, and wonderful person in the world.

But Rhys knew him differently.

Rhys's childhood had been an odd mix of basking in the sun of his father's presence and feeling ashamed when he did not in some way live up to his standards. When he did not wish to go out shooting, and instead wanted to read a book, he was scoffed at, made fun of. More than once, he found the pages of his books ripped out and rearranged. He would find his father and elder brother Francis laughing at the great joke they had pulled on him. His mother was always there to tut over him, but she was constantly distracted by the younger children or her own passions, and Rhys usually had to grin and bear his father's disappointment.

After years of being thoroughly shamed and picked upon, Rhys had a somewhat hardened perspective on his father. But that strengthened him to make his own path. When he wanted to study medicine—as the second son, he was not in a position to inherit anything, and goodness knows his family did not save their income—he was able to brush aside his father's jokes, his mother's sighs of worry. In an odd way, being different from his family had made him his own man.

But it also made him the only person who could save them.

"My father and Mr. Morton—obviously, they did not get on. But my father would not stoically ignore the man, as my mother was inclined to do. Instead, he found ways to pick at him. He would make a game of it. He'd have Francis run over to their property and fish in their stream—daring the man to call them out on poaching. He'd hire away all the servants from the Mortons' home, and the man would have to hire new people at twice the price and half the experience. He even once had every carrot picked from the Mortons' kitchen garden in the middle of the night, because he heard that carrot cake was Mrs. Morton's favorite."

Margaret gave a short chuckle at that, and he nodded. "Yes, you see? What he did *seems* a little cruel, but also funny. But it never was."

"No," Margaret agreed. "He was trying to irritate the Mortons into leaving."

"Exactly. Then my father went a step too far."

"What did he do?"

Rhys took a deep breath. "Nearly ten years ago he was having the fences that bordered the grazing land repaired. Then he had the fences moved six feet into the Mortons' property."

"Essentially stealing six feet of land?" she asked.

"More or less. And no doubt he would have gotten away with it, if his workers had not been caught in the act. Mr. Morton was livid, and confronted my father about it. About everything. He threatened to go to the law and have my father's actions prosecuted. Which my father just laughed at."

Laughed, because who was going to believe an upstart miner over Lord Gray, whose family had lived in the neighborhood for generations?

Rhys remembered the confrontation like it was yesterday. The war had ended, and he'd been home from France for less than a fortnight, hoping for some relaxation in the bosom of his family but having quickly come to the realization that that kind of thing was not possible. He'd just taken a lease on his laboratory space in Greenwich and was coming down the stairs to break the news to his mother, when his father came in the door with Morton on his heels, spitting mad.

"I'll see you prosecuted! I'll see you sent to the gallows!"

And his father laughed. "You think your complaints will be heard? By whom? The magistrate? We've known the magistrate in this county our entire lives. A solicitor? A barrister? A judge? Name him and I'll tell you how his family connects with mine. Tell me how someone like you is going to try a gentleman like me."

"I'll do it as gentlemen do, then. Either apologize for your actions, or choose your second."

A duel. Morton, the insulted party, had every right to call for satisfaction. And Rhys's father was never one to laugh off a challenge like that.

His father chose Francis as his second, of course. And they asked Rhys to act as the doctor, should injury occur. Rhys had refused.

"I would not be drawn into their madness," he told Margaret who had not taken her eyes off his face as he told her his story. "My father should have apologized and I told him as much. After he finished yelling at me for being so unfeeling, and my mother worried herself to tears on my shoulder, my father went and got another doctor from a nearby town—which turned out to be the mistake."

"Why?" she asked. "Was he not reputable?"

"No, the exact opposite," Rhys replied. "He refused to lie for my father."

Margaret, who had maintained an open, calm expression until this point, let one eyebrow go up.

"My father was not about to lose his opportunity to rid the county of the Mortons to chance. So he turned and fired on a count of seven, not ten. And he shot Morton in the back of the thigh."

Margaret sucked in her breath.

"He didn't kill Morton, so he had to defend his story. Said that Morton fired first, and then said he turned to run when he saw that he had missed. Francis backed my father's story. And of course Morton's second backed his version. The doctor, whom I'm certain my father thought would do exactly as he wished, shocked everyone when he backed Morton's version of events. And with that, my father became a cheat. A sneak. And an outlaw."

Dueling was not exactly legal in England, but as long as no one died or was grievously maimed, it was usually overlooked. However, since Lord Gray had fired before the count of ten, and shot as Morton's back was turned, he could not hide behind gentlemen's agreements anymore.

"My father fled the country—he and my elder brother, Francis, who lied on his behalf, are currently in Italy, according to their last letter. And they have been for the past decade. While my mother waited for Sylvia Morton to grow up."

It was the darkest time for his family. His father and Francis had just left in the dead of night, his mother was left with children ranging in age from two to two and twenty, and everything seemed to be in shambles.

The only silver lining Rhys could think of was that it would expose his mother and siblings to the idea that everything his father did was not charming, delightful, or excused by his roguish nature and gentlemanly stature.

He was wrong.

Instead, his mother had spent days alternating between crying on his shoulder and berating him for causing the whole mess.

"If you had not refused your father and acted as physic at the duel, this would not have happened!"

"If Father had not shot Mr. Morton in the back, this would not have happened," Rhys had countered. And of course, it was the exact wrong thing to say.

"He shot him in the leg, not the back!"

"And if Mr. Morton does not succumb to sepsis, he'll walk with a cane the rest of his life."

But his mother simply sniffled harder. "What did you expect your father to do? To refuse to face the man and dishonor his family? Or would you rather that he let himself face a bullet when he's the father of seven and husband to a wife who needs him very much? Oh, I'm just glad that I got Eloisa married off last season. But think of Jubilee and Delilah! What are their chances?" At this she dissolved into tears and again began to soak the lapels of his coat. He wrapped his arms around her. Regardless of her opinions about what happened, she was his mother. She was facing the questions of her children, the censure of society, and possibly a lifetime alone—and she was scared.

"I need your help, Rhys. Until your father and brother come back . . . you are the head of the family."

He'd held her as she wept. Then he found himself saying something that would change his life irrevocably.

"Mother, please don't cry. You know I'll do whatever you need. We'll make this better. You'll see."

Three days later, he found out exactly what that would be.

His mother, being far more politic than his father had ever been, called on Mrs. Morton, who was also more practical, and knew the best path to the top tier of society again. And after a few afternoon teas, everything was arranged.

Rhys Gray, son of Lord Bellamy Gray, would marry Miss Sylvia Morton.

"I'm not marrying anyone!" Rhys blustered when he'd heard. "Especially not Miss Morton—she's still a child!"

"She won't always be," his mother countered breathlessly. "You are not expected to marry her now, of course—but when she comes of age. And then . . . and the fences between our families will be mended, and your father and brother can come home."

"Why me? Why not Francis? Or Daniel, even?"

"Francis? You expect us to give the Mortons the Gray heir?" his mother scoffed. "Mrs. Morton knew better than to ask for that. And Daniel is so young his character is not yet formed. No, with you—solid, respectable young doctor, army hero . . . the Mortons know what they are getting. No one else will do."

She must have seen his aversion to being traded like livestock, because her eyes welled with tears again.

"You said you'd do anything to help," his mother sniffled, her voice becoming alarmingly high and weak. "This is the only way Mr. Morton will not press charges. Your father cannot set foot on English soil without being hunted. Your brother . . . bearing the weight of his mess too. Whatever will I do?"

Every argument he had—*His work was too important. What if he met someone he wished to marry in the meantime? What if Miss Morton did? What if Father just owned up to his idiotic behavior and apologized?*—ran through his head, but ultimately died on his lips when he'd looked into his mother's huge wet eyes.

"Mother . . . we can talk about this later." Years later, he prayed. Or never. "When you're more sensible."

"But you'll consider it?" she said hopefully, clasping her hands to her chest.

"Fine, but . . . like I said, we will talk later."

But later never really came.

Because he ran.

He ran to Greenwich. He established his practice. He once even attended the queen. Even though every time he saw his family, during speedy holiday visits and the occasional stop through Surrey, his mother mentioned the Mortons and how they were spending their Christmas, he simply hummed and nodded and directed the conversation toward what Daniel was doing in school, or what book Jubilee was reading, or how his mother doted on little Rory, her only grandchild.

Eventually, she stopped mentioning the Mortons altogether.

The conversation that could have changed everything had never taken place.

"You never told any of this to Lord Ashby, or Mr. Turner?" Margaret asked.

"They know about the duel, and my father and brother fleeing." Rhys gave a weak laugh. "But that's fairly public knowledge. They don't know the rest. Yet." No doubt he was going to have to tell this story more than once this evening.

"I'm sorry," she said.

"Don't be . . . it was my father's doing. I never let it touch me. I remain to this day the respectable Gray."

"But you bear the weight of it. And you did it alone for so long."

"Like I said, I mostly forgot," he said. And looking down, he realized that his hand was covering hers. He did not move it. "I haven't made any decis—"

"Yes," she replied. "You have. You are going to marry Miss Morton. You love your family too much."

"I haven't decided," he said firmly. And thankfully, she did not question it. She just sat there, volumes of space between them, with their hands reaching into the void and unable to resist touching each other on the soft velvet of the couch.

A zing of feeling ran from where his fingers warmed hers, all the way up his arm and into his chest. If he were thinking medically, he would wonder if he was having heart palpitations. But he was not thinking medically, and his heart remained a steady, strong *thump thump thump*. Instead a stray question reached from the back of his consumed brain and pushed its way to the front.

What would it be like to kiss her?

He quickly tried to smother the thought. It was a result of the situation, of the dramatics of the night that this was how his mind tended. Because kissing *Margaret* was not something to be thinking! She was a very good friend, but that was all—and they had spent a good portion of the evening establishing that as fact. But still he could not stop his memory from slipping back to the moment that they had stood under lamplight, the rest of the crowd minding their own business or enthralled by fire-eaters, when her eyes had dropped to his lips and he felt that delicious punch of anticipation in his gut.

Before he put a stop to it.

He was right to do so, he knew. But still, in that moment, with her hand under his and her gentleness allowing him to tell his tale, he could not help regretting, for just a fleeting second, that he had not found out what it was like to kiss Margaret Babcock.

Because . . . once he officially agreed to marry Sylvia Morton, he would never have the chance.

All of this wracked his brain as he silently studied her profile, lit by candlelight, utterly inscrutable.

"Thank you for telling me," she said eventually. "I cannot imagine what you've been through."

"You must hate me," he whispered.

"Why?" she replied.

But to that he had no answer. Not one that he had words for, anyway.

"We are friends, are we not?" she said. "I don't have many, true, but I should think that in a situation like this, friends are what I would want the most. What . . . I would need the most."

Friends. And yet why he felt the need to explain himself to Margaret first, and Margaret alone, was something he did not have the analytical capacity to contemplate. He just knew he was glad. Glad that she was the one who had heard him. Glad that she was the one who was sitting quietly by his side, gently giving him enough room to breathe.

It was something his family—with their cacophony and needs—had never afforded him. It was something he had only ever found in Greenwich.

Or in a greenhouse in Lincolnshire.

Why didn't you kiss her?

"Miss Babcock," he said, raising her hand to his lips before he could stop himself. "Please know, I am forever grateful to count you among my friends."

He looked up and found her eyes on him. Surprisingly, she did not blush. Instead, her complexion was as soft and clear as her voice.

"I am grateful too."

8

$\mathscr{H}$ere you are." Leticia's voice came from the doors to the conservatory. "I knew I'd—*achoo!*—find you in here."

Margaret turned around. She knew she looked a mess in her long apron and work trousers, but she did not care. She was hard at work, and intended to be for as long as it took her to feel right again. In fact, she was inches away from plunging her hands into the barrel of fresh fish heads that Frederick had procured from the market that morning. He had followed the detailed instructions she had written out last night after her talk with Rhys. His words had been honest, frank, and difficult to hear—but not knowing had been worse. Afterward, Margaret had let Rhys go to his friends so he could tell them his story, and she went up to her room and made a list.

A list for Frederick. Everything she would need to make her special fertilizer tea, which she would spray on her roses to keep them in optimum health and vitality. Luckily, Lord Ashby's stablemen were more than happy to let her have the necessary ingredients from their morning mucking out, but other things had to be purchased, and Frederick was still out. Fresh hay was apparently more expensive in the city than it was in Helmsley.

She was in London for a reason, after all. She must not let herself forget that.

"Where else would I be?" she asked Leticia, who hovered on the edge of the garden, as hesitant to step out onto the grass path (that Margaret was going to have cut and reseed because it was horribly patchy) as a kitten was to put its paw in a puddle of water.

"I'd hoped you would be in your room," Leticia replied. "There the flowers can be easily removed by just handing them to Molly."

"There are flowers in my room?" Margaret replied. Normally, she did not like cut flowers. It seemed so unkind to do that to something simply so you could borrow its beauty, however briefly. But most people considered them a sign of something romantic. Which begged the question, "From whom?"

"From a Mr. Morton," Leticia replied, throwing caution to the wind and stepping out onto the lawn. "By way of thanks. Apparently, you were instrumental in helping his daughters last evening."

"Oh," Margaret replied, letting one of the fish heads slip out of her fingers and back into the barrel. "Yes, that makes sense."

"Last evening . . . last evening was a shock for you, I'm certain," Leticia said, approaching with her nose held until Margaret realized why and put the lid back on the barrel.

"Yes," Margaret replied. "But once I realized the boy was young and had no weapon, it was easy enough to scare him off."

"You know that's not what I was talking about," Leticia replied gently.

Margaret sighed. "And yet that was the only thing last night that was truly shocking."

"Don't you dare," Leticia said. "Don't you dare try and pretend you feel nothing. I know you have more feeling in you than you dare tell anyone."

"It was a shock," Margaret conceded. "But I think it was more of a shock to Rhys than anyone else."

"I'm not concerned with Rhys's feelings at the moment," Leticia said. "Honestly, he deserves a shock. I know he can be a bit scatterbrained when it comes to anything that's not work, but really! One thinks he would remember an engagement!"

"He's not engaged," Margaret said automatically. "It's more of an . . . understanding between their families."

"Yes, I gathered that when John told me about it," she replied. "Although when I had my own conversation with Rhys, I could barely hold in all my questions and he was annoyingly enigmatic on the topic. Would only answer with *hmm*s and 'that's a private matter.' Most frustrating."

As Leticia sniffed in frustration (and sniffed in something pollinated, causing a short round of forceful sneezes), Margaret's head came up in alarm. "You had your own conversation with Rhys? Leticia, please don't tell me you cornered him."

Visions of a red-faced Leticia giving a trapped and frightened Rhys what for flashed through Margaret's brain. She couldn't even imagine what Leticia would say, thinking she was speaking on her behalf. She pinked at the very idea of it.

"Don't worry," Leticia said, seeing the red flood into

Margaret's cheeks. "I didn't attack him. At least, not like you think. But I did need to speak with him, as a doctor."

"As a . . . are you ill?" Margaret asked suddenly. "I know the roses made you sick on the drive down, and I'm so sorry, but I thought—"

"No—it's not that. Well, rather, yes the flowers did make me a bit queasy, as you know. But that was more of a symptom than a cause. I've been terribly tired lately—as everyone no doubt noticed. That, coupled with the queasiness and some other symptoms . . . well, let's just say Rhys confirmed something I'd just begun to suspect."

The nervous smile on Leticia's face spoke louder than the words she coyly refused to say. Soon enough, Margaret's smile matched her friend's.

"You're . . . but how?"

"The usual way, I imagine," Leticia said. For a fleeting moment her smile faltered. "Although I'm as surprised as you."

"Why?"

"I . . . I don't know. John and I certainly—well, there's no need to go into that, but suffice to say, a baby should not come as a surprise. But . . . I am not a young debutante, and as it had never happened with my first husband, I had begun to wonder whether it was possible at all. Whether I was even meant to be a mother." She shrugged, gave a watery little sniff. "I'm not the most maternal creature, you know."

"That's true," Margaret said, and Leticia burst out laughing.

Her face fell immediately. "What? Did I say something wrong?"

"No," Leticia said through gasps of breath. "You said exactly what you thought and that cannot be wrong."

She felt her brow come down. "It feels like I said something wrong."

"No, dearest. If anyone would know about my maternal instincts, it would be you."

"But, you didn't have time to practice with me. You were my stepmother-to-be for approximately three weeks. You'll have absolute loads of time with your own child."

"Yes." Leticia sniffled again. "I will have loads of time. But that brings me to the other bit of news I have to tell you."

"What?" It was doubtful anything could be as momentous as the news Leticia had just imparted, but she looked even more nervous than she had before.

"That we are leaving. Going back to Helmsley."

"Leaving?" Margaret asked. A strange, plunging sensation filled her stomach, like she had just taken a step off a cliff but hadn't yet fallen. "But I haven't met with Sir Kingsley and the Horticultural Society yet, and . . . and the roses have just been transplanted. Frederick has absolutely no idea how to care for them and—"

And she wouldn't see Rhys again.

"No, dearest," Leticia interrupted. "John and I are going home. Phoebe and Ned have said they would be delighted for you to stay."

"But . . . why?" Margaret asked. "We just arrived, and you adore London."

"Yes, but . . . when John found out about the baby, he became quite emphatic. He wants me home, and away from the city air." She smirked. "Meanwhile, of course, I will be sneezing incessantly in the country air, but that does not seem to concern him nearly as much."

"Although that's not the only reason," Margaret said, watching her closely.

"Don't be silly. You know I wouldn't leave you for anything less."

"Leticia . . . I heard those ladies. In the store yesterday. And you heard them too."

Her perfectly composed expression faltered. But very quickly, she rolled her shoulders back and made herself taller. As if nothing in the world couldn't be faced as long as it was faced head-on.

"Yes, I did. And I don't know what I was thinking. That I'd be forgotten? That no one would remember me, so I would be able to enjoy my visit without facing ridicule?"

"I thought you didn't care about that kind of thing anymore. People talking," Margaret replied. When Leticia had married John—a countess marrying a miller—she had basically declared to the world that she didn't give a fig what they thought. Or at least that was what Molly, the maid, had told her, with awe. Margaret very rarely cared what anyone thought, so she was surprised that Leticia did.

"I don't. Not about me at least. But it occurred to me, after you frightened the ladies off, that my presence here would affect you far more than it would me." Leticia reached out and took Margaret's hand, even though it was smudged with dirt. "I want you to have the most wonderful time here in London. I want you to experience everything the *ton* has to offer to a young woman of your standing. And that might not be possible if you are associated with me."

"But . . . I'd much rather be associated with you than with those horrid women in the store."

"I know, and that's what makes you darling. But I still think it's best if I leave. John is chomping at the bit to have me safe at home and keep me from doing anything strenuous for the next several months. He's meeting with the bank right now to finalize the paperwork to purchase the new mill, but our trunks are packed and we are to set out this afternoon."

"This . . . this *afternoon*?" Margaret dropped her hand in shock. "But . . . but the Davenport Ball is tonight!"

The Davenport Ball. Margaret couldn't even think about it. Yes, she'd agreed to go when Phoebe mentioned it—all the little whispers in her ear about how she should at least experience one London ball had worn her down, and after all, what's the worst that could happen? But she'd thought Leticia would be there. Letting her know when her hem had gotten bunched or if she was dancing a quadrille when she should have been doing a Scotch reel.

The Davenport Ball would have been perfectly fine if she was surrounded by people she counted as friends. But without Leticia and John, that number dropped precipitously. And now that Rhys . . . Well, who even knew if Rhys would come and speak with her, let alone dance with her?

Who knew if he would even want to?

"Do you know what I think you should do?" Leticia said, a knowing look on her face. "I think you should go to the Davenport Ball, wearing that gorgeous gown that was just delivered this morning, and make everyone else absolutely fall at your feet."

"How am I supposed to do that?" Margaret asked, a forlorn note creeping into her usually defiant voice.

"By being your usual self," Leticia said, and went up on her tiptoes to place a kiss on Margaret's cheek. "Make Rhys rue the day he ever 'forgot' he had a fiancée."

"They are not engaged," Margaret said again, rolling her eyes. "And for heaven's sake, Rhys and I are just friends. One of these days, you'll believe me when I say it."

Leticia gave a short laugh. "That day will only come when you believe it yourself."

9

$\mathcal{I}$f Margaret Babcock had been the type to gawk at architecture, or ornaments, or chandeliers, or ball gowns, goodness knows she would be drop-jawed at the sight of the Davenport Ball.

As it was, she was frowning at the flower arrangements.

"Those peonies are drowning in that vase," she said.

"What's that, my dear?" Phoebe said, following Margaret's gaze. "Oh yes, well, the vase is a little large . . ."

"No, they are literally drowning. Those flowers are not meant to take that much water, even when cut. No wonder they are drooping."

"Why don't you tell Mrs. Davenport that?" Lord Ashby said, a twinkle in his eye. "We are about to be introduced, after all."

"Ned, be serious!" Phoebe whispered harshly.

"It would make an impression," Ned replied, and suffered grievous injury as his wife pressed her heel into his toe.

"Don't worry, Lady Ash—I mean, Phoebe," Margaret said. "Even I know better than that."

To be fair, she thought as they inched forward in the line to be received by the Davenports, it was something she might not have known better about even as little as a year ago. But Leticia's firm hand and her own awakening to the world around her had her catching up at an accelerated rate.

The thought of Leticia had her stomach flopping over. The carriage had borne them out of London that afternoon, as scheduled. She was probably well up the North Road by now—halfway into Hampshire. Or not, depending on how slowly John made the driver go. Still, she wished she could feel Leticia's presence. Or John's. Or anyone other than the virtual—if incredibly nice!—strangers who had taken up her care during her stay in London.

"Of course you do," Phoebe replied. "The only person here who doesn't know better is the only one who could get away with it." She shot a dark look at her husband, who grinned back at her.

"Is it my fault I'm naturally charming?" Ned asked.

"I don't know if 'charming' is the right word, but 'fault' certainly is," Phoebe replied, and was rewarded with a completely uncouth kiss on the cheek.

"I can get away with that too," Ned replied. And it was true. No one said a word about a husband kissing his wife on the cheek. Not even Mrs. Davenport, as they took one final step to face her.

"Lord Ashby," she said with a voice so commanding there was no doubt that had she ordered them to, the peonies would have stood straight up at attention. "How delightful to see you. And your bride, of course. Lady Ashby."

Phoebe dipped into a curtsy—somehow without seeming to lower her body at all. Really, it was quite a feat. "Mrs. Davenport. How delightful to see you again."

Mrs. Davenport's face was made of crepe paper, and it

creased into the smallest of smiles. Her assessing gaze fell on Margaret, looming behind the earl and countess.

"Mrs. Davenport, allow me to introduce a friend of the family. Miss Margaret Babcock, of Lincolnshire," Phoebe said, leading Margaret forward.

"Miss Babcock. Of course. There are so many new people here tonight I don't even know where to begin."

"Mrs. Davenport," Margaret murmured, and dipped to a curtsy. She of course actually did have to lower herself, else she would just be hovering a foot over the older woman's head. She knew when she rose again she had to say something else. Unfortunately, the only thing in her head was . . .

Don't tell her about the peonies, don't tell her about the peonies, don't tell her about the peonies . . .

"You have a beautiful home," she finally managed.

"Thank you," Mrs. Davenport said, already eyeing the next set of people in line behind her. But for some reason Margaret stood stock-still, flanked by Ned and Phoebe.

"Your decorations . . . and the flowers . . . are all very lovely," she continued.

"Thank you again," Mrs. Davenport replied. "I hope you enjoy yourself this evening."

She gave a small wave to the couple behind them in line.

"Thank you," Margaret said. And then, she couldn't help it. Something about the way everyone was looking at her and not looking at her and the heat of the crush . . . it just overcame her. "Although if I were you, I would take those peonies out of the water before they fall over—"

"We won't hold you up any longer, Mrs. Davenport, but save a dance for me, won't you? Can't wait to waltz you across the room, ta for now!" Lord Ashby said. And without pausing for breath, he took one of Margaret's elbows and Phoebe took the other and they hurried her away.

"Well, you certainly know how to start things off right, don't you, Miss Babcock?" Lord Ashby said, finally stopping. Margaret looked up from her toes, fire burning across her face.

"I'm sorry, I don't know what came over me, it just slipped out . . ."

But then she saw that Lord Ashby was laughing.

"That old bat hasn't heard a word of criticism since she was in pigtails, I'd wager. She's turning blue at the thought of having drooping peonies. Look!"

Margaret chanced a glance behind her. Mrs. Davenport was paying absolutely no attention to the couple in front of her; instead her eyes swung back and forth between the peonies and Margaret, who stupidly caught her eye.

The woman did not look blue. Her hue was of a far more livid shade.

"It will be all right," Phoebe whispered. "She will have so much to do, and so many guests to attend to, that she will forget that you said anything at all."

But Margaret didn't think so. Just before she regained some sense and turned away, she met Mrs. Davenport's eye as she turned to say something to another staunch-looking older lady who had come over to whisper behind her fan. The look on the second martinet's face made shivers run down Margaret's spine. Shivers of dread—which was a feeling with which Margaret was all too familiar.

"I'll give you this, Miss Babcock," Lord Ashby was saying as they threaded through the front rooms and toward the ballroom. "You certainly say what you think."

But at that moment, Margaret couldn't say what she was thinking. Mostly because she couldn't put words to her thoughts. As they rounded the corner and finally emerged into the ballroom, a dance was just ending. Pairs of ladies and gentlemen, all neatly coupled, held hands and came to a stop, bowing to each other before applauding the musicians and their own dancing prowess.

It was a sight that should have been unexceptional, considering the setting.

But there, in the middle of it all, was petite, perfect Sylvia Morton. And her hand was being bowed over by none other than Dr. Rhys Gray.

And even flanked by Phoebe and Lord Ashby, even knowing she had never looked better than she did in her new London dress and with her hair coiled and curled by the evolving genius Molly, and even with Leticia's words of encouragement echoing in her ear, Margaret had never felt more alone.

Rhys knew the moment that Margaret entered the ballroom. Not because Ned's booming voice carried over the final strains of the music (although it did), and not because he heard people greeting the Countess of Ashby (although Phoebe was always well regarded wherever she went, something hard earned for a former governess, and very pleasing to see). No, he knew Margaret was there because Sylvia Morton saw her first.

"Look, Dr. Gray, Miss Babcock is here!" she said with shining eyes and a wide smile.

Rhys turned. There was a sensation not unlike what he felt before he started a surgery. A sense that the next few hours would be long and tense, but more than anything he wanted it to go well, most especially for the person at the center of it all.

"Come, will you take me to her?" Sylvia asked. Before he could reply, she had put herself on his arm, and he had been steered toward his friends—impressive, considering he was the one who was supposed to be doing the steering.

"Rhys!" Ned cried, coming forward to slap him on the back in his normal gregarious fashion. "Didn't expect to see you here."

"I know," Rhys said. He had not mentioned the ball to Ned for two reasons. The first was that when he'd left Ned and John the night before, they'd been in such shock from what Rhys had told them that Ned had been reduced to the occasional ejaculation of "What!" and "How?" and as such giving him a detailed schedule of his social obligations seemed a little bit much.

And the second reason he didn't tell Ned he would be at the Davenport Ball was that he himself did not know of it.

"My mother arranged the invitation—she wouldn't hear of me not coming."

"Lady Gray is here?" Ned's eyebrow went up.

"Yes, and my brother Daniel—somewhere." His best guesses were either the card room or near the punch bowl.

Ned's other eyebrow joined his first on the upper reaches of his forehead, and he was about to make another comment, but thankfully, Phoebe stepped in.

"And who is this lovely creature, Rhys?" she asked, smiling at Sylvia—if not with her eyes.

"Yes, Lady Ashby, may I introduce Miss Sylvia Morton?" Rhys said, and Sylvia blushed prettily as she curtsied. "Miss Morton, this is Lord Ashby, Lady Ashby, and Miss Babcock."

Finally, he let his eyes fall on Margaret. She looked . . . different. It wasn't just the dress—although it was a very smart thing, with long lines and perfect seams that bespoke its London provenance. It was something new, and raw. If she were his patient, he would say that she looked a hair too pale, or a bit too skittish to be completely well. But there was something else too—standing in the middle of this completely new environment, as innocent as a babe, and yet her face was open, accepting.

It was possibility, he realized. Margaret Babcock was the most possible thing at the Davenport Ball.

"Oh, but of course Miss Babcock and I need no introduction," Sylvia said. She let go of Rhys's arm, stepping forward to take Margaret's hand. "After all, we had the most exciting of all introductions just yesterday. One could not forget it."

"Yes, indeed. Quite memorable," Rhys said, fighting against the impulse to frown. The thought of Margaret— who had been in his charge!—lost in the dark walks of Vauxhall was enough to set his stomach churning. But then to have her actually meet with a thief, and talk him out of robbing them . . . well, it was so quintessentially Margaret he was almost sorry he had missed it.

Then again, what followed after was something he would have been happy to miss altogether.

"Miss Babcock, I'm determined we are going to be great friends," Sylvia said, her eyes not leaving Margaret's face. Margaret blinked twice. "And we are going to start by braving the refreshments table together. I was told that Mrs. Davenport's cook has the best tarte au citron, but I have yet to manage to snag one. Together, I'm sure we can do it."

"You mean you need someone tall to hail a waiter for you?" Margaret asked, her voice uncertain.

"Miss Babcock, I promise I like you much more for your directness than your height. Although the latter will prove useful."

Margaret sent Rhys a searching look. He had no idea what she saw in his face, but she ended up simply saying, "Let's find some lemon tarts, then." And let herself be led away.

"Wait," Rhys found himself saying. Both ladies stopped and turned. "Er, Miss Babcock. I . . . have some news. About the Horticultural Society. So . . . save me a dance, if you please? Any dance of your choosing."

"Of . . . of course," Margaret replied. Her dark blue eyes, strangely gray in the light of a thousand candles, never left his. And then . . . she was gone. Disappeared into the crowd by the famished Miss Morton.

"Goodness, that wasn't awkward at all," Ned said as soon as they were alone—well, as alone as three people could be in the middle of a crowded ballroom.

"Ned, hush. So, that's Miss Morton, is it?" Phoebe said, turning to Rhys. He confirmed with a nod. "She seems lovely. Which . . . is good, yes?"

"She is lovely," he agreed. Which just made everything more difficult. If she'd been horrid, he would have had a way out. He could have told his mother that he would take a seat beside Satan himself before he married the girl. But no, she was—rather distressingly—a very good sort.

And as if summoned by his very thoughts, suddenly his mother appeared at his elbow.

"Rhys, my love!" she said. "There you are! I had thought you were on the dance floor with Miss Morton."

There was a chiding in her voice. A worry. One he decided against acknowledging.

"I was, but the dance ended. Mother, may I present my friend Lord Ashby?"

"Lord Ashby," she replied, and turned breathlessly toward Ned. "Of course—but I'm sure you don't remember me. You were barely more than a boy when I last saw you! And now you have quite grown into your title."

"Lady Gray," Ned replied, bowing. He seemed to be struggling with his normal cheeky charm. "I could never forget you. May I present my wife, Lady Ashby?"

Curtsies were exchanged. "Dare I ask why you find Lady Gray unforgettable, my dear?" Phoebe asked.

"Because . . . because of her outstanding personality of course," Ned answered.

"Or it could be because when Ned first met my mother she insisted on showing him a particular portrait of herself, wherein she's wearing little more than a veil," Rhys drawled. "Which is exactly what you should be showing your son's friends."

Phoebe held in a shocked laugh, while his mother waved away Rhys's comments. "You owe your existence to that painting. It's what made your father fall madly for me," she said, sighing dramatically. Rhys silently prayed she would not start recounting the whole story. Then, with a decidedly lascivious look, she added, "Besides, Lord Ashby was much taken by the painting's artistry, if I remember properly."

Ned, for once, was completely without a witty reply. Instead he turned beet red and grabbed Phoebe by the arm. "Oh listen, darling, is that the cotillion? I believe this is my dance."

Then, with quick bows and an apologetic look to Rhys, Ned and Phoebe practically ran to the dance floor, leaving Rhys to the tender mercies of Lady Gray.

"Well, you abandoned Miss Morton as soon as you were able," his mother said. "Did she step on your toes?"

Rhys's mouth tightened. "No, Mother. As a matter of fact, we danced twice. Then she abandoned me to take Miss Babcock to the refreshments table."

"Your, er, friend Miss Babcock?" she asked. At Rhys's nod, she gave the smallest smile. "Clever girl."

He refused to be drawn into his mother's machinations and ask what she meant by that—although his curiosity had spiked. Instead, he attempted more banal conversation.

"Are you having a good time?"

"Oh yes," she replied, her eyes becoming as soft and wide as her smile. "It's absolutely wonderful to be back."

Rhys felt his posture softening. There was no doubt that his mother had suffered over the past however many years. Unable to face society after her husband's duel and flight, she'd put herself into seclusion, not leaving Gray Manor (and no doubt cultivating an air of tragedy). But she had always been a very social, lively creature, so she must have missed this. The ballrooms, the music, the noise of a party, seeing and being seen. It was never something Rhys sought out, but it had always made his mother come alive. Like she was now.

And if he agreed to the marriage, she would be able to have that life again.

But he had not yet agreed. He'd made that very clear to his mother the previous evening, once he got back from Vauxhall. And once he'd correctly guessed her involvement therein.

"The Morton girls were assaulted by a robber!" his mother had said with her usual breathlessness. He had found her in the sitting room, purportedly composing letters, but really it was the best vantage point to the front, to see when his carriage pulled up. "How utterly horrible! Thank goodness you were there!"

"It's more lucky that Margaret Babcock was there," he replied. "But I'm more curious as to why the Mortons were there."

"Whatever do you mean, my love?" she asked, blinking in overacted innocence. "They were enjoying the gardens, I presume."

"And yet, according to you, they were supposed to be enjoying a party at the Ketterings'."

His mother had had the grace to blush, but the intelligence to not provide an answer.

"Tell me, did the girl make an impression on you?" she asked coyly instead.

"She doesn't need to make an impression on me, we know each other quite well."

His mother's brow came down in confusion. "You do? I didn't think you'd spoken to Miss Morton in years."

"Oh!" Rhys replied. He felt two spots of heat on his cheekbones. "Oh, you mean Miss Morton. To be quite honest, we didn't get to spend much time together. What with the attempted robbery and all."

"Well," his mother said definitely. "That is something we will have to rectify. After all, she will be your bride, so a conversation would not be out of order."

"I haven't agreed to that," he said sternly. "Listen and hear me, Mother. I have not yet agreed to the marriage. I have not proposed. And when I choose to marry—*if* I choose to marry Miss Morton—I will be the one doing the asking. Are we clear?"

His mother blinked, taking a step back. Then, with all the grace and training of a lady of society, she recalculated. "Of course I understand. But . . . you are not absolutely decided against it?" she asked carefully.

Rhys's eyes dropped. "No. Not absolutely."

"Oh, my love—it's enough that you are willing to try. And you are willing to try, aren't you? But it is only natural that you want to have an affection for the girl, and for that to occur, you must know her. So I will do everything in my power to assist you, and hopefully you will come to the decision that you want to save your family from the ruinous cloud we live under."

And so the invitation to the Davenport Ball was procured not only for themselves, but somehow for the Mortons as well. And Rhys went without complaint. When they'd walked through the door, they'd barely spoken to

Mrs. Davenport before his mother spotted the Mortons in the crowd and made a beeline for them. There, Sylvia Morton was everything a young lady of good breeding should have been: sweet, shy, and the correct sort of nervous—a kind of eager retiring that always bewildered Rhys. If one is excited, be excited. If one is not, don't—it's as simple as that.

But he knew he was being overly critical, because Miss Morton was only acting exactly as she should. And while his mother waxed rhapsodic to Mr. Morton about the music and the heyday of her youth when she would dance holes in her slippers, Rhys sighed, took the hint, and asked Miss Morton to dance the first two.

And it had been fine. Not amazing, not thrilling—but not horrible either.

He'd told his mother he would try, and he did his damnedest to find the bright side in the prospect of Miss Morton.

She was a very pretty thing. Her features were unblemished and symmetrical. Her skin was firm—indicating working muscles beneath. And she flushed at appropriate moments, indicating a healthy circulatory system.

By medical standards, she had all the textbook indicators of beauty.

And Rhys liked to think of himself as a man who appreciated beauty in women. But often, Rhys had found that beauty was enhanced—or indeed was created—by something beneath the skin. So he attempted to find it.

"Are you enjoying London so far, Miss Morton?" he'd asked during a turn.

"Oh yes. I haven't been in town long—three days only—but I think I like it very much," she replied. And then, after a moment, "Are you? I understand you do not live in town, but close enough to visit."

"Yes, I find town can be exhausting. And I need time for my work."

"Of course. That makes sense."

And then they were silent for a time.

After a while, Rhys managed to think of something else to say. "Your family seems to be doing well. Miss Alice is quite grown."

Miss Morton gave an impish smile, showing a dimple in her left cheek. "She seems to think so. And your family? I saw your brother earlier; I had thought he was at school."

"So did I. He seems to think he's quite grown too."

They managed to meet each other's eyes this time, and shared a knowing, amused look. But just as quickly as it appeared, it was gone.

"Tell me about your work, Dr. Gray. I imagine being a physician is quite exciting."

"Not unless you consider hours of lectures and scientific experiments exciting," he countered.

"Not usually," she admitted. "But try me."

That at least was surprising. And so Rhys talked for the next twenty minutes about his work. He had no idea if Miss Morton was listening to him, but she did say "hmm," and "that's interesting" at specific intervals, coupled with a furthering question.

In the end, he felt he was telling her a lot about himself, but ended up knowing nothing at all about her. Their stilted conversation centered on him, which was not a natural place for Rhys to be.

So when Miss Morton took off with Margaret, he was one part wary of what they spoke, one part unhappy that he did not get a few moments alone with Margaret to assess how she was doing, and one part relieved that he had no need to keep talking about his lecture schedule and his patients' various maladies.

"I find Miss Morton delightful, don't you?" his mother said, and Rhys, not willing to verbalize the entirety of his thoughts, simply gave a curt nod. "I was just telling Daniel that she will make an excellent physician's wife. She will know exactly what you need before you need it. And she will be a perfect hostess to all your academic acquaintances. Why, with a woman like that by your side, who knows how far you'll rise?"

"How far I'll rise?" Rhys replied. "Am I going somewhere I'm not aware of? A hot-air balloon trip, perhaps?"

But his mother simply shrugged off his sarcasm. "Your brother understands. Although I lost track of him while you were dancing. Where is Daniel, anyway?"

"I have no idea. I haven't seen him since we stepped out of the carriage."

"That boy." She shook her head. "He's going to live up to his father's reputation, mark my words."

Rhys's vision darkened. He didn't know what troubled him more—the fact that his mother was likely right or that she said that like it was a good thing.

But at that moment, he couldn't worry about Daniel. He had his own future to ponder—and who the woman was that he wanted to share it with.

❧❧❧

BY THE TIME Margaret made it to the refreshments table, she too was craving a tarte au citron. She was craving any food, really—pushing their way through the crowd had proved exhausting, and if she was going to be subjected to such a squeeze, there had damn well better be something worthwhile at the end of it. Miss Morton was trying to chart a path for them, but as she was so petite, she kept getting jammed up into corners. So Margaret, with the gift of being able to see over most everyone's heads, finally took Miss Morton by the elbow and pulled her through.

At last they had their tarts, a glass of punch each, and Miss Morton, through some lucky happenstance, found them a pair of seats along the wall, where they plopped down and sighed in relief.

"I confess, I now understand why men are sent to fetch refreshments!" Miss Morton laughed. "I would have asked Dr. Gray to go for us, but I wanted you all to myself."

"Really?" Margaret asked. "I cannot imagine why." Unless it was for her tart-reaching capabilities.

"Because I have to confess something to you," Miss Morton said.

Margaret froze. What could she possibly have to say? She watched as the other girl lifted the tart to her lips, then put it down again, unable to take a bite.

"Miss Morton," she ventured. "I'm sure whatever it is, it's not so bad as to put you off your tart." Unless, of course, it was.

She laughed again, and shook her head. "Please call me Sylvia. And I feel too ashamed at the moment to eat. You see, last night—I was the one who made Alice go into the dark walks with me, not the other way around."

"Oh," Margaret replied. She felt relief spread across her chest, which surprised her, because why on earth should she be relieved? "What does that matter? I was alone on the dark walks too."

"Yes, but you proved you don't need an escort," Sylvia countered. "Me, I'm so silly—I simply wanted to experience something exciting, before . . . well, suffice to say, it was utterly stupid. Especially to involve my little sister."

"Involve her by putting the blame on her, or bringing her along in the first place?"

"Both!" she cried. "Alice is quite forthright, like you. She would have given me away if I had not stopped her. I know it was wrong, but I didn't want to admit to something so idiotic in front of Dr. Gray."

Margaret felt her face cracking a smile. "Is that all? I promise Dr. Gray would not admonish you for such action. He's much too understanding for that. After all, he didn't admonish me, and he gave me explicit instructions to not go into the dark walks alone."

Sylvia met Margaret's eye. "Yes, I suppose you're right," she murmured.

"If I know Rhys, he would simply say that if a lesson was learned there's no need to harp on it. That's one of my favorite things about him," she said with a small smile as she took a bite of her tart. "He see people's mistakes—he wouldn't be a very good physician if he didn't—but he does not let it be the only thing he sees."

The smile froze on Sylvia's face as Margaret spoke. Her eyes dropped, and she began playing with the lace trim of her overskirt. "Tell me, Miss Babcock—Margaret. You say you know Rhys . . . how well do you know him?"

Margaret stilled, her tart halfway to her mouth. And she waited for an answer to come out.

As much as it seemed to the outside world that Margaret let any and every thought she had spill out of her head, in fact, quite the opposite was true. She always thought about what she would say. Before she said it. While she said it. And all too often, for hours and hours after she said it. So it was that she carefully considered what she would say now.

She could demur. She could shrug and say they were academic acquaintances. Or, for the first time since coming to London, she could tell the truth.

She took a deep breath. "I know Rhys well enough to

know about . . . the arrangement between your families. And what he's being asked to do. What you both are."

Margaret watched Sylvia's face very closely. For a hair's breadth she seemed shocked. But then her face broke into the widest, most brilliant smile.

"Oh, thank goodness!" said Sylvia.

Margaret looked askance. "You're . . . not unhappy that someone knows?"

"Quite the opposite." Sylvia reached out and grabbed Margaret's free hand. "I've been dying inside, not being able to talk to anyone about this. While my father of course is instrumental in the whole affair, he doesn't exactly open himself up to talking about feelings. And my little sister, Alice, is . . . twelve. And I've been told for years now that I am to marry Dr. Gray, and I've been told I cannot want anything else. It's terribly strange too, because while Dr. Gray seems so kind, I do barely know him, even though his family is neighbors to mine. I'm afraid that I've spent so much of the past weeks just wishing that . . . wishing I still had my mother here."

She ran out of air at the same time she ran out of words. And Margaret found herself feeling very much for this young lady. After all, she was stuck in the same situation as Rhys. Told that she can help her family through a marriage she wasn't sure she wanted. But she felt for her too because she knew what it was like to be standing in a strange place and wishing you had someone to talk to.

"Your mother passed away?" she asked quietly.

Sylvia's chin wobbled slightly as she nodded, her eyes on her uneaten tart. "Two years ago. It's why I could not make my come-out earlier. My mother passed, and then my grandmother, so I spent two years in mourning."

"My mother passed almost three years ago," Margaret ventured tentatively. "You never get used to it, do you?"

"To what?"

"The quiet."

Sylvia shook her head, looking out over the raucous party. "No, you don't."

"I still hear her sometimes," Margaret said. "Daring me to step outside of myself. It's why I'm in London right now."

Sylvia nodded. "So am I. My mother—she and Lady Gray are the ones who made this arrangement. Brokered peace between our families. And I want nothing more than to live up to her expectations. And until now it has been so very difficult. But now that I know that you know, I have someone to share my secret with."

"Yes," Margaret answered hesitantly. "I suppose so."

"And thank goodness it's you and no one else. I don't know what I would do if everyone here was whispering about me and Dr. Gray."

Margaret was about to point out that not only was she aware of the situation, but the entire Gray family knew, and Rhys had told his closest friends Lord Ashby and John Turner, and their wives. But Margaret couldn't imagine any of them not keeping their counsel, so there was no reason to expound upon it.

But there was one thing that stuck out in her mind.

"So you're not upset? That Rhys asked me to dance?" Margaret said.

"Of course not!" Sylvia replied. "Dr. Gray just danced the two with me—if he danced with me again the newspapers would be expecting an announcement. And as you said, you are friends."

"Yes," Margaret repeated. "Friends."

Friends who lean on each other, Margaret thought, her heart picking up speed. Friends who hold hands while alone in a room, and not a word said between them.

"But we both need other people to dance with tonight,"

Sylvia said, her voice lifting and switching from serious to impish. "So let's see if we can't make this night more interesting. Who among all these eligible men has captured your attention?"

None of them had. Even if Margaret had been inclined to look, she really hadn't had the opportunity. "I don't know . . ." she said, demurring.

"Oh, come now, there must be a man in this house who can sweep you off your feet."

Yes, there was.

Ruthlessly she shook her head and shoved the remains of her tart into her mouth. "I am not in London to seek a husband. I'm here to present my rose bushes to the Horticultural Society."

"Really?" Sylvia's eyes widened. "How interesting. You must tell me all about it. However, I didn't say you needed to marry the person. You just need to dance with them."

"Do you think we can find one that is tall enough?"

Sylvia gave a laugh. "Let's see." She scanned the crowd. She opened up her fan and hid her mouth behind it. "There are two over there. In the corner, gossiping no doubt."

Margaret eyed the two men. They were tall, yes. But they were also very refined. Their coats were cut so perfectly they would probably shudder if a single wrinkle marred their outfits. Their expressions were snide, and as they seemed to look over at her and Sylvia, one of them chuckled to another, who snorted in reply.

They looked like every single reason Margaret avoided balls in the first place.

"No," Margaret said suddenly, dusting off the remaining crumbs from her hands and fishing her dance card out of her pocket. She opened it up, careful to hide its blank pages from Sylvia. "I . . . I forgot, I put Rhys down for this dance."

Sylvia tore her gaze away from the young gentlemen, lowering her fan. "You had better go and find him, then," she said after a moment. They rose to their feet. "I should find my father—after last night, he's barely willing to let me out of his sight."

With relief, Margaret turned into the crowd to seek out Rhys, more confused than she had been in a long time. But before she lost sight of her, she saw Sylvia heading toward the two gentlemen in the corner, her fan waving flirtatiously, and her uneaten tart left behind.

10

$\mathscr{I}$'m very glad you put me down for a waltz," Rhys said as he took Margaret's gloved hand in his own, placing his other hand on her waist. "Other dances you have to move apart and come back together—it's very difficult to hold a conversation. I'd much prefer to talk with you."

The feel of her hand in his was very different on a ballroom floor than it was the night before in Ned's study. Previously, where they had found their hands clasped out of solace, now they were clasped in anticipation of a three-count musical rhythm and being jostled by a crowd. One could almost call it ordinary.

But that same zing of feeling spread from where they touched across his skin, making him far too aware for a friendly dance. Thank God the music started as soon as they took their positions, nudging his mind away from his hands and toward his feet.

"Oh," Margaret replied, her expression blank. "That's not why I chose this dance."

"Then why?" he asked, his brow coming down.

"Because I'll be hanged if I can remember the steps to the quadrille."

Rhys threw his head back in laughter.

"You are the third person I've made laugh today," she said, her eyes shining with mirth. "I must be quite amusing."

"You are—I don't mean that in a cruel way. I don't laugh at you."

"I know *you* don't," she replied.

"Did someone else?" he asked. His hand tightened involuntarily against the small of her back.

"No," she replied. "But I am forever expecting them to."

He considered that. He knew the way she felt, could see the way her eyes darted back and forth across the crowd, looking at no one and everyone. It was the way she had looked when he'd come across her slipping back into the ballroom from the refreshment tables. She'd seemed so skittish, so unsure, and then she saw him.

"I was looking for you," she had said, a transformative smile spreading across her face.

She had been utterly relieved to see him. And somehow, that feeling transferred to his chest, and he was relieved too.

"I was looking for you as well. Are you ready to dance?"

And so they were.

He felt his muscles relax, just being able to finally have five minutes without having to worry about his family, Miss Morton, or indeed anything else. He felt for the first time that evening his mind engaging, knowing he was about to have a really good conversation. Even before she said a single word.

How very strange.

"I would rather have you defying those expectations, Miss Babcock," he said, taking her through a turn.

She shook her head. "I will do my best."

"Come now, the party isn't so bad," he said, trying to cajole her into smiling again. "Mrs. Davenport certainly pulls out all the stops."

"I suppose so," she replied. Her brow furrowed.

"What is it?"

"It's strange," she said, smiling. "I feel like this is something I would describe in one of my letters to you. Telling it to you in person feels very odd."

"On the contrary—it makes perfect sense. Seeing your face is different from seeing your handwriting. We cannot think out what we are going to say and perfect it. We have to take each other at face value . . . mistakes and misused words and all." He watched her closely. "What would you say, if you were writing me a letter?"

She cocked her head to one side. "I suppose I would say . . . Dear Rhys. Thank you for your last letter. I am very gratified to know that Sir Kingsley at the Horticultural Society is willing to view my roses. I am eager to discover what day precisely we will meet."

"My apologies," he interrupted. "I have traded messages with Sir Kingsley. I'm certain I will know by tomorrow the day."

"Excuse me," she said, a mocking look on her face. "But I'm in the middle of a letter."

"I apologize again," he said. "Please, proceed."

She cleared her throat. "In the meantime, I have seen Vauxhall, and was particularly impressed with their dark walks"—he managed to smother his smile at that—"and have attended my very first London ball. Which was . . . perfectly fine."

"Only 'fine'?" he asked. "And before you chide me for interrupting, if I were to reply to your letter, I would ask for further explanation."

"If you must know . . . I find it rather hot. And noisy."

"God, yes, it is," he agreed. "How do people think in all this cacophony?"

"I'm convinced they don't," she replied. "And I managed to embarrass myself with the hostess, by pointing out the drooping peonies."

He held back a chuckle. "She's likely forgotten it by now, if it's any consolation."

"That's what Phoebe promised me." She sighed. "But other than that . . . it's exactly what I pictured a London ball to be, and therefore it's fairly uninteresting."

"That is an interesting observation. What do you mean by it?"

"Just that . . . there's music and dancing and food and people, and all of it seems terribly rote. Not a surprise to be had."

"And since it matches your imagination, that makes it ordinary?"

She nodded.

"And does ordinary equate with unpleasant?" he asked.

"No, of course not. At least, dancing with you is not unpleasant. Although for all my missteps, I doubt you could say the same."

But he could. For whole minutes he'd forgotten about the rest of the world, which let him see the ball through Margaret's eyes—or rather, through her letter. And they were dancing quite well, come to think of it. She fit in his arms like she was made to, and every one of their steps was in sync. Her stride matched his, he didn't have to shorten or mince his steps or be afraid that she was going to be lifted off her feet by his pace. He didn't even have to worry about dancing badly, because he knew he was with a partner who would forgive him for it.

There was no difficulty being with Margaret. No pressure. It was just . . . exactly where he wanted to be.

And it was that stunning realization that made him trip over his feet.

"Are you all right?" she asked as he recovered his steps and found the rhythm of the music again. Luckily, the music was in its final strains, and he managed to hide his faux pas.

"Yes, my apologies," he murmured, blushing as they came to a stop. "I seem to be doing that a lot tonight."

"Tripping? Not so I'd notice."

"No—apologizing."

She smirked as she took his proffered arm. "Luckily you can just blame it on me; no one will know the difference."

He slowed, growing serious. "You have to stop doing that."

"Doing what?" she asked.

"Deprecating yourself. You've danced sublimely. You look beautiful tonight, and there is no one I'd rather be with. I refuse to let you pretend otherwise."

She looked up at him with wide eyes, darkened in the candlelight. "Well," she said softly. "I guess there is something at this ball that is out of the ordinary."

It absolutely took his breath away.

And . . . that was not something he could allow himself.

"Yes . . ." he said, putting another inch or two of space between them. Cold, unwanted space. "Let's see . . . what else is out of the ordinary at the ball, do you think?"

She looked around the room, searching for something exemplary. Finally she looked up and smiled.

"The chandelier," she said definitively. He looked up— the large circular chandelier shone with hundreds of candles, crystal sparkling and polished brass shining.

"I have never seen a chandelier of that size," she said.

"And how do they keep the wax from dripping on all of us?"

"It's a scientific mystery," he replied, following her gaze. "What else?"

She reflected. "I saw a man wearing purple satin knee breeches while I was getting my lemon tart."

"I didn't even know they still made purple satin knee breeches."

"He—and they—looked quite old."

"Perhaps he's trying to bring them back into fashion," Rhys replied. "And how were the lemon tarts?"

She grew serious. "They were . . . educational," she replied softly.

The feeling of ease he'd been enjoying slid away. Replaced by the cool recollection of what had brought him to the Davenport ballroom in the first place. He moved them off to the side of the room, found a close corner where they could whisper in confidence.

"I assume you have an opinion of Miss Morton too?" he asked, trying to keep his voice light. "Everyone else does."

"I do." She nodded once.

"Well?" he asked. "Don't keep me in suspense, I beg you."

"I think that you're not the only one stuck in an awkward situation."

Shame. Complete and utter shame wracked his body. Usually, he was the one to listen and carefully consider as many sides of the story as possible—after all, that was the only way to get a correct diagnosis. But when he had been faced with his own difficult situation, he couldn't see beyond his own nose.

He'd never considered Miss Morton's feelings on the matter. That she might be having as hard a time adjusting as he. Instead, he'd assumed she'd been as happy with the arrangement as their families seemed to be. And it was only with Margaret's wide eyes watching him, and her wise words penetrating his brain, that he'd seen it.

"I've been a horse's ass, haven't I?" he murmured.

"Not at all," she replied. "You've just been a little blind-sided."

Blindsided. Yes. But now he felt like he was having his eyes opened to many things.

Like how their waltz, and the silliness of her "letter," had been the only time that Rhys had felt like himself. Not just himself, but his best self.

Like how he had just noticed that Margaret had the most perfectly formed lips of any human he had ever seen. Symmetrical, with a full lower lip and a pillow upper, that dipped sharply in the middle, a divot shaped exactly for the soft trace of a lover's fingertip.

Like how this was the world's most inopportune time to be thinking this way.

Hell, wasn't it only last night that he'd told her that she should not have any expectations of him during her visit? And she absolutely shouldn't.

If only he could remember that.

"Margaret," he began, struggling to keep from drowning in those eyes. "I . . . I want you to know that—"

"Rhys, my love! Thank goodness! There you are!"

The bubble around them broke, and his mother stomped on the shards as she pounced on them.

"I need your help! It's an absolute emergency."

"What is it? What is wrong?" he said immediately.

"I . . . oh, I'm sorry, I didn't mean to interrupt," his mother said breathlessly as her eyes fell on Margaret.

"Mother, my friend Miss Babcock. Margaret, this is Lady Gray." Rhys was quick about the introductions because for once, his mother did not seem as if she were being dramatic. Well, she was always dramatic, but this time, it seemed like she had come by it honestly.

"Miss Babcock? Oh, well—I'm very pleased to meet you; my son has spoken of you highly," she said, her manners at war with her mannerisms. She eyed her son carefully.

"Mother . . ." Rhys said.

"It's your brother. Daniel," she said, snapping back to what had sent her running their way in the first place. "He's gone!"

"Gone?" Rhys asked. "You mean he's left the party?"

"Yes," his mother sobbed.

"Why is that cause for such alarm?" Rhys asked. After all, Daniel was a young man who'd been given free rein most of his life, and he had no pressing reason to stay. "Did he take the carriage?"

"No—he left with Haverford!" she wailed, bringing the attention of others nearby.

Rhys glanced to Margaret, who shook her head briefly in equal confusion.

"What does that signify?" Rhys asked. "Haverford is Daniel's friend. They've been in each other's pockets all week."

"Well, isn't that perfect?" His mother laughed hysterically. "My poor baby might as well be headed for the gallows!"

She was so distraught, and sobbing so loudly, that everyone around them stopped what they were doing. Rhys was flummoxed, when Margaret took control of the situation.

"Lady Gray, come sit down," she said. Her plain, firm tone and her general towering over his mother made her someone who could not be contradicted.

She wept into her handkerchief, but let herself be led to the chairs by the wall. Luckily, Margaret knew where she was going, and headed directly for a pair of open chairs right where Phoebe was sitting with Ned, who was watching them approach with concern.

"Rhys?" he asked. "Lady Gray? What is wrong?"

"Daniel's gone missing," Rhys said through gritted teeth.

"He ran off with Haverford!" his mother managed through sobs.

"Haverford?" Ned said, then sucked in his breath.

"Who is this Haverford?" Margaret asked.

"He's Daniel's friend from school." Rhys blinked in surprise.

"He's also completely ransacked," Ned replied.

"It's been all over the society pages," Phoebe supplied. "The Haverfords lost their fortune in a land swindle, and the youngest son is suspected of trying to pay his bills by imposing on his friends."

Rhys's pulse went up. "Let me guess . . . by getting said friends drunk and then playing faro?"

Ned nodded. "Lord knows how he even got into the Davenport Ball—someone probably snuck him in."

Rhys's vision darkened. He wouldn't be surprised if that someone was Daniel.

"We'll find him, Mother," Rhys said, meeting Ned's eye, who nodded. "Do not worry. We'll start at the regular clubs and go on from there."

He turned to Margaret. "We'll be fine," she assured before he could open his mouth to say . . . something.

"Yes," Phoebe replied. "You take the carriage. I'm sure Lady Gray can accommodate us."

Rhys glanced at his mother. She had overcome her hysterics enough to transfer her weight from Margaret's arm to Phoebe's. Even in times of crisis, the woman always knew how to play it to best advantage. "Yes, of . . . of course, Lady

Ashby," she said, dabbing at her drying eyes. "Oh, but you must bid farewell to the Mortons! It would not do to just have you leaving and asking questions."

"Mother, time is of the essence—"

"I'll do it," Margaret piped up. Every eye turned to her. "I can make your good-byes to Miss Morton. I assume we all will be leaving the ball shortly, in any case."

Phoebe nodded. Rhys felt a pang of regret at taking Margaret away from her first London party, but it was obvious that even though the festivities would go on long into the night, there was little chance they would be able to enjoy them any longer.

"Thank you." He took a risk and reached out and squeezed Margaret's hand. He held it, and her gaze, for as long as he dared.

Why didn't you kiss her?

Then he let go.

"Come on, Ned," he said, marching toward the door, "let's go find my idiot of a brother."

IT ONLY TOOK a few minutes for Margaret to find Sylvia in the crowd. She was standing with her father, who beamed heartily and reached out to shake Margaret's hand the moment he saw her.

"Wonderful! Wonderful!" he said, pumping her arm as if it were a well. "I understand that you and my Sylvie are becoming good friends! A better partnership I cannot think of! A good strong mind like you can only keep her out of trouble, eh?"

"Father," Sylvia chided with a laugh. "Give us a moment, would you? We have 'good friend' things to discuss."

She pulled Margaret away into the crowd. "I'm so glad

you're back! Do you remember those two gentlemen we eyed? The ones in that corner over there?"

"Yes," Margaret replied, her stomach dropping to her knees. "You didn't talk to them, did you?"

"No, of course not!" she cried. "We have not been introduced, so I very well could not speak with them—at least not without an excuse, which I couldn't think of. But I did stand very near them, and I know that they noticed me."

"Oh," Margaret said, more than a little confused. "That's . . . good?"

"Yes," Sylvia said. "So, my idea is that if you and I both stand right here, they will notice both of us. Come, let us laugh as if we just heard the funniest joke." When Margaret did nothing, Sylvia's face fell. "It's just for fun. There's no harm in a little conversation, and really, we're doing this for you, not me." She leaned in close and waggled her eyebrow. "The one on the left is the absolute perfect height for you."

Margaret shook her head, not entirely sure where to start. But before she got drawn into laughing at some unheard joke, she remembered her purpose and guided Sylvia behind a potted palm. "Actually, I'm terribly sorry, but I am here to bid you good night."

"Good night?" Sylvia repeated. "You're leaving already?"

"I'm afraid so. And I have been asked to convey Dr. Gray's regrets—he's had a family matter arise and—"

As Sylvia's face fell into a little pout, she reached out to take Margaret's arm. And Margaret was certain the perfect expression of lost opportunity was about to come out of the girl's mouth . . . if only they hadn't been positioned close to a certain corner, where two young gentlemen were conversing, while they were concealed behind a particularly leafy palm.

". . . where'd that girl go? The little minx who was eyeing us over her fan?" one said in a bored drawl.

"I saw her talking with that beanstalk we saw her with earlier, then they disappeared," the other answered. "Don't bother with that one," he continued. "She might be lovely, but her father's a merchant."

Margaret glanced down at Sylvia. Her lips were pursed, but other than that, she seemed bored by what they were hearing. As if it could not faze her.

The other gentleman paused to consider. "There's money in the merchant class."

"I also hear she's spoken for."

"Ah . . ." Then, "What about the beanstalk?"

"Lord—now there's a mess." The gentleman chuckled, although his gentlemanly nature was being called into question by the second. "She's a nobody from nowhere, with no polish—I had it from Mrs. Davenport herself that when she went through the receiving line she decided to pull the flowers out of a vase and claim them as her bouquet."

"What an oddity," was the reply. And Margaret felt her face flame. Everything around them had grown so silent. The only thing in the world was the conversation taking place on the other side of the palm, and their ears straining to hear it—however much Margaret might not wish to.

"That's being kind. She's with Lord Ashby—friends of friends or some such thing."

"Ashby—is he the one who married the governess?"

"Hmm . . . and now he's saddled with another mediocrity."

"What's her name? The mediocrity."

"Ah . . . Babcock, I believe."

"There's a Sir Bartholomew Babcock, from the north, if I remember Debrett's. Very large estate. One daughter."

"You're such a woman, memorizing Debrett's. And if he only has one daughter, the estate is entailed away. She's likely as much a pauper as she is a mediocrity."

Margaret caught Sylvia's eye again. Now, instead of looking bored, she looked utterly livid. The angry pink on her cheeks highlighted the dark flashing in her eyes. And the way her breast rose and fell with sharp breaths, she obviously could no longer keep their positions a secret.

"Now see here!" she said, storming around the palm fronds to confront their detractors. "How dare you say such horrendous things about my friend! I might be from merchant stock, but you are rude, and . . . and . . ."

"And wrong," Margaret added.

"That's right, Margaret." Sylvia nodded hotly. "You are in no way a mediocrity!"

"Certainly not in size," one of the gentlemen snickered.

"I meant about Mrs. Davenport's flowers," Margaret replied. "I did not go near them, simply mentioned they were overwatered. Also, you're wrong about the entail."

"The . . . entail?" the taller of the two gentlemen asked, the smirk of self-satisfaction falling from his face.

"Yes, my father's estate is not entailed to the male line, but instead to any heir. Which, in this case, is me." She cocked her head to one side, thinking. "So one day I'll be the largest landowner in Lincolnshire, I suppose."

Three sets of eyes blinked at her, the faces still with shock.

"Really, if you're going to gossip about people"—she shrugged—"you should at least have all the facts."

It was as if the entire room froze—or at least, a circle of five feet, with Margaret at its center. Then, one perfect peal of laughter broke through it all.

Sylvia was the one laughing. And she was laughing at the flustered looks of shock still covering the two men's faces.

"For heaven's sake," Margaret muttered. "What did I say now?"

11

*R*hys and Ned had been to every gambling hell Ned knew of before they finally caught up to Daniel. This was partly due to the fact that Ned was decidedly out of practice when it came to hells.

"I haven't been to one since I married," he said by way of explanation. "And as a business, gaming hells don't seem to have much in the way of longevity. New ones keep popping up to replace the old."

Of course, they hadn't started at the hells. They started at the gentlemen's clubs, where a man could get a decent supper. "Your brother would want to fortify himself before embarking on debauchery, possibly?"

"Or possibly you wanted to grab a slice of ham and cheese before we headed out?" Rhys had grumbled irritably.

"We didn't go to get sandwiches," Ned replied, swallowing the last bits of his food. "We went to speak with Faber. He knows all the best—or rather, worst places to go. The sandwiches were just a bit of luck."

"Yes, you always did have that kind of luck," Rhys admitted. Faber was the underbutler at White's, and he knew everything about London—the one that sat in cushioned chairs that looked out of marbled windows onto clean streets, as well as the one that scuttled and seduced beneath. He gave them a list of hells as long as Rhys's arm. They started with the names Ned recognized, but after those three did not yield results, they continued on with the rest of the list, going from most disreputable to least.

They found him in the second one on the list.

"Well," Ned said weakly, "at least it's not the worst?"

They found Daniel at the faro table, surrounded by eager young lads watching the play. To his left sat a woman who could have been twice his age or could have been half—it was impossible to tell under all the paint. But her eyes were older than she could possibly be.

To Daniel's right was a man about his age, with wispy dark hair and the hungry look of someone trying desperately to not salivate over the money on the table.

Haverford.

Rhys was surprised that Haverford hadn't created an ocean on the baize, considering the sum of bank notes piled up in the center.

"Daniel," he called out, drawing the attention of absolutely no one, since they were all focused on the cards. "Damn it all," he muttered, and pushed through the crowd to where Daniel sat. He clamped his hand on his shoulder.

"What on earth—" Daniel slurred, turning. "Oh hell," he muttered, seeing his brother. "You here to bother me? Or are you here to take part in the underbelly's more savory side?" He grinned and leaned over to the woman at his left, then proceeded to give her the most slavish, drunken kiss to which Rhys had ever been unfortunate witness.

"It's the former," he said. "And what are you doing, licking the inside of her cheek?"

"You should try it," Daniel said when he came up for air.

"No one should try that," Ned piped up. "Ever."

"Come on," Rhys said, pulling Daniel up by the arm. "We're going home."

"Like hell we are," Daniel replied. "I'm still playing."

"Quite right," Haverford said. "We're in the middle of a round!"

"I wouldn't talk if I were you, Haverford," Rhys growled. "You're not getting any more money out of my brother than what's on that table. Be grateful I don't send for officers."

Haverford looked sufficiently cowed. Daniel, however, was not. "Now see here, Rhys, I haven't lost yet!"

Daniel pulled against Rhys, intending to sit back down. But Ned slipped into Daniel's open seat right before the boy could sit on his lap.

"Let me take this round for you. I've always had the devil's own luck at faro." Ned examined the cards on the table in front of him. "Go with your brother, he has something urgent to say to you."

Rhys met Ned's eyes, and nodded at him in thanks. Daniel had little choice but to follow where he was dragged, which was a slightly less crowded corner of the hell.

"What is it?" Daniel said, blowing a lock of blond hair out of his eyes. "I have a game to win."

"You wouldn't have won that game," Rhys replied. "Oh, you might have won that hand, but over the course of the night, your drinks would have gotten stronger and your cards weaker."

"So?" Daniel said, defiant. "What of it?"

"What of it?" Rhys repeated. "You're being deceived by your supposed friend, you know. And you're losing your entire allowance in a card game."

"Haverford *is* my friend. And you didn't give a damn if

I spent my time with him before Mama showed up to force you into doing her bidding."

"I didn't know of his deceit before . . . and I do not do Mother's bidding."

"You're marrying at Mama's bidding."

Rhys bit his tongue in his effort to keep from skinning Daniel alive as the inebriated idiot grinned in triumph.

"You're quite the philosopher when you're drunk and being swindled."

"And you're quite the moral stick-in-the-mud when trying to end a man's fun."

Daniel's petulance was matched by the glassy-eyed look on his face. Rhys glanced over at Ned, who called out, "Oh, look at that! I won again!" and raked the pile of money toward himself. Ned was occupied, Daniel was drunk, and Rhys knew that arguing would have no effect whatsoever.

"My stuck-up morality is the only thing that is saving you from ruination at the moment. Now come along!"

Rhys yanked on his brother's arm again and made for the door. However, this turned out to be the wrong course of action. Because of being jerked back and forth during the last few minutes, Daniel had been decidedly off balance. And his lack of balance must have unsettled something in his liquidated stomach, because suddenly he turned quite green.

"No," he muttered weakly. "I have to—"

And he ran to a large vase that was situated next to the staircase and promptly cast up accounts into it.

The vase held several umbrellas. It was a rather homey touch for such a sordid place. As his brother retched, Rhys could only hope that some poor soul who just lost all his winnings would not go the vase, open up his umbrella, and be greeted by the contents of Daniel's stomach raining down on his head.

While he was waiting patiently for Daniel's digestive system to finish rejecting the substances he'd spent the evening ingesting (apparently Daniel had enjoyed several of Mrs. Davenport's lemon tarts), a tap landed on his shoulder.

He turned to find himself staring down at two identical young gentlemen, neither of whom he recognized.

"Excuse me, sir, but are you Dr. Gray?" the bolder of the two said. He bore highly flushed cheeks and a tousled set of curls that made him look younger than he likely was—although the fuzz on his chin did nothing to help the image. "I'm Richard Thorndike; my uncle Stuart served with you in the army." At Rhys's blank look, he blushed and continued. "Stuart Thorndike? He runs the *Gazette-Post* now? But that's neither here nor there. Anyway, this is my brother Henry."

Both young men bowed. Henry, identical except for a self-important sneer, said, "*Lord* Henry Thorndike. At your service."

"Right," Rhys replied, and quickly returned their bows. "Do give my regards to your uncle, but I'm afraid I'm in the middle of—"

"Wait," Richard said, turning Rhys's attention back to him. "We need a doctor. Urgently."

That had Rhys's attention. Daniel was moaning over the vase; he wouldn't be trying to run back to the tables again. "What can I assist you with?" he asked, assuming his most professional demeanor.

"It's Henry, sir," Richard replied. "He has just suffered the most grievous injury."

Rhys looked over the other twin. He stood tall, did not exhibit pain. He did not seem to be in the throes of a medical emergency. "Injury, you say?" Rhys answered. "Where?"

"To my good name!" he replied hotly. "Carhartt spread

a rumor about my horsemanship. Said I treated my horses ill to everyone at Tattersalls!"

"You did forget to give Chauncey oats three times in a row," Richard piped up.

"When I was seventeen!" Henry replied. "I was but a child. And Carhartt knows this. But he decided to spread the rumor anyway—I had no choice but to call him out."

"Thus is our dilemma, sir," Richard said, trying very hard to not roll his eyes but not succeeding. "My brother insists on satisfaction. Carhartt's second has arranged the time and place. We are to bring the pistols and the doctor. And we don't know of any doctors."

"No," Rhys said. "Daniel, let's go."

"Please, Dr. Gray—my uncle says you saved his life in France."

"And I'm saving your life now," Rhys said, meeting Henry's defiant eye. "Go to your friend, rescind your invitation to the dueling ground."

Henry cocked his head to the side. "I told you he wouldn't do it," he said to his twin. "He wouldn't for his own father. Come on."

"No." Richard shook his head. "Dr. Gray—it's Henry's first duel . . ."

"Won't be my last." Henry's chest puffed out with pride.

"And we'll be laughingstocks if we show up without a doctor."

Rhys sighed. "Do you know why you need a doctor there?"

"To declare my opponent as having lost." Henry smirked.

"You young fool—" Rhys turned away from the brother for a moment, his eyes narrowing in on Henry and his second. "Do you know what a bullet does to the human body? It doesn't slice neatly, it doesn't poke. It rips. It shatters."

"Carhartt is a terrible shot," Henry replied. "I, on the other hand—"

"You might end up wishing that he was a good shot," Rhys interrupted. "Let's say you both turn and fire, not in the air, but at each other. You shoot him straight in the chest and he's dead in seconds. Meanwhile, you've been nicked in the shoulder."

Both twins were silent. Riveted.

"Now, you may initially be relieved. After all, you're living and breathing, and Carhartt is not. You are lucky that the bullet missed the major arteries. Instead, it ripped into the muscle and sinew of your shoulder. So now you cannot feel your arm. And it hit your collarbone, shattering it. A dozen bone shards are sticking into your tissue, stabbing you like hot needles. And the bullet? Well, the bullet is still in there. You will need to have an operation to have it removed. But with the excitement of the duel and the injury, your heart is beating fast, and you are losing blood quickly.

"So you're thrown into the carriage and head back to the closest safe place. It could be your home, it could be the doctor's rooms, it could be a pub. But in general you won't care, because your shoulder will be screaming with pain by now and you won't give a damn where you are.

"The doctor you brought—let's say it's not me, because it won't be—he's slightly tipsy, because it's a cold morning and he wanted the warmth of whiskey. So his vision will be double by the time he gets you onto a table, to examine the wound with his instruments. The only bit of luck you will have is that the pain is so great that you finally lose consciousness."

By now both twins had lost their ruddy, high color. And Henry had lost his smug sneer.

"When you awake, you'll find that the surgery is over. You have black thread holding your skin together, and you have to pray that your bleeding will slow. You are weak from the blood loss, and you still can't feel your arm. What you don't know is that you never will again. Shards from your collarbone severed the tendons that connect it to your body, so it just hangs there like a dead animal in a sack.

"You might think you are through the woods, because at least you're still breathing. But now the fever comes. And it doesn't abate. Because another thing you don't know is that a piece of your shirt was lodged in your shoulder along with the bullet, and your drunken doctor missed it. It's inside you, festering even as your body tries to heal, and your entire shoulder is raw with infection.

"So they try to bring your fever down by bleeding you, although you don't have enough blood anyway, but they have to try. It doesn't work. And now the infection is starting to spread down to your arm—this dead thing, lying by your side.

"Have you ever seen someone have a limb amputated? It's not pretty. You'll wish for death as a doctor takes a saw to your skin. Since the arm is dead anyway, they won't try to save any of it. They will cut as close to your wound as they can. It will take twenty minutes to cut through your bone. And this time, they do not let you fall into unconsciousness, because if they do, they know the odds are you won't wake up."

By now, more than the twins were listening. Everyone around them had paused. Rhys could feel Daniel, listing by his shoulder.

"If you survive this—and those odds are not good—you still have an infection. You are still fevered. So they bleed you again. They will do this until you die or until the fever breaks. But the entire time, you will be wishing that you could have ended on the field like Carhartt.

"And if you do survive, you'll be charged in your friend's

death. You'll have to run to the Continent—perhaps your brother will help, but chances are, he'll be too busy assuming the role you were supposed to occupy.

"Your health will never return fully. You will always tire easily. The fever lasted so long you have forgotten things. Your mind falls to confusion much easier than it used to. You will never come home. All because you were embarrassed that you forgot to give Chauncey oats when you were seventeen."

Everyone was struck dumb. Young Richard wore his shock openly, but Henry looked as if he was about to need Daniel's vase of umbrellas.

"Where is Carhartt?" Rhys asked.

"I . . . I don't know," Richard said, shaking his head. "At the club, I imagine."

"I suggest you find him. And make your amends."

"Yes, sir," Henry said, swallowing his pride, and his bile.

With that, the Thorndike twins mutely slipped out of the building, off to find their friend and negotiate a truce.

"Well done, Rhys," Ned said in a hushed tone as he appeared at his left. "We had better go. I won the table, and if I recall correctly, hells tend to look down upon people winning."

"Well done?" Daniel scoffed as they headed for the door. "You and your morality stick have just destroyed a man's pride. He'll be the laughingstock of London tomorrow."

"At least he'll be alive."

"You'll never understand, will you?" Daniel said. "Come tomorrow, Thorndike will wish he had the courage to die, once this story gets around."

"Stand on a battlefield," Ned said, his voice hard as granite. "Then tell me about the courage to die."

Daniel merely shrugged as they took him by the scruff of the neck and threw him into the carriage. Rhys turned to his friend, shaking his head. "Don't argue with him, Ned—it's pointless."

"After all your family's been through," Ned said, his eyes hot. "After all *you've* been through. He should know better."

"True," Rhys agreed. "But this is one lesson most Grays refuse to learn."

"Hold on," Daniel said, popping his head out. "Did you say you won the faro bank? Since you were playing for me, really I won, didn't I?"

Rhys didn't reply as he shut the door in his brother's face.

12

The next morning, Margaret Babcock found herself surrounded by more varieties of flowers than she had ever seen before.

And that was no small feat.

Just off the top of her head, she saw roses, delphiniums, clematis, primroses, violets, tulips, calendula, daisies, sweet William, hollyhocks. She decided she liked the daisies best—for their bold simplicity in the face of overwhelming competition.

There were obviously cultivated purple saxifrage next to the florist's favorite carnations, the latter she personally found terribly sad. All petal, no purpose. Amazingly, there was also an Indian lotus! Margaret had only seen drawings of Indian lotus before. However, in the drawings they were floating in water, not tied into some kind of posy. Margaret lasted three seconds before she crossed the room, ripped the lotus from the nosegay, and placed it in a jug of fresh water.

Chances were slim, but with luck, she might be able to salvage the flower, or a cutting.

This cornucopia of blossoms occupied the sitting room, and the parlor, and leaked into the breakfast room, which was where Margaret first encountered it, coming down for a bite to eat before she headed to the garden, dressed in her trousers for a day of long work.

The first thought she had was, *Thank goodness Leticia was already counties away*. The second thought was . . .

"What on earth . . . ?" she asked, finally free to examine the flowers, now that she had fixed the lotus.

"They've been arriving since dawn," Phoebe said, coming into the room, carrying the baby. "Of course, we've been up since four, haven't we, my little love?" She nuzzled the baby, who gurgled in a way that made Margaret think he had been delighted to be awake since four. "Nanny had been awake for twenty hours; I decided she needed a reprieve."

"Who are they for?" Margaret asked.

"You, of course."

"Me?" she cried. The familiar sensation of bewilderment rushed over her. "Why?"

"Because of what you told me you said to those two gentlemen last night."

"About Mrs. Davenport's peonies?"

"No, darling." Phoebe laughed. "About how you are the heir to your father's estate. You suddenly shifted from just 'someone at the party' to a significant heiress and eligible young lady of stature."

"Usually when people talk about my stature, it's not a comment on the size of my fortune," Margaret replied.

"Some of the flowers came with cards, if you were curious as to who sent them." Phoebe nodded toward a pile of perfect rectangles spilling over their silver tray. Cautiously, Margaret went and thumbed through them.

"I don't know a single one of these people," Margaret

said. Then, "This one is a duke! What would a duke want with me?"

"I haven't the foggiest," Lord Ashby said, yawning as he entered the breakfast room. "Good morning, my love." He leaned down to kiss Phoebe. "Good morning, my little rooster," he said, kissing the baby's head.

"Rooster?" Phoebe asked.

"Because he's what wakes us up in the morning," he replied, shrugging. "I'm trying it out."

"Try something else." Phoebe smirked.

"What's this about a duke and Miss Babcock?" Lord Ashby said as he stuffed a piece of toast into his mouth and loaded his plate with sausages and eggs. "Does it have anything to do with why she's wearing trousers?"

"Ned!" Phoebe cried.

He froze, looked to his wife. "Is that one of those questions I'm not allowed to ask?"

She nodded.

"I'm wearing trousers because they are my clothes for working in the garden," Margaret offered. "And apparently a duke sent me flowers."

"Interesting." Lord Ashby's eyebrow rose. "Where did you meet him?"

"I haven't."

"After you left last night," Phoebe explained, "some information about Miss Babcock's situation as one of the largest heiresses in the north was revealed to the general public at the Davenport Ball."

"It wasn't the general public," Margaret said. "It was two gentlemen, who—"

"Who told absolutely everyone else they could find," Phoebe said, shaking her head. "Face it, Margaret—you are the sensation of the season."

"But . . . I'm not here for the season!" she cried. "I'm

here to present my roses—which I desperately need to check on; I left Frederick specific instructions about the mulching—and I wanted to see some sights, and that's all."

"Well, you're one of the sights now," Ned replied through bites of food. He reached for a pitcher on the table. "Why is there a flower in this water?"

Phoebe rolled her eyes, plopped the baby in her husband's lap, and crossed the room to Margaret.

"I know this is overwhelming, and you are under no obligation to answer or even accept any of these cards," she said, gently laying her hand on Margaret's arm. "But if you were perhaps interested in amending your plans and seeing what the *ton* has to offer, you'll not be alone. I would be happy to accompany you anywhere you wish."

While Margaret took in what Phoebe said, over her shoulder the baby made a retching sound and spat up warm milk onto his father's lap.

Lord Ashby looked down into his son's smiling face. "Thank you for that. Most generous," he said, and put another sausage into his mouth.

Margaret felt it best to leave the perfumes and pressures of all the hothouse flowers that crowded the house—more were arriving by the minute, and taking over the hallways now—and go about her day as if nothing out of the ordinary was happening. Therefore she headed to the conservatory and the garden.

At her direction, Frederick had located and purchased several dozen clay pots of varying sizes. It was not the time of year for planting, but beggars could not be choosers, and the rosemary, mint, and thyme cuttings Frederick had also managed to obtain from the grocer would make an excellent start to building a decent herb garden.

She had no doubt Lord Ashby would thank her when his eggs had flavor.

She was in the middle of setting the cuttings in water to force root growth when Sylvia Morton walked into the conservatory.

"Now you'll want to change the water on these every few days, Frederick, and in a few weeks' time—"

"Well, isn't this marvelous?" Sylvia's voice floated over the high space, echoing against the glass walls. Margaret turned and saw she was admiring a pot of ivy that was hanging from the ceiling. One of the few plants that could even survive Frederick's gardening before her arrival.

"Sylvia," Margaret said. "How good to see you."

"I passed a veritable hothouse on the way in," Sylvia said. "If that is your handiwork, the Horticultural Society will throw you a fete."

"It's not," Margaret said, eyeing the brown pots filled with dirt and no flowers. "My work doesn't have much in the way to show for it at the moment. Except for those."

She nodded toward the doors to the back garden, which were open to allow in some of the sweet morning air. There, the hybrid roses sat proud in their mulch, feasting on the sun and their new London soil.

"Oh my," Sylvia said. "How interesting. But where did all these other flowers come from?"

"They are from . . . people," Margaret replied.

"People?"

"I don't know any of them. But they sent cards as well." She shook her head. "One was a duke."

"A duke?" Sylvia's lips formed a perfect O. "But this is fantastic! You are being courted."

"So I've gathered," Margaret replied, wiping her hands of water and dirt onto her apron. "It's all very silly."

"Of course it's silly," Sylvia replied. "That's what makes it fun!"

Margaret felt her eyebrows shift up.

"The flowers come in the morning. And then the men come in the afternoon." Sylvia clapped her hands together. "You are about to be inundated with the most eligible men London has to offer. Oh, I am so envious!"

"I . . . I don't want to be inundated," Margaret said, panic rising in her chest. "I have these herbs to propagate, and I was hoping to experiment with my lotus blossom, and—"

"Oh, Margaret," Sylvia said, stepping forward to stand on the opposite side of the table from her. "I did not mean to make you uncomfortable. Of course, you need not receive anyone if you don't wish to. I was simply curious who would be so bold as to show up at your door today. Aren't you?"

Margaret looked down at the pots in front of her. Her hand went unconsciously to her braid, and she began twirling the end around her thumb.

"You *are* curious, aren't you?"

"No. Not really," Margaret said. "Except—have you ever seen a duke in real life?"

Sylvia shook her head, grinning. "Do you think they wear their ermine when paying calls, or just when sitting for paintings?"

Margaret snorted a laugh. Then, "But I have no wish to receive anyone. And I have so much work to do here and—"

"Maybe you don't have to see anyone," Sylvia replied. "Do you realize that one of the rooms on the second story directly overlooks the front entrance? We could simply sit up there by the window, watching everyone who comes to the door. The butler will tell them you're not receiving, and they'll go. You could even bring your plants to pot while we watch."

It wasn't a bad plan, as far as plans go, Margaret thought.

They would not be seen, but her callers would. And she could remain blissfully anonymous.

"Oh please," Sylvia begged prettily. "I'm absolutely dying of curiosity."

Margaret smiled ruefully. "All right," she said as Sylvia gave a little hop of glee. "Frederick, grab about a dozen pots, that bucket of soil, and the mint cuttings. We'll be working in the upstairs parlor."

Margaret stepped out from behind her bench, taking a few pots in hand. As she did, Sylvia caught sight of what she was wearing, and her eyes grew wide.

"Oh my goodness!" Sylvia said. "Trousers?"

"They're for work," Margaret said, slightly defensive. "I can get them dirty."

"Well, it's a good thing that no one will see you," Sylvia said, reaching forward to take a pot. "They'll all fall madly in love with you on sight. And that would be an utter disaster."

Thus the afternoon was spent in a haze of mirth and mint potting.

Sylvia and Margaret set themselves up in the upstairs sitting room, which was generally unused, since the family rooms were all downstairs. But as Sylvia had pointed out, it had a perfect view of the front steps and square. They could see anyone approaching from either direction.

"This is perfect," Sylvia cried. "Oh, you could know everything about everyone on the street from up here!"

"I suppose," Margaret said as she pulled a small side table out from its position by a stuffed chair. "But what business is it of mine?"

"It's the business of everyone," Sylvia replied. She left the window to come over and help Margaret move the table into a ray of sunlight. "Information is currency. If you see, let's say, one of the patronesses of Almack's walking with her dog, then when you are presented to her, you'll have something to say."

"Oh," Margaret replied. "That does make sense." Although the last time she had tried to make conversation with a hostess, it hadn't gone that well.

"Imagine you see something on the street one day, and you can confirm it happened to anyone who asks before it even hits the papers."

"I've always wondered—if everyone is talking about something, why does it need to be printed in the paper?" Margaret asked as she placed the pots and the mint in neat rows on the table.

"Because once it's in the paper, it's unquestionably true."

Margaret took her notebook out of her apron's pocket and began to jot down what she was planting, how, and where. Her records were always meticulous.

However, as the time ticked from before to after noon, the notebook fell by the wayside, and the mint left to take root in their pots without Margaret's diligent attention. Because as Margaret soon discovered, sometimes it was fun to look out the window with a friend and see who was walking by.

"Oh! There's one!" Sylvia cried. "He's wearing a gray coat and hat. And . . . he's knocking . . . and the butler is telling him you are not receiving today." She pushed closer to the window, her nose almost touching. "He's taking off his hat . . . decently good-looking, although his chin is a little weak."

Margaret relented and glanced at the window. "He's also five feet tall!"

"His hat obscured his height," Sylvia said, frowning. "He's going—oh, but he left his card. Can we have all the cards left by gentlemen brought up here? So we know who they are?"

Soon enough, Molly was running up and down the stairs every ten minutes, bringing a half dozen new cards with her every time. When peckishness began to distract them, tea and a tray of sandwiches were brought up as well.

Before she knew it, Margaret was seated in the window bay, cup of tea in one hand and a cucumber sandwich in the other, as she laughed with Sylvia over the parade beneath them. It was, for once, as if she understood those girls on the streets of Helmsley, walking in packs together and whispering and giggling. She was let in on the secret she had long been denied.

"I think that's Lord Thorndike," Sylvia said. "He has a twin, so he's easy to spot."

"Not if you cannot tell them apart."

Sylvia laughed. "I heard he was supposed to fight a duel this morning but recanted. Most embarrassing."

"More like most intelligent," Margaret replied, laughing.

"Believe me, I agree with you most fervently on the topic of dueling," Sylvia mused. "But still . . . embarrassing."

Margaret suddenly remembered with stark brightness the story Rhys had told her about his and Sylvia's fathers. The reason he and Sylvia were being pointed toward marriage.

And then of course, her mind turned to the warmth of Rhys's hand at the small of her back as they danced . . .

"Oh goodness!" Sylvia cried, almost jumping from her seat. "There are those two men from last night! The cruel gossips!"

"Why on earth are they here?" Margaret frowned. "They must know I wouldn't receive them even if they brought me the gardens of Hampton Court Palace!"

"They are coming to eat crow. One or both must be quite hard up for money."

Their names, it was learned when Molly came back up

with the cards, were Stanhope and Corduff, and Margaret made a mental note to never speak to anyone ever named Stanhope or Corduff, as Sylvia gleefully ripped up their cards.

A carriage rolled up. A very grand, very fine carriage.

"Who might this be?" Margaret mused.

Sylvia gasped. "That's a ducal crest on the carriage. That's your duke!"

They both dropped their sandwiches and peered out the window. They watched as a liveried servant jumped down from his perch and went up to the door. The carriage remained closed, only the curtain from the window floated in the breeze.

"Oh pooh, we shan't see the duke," Sylvia said.

But they did manage the smallest glimpse of the duke, for when the liveried servant went back to the carriage, the duke laid his hand on the window's edge.

"Is he wearing gloves?"

"No, I just think his hand is quite . . . wrinkled. And spotted."

"That is an alarming amount of lace at the cuff."

"Was that purple satin on his sleeve?"

Margaret and Sylvia met eyes. And together they burst out laughing.

And that was how Rhys found them when Molly showed him up to the second-floor sitting room.

"I'm terrified to ask what you are laughing at," Rhys said, after knocking lightly on the open door.

Margaret turned and watched him cautiously enter the room. He had his hat in hand, and was observing them both with a look of true befuddlement on his face.

"Oh, Rhys!" Margaret said, leaping to her feet like a child caught being lazy. "How did we miss seeing you? We've been watching the front steps and—"

"Why have you been watching the front steps?" he asked, his eyes swinging from Margaret to Sylvia.

"Because last night I accidentally told people that I'm rich," she answered haltingly, although she was fully confident Rhys would understand.

Rhys blinked twice, then nodded. "Ah, I see."

"Miss Babcock is quite popular, Dr. Gray," Sylvia said smoothly. "All the flowers downstairs, the invitations that I'm sure have been arriving. We have been watching the gentlemen callers come and leave their cards."

"Anyone of interest?" Rhys said, his eyes meeting Margaret's.

"No, of course not," she replied immediately.

"Don't say that," Sylvia chided. "You never know until you give them a chance. Who knows, your future husband could have just knocked on your door."

Margaret blushed furiously and did her damnedest to avoid anyone's eye.

"But, I second Margaret's question," Sylvia asked. "How did we miss seeing you?"

"I came in through the garden," Rhys replied.

"The garden?" Sylvia asked when Margaret shrugged.

"There's a hidden door by the back wall. There was a bit of a crowd out front, you see."

And Rhys was so very used to coming and going as he pleased in Lord Ashby's house, it was second nature to come via the more casual path.

"How delightful to see you, sir," Sylvia said, breaking through the silence. She stepped forward gently, folding her hands in front of her demurely. "My father was quite disappointed that he did not get the chance to speak with you at length last evening."

"Yes." Rhys grimaced. "I regret having to leave so abruptly, but—"

"Have no fear—Margaret made your excuses."

"As always, Margaret, I am in your debt."

Margaret blushed again. Really, this was becoming unseemly.

Sylvia came to her side, lacing her arm through Margaret's. "To what does Margaret owe your visit?" she asked, overly bright. "I assume you came to speak with her, of course. Since you no doubt thought she was in the garden."

Margaret glanced up through her lashes, and was surprised to see Rhys blushing now.

"Yes. I did come to speak with Margaret," he said, once he recovered his voice. "But it's nothing you cannot hear, Miss Morton."

Margaret could feel Sylvia's body relaxing against hers. She nodded, prompting Rhys to continue.

"I simply wanted to let you know that Sir Kingsley from the Horticultural Society of London will be coming to call and view your roses a week from today," he said. "It will be an unofficial visit, since they have horridly old-fashioned rules about allowing women into their circle."

"Goodness, if they are that old-fashioned, they will be completely scandalized by your trousers, Margaret."

Margaret glanced down. She had completely forgotten she was still wearing her work clothes and her apron. "Oh, I shan't wear this when they come. I do have some sense of etiquette. But . . . if they are coming in a week, I have a great deal to do before then!" The conservatory was nowhere near ready. She had to mix up more batches of fertilizer tea. She would like to take cuttings from her roses and test them for how well they responded to the light in the southern part of England as opposed to Lincolnshire. And she'd be damned if she'd let Phoebe be shamed for her lack of proper garden.

"Oh, but . . ." Sylvia said, looking down at her hands.

"The Medfield Ball is tonight. I was so hoping you were going to be there."

"I . . . I don't believe I've been invited."

"From what I've seen today I doubt you need to be. But chances are there is an invitation in the pile that came in the last hours," Sylvia countered. Her eyes became wide, vulnerable. "I won't know another soul there, and it's terribly daunting."

Margaret looked from Sylvia to Rhys. On the one hand, she did have a great deal of work she wished to do. And she had already experienced a London ball and found the evening rather dull—excluding its consequences. She saw no need to go to another.

On the other hand, she might not have had much experience with having friends—female friends her own age—but from observation, they seemed to require each other's support. And Sylvia was asking for hers.

"I would need to speak to Phoebe," she said. "But I suppose . . ."

"Wonderful!" Sylvia cried, unable to hold back from embracing Margaret. Although Margaret wasn't certain she had tried very hard. When she pulled away, she turned toward Rhys. "And you, Dr. Gray? Will you be attending the Medfield Ball?"

Rhys looked to Margaret. And Margaret tried to send him a silent plea. Because if she must attend the Medfield Ball, at least there would be a spot of sunlight in an otherwise dull evening if Rhys was there.

And maybe they could dance again.

His hand on her back . . .

Luckily, he was fluent in silent pleas—at least he was fluent in Margaret's—because he nodded slowly, clearing his throat.

"Right," he said. "I would have to find out if I have a

pending invitation, but I would be happy to attend, Miss Morton." Then he turned to Margaret, and finally his eyes met hers. And that same strange sensation that she felt before thrilled through her chest. Standing under fireworks in Vauxhall. Dancing a waltz under the Davenports' chandelier.

Under a spell.

"Delightful!" Sylvia said, shattering Margaret's thoughts with her cheerful verve. "I'm so relieved you both will go."

She stepped forward, pulling Margaret with her. Impulsively she reached out and laid her hand on Rhys's arm, linking the three of them in a chain.

"Margaret, Sylvia, and Rhys." She swung her smile back and forth between them. "What a threesome we shall make!"

13

Over the course of the next several days, Rhys went to more balls, routs, card parties, dinners, salons, and informal gatherings in evening wear than he had in all his previous London visits combined.

His mother was ecstatic.

"You've become quite the social butterfly," his mother said, winking at him over her tea one breakfast.

"Yes, it's almost as if you are trying to curry a female's favor," his sister Eloisa said, the vinegar that normally flavored her voice suddenly swapped for honey.

Rhys felt his back stiffen even as his cheeks blushed. "I am merely enjoying my time in London with my friends. Miss Morton has nothing to do with it."

"I wasn't talking about Miss Morton," Eloisa said.

Rhys froze. "Then whom?"

"Why, Mother, of course." She smiled at him, syrupy again.

"Miss Morton aside," his mother said. "Although I know it must be very difficult for you to put her aside, your appearing in society does us all a world of good. It lets everyone know that the Grays are still very much a part of things, and paves the way for your father's and brother's return."

"Uncle Rhys—" came a small voice from beside the table.

"Well, if going out in society is what we must do for the family good, I am happy to do my part," Daniel said, grinning. Then wincing. He had an awful head from his carousing the night before.

"Your kind of 'going out' does not assist anyone, unless it's card sharps and courtesans."

"Rhys, would you be so kind as to not speak of card sharps and . . . the demimonde in front of your youngest brother?" his mother chided, nodding toward Benjamin, who was engrossed in building the largest pile of potato mash on his plate as humanly possible. Not eating, just . . . piling.

"Uncle Rhys."

"The demimonde?" Delilah asked, eyes sparkling. "Ooh, what's that?"

"It's exactly what you think it is, Dee," Jubilee said, her eyes coming up from her book. "And apparently Benji's ears are more sensitive than ours, because Mama told us all about it when we were fifteen."

"Uncle Rhys."

"Benji is my baby," his mother said, her eyes getting misty. Then she cleared her throat. "But for girls, fore-warned is forearmed."

"Oh, perhaps that philosophy is one the young ladies in your life should be made aware of, Rhys," Eloisa said.

"Uncle Rhys."

"Yes, Rory?" Rhys said finally, turning to his nephew. He prayed that the boy had something of interest to say. Something to pull him out of the endless round of pointed quips and questions that were aimed at his head.

"I can whistle now."

Then of course, he remembered that the boy was four. But still it was a welcome distraction, and Rhys took a certain amount of unclely pleasure in watching Rory purse his mouth and proceed to blow spit all over himself in pursuit of a high pitch.

As Eloisa took her whistling son onto her lap, Delilah put her hands up over her ears, knocking Benji's elbow as she did. Which caused him to put his entire hand into his mountain of mash. Then, with great disgust, Benji wiped his hand on his sister's shoulder.

Rhys couldn't contain his grin. *This* was what he had missed. This was his family. Being loud and silly and completely comfortable with each other. It was times like this when he felt that pang—that he had somehow done himself a disservice by staying away from them.

"We should really settle on a date to invite the Mortons over for dinner. Make our families . . . that much closer," she said, leaning forward conspiratorially.

And that was the reason he was spending so much time out of the house. He was trying this morning to hold off the questions about his supposed marriage, but they would always be there. Even when he wasn't going out to dinner or to the opera in the company of Margaret and Miss Morton, he was so often at Phoebe and Ned's home that they began setting a place for him at every meal, the staff knowing it was as likely as not that he would be there.

It was also increasingly likely that Miss Morton would be there. She had attached herself to Margaret in a way that he would have found alarming—if not for Margaret seeming to enjoy Sylvia's company. To be fair to the girl, she and Margaret seemed to enjoy a fast friendship, regardless of the obvious situation that everyone was aware of. A situation that was never named, never spoken of, but was beginning to weigh heavily on Rhys.

Whenever he wanted to speak to Margaret, Sylvia was there. And he wanted to . . . oh hell, he didn't know. He wanted her presence. He wanted to ask her questions and hear what she had to say. He wanted to tell her about his nephew's exceptional prowess at whistling. Instead, he found himself following as Sylvia declared she wished to attend some function, and Margaret promising to attend as well.

So first it was the Medfield Ball.

Then an afternoon salon the next day.

Then Ned and Phoebe's box at the opera.

Then the next day a soiree held in Regent's Park, in the late afternoon.

Then a ball, then a dinner party, then a ball . . . He went to all of them, neatly packaged into the party with Ned and Phoebe. Mr. Morton, it seemed, was happy to allow his daughter to be de facto chaperoned by Lady Ashby, and sat out most events if they went past nine o'clock. He was still very much accustomed to country hours. Much like Rhys's mother, he seemed to be of the opinion that as long as Sylvia was with Dr. Gray, it was all to the good.

Also, Mr. Morton and Lady Gray were not the only people to notice. Whispers were beginning to circulate, as people remembered the past, and why the name Morton was so familiar when one said it next to the name Gray.

"The fathers . . . it was a duel, you know . . . Lord Gray's been living on the Continent ever since."

"And the Mortons are willing to forgive it?"

"I don't know, but Dr. Gray dancing with Miss Morton is a good sign, don't you find?"

"It's like Romeo and Juliet—oh, how romantic!"

And so on.

Such whispers made every attempt to reach Rhys's ears, and he found it quite disturbing. He was not unused to whispers—his family reveled in their passions, and that often meant there was a casual disregard for the rest of the world watching. But *he* had never been the subject of the whispers before.

Unlike the rest of his family, he found himself very aware of the eyes on him.

It made him miss Greenwich. It made him miss his laboratory, and his work. But he knew he could not step away now, not even for a day or two.

Not when Margaret was so unhappy.

It was not something she showed to the outside world. To the outside world, she smiled politely, and danced when asked (and suddenly everyone was asking), and tried to make conversation. To them she was Miss Babcock, the surprisingly most eligible young lady of the season, and she was having a marvelous time.

But Rhys could see differently.

"I never took her for a social butterfly either," Phoebe said as they made their way through yet another party—the name of the hosts Rhys had completely forgotten, not as if it mattered anyway. "But she's the one who comes to me and says that she wishes to attend these parties."

"Yes," Rhys grudgingly agreed. "However, I cannot help but feel that it is Miss Morton who wants to go to these events, and Margaret obliges."

"That is decidedly possible," Phoebe murmured slowly. "But perhaps that has more to do with trying to please you than with pleasing Miss Morton."

Rhys looked up.

"We are trying, you know. Learning of your . . . connection to Miss Morton, it threw us all. But Margaret is the one who made the effort to befriend her. Perhaps she is trying to make this time easier for you. Easier to be in company with Miss Morton, easier to get to know her."

Rhys was dumbstruck. "I . . . that's not what I want for Margaret. I don't want her worrying about that."

"We all worry about that. It's what friends do." Phoebe glanced at Rhys's face, hesitant. "If it's worth anything at all, I've spent the last week in Miss Morton's company, and she is everything a young lady is brought up to be. She could be a good wife to you. If that is what you want."

Rhys didn't have an answer for that. Simply because it was the same conclusion he had come to. And that had settled on him like a cold chill. Not unpleasant, but as if he was slowly being made dormant.

"I would rather Margaret be doing as *she* wished, instead of trying to please others," he said gruffly. "Especially me."

"Have you spoken to her about it?" Phoebe replied.

"I will. Right now."

But as he set off across the floor, looking over the tops of people's heads for Margaret, he did not see the person coming up to him, who then walked straight into his chest.

"My apologies," Rhys said as he extricated the young lady from his arms. She clung delicately to his side, trying to keep her balance.

"Dr. Gray," Miss Morton said, smiling up at him once she had her bearings. "It's quite all right. Out of all the people I could run into, I count you among my favorites."

She smiled at her small joke. And he smiled too, in spite of himself. "Miss Morton, I was looking for Margaret."

"She's . . ." Miss Morton's face clouded. "She's dancing and having a marvelous time, I'm sure. In fact, that was why I came to find you. It's our dance, I believe."

"I . . ." Rhys was torn. On the one hand, he wanted to find Margaret, to speak with her. But he did promise a dance to Miss Morton.

In fact, he realized, he'd danced with Miss Morton at every outing this week. She managed to get him to promise a set to her before they even stepped out of the carriage.

No wonder people were whispering about them and his mother was so ecstatic.

Miss Morton was looking up at him with wide-eyed hope. And he found himself unable to disappoint her.

"Happily, Miss Morton," he said, and took her arm.

The dance was a quadrille, so Rhys spent most of the time concentrating on remembering the steps. Miss Morton seemed pleased enough by this, and did not press him for conversation.

In fact, she rarely did.

"Are you enjoying the evening, Miss Morton?" he asked as he counted steps and kept his eyes peeled for the tall, blond form of Margaret, likely counting steps too.

"Of course, Dr. Gray. How could I not?"

Indeed. At least one of them was.

"And . . . what did you do with your day today?"

"Margaret and I went shopping, and then we met you for dinner at the Ashbys'," she replied. "Terribly uninteresting to you, I'm afraid."

"Not at all." Yes it was. "But I would think that dances like this are a prime opportunity to get to know one another better."

"Do we need to?"

That brought him to a stop, in the middle of a turn. Miss Morton blushed, furiously embarrassed, and guided him back into the steps.

"I meant no offense," she said in a rush. "Of course we need to know each other as best as possible. I simply meant that . . . having been in each other's constant company, there is not much I could say that you don't already know."

"Yes," he agreed. "But I don't know how you feel about it."

"How I feel about it?" she said, shaking her head. "Today I went shopping in London and now I'm dancing in London. How could it be anything other than grand?"

"And Margaret?" he found himself asking.

"What about Margaret?"

"How does she feel about it?"

"Well . . . she loves it, of course! Why else would she be here?" Miss Morton exclaimed, a spot of frustration showing through.

And further darkening Rhys's vision. Obviously the girl was not paying any attention to her friend. He again raised his head, looking about for Margaret.

"But she's not here," he replied. "Not dancing, at any rate."

"Oh for heaven's sake, Margaret is fine. She wanted to see the gardens, so Mr. Bainbridge took her."

Rhys came to an abrupt stop again. This time, Miss Morton stopped with him, and they stepped fully out of line.

"She went with Mr. Bainbridge to the gardens?"

"Yes," Miss Morton admitted.

"And you let her?"

"But . . . but Mr. Bainbridge is a gentleman," she said, flustered. "And Margaret—well, she wanted to go, and she's obviously able to take care of herself, so . . ."

But he did not hear the rest. Because he was gone.

He moved with all possible haste to find the garden. He dodged and weaved through the crowd and into the dining room, before he finally found the French doors to the terrace, which stepped down into the gardens.

It was black as pitch with a waning moon, and his eyes searched the gardens for any sign of movement.

There was perhaps a bit more movement than he was prepared for.

"Oh!" he said, disturbing one couple who were obviously not anyone he knew. "Sorry."

The gardens, for a London home, were impressive, at least in size. He had absolutely no idea what kind of plants were growing because of the dark . . . but then he realized he knew someone who wouldn't let a little lack of light stop her from proper identification.

All he had to do was listen for it.

". . . These pots are much too small, the root will ball up and choke the poor thing . . ."

"Miss Babcock," came the scratchy voice of young Bainbridge. "Did I tell you your eyes look beautiful in the moonlight?"

"There's very little moon and I'm not looking at you, so how can you possibly tell?" Margaret answered.

"I . . . I . . ." was the reply from a young swain trying his hand at seduction obviously for the first time.

"I agree, Miss Babcock," Rhys said, coming around the corner. Margaret had taken one of the potted plants, was holding it up to examine in a faint beam of light from the party inside.

"About what?" She looked up at him, and his breath caught.

"That there is no way Bainbridge could know your eyes look beautiful in the moonlight."

But they were. Wide, dark orbs, the whites luminous in what little light the crescent moon threw off. Some of the yellow warmth from the party inside in the distance caught her skin, emphasizing her striking cheekbones, which until now had never actually struck him. And the way she smiled when she saw him . . . Like he was the only person in the world . . .

He had to stop noticing things like this. It was distracting. Unfair to everyone. And it only made him more irritable.

"D . . . Dr. Gray," Bainbridge said, taking a precautionary half step away from Margaret. "Good evening." He bowed nervously.

"Good evening, Mr. Bainbridge. I trust you are healthy."

"Yes," Bainbridge said, his mouth trembling into a quasi-smile. He then turned to Margaret by way of explanation. "I was thrown from a horse a few years back, and Dr. Gray here set my bones. My family seat is near Greenwich and Dr. Gray is, of course, the most renowned physician in England."

"Really?" Margaret's eyes went wide. "And here I thought Dr. Gray was only renowned in the southern counties."

"Only the best for us Bainbridges." He smirked.

"You suffered quite dreadfully from a fever too," Rhys said, trying to keep from smirking in turn. "And incontinence if I recall correctly. I assume that resolved itself?"

"I . . . I . . ."

"Well, as I find you this far from a chamber pot, I suppose it must have."

"I . . . I was only showing Miss Babcock the gardens . . ."

"And yet that wasn't what you wished to show her, was it?" he said.

Bainbridge, looking ever more the boy, stuttered. "I . . . I would never . . ."

"Never what?" Margaret asked, turning her attention from Rhys to Bainbridge. Her innocent question seemed to be the undoing of the youth, and he stumbled over his feet as he swiveled, trying to figure out which person he should take his leave of first. Finally, he managed to bow to both Margaret and Rhys and left, muttering something about his father hearing about this.

"What was that about?" Margaret asked, watching as the boy disappeared into the darkness.

"His own inadequacies," Rhys said, smiling for the first time all evening. "What do you have there?"

Margaret glanced down at the pot in her hands. "A member of the Asteraceae family." At his raised eyebrow, she translated. "A plain old daisy. Whose root base is far too large for this pot."

"Tell me, how difficult is it for you to refrain from pulling the whole thing out of the offending pot right now and putting it into a more hospitable bit of earth?"

"You have absolutely no idea," Margaret replied with a conspiratorial blush. "If I was not wearing this gown I would have already done so. Just picking up this pot has no doubt ruined my gloves."

"Let me see." He took the pot from her and set it on a low wall. Then he took her hands in his and flipped them over, examining the palms.

"Hmm," he said.

"That bad?" she asked.

"In my professional medical opinion?" he replied. "These are past saving."

"Drat," she said, "I knew it."

But he didn't let go of her hands. And neither did she pull away. Instead they just stood there, in the dark of the garden, holding hands like they were dancing a reel.

The slowest reel known to man. Just a slight sway to the sound of a breeze rustling the leaves in the trees. A distant laugh. A pair of moonlit eyes.

"Ah . . . what are you doing?" Margaret asked him eventually.

"Doing?" Rhys said, shaking himself out of his reverie.

"Out here, in the garden?"

"Oh yes," he replied. "I came to look for you, actually. I was told you were out here unchaperoned."

"Oh . . . oh *no*," Margaret said, her mouth dropping open. "I mean, yes, I was unchaperoned. But I wanted to see the garden—I thought I would just pop out and take a look, but then when I glanced up, Bainbridge was there too. Oh God, does this mean I will have to marry him?"

"What?" Rhys said, shocked. "No!"

"Really? Because I have been told quite explicitly by Leticia and Phoebe and Helen and Sylvia that being caught with a gentleman unchaperoned would mean utter ruin or marriage or in this case both."

"Margaret, I assure you," Rhys said, his hands moving to her arms, gripping her tight. "I would never allow something like that to happen. Should it come to that I would testify in a court of law that I witnessed nothing untoward between you and Bainbridge and . . . and you're making fun of me, aren't you?"

She broke into helpless giggles. "Yes, but I'm awfully glad that you caught on. You're the only one who ever does. No one else can tell when I'm making a joke."

He grinned in spite of himself. "I should have known you wouldn't give Bainbridge any chance to . . . act ungentlemanly."

"If he was, I doubt I would have noticed," she replied. "Which, come to think of it, would be necessary for ungentlemanly acts against a lady. Don't you think? If a woman does not notice or is unaffected by a man's actions, did they even happen?"

"Philosophizing about society," he replied, his eyebrows going up. "You have been in London a bit too long, I think."

"I could not agree more," she said, still smiling at him, but . . . something tinted the edges of her posture.

"Come," he said gently, "sit." He guided her to a nearby bench. There he angled his body toward her, their knees making the lightest of contact through distracting layers of cloth.

"I was wondering if you were enjoying yourself," he said finally.

"I am now," she said. "Thankfully they have a garden here, else I would still have to be inside and listening to the unreality that spouts from people's mouths."

"Unreality?"

"The things they say," she replied, her face faltering just a touch. " 'Miss Babcock, you are luminous!' 'Miss Babcock, you are so very witty, it's delightful!' And, 'Miss Babcock, you are just the epitome of style and taste, tell us where you got your gown or shoes or bonnet!' "

"And such praise makes you uneasy?"

"How could it not? We both know I am not luminous, nor is my wit delightful, nor do I have any particular care about my gown or shoes or bonnet." She shrugged. "I'm absolutely no different than I was before the world realized my worth. And yet."

"First things first," Rhys said, clearing his throat. "I find your wit delightful, at least when you refrain from scaring the life out of me by proposing marriage to Bainbridge. And your luminosity is completely dependent of the moonlight, which is proving perfectly adequate this evening."

"Thank you, but I was not fishing for compliments," Margaret replied, looking at her hands.

"And I offer none, merely facts. If I was trying to play up to you I would commend your choice of gown or shoes or bonnet, when we both know your taste is rather dismal."

She cracked a smile again, still looking to the ruined gloves in her lap. And it made warmth spread through Rhys's chest.

"But instead I will tell you that your worth is not based on your father's fortune," he said, his voice barely more than a whisper. "And anyone who doesn't realize that is not worth your time."

That brought her eyes up to meet his. Their faces were alarmingly close together. So very close, as if their whispers had to be held tight, like a conspiracy against the rest of the world.

A breath away.

A heartbeat passed before Rhys remembered himself and moved back the barest inch. But a terribly important inch. "You know that if you don't want to attend these things, you don't have to," he said.

"I know," she replied, nodding sharply. "I don't mind, you know. Sylvia wants a friend to go with her, and Phoebe enjoys it more than she says. I find it . . . interesting."

He gave her a knowing look. "You find it exhausting."

She didn't say anything in reply. She didn't have to.

"I have often thought," Rhys mused, "that there are people in the world who find being in the middle of the excitement invigorating, and there are those that find it draining, and must have a bit of space and quiet to refill their cups."

"And you have your laboratory," she replied.

"And you your greenhouse."

"Yes." She sighed, looking up at the moon. "I confess I miss it. Phoebe and Lord Ashby have been so gracious in giving me use of their conservatory, but it's not the same. I almost wish I would have gone home with Leticia, and then come back for the meeting with the Horticultural Society."

He felt his stomach drop to his knees. Somehow the idea of her going away threw into sharp relief the brightness of the time he did get to spend with her.

"You would not find such travel intolerable?" he asked, and she shook her head. "I'd find it intolerable on your behalf."

"Still," she said, leaning back on her hands, allowing her face to tip fully up to the faint light of the moon. "I think I would find it easier if I had something to look forward to. Instead of this endless parade of parties. And people fawning all over me." She looked perplexed for a moment. "And the men constantly trying to fetch me punch. One time it tasted strange, so I don't drink them now."

"Likely a good policy. But, you *do* have the meeting

with Sir Kingsley," Rhys pointed out. "Surely that is something to look forward to."

"That makes me more nervous than anything else," she admitted. "Especially considering I haven't gotten the conservatory and gardens in order the way I would like. Too many calls to pay, too many teas."

He shook his head. "Then you must speak up. Tell Sylvia and Phoebe you need to spend the next few days in. You're not receiving."

She met his eyes.

"You have that right," he whispered. "Everyone has the right to themselves."

"I did not come to London to attend parties," she said softly. "And it's all I'm doing."

He could lean in now. The thought dashed across his brain like a fiery wire. He could close the minute space between them and let himself taste her lips. Her skin. The darkness of the garden, no one would see. It would just be . . . once.

Just so he would know.

He should not be thinking like this. He should not be watching Margaret for every look, every touch, every change of breath.

She was his *friend*, for God's sake. Why, it was the same as if he thought about Ned or John in this manner.

He shook his head. As if the thoughts weren't already disturbing enough.

He needed to think about something else. Something that calmed him, made him focus . . .

"My laboratory," he said suddenly.

"Your . . . your laboratory?" she said, blinking.

"Yes. You need something to look forward to. So . . . once you've presented your roses to Sir Kingsley, I'll show you my laboratory in Greenwich—it's only a day trip up the river; you would be back by the evening." The corner of his mouth perked up. "A little bit of peace in the middle of all this madness. How does that sound?"

"Like Phoebe is going to insist on a chaperon."

"So we bring a chaperon." Rhys shrugged, still seeing her hesitance. "Come now, what's the worst that could happen?"

Her head came up, shocked. "What did you say?"

"I . . . I said 'What's the worst that could happen?'" he replied slowly.

He watched her intently, trying to place what was going through her mind, and why she had reacted as she had. "If you're not comfortable going, please accept my heart-felt apologies. I simply thought it would be something you enjoyed—"

"All right," she said, a slow, wondrous smile spreading across her face. "We'll go to Greenwich."

And suddenly his mind wasn't thinking calm, focused thoughts again.

"Ah . . . then that's what we will do," he said, trying to talk his mind back to normalcy. "You will enjoy it immensely, I'm sure. And I have been away far too long, I am certain that my house staff has disobeyed my direct orders and dusted the laboratory. They do it every time I'm away longer than an evening. I suspect the butler and the maid conspire against me."

"I have no doubt," Margaret said, leaning in. "I'm certain Molly has conspired with Frederick to have me out of the conservatory in time to dress my hair."

Rhys cracked a smile, then a laugh, and then they were both laughing. And so it was that he did not notice that he took her hand. And he did not notice that in doing so, he pulled her closer, so she was lined up against his side. And then he did not notice that he caught her midnight-blue eyes with his own.

What he did notice—finally, after his breath had caught—was a rustling in the bushes behind him.

"What on earth . . . oh. Hello, Rhys."

His sister Eloisa's voice was, for once, not coated in its usual acid. Instead it was surprise and even a bit of worry.

Perhaps her worry was about the rustling that continued in the bushes behind her, fading away as whomever she was with had retreated.

"Eloisa," Rhys said, standing, his body fully aware of the cool air that filled the new space between himself and Margaret. "May I introduce Miss Babcock?" He turned and offered his hand to Margaret. "Miss Babcock, this is my sister Eloisa. Who I did not know was coming to this party tonight."

While Margaret dipped to a perfect curtsy, Eloisa's eyebrow went up. "There's a lot you don't know, Rhys. Yes, Miss Babcock. You're the friend."

Margaret shot Rhys a look of confusion at Eloisa's direct wording. "Ignore her," he said. "My sister's been in Scotland for many years and has completely forgotten how to pretend politeness."

"Oh," Margaret replied. "It's still quite good to meet you."

Eloisa smiled. "Thank you. And while I may have lost some of my manners in Scotland, I haven't lost my good sense. Would you mind terribly walking back into the party with me, Miss Babcock? I feel like it might be prudent. Just give me a moment with my brother?" she said, and pulled Rhys three steps away, out of Margaret's earshot.

"I consider it the greatest of luck that I ran into you in this garden," she said. "And not anyone else."

"I should imagine," he replied. "If you're worried about me telling anyone, don't be. I don't care enough about your amorous activities. However, I do not like you using Margaret as your protection against the eyes of the old ladies at the party."

Eloisa goggled at him. "I didn't mean it was lucky for my sake, I meant it was lucky for *yours*. And hers."

Rhys's face grew hard. "There is nothing untoward going on between me and Margaret."

"The speed with which you jumped away from her when you saw me says otherwise."

He began to turn away, but Eloisa caught his arm.

"Rhys," she said earnestly. "Be careful. You have more Gray blood in you than you like to think."

"What is that supposed to mean?"

"It means . . . you won't tolerate being unhappy. Even if it's by your own doing." She glanced back at the bushes, now still and silent. "Take it from someone who knows."

"I'm not unhappy," Rhys said, confused. "And neither are you. You are simply bored."

"They can be one and the same." And with that, Eloisa straightened her shoulders, and stepped toward Margaret with a bright smile.

"Miss Babcock. Have you seen the ladies' retiring room yet? It's the most awful puce and I cannot wait to show it to you."

Eloisa took Margaret's arm and dragged her away before Margaret could even take her leave of Rhys. She barely managed a single glance over her shoulder as Eloisa led her through the doors and into the light of the party.

Leaving Rhys in the dark, with nothing but his unfocused, unruly thoughts for company.

14

Dear Miss Babcock—
   Please accept our apologies on behalf of Sir
Kingsley. However, he has discovered a conflict and
cannot attend your scheduled meeting on Saturday
the 21st. We humbly ask your indulgence to postpone
the engagement until the afternoon of Sunday the
22nd. Please forgive this imposition, and if you are
amenable, we shall see you on Sunday.

Sincerely,
The Hortacultural Society of London

*M*argaret moved the pot with the rosemary cutting
for the fifth time that day, trying to find the correct amount
of light to let it thrive. So far, it was the only one of her
herbs that was proving finicky, which was odd, since rosemary was usually heartier and able to grow in a variety of
settings.

Her mother would say that the cutting just needed time. Well, Margaret didn't have time.

Although she had more time than she had thought she would since she received the letter from the Horticultural Society.

The change of plans did not affect her much—at least beyond a vague sense of disappointment. She had gotten the conservatory and herself as ready as possible. After her talk with Rhys in the garden a few evenings ago, she had taken his advice and told Phoebe that she wanted a few days without social obligations so she could work. Phoebe was understanding, if a little harried, writing notes to all the hostesses they would be disappointing. Sylvia's reaction was a bit more surprising.

"Of course you want to do your work! I'm terribly sorry if I have been monopolizing you!" she said. Then she eyed the piles of soil Margaret was busy turning. "Er . . . is there anything I can do to help?"

After assuring Sylvia that she was under no obligation to assist, the girl went off, saying something about spending the next few days entertaining her little sister. And Margaret was free to breathe in the joy of a hard day's labor.

Couches were moved and stands arranged in the conservatory. Frederick himself washed the windows, with Margaret over his shoulder observing and making helpful suggestions the entire time. At least, she thought they were helpful. Frederick's grumblings perhaps suggested otherwise.

She took a cutting of the vine that had grown wild along the garden wall, potted it, and hung it in the sun until it began to flower in perfect little bells of white. She turned the earth in the garden beds along the wall, giving air to the packed hard soil. Then she spread her fertilizer over everything, not just her roses.

And oh, the roses. After two days of coaxing and hoping and wishing, there were new buds beginning on their branches! She had a heart-stopping moment when the temperature dropped the night before, and feared the roses, still not fully used to London and their roots not twined as deep as they needed to be, would huddle back into themselves, forgoing another bloom until next spring.

But no—her hybrid China roses remained hearty. Not just hearty—they thrived.

And somehow, Margaret had always known they would. It was as if all the worry and all the preparation had been worth the risk. Because here they were, her roses and herself, in the middle of a London house's garden, and completely fine.

She would have to thank Rhys, she thought, wiping her hands on the legs of her trousers. The planned trip to Greenwich had buoyed her while she worked to bring the conservatory and gardens up to her standards. It had been a secret ball of happiness, glowing just beneath her ribs, knowing that she would have such an event in the future. Indeed, the disappointment in knowing that her meeting with Sir Kingsley would be delayed was partially due to the fact that it meant the trip to Greenwich would be delayed too.

Suddenly, her mind stumbled back to the way Rhys had looked at her in the garden in the moonlight as he proposed his Greenwich scheme. There had been so much hope in his face. In the way he'd leaned into her. The way his hand had fallen on hers.

What's the worst that could happen?

She had felt a shiver run down her spine when he'd said those words. And a reckless thought had come unbidden into her head. *Nothing,* it said. *Absolutely nothing bad could happen.* Not as long as she was with Rhys.

She'd hoped he'd received her letter. She'd sent it as

soon as she received the note from the Horticultural Society. It was funny, but she assumed the missive would have been sent to him, not herself. And she assumed they would know how to spell the word *Horticultural*.

But these worries were far, far at the back of her mind, as she and Frederick endeavored to move a large tub Margaret had located in the cellar into the proper position under the garden wall.

"But, miss—this is a bathing tub!" Frederick had said, appalled.

"One with holes rusted into the bottom," she'd replied. "Which means it will never bathe another person again, but makes it ideal for what, Frederick?"

"Drainage, miss?" Frederick said.

"Very good!" she said. Perhaps Frederick could be made into a decent gardener after all. Although the fact that she had to teach him about drainage at all was a worry she would not think too hard on. No, only positive, good, garden-type thoughts today.

They had positioned the tub in a corner of the garden, next to the wall where an old dead vine had recently been removed, leaving a horrid blank space. A bit of whimsy tucked into a nook of a grand and impressive house. She had the feeling Phoebe would appreciate it, and Lord Ashby would . . . likely never even notice. Margaret had grand plans for that tub, with a potted miniature orange tree that could be brought indoors in the less temperate months, but at that moment they were merely preparing the soil in the tub.

And so it was that Margaret was elbows deep in a mixture that was more manure than not when Phoebe ran out to her, the baby on her hip and Rhys on her heels.

"Margaret! Oh goodness! You are not ready?"

"Ready?" Margaret asked, standing up. "Ready for what?"

"Your meeting, of course!" Phoebe said, her eyes practically popping out of her head. "Sir Kingsley is here!"

"What?" Margaret looked from Phoebe to Rhys. "The Horticultural Society? Here? Now?"

"Did you forget the day?" Rhys asked, a look of concern furrowing his brow.

"No, I received a letter this morning postponing it," Margaret replied. She fished in her pocket and brought out the letter in question. "See?"

Rhys eyed the letter briefly. "Perhaps there was some mix-up with the society?" he muttered to himself, flipping the page over, looking for more (sadly nonexistent) clues.

"That hardly matters now, Rhys," Phoebe was saying. "Because you've left Sir Kingsley and his fellows in the drawing room admiring the tea cups, when they are chomping at the bit to admire the roses."

"They said that?" Margaret asked, a thrill running through her chest.

"Yes," Rhys said grimly. "Rather in the context of how they wanted to get this over with, but—"

"Rhys!" Phoebe exclaimed, swatting at his arm. This caused the baby to giggle and drool through his two teeth. "You cannot tell her that!"

"It's best she know the truth," he countered.

"Yes, it's best that she does," Margaret said dryly. "I have no illusions that I am a welcome addition to Sir Kingsley's day."

"Well, the truth is Sir Kingsley and two other Horticultural Society gentlemen are looking at the clock on the mantel in the drawing room, wondering just how long this will take," Phoebe said. "And you are covered to your elbows in dirt from . . . is that a bathtub?"

"It's not dirt," Frederick piped up. "It's a specific mixture of soil and minerals to promote the growth of citrus plants."

"Very good, Frederick!" Margaret beamed at him, and Frederick grinned with pleasure.

"Yes, Frederick, your trade is improving immensely." Rhys nodded at they boy. "However, I think Phoebe's fears are that you will not be able to bathe, change your outfit, and clean up the garden before Sir Kingsley has to attend to his next appointment."

"His appointment with his lunch," Phoebe muttered.

"Margaret, what do you wish to do?" Rhys asked her, stepping forward and putting a hand on her arm. "We can ask Sir Kingsley if he would be willing to reschedule."

Margaret looked at Rhys, then to Phoebe, and then Frederick. They were all watching her, waiting for a decision.

On the one hand, she felt completely taken aback. She was prepared, yes . . . but not as prepared as she could be. Not as prepared as she would have been had she not been misinformed about the day. Surely she should try to put her best foot forward, yes?

On the other hand, she had come to London to meet with the Horticultural Society. That was it. And considering all the trouble Rhys had gone to to make this happen . . . she could not ask any more of him.

"There is no need for all that," Margaret said, taking a deep breath. "They are here to see the roses. And the roses, at least, are ready to be shown."

"Are you certain?" Rhys asked.

"Of course," she said with a shaky smile. "If the Horticultural Society cannot handle a little dirt, then they are hardly worthy of the name."

Rhys nodded and returned her smile with one that gave her strength.

"In that case, I will be right back with our guests."

As Rhys disappeared through the conservatory doors, Margaret darted to a pail of water and a rag, and began to wash her hands.

"It will be fine," Phoebe was saying, shifting the baby from one shoulder to the other. "You will present the roses, and we will say the tub is there for . . . Frederick, because he needs to bathe. And of course they will be utterly charmed by you, how could they not be? And it—"

Suddenly, Phoebe stopped talking. Margaret glanced at her. She was looking down toward Margaret's feet. Then, when she brought her head up, her face was stark white. "Good God, Margaret, I didn't even think! You cannot receive Sir Kingsley!"

"Why not?" she asked, bewildered.

"Because . . . *You're wearing trousers!*"

Margaret froze. She wore her trousers all the time when working; of course she put them on today. No one minded—Phoebe and Lord Ashby had blinked a few times but gotten used to it. Frederick had stopped blushing like a schoolboy. Even Rhys took no notice of it. But lord knew, Sir Kingsley was not likely to be so willfully blind.

And judging by the look on his face as he stood in the conservatory doorway, he most certainly had the gift of sight.

"Too late now," Margaret whispered. "Come now, what's the worst that could happen?"

She said it to herself, almost like a prayer. Then, pasting a nervous smile on her face, she took every lesson she had learned from the past few weeks of being in London and greeted their guests.

"Sir Kingsley," she said. "Gentlemen. An honor to meet you all."

There was no reason for the morning to go as well as it did. Considering the way Sir Kingsley's eyes were about to pop out of his head upon seeing Margaret's trousers, Rhys would not have been surprised if he turned around on his heel and ran as far as his feet would carry him. And perhaps he'd considered it. Perhaps he'd even tried. But Sir Kingsley was not particularly quick on his feet.

"Miss Babcock, I presume," he said as he came forward. He was a large man, nearly as wide as he was tall—and he was rather tall indeed. An imposing presence in Horticultural Society meetings no doubt, but he leaned so heavily on his spindly cane it's a wonder it didn't snap in half. But Rhys knew the truth—as overwhelming as the man could be, he was as gregarious and open as Margaret's own father. And possibly Margaret saw the resemblance, because she managed to extend her hand and dip to a curtsy without the least bit of nervousness.

The gentlemen with him, however, were less warm. The entire ride over to Ashby's, the only thing they had remarked on was how they hoped this would be a visit of short duration. Now, of course, they both had their eyes popping out of their heads.

"Er, Miss Babcock," ventured Mr. Coddington, who had a blinkered face that was eerily reminiscent of a codfish, and thus Rhys was able to keep him straight from the other gentleman, Mr. Swindon. "Do you perhaps wish to excuse yourself to . . . Erm, that is, your wardrobe . . ."

Coddington blushed profusely as Rhys's blood shot to his ears. He was in the act of raising his foot to step into the fray when a hand landed gently on his arm.

Phoebe met his eyes, and she gave the slightest shake of her head.

"Thank you, Mr. Coddington, for stating the obvious," Margaret said, one corner of her mouth coming up. "If you hadn't, I was afraid you gentlemen would spend the morning with your eyes on the clouds above to avoid a chance sighting of my ankles."

Now it was Rhys's turn to have his eyes bulge out of his head. Margaret had always been direct—in his opinion delightfully so—but the sparkle in her eye made her almost cheeky.

Perhaps she didn't need his intervention after all.

"My wardrobe is exactly what I wear when I'm working," she continued with a small shrug. "If you are of a mind that I would somehow be able to dig in the dirt and plant trees and shrubs and build trellises in a skirt, I would recommend you try it sometime."

Mr. Coddington turned purple. Now Rhys—as a medical professional—stepped forward and slapped Coddington on the back, hard enough so he had to inhale to steady himself. "That's better," Rhys said. "A nice normal color. I was afraid you had swallowed your tongue."

And Sir Kingsley gave a great harrumph of a laugh. Mr. Swindon, seeing Sir Kingsley's reaction, erred on the side of safety and laughed along with him.

"My darling girl, if you've ever built a trellis, I would eat my hat," Sir Kingsley said, holding his arm out to her.

"Sir Kingsley, I hope your hat is well salted, because I have in fact built a trellis," she replied. "It's in my greenhouse at my home in Lincolnshire, and I hammered my thumb more times than I can count in the construction."

Rhys didn't know where this confidence, this forthrightness, was coming from, but it was a sight to see. To his mind, Margaret should for all the world be monumentally uncomfortable appearing in her work trousers in front of these men. But then again, perhaps it *was* the trousers. She was comfortable. There was no hiding, so there could be no worrying about how she was presented. The only person she had to be was herself.

It was glorious.

She was glorious.

Sir Kingsley laughed again, and then he said, "Well, girl. Show me these roses I've heard so much about. Dr. Gray told me of them every time he came to visit for the last six months."

"To visit?" Margaret said, turning her head to look back at Rhys. He put his hands behind his back, and suddenly became very interested in a lavender shrub by his feet. "I thought you met Dr. Gray when you were a visiting lecturer at Greenwich."

"I did," he said, looking up at her from under his lashes.

"And when he heard me speak, he knew I had spent the last several weeks with a cough that wouldn't go away. He began to treat me after that—and treat me to tales of you and your roses." He leaned in close. "He's a very determined sort, for so quiet a fellow."

"So I've observed," she said, and gave a soft glance at Rhys.

Pride ran through him like a stampede, flooding his limbs. Then something else—something driven just by the look in her eyes.

"It's a terribly far walk to the roses I'm afraid, all the way to the other side of the garden," she said to Sir Kingsley, only babbling slightly. "But time flies when one is in good company, or so my father often says. And look, here we are!"

She steered him over to where the rose bushes had been planted, along the garden wall. There they stood, new buds willing their way forward. No rot. No caterpillars had taken so much as a nibble of the leaves. Rhys could practically hear her heart thudding in her chest. These plants represented the work of years. The work of both herself and her mother. And now they were being seen by someone who would finally recognize their worth.

Or perhaps not.

"Oh," Sir Kingsley said, cocking his head to the side. "Er . . . Is that it, then?"

Margaret's smile fell as she crossed her arms over her body, folding in on herself.

"Yes," she said, her voice smaller than before. "These are my roses."

"You'll have to forgive me, my dear, but I assumed they'd be a bit more . . . impressive."

"Yes," said Coddington, stepping forward with his fish face and planting it mere inches from the closest rose bush. Margaret started when he took one leaf and rubbed it between his fingers, snapping it off. "It is a China rose, to be sure. But we have several of them in our hothouse."

"But . . . you'll notice these are not in a hothouse," Margaret tried to reply.

"And the blooms are rather small," Coddington continued, without paying heed.

"Quite right," said Swindon, obviously feeling he had to contribute something to the conversation. "And this late in the year too."

The looks on all three men's faces—Coddington, bored; Kingsley, pitying; and Swindon, an amalgam of the two— did not bode well for the roses or for Margaret. Rhys almost stepped forward again, lent his support. But he remembered the hand that had landed on his arm before, and its meaning.

He had to let her do this.

Margaret took a deep breath and launched into a speech she had no doubt been practicing since the moment she decided to come to London.

"As . . . as you know, the benefit of the China rose is that they rebloom several times during the summer, giving one a flowering garden for months, not just the few weeks that our ordinary English roses give."

"Our roses are not ordinary!" Coddington cried, his expression crashing down into a frown. "English roses are the staple of the garden! I have developed and bred almost a dozen varieties of English rose myself."

"Yes," Sir Kingsley agreed. "I brought Coddington along because he is the Horticultural Society's leading authority on roses."

"Of . . . of course," Margaret said. "I did not mean to imply that English roses were in any way ordinary. But you have to admit, they are limited, having only one bloom."

"What you call a limitation I call a natural survival instinct. Roses cannot flower in the edges of the season. They are not hearty enough." Coddington veritably sneered. "And the fact that I have to explain this to you is a rather dull use of my time."

"Yes!" Margaret agreed. "I mean, no, you don't need to explain it to me. Which is why I have spent years—as did my mother, before she passed—learning to hybridize roses. I collected the pollen from my China rose, and used it to seed an ordinary . . . I mean, a *traditional* hearty English rose. And voilà!"

"Voilà?" Coddington sniffed. "You obviously don't know very much about hybridizing roses, if you think it ends with a 'voilà.'"

"Yes, my dear," Swindon said, an echo of condescension. "Surely you realize there is more to hybridizing than seeding a rose and hoping for the best."

"Obviously she doesn't," Coddington muttered.

Rhys thought for the briefest moments that they were done for. And he wanted to run over to her and take her away. Make her safe and unscrutinized. The hardest thing he had ever done was stand still.

Then, he saw it. That spark in her eye that gave him a jolt down his spine.

Watch this, he thought.

"Actually, there is not much more than that," she said, blinking innocently. "Oh, of course there is the collection of the pollen from the China rose, the preparing of the seed parent bloom on the English rose by removing all the petals and delicately removing all the pollen sacs lest there be cross-contamination. Then of course the pollination—I like to pollinate at least once a day for three days, but I'm sure you have your own methods. Then waiting four months for the rose hips to mature. Then collecting and storing and then shelling the rose hips—have you ever used a serrated blade for shelling? I found it worked quite well. Then there is the planting, done in Lincolnshire in March after the first thaw; you really can't wait any longer. But after that I can only tend their soil and give them water. I cannot force them to grow, and I cannot choose which traits they will have gotten from their parents, any more than a father can choose the sex or hair color of his child. At that point, it's simply not up to us."

Coddington gaped in a rather fishy manner. Swindon grunted and looked at the ground. Off to the side, Margaret glanced at Rhys grinning and Phoebe smothering a laugh by rocking the baby to sleep in her arms.

"Well, ah. Quite," Coddington said. "Er . . . Sir Kingsley? You were saying?"

Sir Kingsley seemed jarred back to the present. "Oh, er . . . well, it certainly has the size of a China rose," he said. "Pray, what are the characteristics it inherited from the English?"

"If any," Coddington was quick to add.

"As I've said, these roses do not live in a hothouse. And look, they are blooming."

Sir Kingsley peered out from under his hat, truly looking at the roses for possibly the first time.

"Er, yes they are, dear. A little late in the season if I'm not mistaken, though."

"Quite late in the season," Coddington sniffed. "No doubt they started when they were brought down south to more hospitable climes."

"Perhaps," Rhys said, unable to stop himself. "This is not the first bloom, but the second."

"Oh." Kingsley's eyebrows went up. "That *would* be interesting."

"I'm afraid, however, that this isn't their second bloom of the year," Margaret said, her face falling and taking Rhys's with it.

"Ha!" came from somewhere in the vicinity of Coddington and Swindon; it was impossible to tell which.

"This is their third," she said, and waited patiently for Coddington's head to explode.

"Third?" he said. "But that's . . ."

"Amazing?" Rhys finished for him. "Simply remarkable? Utterly fantastic?"

"All of the above," Margaret said. "The buds began so early this year I was shocked—especially considering they were grown in Lincolnshire soil. We had frosts as recently as six weeks ago!"

"We had a frost too, didn't we, Margaret?" Phoebe prompted. "Just last week."

"A very chilly night, if I recall correctly," Sir Kingsley added. "Are you telling me, Miss Babcock, that these rose bushes not only bloomed three times already this summer, but can survive the temperamental English climate?"

"So far, they have," Margaret said, unable to hide a glowing smile. "They are hearty plants, sir, and eager to be seen."

This began a many-sided discussion among the gentlemen of the Horticultural Society and Margaret about how this could change the state of the English garden, how they should present this find to the rest of the Horticultural Society—either in a paper or by having their codes broken and allowing a woman to present her findings—and what Margaret would be naming her hybrid China rose.

"I'll have to think on that," she said as the men surrounded her.

Not even Coddington could hide his enthusiasm anymore. "Tell me, in your process, how did you clean the seeds? I have always found that a thoroughly cleaned seed yields—"

It went on like this for several minutes—and would have gone on like this for several hours, if Phoebe had not interceded.

"Gentlemen, I was given to understand that you had another appointment after this?" she asked softly in deference to her sleeping son, but with enough steel to let them know she would not brook any opposition.

Of course, they tried to brook some opposition. "Er, yes. That is, it's nothing important," Coddington was saying.

"Only my son's engagement luncheon," Sir Kingsley added. "Surely they will not mind."

"Your son may not, but your new daughter-in-law will be in tears, I've no doubt," Phoebe said, steering the gentlemen toward the conservatory doors. "Come, I'm sure Miss Babcock would be happy to receive you tomorrow if you have any further questions . . ."

The moment the conservatory doors closed behind Phoebe and the gentlemen, Margaret burst into a squeal of delight.

"Oh my goodness! I had no idea I could do that!" she said, pressing a hand to her breast.

"I did. I knew you would be absolutely brilliant!" Rhys replied, grinning like a loon as he lifted her off her feet and spun her in a circle.

He was so thrilled—so damned proud—that he didn't care that lifting and spinning Margaret wasn't proper. It was *right*.

But when her feet finally met the ground again, she still held fast to his shoulders. She looked up into his eyes, and before he could comprehend it, she had pressed her lips to his.

Perhaps she hadn't intended it to be anything other than a friendly kiss. Perhaps she hadn't intended anything at all. But it was happening, and it was more than friendly. That, he knew for damned certain.

He knew she should let go. That he should put air between them, space. Several feet, if possible. But he didn't. In fact, he didn't move. And slowly his hands went from holding her still to clasping the back of her head, twining his fingers in her hair, loosing her braid.

His mouth opened, ever so slightly, giving him a true taste of her. She opened in kind, and pressed herself even closer. Her belly against his, her back arching into him.

One of Rhys's hands left her hair, and drifted lower. Down her spine, to the small of her back, to where her trousers met her shirt.

And that was what did it. Those damnable trousers. At once so delightful, but reminding him of where he was. Forcing him back to now, and the cold realities of his life.

They both opened their eyes, stopped. Slowly, breathlessly, they drew back.

Then Rhys pulled his hands off her quickly—as if keeping them on any longer would leave him singed.

"I . . . I'm sorry," she said immediately as he took an unsteady step back. "I was just . . . excited. About my roses."

"No," he replied, forcing himself to keep his bearings. "I'm the one who should apologize. I was caught up in the events as well."

"We both were," she reasoned. "Yes. We both were overly enthusiastic about the way the visit went and . . . got confused."

"Confused," he repeated. *Confused* was not the word he would have used. Because like it or not, he had known exactly what they were doing.

"Yes," she said, nodding fervently. "I was excited and it is all my fault, and could you please stop pacing now?"

He looked down, somewhat shocked to discover he had practically paced a hole in the grass. As if he had too much in him to not be moving in some way.

And if he wasn't going to move toward her, he had to do something with all his feelings. The grass could take the beating.

But he did stop. He took two great deep breaths, straightened his coat, and turned to face her.

"I am the one to blame," he said. "I should not have reacted so . . . enthusiastically. It was wrong, especially considering my responsibilities and . . ."

His voice trailed off, but he didn't have to say it. He didn't have to say her name.

Sylvia. His family. And what this would do to them.

"We can . . . we can simply forget that it ever happened," Margaret said. And instantly something in him felt horrifically sad. Could she really forget that easily? Just . . . voilà?

"Yes," he agreed with a short nod. "That is for the best."

He gave a bow and reached out to take her hand. But then he stopped himself—because if he touched her now, he might not be able to let go.

"It will be forgotten entirely," he said. And then he turned away and stalked to the conservatory doors, his footfalls thumping in time with his heartbeat.

It will be forgotten, he thought, *just as soon as I figure out how.*

15

 he next few days were quiet in the Ashby household. Where some young ladies might have sought the delights of the season to distract them from their thoughts, Margaret found she preferred to wallow in them quietly. Since she had called a moratorium on going to parties and balls, it was no trouble at all to simply extend it and give herself another few days of peace and quiet. Phoebe did not mind, and Lord Ashby seemed grateful to have his wife back home and not running herself ragged around town.

Calls were still paid, of course, and Margaret received them dutifully and gratefully, but the one person she wished and dreaded seeing never came.

Instead, the Horticultural Society took up most of her morning receiving hours.

"Goodness," Sylvia said, pressing a hand to her breast. "I've never seen so many gentlemen interested in flowers!"

Sylvia had come over to keep Margaret company the past few days, although it turned out Margaret had more than enough company to keep her occupied. Every single member of the Horticultural Society wanted to see the roses. And as they could not come without an introduction, Sir Kingsley had practically had a bench reserved for his own particular use in the small garden area of Lord Ashby's townhouse.

Apparently, since the bushes had been transferred successfully, it was decided among the society's members that it was better to come to it than to have it come to them. So Margaret dutifully and happily took each of the gentlemen through her process on cultivating and hybridizing the roses, where the parent roses had come from, and how she had been trying to successfully combine them for years. Every gentleman was politely enthusiastic, every one of them wanted one of her roses for their own. An illustrator for the society's pamphlet had come by to sketch the blooms. There was even talk of allowing Margaret to have special dispensation to attend Horticultural Society meetings when she was in London, regardless of her gender.

It was extremely gratifying. She should be pleased beyond measure. But how could she be pleased when she hadn't heard from Rhys in two days?

"Margaret?" Sylvia's voice came through her fog. "Margaret, are you quite well?"

It was just before tea. Sylvia had spent the whole afternoon at the Ashbys' with her, suffering through an endless parade of flower enthusiasts.

"Yes!" Margaret replied, perhaps too brightly. "My mind was simply elsewhere."

That somewhere else was that exact garden, two days before. When she had kissed Rhys Gray, on that spot on the grass, right over there.

She didn't know how it had happened. She had been so nervous to speak to Sir Kingsley. And then, she had been so not nervous. And then suddenly Rhys's arms were around her and her feet were swinging in the air.

It was the *best* feeling—there was no other way to describe it. To have been as utterly confident as she had, to have her roses—her work and her mother's work—praised by Sir Kingsley, and to have Rhys's arms around her, lifting her as if she weighed nothing and spinning with her until she thought she might take flight . . . there was simply nothing better.

Except . . . maybe there was.

Because when she had kissed him, she had found out that there was indeed something better. Something she felt inside and out.

She had done it without thought. It wasn't as if she had woken up that morning thinking *this is the day I will kiss Rhys*. It was simply the only thing she could do with all of these wonderful feelings she had.

Then it ended.

And with it, possibly their friendship.

What's the worst that could happen? The words echoed in her head.

Rhys could never talk to her again. That was the worst. And it seemed to be happening.

"Sylvia," Margaret asked suddenly. "Have you ever done something . . . wrong?"

Sylvia gave a soft laugh. "Of course I have. My governess was always bemoaning my mistakes at my lessons. Is this about your trousers?" Margaret hadn't told Sylvia about being caught by the gentlemen in her work trousers, but in true London fashion the story had made its way around. "Because I don't think you have to worry about that—if anything it's made you even more popular! I heard that Madame Louise has had orders for trousers from several young ladies copying you." She gave a little laugh. "Only you could get away with it!"

"Not like that. Have you ever done anything that you . . . that you wish you could take back?"

"Take back?" Sylvia's smile faded into concern.

"Well, not 'take back' per se," she corrected. Because the kiss wasn't something she ever wanted to take back. No, she wanted to live in that moment forever. "But . . . have you ever done something that caused change? And you wish you could go back to the way things were before?"

"Margaret," her friend said gently. "What is wrong?"

"Nothing," Margaret said, shaking her head with what she hoped looked like a natural smile. "I'm woolgathering, that's all."

As much as she might wish to speak to someone—a friend, a female, someone who could tell her how to feel—there was no one. Leticia was over a hundred miles away. Phoebe would listen, but she was so much more Rhys's friend than hers, it did not feel like she could help. And she couldn't talk to Sylvia. If it were about any other man in the world, Sylvia would relish knowing Margaret's secrets. But she couldn't have secrets about Rhys.

He didn't belong to her.

But . . . on some level he did, didn't he? She had been friends with him before Sylvia Morton had come into their lives. At least, before she had been more than an abstract thought to Rhys. And don't friends deserve pieces of each other? Don't they have a right to know what the other is thinking?

Why they would just leave like that? For so long?

She was halfway to being good and angry at Rhys when Frederick came into the garden with a letter in his hand.

"Frederick, what are you doing bearing letters?" Margaret asked upon seeing the lad. "You are no footman now, you are head gardener!"

"Most footmen would consider that a step down," Sylvia said into her tea.

"Not this one," Margaret replied.

"Chalmers was going to leave this for you in your room, miss," Frederick said, out of breath. "But I told him you'd want it straight away."

"Oh?" Sylvia's eyes lit up. "Is it from one of the flower-loving gentlemen? I observed Mr. Coddington making cow eyes at you."

Margaret knew that handwriting. Knew it almost as well as she knew her own. She snatched the paper as nonchalantly as she could and unfolded it.

It did not have any effusions, any *my dearest*s or *darling*s. There wasn't even a *my friend*. It was simple and straightforward, and it brought every one of Margaret's senses to life.

Margaret—

Please forgive me for being absent for the past few days. I have been busy arranging our promised trip to Greenwich. If agreeable with you, we will leave in the morning tomorrow and be back before dinner, which should allow you to attend any evening activities that you have on your schedule. I will call at nine in the morning to collect you. Please dress appropriately for river travel. And as Phoebe has declined to join us, she has suggested your maid, Molly, as an appropriate chaperon—and before you roll your eyes, I think you will agree with me that yes, a chaperon is required.

Sincerely,
Rhys

Greenwich. In the aftermath of her horrific blunder, she had all but forgotten Rhys's promise to take her to Greenwich once the interview with the Horticultural Society was over. But he had—and if there was one thing that had been proven to the world at large, it was that Rhys Gray was a man of his word.

Which is why it was somewhat distressing when Sylvia leaned over her shoulder and said, "So? Who is it from? Is it a love letter?"

"Nothing of the sort," Margaret said, quickly folding the letter and shoving it into her pocket. "It's about an appointment for tomorrow. Will you excuse me for a moment?"

She didn't wait to hear if Sylvia would excuse her, just left the girl sitting there, slack jawed in surprise.

Margaret moved quickly through the conservatory, into the central part of the house. She poked her head into each room until she found Chalmers in—appropriately—the butler's pantry, where he seemed to be deep in the throes of a novel.

"Oh! I'm sorry, I didn't mean to interrupt," she said.

Chalmers turned red to the tips of his ears as he stood and hurried the novel out of sight. "Yes, Miss Babcock? How can I assist you?"

"I . . . I wanted to know if the messenger who brought my letter was still here," she said, trying very hard not to notice the older butler's mussed hair and rolled-up sleeves, as she hoped he would not notice her breathlessness from running through the house.

"If he is not, we can easily send a messenger out with a reply," he said. "Would you like to write a quick note, and I will see to its prompt delivery?"

"What?" she asked, bewildered. "Oh! Of course. I didn't even think."

Their entire friendship had grown from letters, and

suddenly she forgot that the proper way to reply would be with a written missive, not a verbal one.

She hurried off to grab a piece of paper and pen from Phoebe's writing desk in the sitting room. Luckily it was unoccupied, because Phoebe had shooed the last of the visiting Horticultural Society members and suitors with the stench from her son's nappy. She didn't even have to sit down. She knew her reply.

Rhys, it said in much the same, straightforward tone as his own note—

I am amenable.

Sincerely,
Margaret

MARGARET COULD BARELY sleep that night, knowing what pleasures awaited her in the morning. She had a small moment of uncertainty when she questioned what attire would be appropriate for "river travel," but was soon assured by Phoebe and Molly that they had no idea what was meant by that either, and decided her usual traveling cloak and hat would serve her well enough.

Phoebe, in particular, was delighted by the outing.

"It's going to be ever so interesting. Did you know, not even Ned has been out to see Rhys's laboratory? Rhys has always been so private about it. I'm terribly jealous."

"If you're so jealous, why don't you join us? Rhys said you declined."

"Oh. Yes. I feel a slight cough coming on." And as proof, she coughed delicately into her hand.

Margaret could see what she was doing. But whereas before, she would have made a point to call Phoebe out on her assumptions, making certain to reinforce that she and Rhys were just friends, now she stayed silent. Because she knew they were more than simple friends. And it had, as of their last meeting, become impossible to deny.

At least, it was impossible to deny to herself. And as she had never been a particularly good liar, she thought it best to simply hold her tongue. And daydream about what was to come.

So it was that Margaret Babcock was standing in the foyer of Lord Ashby's townhouse ten minutes to nine the next morning, dressed in her traveling clothes and ready for whatever adventure awaited. When she heard footfalls on the steps, she flung the door open before there was even a knock.

"Oh," Rhys said, blinking back in surprise. His hand was raised to reach for the knocker. "Hello."

"Hello," she replied in kind. Then remembering herself, she dropped to a quick curtsy.

"I see you're ready to go," Rhys said, eyeing her traveling cloak. "But where is—"

"Right here, sir," Molly said, popping out from behind Margaret, giving her a start. Margaret hadn't known she was there. To be fair, the girl was so small she easily could be hidden by Margaret's shadow. "I'll let Lady Ashby know that we are departing, shall I?"

Molly gave a quick curtsy, then trotted off into the house. Leaving Margaret alone with Rhys. And the hand he extended to her.

She took it.

And suddenly she remembered everything that she had promised Rhys would be forgotten. The kiss. The way her body felt against his. The way he let her go.

She knew she had to speak. Because her silence spoke too loudly.

"I am terribly excited about this trip," Margaret said, hoping she didn't sound like a ninny. Which was something she had never had to worry about with Rhys before. The rumbling in her stomach worried her more than her worry did. What if . . . what if she was not able to speak with Rhys as she normally did? Because she needed a friend to talk to—and he was the only one to whom she could apply.

But what if nothing was ever normal between them again?

"I could tell," he said, squeezing her hand with his as they moved slowly toward the waiting carriage.

"I'm so pleased that I get to meet your laboratory."

He laughed aloud. A guffaw of surprise.

"I know that sounds odd," she said, immediately mortified.

"No, it doesn't. Not to me. My laboratory will be pleased to meet you, I'm sure." He hesitated, and added, "I hope it will be pleased to meet you both."

"Both?" Then her brow cleared. "Oh, I'm not sure Molly will be interested, but she is ever so excited to be having a day in the country."

"No," he said. They reached the steps of the carriage, and he stopped, turning to her. "There has been a slight change of plans."

"Oh," she said. "In what way?"

"I'm afraid my mother got wind of my plan for the day, and made some adjustments to it."

"Your mother is attending?" Margaret's eyebrow went up.

"No," he admitted. But before he could open his mouth to say another word, the carriage door swung open, and there, with perfect posture and a look of true delight, sat Sylvia Morton.

"Margaret!" she said with a wide smile. "Isn't this delightful? An outing just for us!"

16

The town of Greenwich sat less than seven miles outside of London, but it might as well have been an entirely different world. Margaret marveled at the changes in the landscape as they drifted up the river (although, since they were heading east, it was technically "down" the river, and the ease with which they floated on the current spoke to it). The stately buildings that lined the Thames along the Savoy went by, as did the Tower. They gave way to docks and warehouses, which in turn gave way to pastures and cows. Of course it wasn't all an agrarian paradise, because as the town of Greenwich came into view, and the grand buildings of the maritime college broke the landscape, Margaret heard Sylvia's relieved sigh.

"Oh thank goodness," she said. "I was afraid Greenwich would not be any more than a country village."

Rhys turned to her. "Greenwich has a very rich history," he said. "You shan't be bored, I promise, Miss Morton."

"Of course not!" Sylvia replied with a laugh. "But anything compared to London will have a hard time standing out."

"Greenwich will have its own charms," Margaret added. "Just like Helmsley does for me, or your home village does for you."

Sylvia simply wrinkled her nose and wrapped her cloak around herself tighter. It was terribly windy on their ship, a river-cruising yacht with short sails that on the way down the river relied mainly on the current, and on the way up had some very large oars stashed away to "help."

But instead of wanting to huddle against it, Margaret had to restrain herself from spreading her arms and fingers and embracing the wind and air around her. It was a beautiful day—not too hot, lest the river smell, and not too cold, lest their noses and ears go as pink as their cheeks. Large, beautiful clouds towered against a dark blue summer sky, and the air had a touch of weight to it—promising a little bit of weather to come, but held at bay. As if the sun was saying "not yet" and letting the little humans below stir in the out of doors.

It took a good two hours for the yacht to meander to its dock at the Greenwich pier. When they finally came to port, it was within shouting distance of those grand towers, sitting at the top of a green hill.

"What are those?" Margaret asked.

"That is Greenwich Hospital," Rhys replied, helping to hand both Margaret and Sylvia off the yacht. Sylvia held onto Rhys's arm as they walked down the dock, and Molly (who had survived her first boat ride with aplomb) walked at a respectable distance behind them. "I spend a great deal of time there."

"Whatever for?" Sylvia said. "Granted, it is a very grand building—is it where you give your lectures?"

"Some." Rhys smiled. "The Greenwich Hospital does play host to the Royal Hospital School."

"And do you teach serious gentlemen to become men of medicine like yourself?" Sylvia asked.

"Not quite," Rhys replied. "The Royal Hospital School is a school for boys, most intended for commissions in the navy. I mainly lecture bored children on how not to die of dysentery when they are onboard a ship."

"Oh." Sylvia looked a mixture of shock and disgust. Although what she was shocked or disgusted about was uncertain.

"But the Greenwich Hospital is home mostly to retired sailors—many of whom are my patients."

"Patients?" Sylvia replied. "You see aged sailors in your practice?"

"Of course," he said. "I see whoever needs seeing."

"I imagine there are a number of interesting cases they can give you," Margaret added, her eyes never leaving the Greenwich Hospital buildings.

"There are!" Rhys replied, happy. "These are men who have been across the world—they bring back so many habits, and occasionally even diseases that I've never—"

"I'm sorry," Sylvia said. "But I thought you lectured at a university . . . and that you once attended the queen."

"I did," Rhys replied. "A long time ago, when we had a queen. And I do give lectures occasionally for the Medical Society of London, but if I didn't see ordinary patients, what on earth would I have to lecture about?"

"Oh," Sylvia said, her brow clearing as she smiled. "Yes, of course. That makes complete sense." Then . . . "How often do you lecture in London?"

"Every month or so," he said, and was met with another bright smile.

"Oh, well that's fine, then!" she replied cheerfully, and let Rhys lead her farther up the hill.

"Where is the carriage?" Sylvia asked as they strolled along.

"I don't keep a carriage," Rhys replied. "I hire a hack when needed, but Greenwich is fairly small—not like London. I can walk to just about anywhere I need to go."

Sylvia slowed, gave a small petulant frown. "But . . . what if there is an emergency? With your, er, patients?"

"Oftentimes I'm faster on foot," he said with a shrug, "than waiting for a carriage to be called and the horses brought out."

Sylvia seemed to take that in. But her silence was unusually fraught.

"Of course," he added, after a cough, "a carriage can be easily acquired, and likely will be, once I move to . . . family accommodations."

"Yes, that makes sense," Sylvia replied, and leaned more into his arm as they walked across the flat dirt path.

Margaret felt very strange, being privy to these conversations. It seemed like intimacy between strangers—a negotiation. And the only thing she could think was that she herself was fine without a carriage, and walking was excellent exercise. But she had learned enough to not say that out loud.

They walked along some distance away from the river, passing wide green fields, when in the shadow of a compact red brick building, Rhys stopped.

And waited.

"Why have we stopped?" Sylvia asked.

"What is that building?" Margaret said at the same time.

Rhys smiled. "That is the Royal Observatory of Greenwich. And you are standing directly on the prime meridian."

Margaret's face split into a wide, amazed smile. "We are?" She looked down at her feet on the path. It seemed terribly ordinary, just dirt hedged by grass and brush, with wheel pits and footprints in the damp ground.

"I know, it doesn't look like much," Rhys said, reading her thoughts.

"Sometimes the most extraordinary things are hiding in plain sight," Margaret replied with a smile.

"I am sorry," Sylvia said. "But what are we standing on?"

"The prime meridian," Rhys repeated. "It's a line that goes all the way around the earth, the first line of longitude."

"And the last," Margaret added. "The means of navigating the globe—latitude and longitude—were invented right here!"

She turned her eyes to the red brick building, and all at once she took notice of its delightful oddities. White window frames and cornices broke up the red, and the main part of the building was octagonal in shape. It looked like no other building Margaret had ever seen, and so utterly quirky it absolutely belonged.

Margaret wondered if they had a garden.

"I'm told the Astronomer Royal is working on a device to signal the ships at sea accurate time," Rhys said, letting go of Sylvia's arm and leaning closer to Margaret.

"Oh, that's interesting. So watches could all be wound at the same time," she said, nodding.

"What's so important about watch winding?" Sylvia said, looking from Margaret to Rhys with a queer expression on her face. "Are sailors such sticklers for teatime, then?"

Rhys glanced to Margaret. "Accurate time is necessary for accurate navigation. Knowing what time it is helps you know where you are."

"Hmm," Sylvia said, shrugging. "Well, I know where we are—but what time are we supposed to be at your laboratory? Surely we must be running late."

"Actually, I arranged for a tour of the observatory," Rhys said.

"Really!" Margaret said, delighted.

"Really?" Sylvia said in a notably different tone.

"Yes. I know one of the men who maintains the observatory; he's graciously agreed to show us around."

"A patient, no doubt," Sylvia said flatly.

Margaret could feel the glee bubbling in her chest. Sylvia, however, was not as eager, and her face (and comment) showed it.

"Sylvia," Margaret asked quietly. "Are you quite well?"

"Oh, I'm fine!" she replied brightly—perhaps too brightly. "I was hoping to attend Almack's this evening, is all. I finally got a voucher." She bit her lip and brought her big eyes up to Rhys's face. Then to Margaret's. "And that you would come with me, Margaret. I know you've had a voucher but haven't gone yet."

Margaret felt the air seize in her chest. Luckily, Rhys stepped in and spared her from disappointing either herself or Sylvia.

"Have no fear, Miss Morton," Rhys said, taking the girl's arm. "I have arranged the timing precisely. We have a short tour here, then we will have an early luncheon and see my laboratory, before we catch our ship back home. We will be back in London with plenty of time for you to prepare for an evening out."

Sylvia's face cleared of all worry as she put her hand on Rhys's arm. "Of course you would be so considerate. You always know exactly what you're doing."

The tour of the observatory was delightful. At least, it was delightful for Margaret. She got to ask impertinent questions and peer into telescopes. And the tour allowed her to focus on something other than Rhys, and Sylvia, and her own confused feelings.

Rhys seemed to enjoy himself as well, laughing as Margaret commandeered their guide's attention for the fourth time to ask some question about equatorial weather conditions. But his attention was split between Margaret's enthusiasm and Sylvia's lack thereof.

Margaret couldn't help feeling a little sorry for Sylvia. It was obvious that maritime navigation wasn't at all interesting to her. Of course, it wasn't to Margaret either, but her natural curiosity bridged across subjects, and she found herself enjoying learning something new.

Molly, for her part, kept her distance and her own counsel.

Except for once.

It was as luncheon was being served at a local tavern, located right outside the observatory's park gates on King William Walk. Rhys had arranged a private room, but the space still felt intimate and tight. Right before she took her plate to a chair along the wall—so as to not interfere with their conversation, but still be able to chaperon—Molly whispered to Margaret.

"Are you having a good time, miss?" she asked.

"Oh yes," Margaret said. "It's delightful!"

"Good." Her maid nodded. "He did this all for you, you know. Don't let her take it away."

Margaret's brow came down, but before she could comment, Sylvia seated herself between her and Rhys.

"Well, I'm famished. A lovely, quick cold lunch should do the trick." She squeezed Margaret's arm under the table. "You know quite a lot about celestial navigation!"

"Well, I do now," Margaret said with a smile, meeting Rhys's eye. "Although I expect it is Rhys who has an untapped yearning to go to sea."

Rhys chuckled. "I did briefly consider life as a ship's doctor," he said.

"Why am I not surprised?" Margaret replied, rolling her eyes.

Rhys looked like he was going to answer, but Sylvia turned to him, her head blocking Margaret from view. "Dr. Gray, I was told that there are some lovely manor houses in the area. Do you think you would let one? In the near future, I mean?"

Thus luncheon went quickly, although not quickly enough to satisfy Sylvia. And truth be told, not quick enough for Margaret. As Sylvia commandeered the conversation, Margaret began to feel like an interloper on her own outing. And she began to wish they were walking, moving, discovering new things. Because being in that close room—as pleasant as it was; the tavern keeper had put some lovely pansies in pots near the windows—meant that there was no escape from her own thoughts.

But luckily, soon enough they were outside the tavern and making the short walk through the streets of Greenwich to Gloucester Circus, and the address that Margaret knew so well by her letters.

"Well," Rhys said, throwing an arm wide. "Here it is!"

It was a plain brown brick building, the first in a row of townhouses that rounded the circus, and a small, overgrown park at the center.

Margaret itched to go into that park and see how she could tame it.

Rhys went up to the bright blue door—the only bit of whimsy in the whole block, and she was pleased to see that it belonged to him.

"What a lovely blue," Sylvia said, for once her mind and Margaret's working along similar themes.

"Thank you!" he replied, pleased. "I like it. It's quite useful too, as I need only mention the blue and my patients know which door to knock on."

Sylvia's smile held still at the mention of patients. She shrugged it off, and instead asked, "Dare we hope that the interior is as bright and cheerful as the door?" She gave a little wink to Margaret.

"The inside is annoyingly practical," Rhys replied. "But I hope it meets with your approval."

He opened the door, and Sylvia, followed by Molly, walked inside.

"I saw you, you know," Rhys said as Margaret passed him.

"Saw me what?" she whispered back.

"Eyeing the park," he replied. "You'd have it in shipshape in no time, I wonder."

"Shipshape is de rigueur in Greenwich, I imagine." She smirked.

He swallowed a laugh. And smothered it completely as Sylvia turned around to look at them.

"I see patients in this room over here, my office," he said, opening up a door to allow a quick glance of an ordinary-looking study, with perhaps more medical texts than your average gentleman might own. "And my personal rooms are upstairs," he added, nodding toward the sturdy polished staircase.

Margaret lingered for a moment, her eyes on those stairs, and where they led. Rhys's rooms. Where he dressed. Where he slept.

Where, perhaps, he read her letters and thought about her.

Quickly she darted her eyes away from the stairs as Rhys led them behind him, toward the back of the house.

"And this," he said, opening a pair of French doors and throwing them wide, "is my laboratory."

Margaret's eyes went wide as she walked into the space. It was like walking into Rhys's mind. It was a warm, bright space. The windows to the back of the house were quite large and faced north, giving him excellent light throughout the day. There was a large cabinet with small drawers, reminiscent of the apothecary on the far side, with neat labels on each one. Jars sat atop it, each containing a different colored liquid, each meticulously labeled. A large table was in the center of the room, a contraption of connected glass tubes and bulbous containers sitting gracefully upon it. A sheaf of notes sat to one side, observations written in a neat hand.

An ornate iron spiral staircase sat in one corner, no doubt leading up to those personal quarters that had so captured her attention. And in the other, was . . .

"What on earth is that!" Sylvia cried, burying her face in Rhys's shoulder.

"It's a skeleton," Margaret answered. The white skeleton hung from a metal frame, grinning at them, its hand raised in a disconcertingly cheerful wave.

"Of a person?" Sylvia wailed into his shirt, her voice muffled.

"Well, yes," Rhys said, somewhat chagrined. He shot a helpless look toward Margaret. "I know it seems morbid," he began, only to be cut off by another wail.

"*Seems* morbid?" Sylvia cried. "There is the corpse of a man in your home!"

"Sylvia, it's not a corpse," Margaret said sensibly.

"Nor is it of a man," Rhys said, and was met with wide-eyed shock from one and a look of complete consternation from another. If Margaret could have mouthed the words *don't help* she would have.

"It's a skeleton. And *Dr.* Gray," she said, reminding Sylvia of Rhys's position in the community, "uses it to study. To do his work. Did you honestly think he only ever looked in books to learn his trade? How on earth do you think the books get written?"

"I . . . I don't know," Sylvia said with a wet sniffle. "I know that you are a man of science, Dr. Gray, but I didn't expect it to be so . . . present."

"For heaven's sake, to grow a plant I have to take manure and fish carcasses and press them through cheesecloth," Margaret replied. "Every endeavor worth doing has aspects that are unseemly."

Sylvia gave a little smile at that. "As I am quickly learning."

"Maybe it would be best if Dr. Gray showed you what he uses the skeleton for," Margaret prodded.

Sylvia drew back nervously.

"Of course," Rhys said with formality. "I use her—*it*—mostly for instruction. I take the skeleton with me to lectures, to illustrate my subject. For example, I can point to the metatarsal bones—the foot—and show how they all work together to help a person move."

"You take it with you?" Sylvia asked, shocked. "Does it ride alongside you on the boat?"

"No." He laughed. "It has a carrying case."

"Perhaps . . . yes, perhaps it is best if in the future the skeleton stays in the carrying case," Sylvia said.

"Yes." Rhys gave a slow nod. "Usually, she—I mean it, is. I just made sure to have her out today because I thought—"

His eyes fell to Margaret. And she knew suddenly exactly why the skeleton had been out of its case. Because he had planned an adventure for just the two of them. For Margaret. And he thought it was something that would make her smile.

And he was right. It had made her smile the moment she saw it—right before Sylvia did. And Margaret suddenly realized what Molly had meant. Rhys had put this trip together for *her*. Not for Sylvia. But it had very quickly become about Sylvia.

And the only one who could stop that happening was Margaret.

So, with a wink and a bit more confidence than she knew she had, Margaret walked over to the skeleton and introduced herself.

"Hello," she said, taking the skeleton's surprisingly light hand and giving it a gentle shake. "Margaret Babcock, very pleased to make your acquaintance. And you are . . . ?"

While Sylvia goggled at her and Rhys smiled, Margaret continued.

"You're very soft-spoken, but I suspect you know anything and everything about this laboratory. Would you indulge me with a tour?"

Rhys took a step away from Sylvia and toward Margaret.

"She'll tell you none of my secrets, Margaret," Rhys replied cheekily. "Miss Crossbones is wholly loyal to me."

"Miss Crossbones? I knew you had an unspoken penchant for the sea, but I never dreamed of piracy!"

As Rhys laughed, he came closer to Margaret's side. Sylvia stood abandoned.

"Now, if you truly want a tour, we will start with the herbs," he said, coming over to the large apothecary cabinet with its neatly labeled drawers. "I've been in contact with a chemist in York for some time who thinks that a powder made from a combination of arrowroot and belladonna helps settle an irregular heart . . ."

"Dr. Gray," Sylvia said, "I . . . I still don't think . . . dear me, this space is making me feel a bit woozy."

"Is it?" Rhys said, coming immediately to Sylvia's side. "Well, we cannot have that. There is a sofa in my study, come." As he guided her to the door he continued, "You can have a bit of a lie-down, and collect yourself."

"Thank you," she said gratefully.

"I'll have my maid of all work bring up some tea."

"You . . . you aren't going to stay with me?" she asked.

"I will of course see you settled. But wouldn't you rather have Molly attend to you?" he asked. "I have promised Margaret a tour, and it would be terribly rude if I left her at odd ends."

"But . . . I mean, yes, of course," she replied. Then after a moment of hesitation, she took a deep breath and rolled her shoulders back. "Do you know, I think I feel a little better," she replied with a wide smile.

"Are you sure?" he asked.

"Yes, of course," she said, leaning into him. "Just a moment of disorientation; it has completely passed."

"Excellent," he said, and brought her over to where Margaret stood by the drawers. "Margaret, open that drawer marked 'dried fungus'—I think you'll find it fascinating."

And so the tour went. Rhys showing every aspect of the lab that he could to Margaret, Margaret peppering him with questions—much like she did the man at the observatory. It was a day of complete fascination and wonder for her.

And Sylvia, standing just behind them.

Occasionally she would ask a question. Such as if there was any other room in the house they might visit, or if the hour was growing late.

And to be fair, the hour was growing later than Rhys had likely planned. After Sylvia mentioned it for the fourth time, he glanced up at the mantel clock.

"Lord, is that the time?" he asked, squinting slightly in a way that made Margaret briefly wonder what he would look like in spectacles. They would suit him, she decided. "Time flies when enjoying oneself, I suppose."

"Of course," Sylvia replied tersely. She straightened her back and was at the door of the laboratory before either

Margaret or Rhys could draw another breath. "But as . . . interesting as it is, we should be going. Margaret and I do not wish to be late and—oh!"

She opened the door and walked almost directly into the bloodied apron of a man waiting in the hall.

"Pardon me, miss," the man said, immediately stepping back and whipping off his thick leather hat. "I was told that the doctor was 'ere, an' . . . oh, they're ye be, Dr. Gray."

"Mr. Thompson," Rhys said, stepping forward. "Yes, I'm here. This Miss Morton and Miss Babcock. Ladies, Mr. Thompson, my butcher."

"Yer girl let me in," Mr. Thompson said sheepishly. "I don't mean to bother. But it's m' Jane. Her hands have been aching from the damp, and she ran out of that powder you made her."

"It's quite all right," Rhys said, straightening, and immediately switching into what Margaret knew was his medical mode. "Ladies, would you care to wait in the kitchen? Molly, can you show them the way—my maid will have tea for you."

"But . . . our ship . . ." Sylvia said plaintively. "And those clouds look threatening."

"It will take absolutely no time at all," Rhys replied, not looking back at them as he escorted Mr. Thompson into his office.

As the girls followed Molly to the back of the house, Margaret tried to give Sylvia a smile, a bit of consideration.

But Sylvia was glum to the point of despair.

They sat in the kitchen. They drank tea.

They waited.

"I thought it would take no time at all," Sylvia said, her eyes once again flying to the window. "I'm not going to miss Almack's! Not for this."

"You won't. It has only been a few minutes, and there

are boats sailing every hour," Margaret replied. Then, after a moment, "I expect this is fairly normal in Rhys's life. In a doctor's life."

"Well, it shouldn't be," Sylvia said in a huff. "Dr. Gray is a man of prestige! And a man of prestige should be able to set his own schedule, go to London and lecture, and not adhere to the whims of . . . of butchers! He's a *Gray*, for goodness' sake."

"He is a man of prestige," Margaret answered quietly. "But he is also a man people need. And a doctor's wife must respect that."

Sylvia looked utterly miserable as she contemplated what Margaret had said. The world echoed between them.

It wasn't long before they heard quick, heavy footfalls in the front hall. The door open and shut again. And Rhys's own lighter steps moving briskly back to the kitchen.

"Well," he said, rubbing his hands together as he entered the small, warm room. Sylvia was on her feet the moment he appeared. "I apologize for the wait, but Mrs. Thompson's hands . . . thank you for your patience."

"No trouble at all!" Sylvia said brightly. "But we really should be going, don't you think?"

"Precisely. If we walk briskly we will make the ship as intended and be back in London by—"

But Rhys was destined to never finish that sentence. Because as they made to gather their things, they heard it. A crack of thunder that shook the walls of the townhouse, and portended the opening of the skies.

17

*N*othing in this trip to Greenwich had gone the way Rhys had planned. First, he had been surprised that morning when he discovered his mother not only awake, but fully attired (she usually wore shockingly little to sleep in, and enjoyed the looks on people's faces if they happened to see her in her gauzy chemises—a particularly awkward circumstance for a son). More surprisingly, she was in conversation with his sister Eloisa, and with Miss Morton.

Then he had been surprised to discover that he was taking Miss Morton with them to Greenwich. But for that, he knew whom to blame.

Eloisa.

He'd returned from Margaret's garden three days prior, entering the house after taking so long a walk it was a wonder that he hadn't trod on every street in London. He'd wanted to forget everything and remember everything and let his blood calm down a bit before he tried to form coherent thoughts. And was immediately pounced on by Eloisa.

"Where have you been?" she asked.

"I had that Horticultural Society meeting," he replied.

"That was this morning," she said. "It's almost tea!"

"Since when do you keep my schedule?"

"Since Mother got a letter from Father today!" she hissed. "She was hoping that he was writing to say he was coming home, but now he's said that he cannot come back until he has absolute assurances of Morton's forgiveness. She's been upset all afternoon! She's gone through all the handkerchiefs and tea cakes in the house, and has been soaking in the bathtub since she ran out of both."

Rhys had closed his eyes. On top of the roiling feelings in his gut, now he had to deal with his absent father's continued manipulations of the family he left behind. And, if he knew the bastard, it was a family he had no intention of returning to. Rhys was exhausted.

He just wanted to go home.

And then he realized he could. Not only that he could, but that he must. Because he'd made a promise to Margaret, and suddenly there was nothing he wanted more than to take a boat ride down the river, and be standing next to her as they did.

Even considering what had just happened between them, that image made him feel peaceful. Made him feel . . . happy.

"No. No," he said with determination. "Unfortunately, I cannot. I have to go to Greenwich. Yes, and urgently. I have to make arrangements for a visit, so—"

"You're leaving me to deal with Mother? How typical. You always run. You're the one who—"

"I'm the one doing the marrying to secure Morton's forgiveness, so you can bloody well speak to the woman who gifted you with your stunning penchant for dramatics!"

He'd said it so harshly—much more harshly than he'd intended. He'd never really spoken to any member of his family that way—ever. Eloisa visibly flinched, and became quiet.

"Wait—a visit. With whom? Who is going to visit Greenwich?" Eloisa asked.

But he didn't have to answer. Because oddly somehow, it was Eloisa—his sharp-tongued sister—who had become the keeper of his secrets.

"You are walking a fine edge," she'd said. "You and Miss Babcock."

"Utter nonsense," he'd replied. "We are friends."

But considering how she had kissed him—and yes, how he had kissed her back—he wasn't sure he believed it anymore.

It had taken everything in him to break that kiss. To not let himself sink into delirious warmth. But he had done it.

Because he didn't have a choice.

And that was the whole of it, wasn't it? He didn't have a choice. He was not putting off his decision to marry Miss Morton, he was simply putting off the act of asking. Because Margaret had been right.

He loved his family. As loud, eccentric, and occasionally bohemian as they could be, they were his. And they needed him.

So while he was disappointed to discover Miss Morton being added to the party, a very small part of him was relieved. Because while he did want to take this trip with Margaret, while he had been looking forward to nothing else for two days, he had to grudgingly admit that Eloisa was right.

It was dangerous.

The surprises, of course, did not stop there. Nor did they end with the sudden downpour. A downpour that did not let up, no matter how much Miss Morton stared out the window of the tavern.

They had rushed as quickly as possible from his townhouse in Gloucester Circus to the Greenwich docks, only to be thoroughly soaked and discover that the river cruises had been abruptly canceled.

The rain wasn't the main problem, the ship's captain had said, although it was a problem. It was the wind that had come with it. Blustery and strong but with no consistency—if a ship did not have to be on the water, it shouldn't be.

Next they repaired to the tavern—the same they had taken their luncheon in. It was the closest and most comfortable place to wait while Rhys attempted to hire a carriage. While Margaret and Sylvia dried off in front of a fire in a private parlor (thankfully, someone had the intelligence to grab an umbrella so the ladies were not entirely soaked—and it should be no surprise that person was Molly), Rhys ran around to every posting house he knew of. And every one of them was happy to take him and his party into London, as soon as the rain let up.

The rain, however, did not cooperate.

It poured on, long after night fell, turning the skies to true darkness.

"Miss Morton, come away from the window," Rhys said gently. "We have wine, and cheese and fruit . . ."

"I don't want cheese or fruit or . . . or anything," she sniffled. "I just wanted to go to Almack's for once in my life. And we've missed it."

It was true. Even if they could leave that minute, they would arrive back in London after the patronesses had closed the doors, sticklers as they were for the rules.

"Well, if it's any consolation," Margaret said, "the storm is likely just as strong in London—so going to Almack's might have been difficult in any case."

"Oh, hang it all," Sylvia said, miserable. "I would go to bed. I'm stuck in Greenwich and the evening is ruined."

"That's a good notion, miss," Molly piped up from her spot along the wall. "Close your eyes knowing that when you open them, the rain will have stopped and the sun will have dried everything out."

They had taken rooms at the tavern. It was a respectable establishment, and it was really the only solution. It was absolutely impossible for two young, unmarried ladies to stay at a bachelor's accommodations for an evening, no matter how well they were chaperoned. It was sidestepping the rules just to have had them there that afternoon for a tour.

Besides, Rhys just didn't have the space to put them up.

"Well, yes," Sylvia replied, sounding relieved for the first time all day . . . and night. "But I should not wish to abandon—"

"I have no doubt we will retire ourselves very shortly," Margaret said soothingly.

"Come, miss," Molly said, steering Sylvia to the door. "I'll help see you settled. It's been a trying day."

"Yes, Molly," Sylvia said, her voice heavy with exhaustion. "It has."

And just like that, Rhys found himself alone with Margaret for the first time all day.

The one thing that he'd been wanting. Now that it was before him, he wasn't quite sure what to do. Or say.

Unfortunately, Margaret seemed to have the same problem. And they stood there for some moments, letting the rain falling and the fire crackling fill the silence.

"Well," he said, his voice weirdly high. He coughed and began again. "I hope she sleeps undisturbed."

"I imagine she will," Margaret replied, her eyes still on the door. "Spending all day being displeased is exhausting work."

His eyebrow raised. Then she met his look.

Then they both laughed.

"I'm sorry," he said, laughing so hard now he was becoming teary. "I know I shouldn't laugh, but . . . did you see the way she looked at me when she first saw the skeleton?"

"I thought she was going to call the police and report you as a grave robber!" Margaret said, smothering her own chuckles. "Oh, I should not laugh, it's not kind."

It wasn't kind, but it certainly felt good. It felt a relief.

"I am certain everything she knows about the medical profession she learned from Gothic novels, and I had suddenly been cast as some kind of evil preying villain."

"Well, to be fair, you're the one who gave your skeleton a name," she replied, seating herself back at the table, close to the fire.

He sat across from her, let the fire—and her gaze—warm him. "What else was I supposed to call her? She's one of the foremost ladies in my life. She's assisted me since I worked in London."

"You worked in London?" Her head tilted to the side, exposing her long neck to the firelight.

"Briefly," he said.

"Is that when you attended the queen?" she asked. "Lord Ashby said you had."

"Yes," he replied, more than a little embarrassed. "An old story that made me want nothing more than to move away. Which is how I found myself in Greenwich."

"I see," she said, nodding. "You don't like talking about it, do you?"

"It's always struck me as odd that the thing I am best known for is something that was a complete happenstance. An utter fluke," he replied after some thought. "If I am to be known at all, I'd much rather be known for something else."

"Something other than being a good physician?"

"Something other than being a good physician one time,

to one single person." He shrugged. "It would be like you growing one single rose. Everything else becomes irrelevant."

"That makes sense." She smiled softly. And to her, he knew that it did.

And then they sat there. Watching each other. Waiting to see who would speak next. And what they would say.

It wasn't unpleasant, this silence. Nor was it dull. In fact, Rhys could not recall a time he ever felt more focused. In the moment.

But moments, as long as they can be, have a tendency to pass.

"Well," she said, watching him as he watched her. The way the light played over her hair. The way the flames made her skin look soft as velvet.

"Well," he replied, shifting slightly in his suddenly uncomfortable seat.

"I think it best if I go up to bed," she said after a low sigh. "Sylvia and I are sharing a room and bath, and I have no doubt all the hot water will be gone if I do not take advantage now."

"Yes," he said, nodding dully. He had taken his own room too, even though he lived three blocks away. He could not imagine leaving Margaret and Sylvia in a tavern—even a respectable one—alone, with only a maid for protection. And after spending an hour in the rain looking for a hack, the idea of a soft bed was tempting.

But somehow he didn't move. And neither did Margaret.

"Or," he said, his eyes never leaving hers, "we could finish our wine here."

She held his gaze. "Our wine?"

"We still have over a half bottle. And we've hardly touched the cheese and fruit. It would be a shame for them to go to waste."

She took one breath. Two. "I suppose it would."

Relief rushed through him, mixed with a touch of something else. Anticipation.

"Stay," he said. "Stay, and I will tell you about the time I attended the queen."

He bribed her with words. He didn't know if it was necessary to do so, but he just wanted this. He wanted to stay in this room, the world outside keeping them in.

He filled both their wineglasses, cut the fruit on the tray. Took his time—their time.

"It was just after the war. We had come back, and Ned and I dutifully received our medals for service in battle. There was a receiving line with Queen Charlotte—she was a patroness of botany, did you know?"

She nodded and he went on. He told her about how, as he bent in front of Her Majesty, he noticed she was a bit mottled in color. How he speculated with his unfiltered doctor's mind that she was having difficulty breathing. And, considering the queen was in her eighth decade, that she was likely too fragile for the corset she was wearing. And how he said so.

"You did not," Margaret replied, her eyes wide. "You did not tell the queen to take off her corset."

"I did," he said. "And as I was being dragged out of the parade by some exceptionally burly guards, the queen had me brought back to speak to her privately."

Margaret was shaking her head and laughing to herself. "Even I know you do not tell the queen to remove her corset. And I routinely wear trousers."

His mind flashed to that morning in the garden three days ago. When he confirmed with his eyes—and his hands—that she was indeed a woman who wore trousers.

"At any rate," he said, after clearing his throat with a gulp of wine, "Her Majesty said that I was the first doctor she had seen to make such a practical recommendation and that she was going to implement it. Then she asked me to take a look at a small spot on her hand—she had scraped it accidentally and it was not healing very quickly. I recommended a salve, and then I was dismissed, and that is the story of how I attended to the queen."

Margaret smiled and took a sip of her own wine, leaning back in her chair. "And after?" she asked.

"After, I was bombarded by everyone. My colleagues, my family . . . the only people who did not treat me differently were Ned and John."

"What I find surprising is that it is worthy of comment at all. That an old woman who seemed to be having difficulty breathing being told that she should perhaps remove the restraints to said breathing, only seems to be common sense to me." She leaned forward on her elbows, resting her chin on her fingertips.

"Ah, that is because you are a sensible person," Rhys replied. "As well as good humored and intelligent. No wonder all of London and the Horticultural Society want your company."

She drew back slowly, coming off her hands.

"What is it?" he asked gently.

"I wish you wouldn't do that," she said, her voice quiet but strong.

"Do what?" he replied.

"Tell me I'm wonderful."

He drew back, serious. Watched her as she sighed, bit her lip, and then looked up at him again.

"Ever since I came to London. Every time I see you, you tell me I'm brilliant, or doing well, or that I have virtues worth . . . recognition," she said.

"You do," he insisted. "I was only—"

"Making me feel more comfortable," she finished for

him. "I know. And at first it helped. At first, I needed a bit of confidence to step out into society and not feel completely awkward and strange. But now—"

"That wasn't what I was going to say," he interrupted. "I . . . did not—*do* not say those things to make you feel more comfortable. And I do not do it to simply buck up your confidence. I say it because it's true. It's how I think of you." When she remained silent, he continued.

"Dammit, Margaret, it's how I feel. And I won't apologize for it."

"I know," she said quietly. "And that's what makes it so hard to hear."

The crackling of the fire was the only sound in the room. Even the rain outside was lessening. It was as if the whole world was holding its breath.

"You tell me I'm wonderful. And I know you are. I've known it, I think, since before we began writing letters. But there is nothing we can do about it, is there?" she said finally.

"Margaret . . ." he said, his voice a low rumble. "You cannot know what you are asking. What you . . . what you want."

"Rhys," she said, her eyes growing suspiciously shiny. "You have never, not once, made any assumptions about my intelligence. You've never treated me like a naïve child. So please don't do so now. Why wouldn't I know what I want? I'm a human being. I have a heart, and I know its wants." She took a deep breath. "I have a body. And I know its wants too."

His heart, that treacherous mechanism, that organ of life, began pounding in his chest. *Tha-thud, tha-thud, tha-thud.* It echoed in his ears, quickly taking over his rational mind. Only leaving space for her words, and the way they lit his body on fire.

"That . . . that kiss," she said, taking all her bravery and putting it on the table in front of them. "That wasn't an accident. And I could not forget it, even if I tried—although I confess I did not try very hard."

"Neither did I," he admitted, before he realized he spoke aloud.

"It was my body winning the fight. The fight I have every time I see you," she said. "To give in to the desire to touch you. To take you in with all my senses."

His hand, purely of its own volition, began to slide gently across the small table. To touch hers, resting there. The long, beautifully strong fingers, the softness on the underside of her wrist. Her fingertips dancing with his placed just as much of a spell on him as her words did.

"I've been hiding it, this fight," she continued, and he realized her foot had inched forward. Her ankle lightly grazing up against his. "Even from myself. Telling myself that we are friends, when we are not."

"We *are* friends," he insisted.

"But not just friends," she replied, her eyes following his fingers as they traced the lines on her palm. "Being friends doesn't feel like this."

No, it certainly did not, he thought. Friendship didn't feel like a drug. A wonderful, terrible drug that shrunk existence down to the person in front of him. To the way her foot felt against his. The look in her eyes. The blazing heat of her hand under his. The hitch in her breath before she spoke. Friendship didn't make him want to throw the small table aside and hold her against his body, feeling the length of her against his, or make him wonder about just how much warmth came from her, or how dark her eyes could become.

Friendship didn't make him *want*. And Margaret . . . Margaret made him want.

Just when the bloody hell had that started? There was no moment he could point to. No one letter that made his heart pump to this rhythm—it was just there, as if it had always been.

"I'm not very good at pretending," she said with a rueful smile. "Even though I've been pretending this long. I don't think I can pretend anymore."

"Pretend what?" he asked.

"Pretend that I don't want more."

His mouth went dry. And he knew that the next few seconds he had to tread very, very carefully. The next few seconds could change his life. "What would you want . . . if you could have more?" he asked, never letting his eyes drop from hers.

She held his gaze. "I would want today back," she said.

"Today back?"

"Oh, I would want you to take me to Greenwich, and to have a tour of the observatory, and your laboratory. And I would want to dally there for so long that we got caught in the rain. And we had to stay at your townhouse, waiting for the rain to clear. With no one pushing us to leave. No one waiting for our return. No one but you and me."

She shrugged gently, and for the first time, he noticed that she had at some point uncoiled the braid pinned to the back of her head. It now lay fat over her shoulder, turning gold and red in the fire. Torturing him with its possibilities.

"And I feel terrible saying that. Because Sylvia has been a friend to me. She doesn't deserve to be wished out of existence. But I can't help imagining what today would have been like, if we'd been given that chance."

What would today have been like, if it had just been the two of them? He didn't have to wonder. In a flash he saw everything. He saw himself giving Margaret his arm while he led her from the boat to the observatory. He saw her not letting go of it—and him not wanting her to. He saw how close they would have stood, while she explored the little drawers in his laboratory. He saw them talking, about little things. About nothing. And he saw their closeness growing, until there was nothing between them. Not air. Not even clothes.

And they would have stayed in his bed at his home until morning. Not in this inn, in this room where their privacy extended only to the door. They would have the whole house, and all of time. Scandalize his maid—and Molly—and neither of them caring. Just . . . being allowed to sink into each other.

To let his body win the fight.

"What would you want, if you could have more?" she asked, unblinking. "If you could let yourself?"

"But I can't. *We* can't."

"Rhys," she breathed. "What's the worst that could happen?"

What would he want? he thought, if he let himself. He wanted everything his mind had just shown him. He wanted her words in his ear, her presence in his house, in his bed. He wanted everything that she—as a maiden—couldn't possibly know but as a scientist had likely guessed. But at that moment, he wanted nothing more than to show her just precisely what it was he wanted.

So show her.

The thought entered his mind and ran straight to his blood. And for once, Rhys's mind and body were in perfect accord.

He sat back. Picked up his napkin and wiped his mouth, even though the last of the wine was long since drunk. Then he stood. Came to her side of the table.

And held out his hand.

She watched him warily as she slid her hand into his.

He pulled her to her feet and fit her body right alongside his. Then he put his hand under her chin, lifting her eyes to his. Those daring, direct eyes had turned the color of midnight as he slid one hand behind her back.

With the other, he reached up and took that braid that hung over her shoulder. He untied the end and let his fingers weave their way through, unplaiting it as he went up. Then he shook out the tresses into full golden waves that fell past her elbows. Then he looked. He let his eyes drink their fill, as want coursed through him.

She looked so much older with her hair down, which was the opposite of what one might expect. The braid she usually wore was serviceable, and how she'd likely been wearing her hair for years. But the soft waves framing her face made her look feminine, and powerful.

She didn't say a single word. She didn't need to. Her body spoke for her.

She leaned into his touch. He lightly traced his fingers down her slender, graceful neck, brushed them gently along her collarbone. Her own hands held fast to his arms, sought purchase lest she lose her balance and fall into him completely.

And then she opened her mouth, just for a moment—the space of a breath. It was all the invitation he needed, and as he lowered his head, he—

"Oh! Excuse me!"

They froze. A mere inch away from each other. Neither of them turned their heads, but they didn't have to. The sound of raucous laughter from outside the room became louder as the door was thrown open, and Molly peeked her head in.

"I did knock," she said sheepishly.

"It's . . . it's all right, Molly," Margaret said, her eyes sliding to her. But she didn't move from his embrace. Not yet.

"I apologize, miss, but it's Miss Morton. She's asking for you. Says she won't sleep without knowing you're . . . well. She says she'll come down here in her robe iffn' I didn't fetch you."

And there it was. Miss Morton. Sylvia. The world, the one they had held so carefully at bay, had come rushing back to them through that open door. And by the way Margaret let go of his arms, she knew it too.

Slowly she took a step back, breaking their contact, and his body wept for her touch. "Thank you, Molly. I'll be right along."

"Forgive me for saying so, miss, but I think you should come with me now. If I return there without you . . ."

Margaret nodded, biting her lip. "Yes," she said, watching Rhys as he watched her. "Yes, you are perhaps correct. Thank you, Rhys . . . for the wine. And for today."

"It was my pleasure," he said automatically. "Truly."

"It was . . . it was wonderful," she said, and he knew what she was saying. It was wonderful to wonder. To let themselves imagine what it would have been like if they'd had the day to themselves. If they'd had nothing in their path.

But as she stepped away to Molly, who quickly pinned her hair up before leading her out, Rhys knew they could not let themselves wonder forever.

Because their path was not clear.

And to pretend otherwise was nothing but a lie.

But could they tread it anyway? His mind wondered as he stood alone in that room, the cool air rushing in from the door left wide open. Or would it be the height of selfishness?

As he let himself ponder that, forcing his body to forget about everything that had almost just happened, Rhys left the room, walked to the front door of the tavern, and out into the night. The rain had slowed to little more than a mist. If Sylvia and Margaret had not already retired for the evening, they might have ventured to the nearest posting inn and hired the promised hack. But it would be better to take the river in the morning. And it would be best of all if Rhys took a walk and got a little air. He would be back in a few minutes, he rationalized, but he needed to think, and it was not going to be easy doing so in the private room with the memory of Margaret's hair in the firelight.

However, if he had not been so lost in thought, he might have glanced out across the main room of the tavern as he passed. And he might have seen a familiar face.

"Haverford!" one of the young man's cronies called out, forcing his eyes back toward the barroom. "Who are you staring at?"

"I believe that was Dr. Gray," Haverford said. It had been an odd turn of events that led him to be in Greenwich that evening. He'd been marked at the bigger London gaming establishments, so he had been reaching further out. A friend of a friend was a navy man, and knew of certain spots in Greenwich that might serve him well. Of course, it had been a complete waste, with no one gambling higher than a crown. Thus he had to wait out the weather like everyone else to head back to town, and *real* fun.

"Daniel's brother?" the crony said. "Whatever happened to Daniel, anyway?"

Daniel had been pulled out of his reach by the very same brother, Haverford thought, his vision going dark.

"Daniel has family in town," Haverford answered amicably. "Apparently his brother Dr. Gray is to be married, and his family descended, thus he cannot play with us anymore." It was a real shame too. The boy had been so predictably bad at faro—and he'd needed that money. Once people knew your pockets were to let, they wanted their bills paid, and on time.

"Really?" An eyebrow went up. "Daniel always said his brother was a terrible killjoy. What young lady would want to marry that?"

"Interestingly," Haverford said, a malicious smile spreading across his face, "it's not the young lady who left the room just before him."

Because he knew the tall female who exited the room only moments ago, with pink cheeks and her hair loose, looking like she had been thoroughly ravished. Everyone in London knew the unique, compelling, and incredibly wealthy Miss Margaret Babcock on sight.

Well, well, well . . . this trip to Greenwich might not have been a waste after all.

18

The next morning, after a decidedly awkward boat ride back up the river to the London docks, Rhys first escorted Margaret to Ashby's doorstep, and Sylvia to her father's thereafter. And while it would have been more expedient to drop the ladies off in the opposite order, he knew he would have to make lengthy explanations to Mr. Morton, and Ned would likely be more forgiving.

That's what he told himself at any rate. But he knew the truth—that he could not risk himself alone with Margaret. Not even for the few minutes it would take to go from the Mortons' to Ned's. He simply did not trust that he could hold on to his restraint.

His walk the night before had proved blood cooling, and head righting. What he wanted—*whom* he wanted . . . he could not act upon. At least not in the way he had last night, if at all. It was disrespectful to Sylvia . . . and it was disrespectful to Margaret. No young lady deserved stolen kisses and moments in a tavern.

She deserved better.

It had been the wine, he decided. And the rain. And the

firelight that opened up that door. Now he had to shut it closed ruthlessly.

So Margaret was deposited into Phoebe's and Ned's care with very little said between them. And Sylvia was deposited into her father's loving embrace.

"I was halfway to turning out the guards!" Mr. Morton said. "But cooler heads prevailed, once I realized the rain was the culprit!" Then he put a heavy hand on Rhys's shoulder. "I'm glad the girl was with you, as I know you're an honorable sort—but I tell you, had Miss Babcock not been there to play chaperon, you and my Sylvia would be standing in a church right this minute."

He was invited to stay for breakfast, but after that fear-inducing dialogue, he declined.

"Thank you, but I expect my own family is very curious as to my whereabouts," he said.

"Knowing your family," Sylvia said, a dimple showing in her cheek, "you'll be walking into a melee!"

Sylvia was likely right, Rhys thought, although, not for the reasons he had posed. The Gray household existed in a constant state of melee. So much so it was entirely possible that the evening had passed and no one had noticed that he was not there.

Thus it was a bit surprising when he walked through the door to be swarmed by all three of his sisters, his youngest brother, and the dog.

"Dammit to hell, Rhys, what did you do now?" This from Eloisa.

"I have no idea," he replied. "You, however, just swore in front of two young ladies and a twelve-year-old."

"Justifiably!" This from Delilah, whose eyes were wide with the stimulant of dramatics.

"Also, we don't care about that," Jubilee added.

"And she swears all the time!" Benji added. "Yesterday she said—"

"Benji," Eloisa said, reminding them all she was the mother of a four-year-old with one stern word. "That does not matter at the moment. We are dealing with a crisis."

"Is this a real crisis or one of mother's 'crises'?"

"That depends," Eloisa replied. "Were you making love to Margaret Babcock in a tavern in Greenwich last night?"

Rhys froze. He stared at his sister.

"What did you say?"

"It's true, isn't it?" Delilah said, gripping Jubilee's arm in morbid delight. "Oh, it simply must be!"

"No, it is not true," Rhys bit out. As much as his body wished it had been. "Where did you hear such a thing?"

"Daniel came in this morning," Eloisa began.

"He woke us all up before sunrise!" Benji added.

"Benji, can you find Rory for me? I think he's out in the garden," Eloisa said diplomatically, but brooking no opposition. "Quickly, before he pulls up all the flowers."

"Rory's been trying his hand at gardening," Jubilee explained as Benji left sullenly.

"Yes, but my son is not the gardening enthusiast we are currently concerned with."

"Please go back," Rhys said. "You were talking about Daniel."

"Daniel came in at some ungodly hour of the morning, straight from whatever den of iniquity he'd been frequenting. Said that one of his friends came in saying that you'd been seen with Miss Babcock at an inn."

"Well, that much is true," Rhys replied. "I was at an inn with Miss Babcock."

Delilah squealed. Even Jubilee's perpetually blank expression gave way to a lifted eyebrow.

"I was also there with her maid, Molly, and Miss Morton." He crossed his arms over his chest. "We were stuck in the rain and could not travel back to London until this morning."

"As apparently was Haverford," Eloisa countered. "You remember, Daniel's not-so-chum? Daniel was told it was Haverford who saw you, making love to Miss Babcock."

"Not Miss Morton, to whom everyone knows you are engaged," Delilah added, wide-eyed.

"We are not engaged," Rhys replied automatically.

"Intended, then," Eloisa said, waving away his objections.

"I just came from Morton's, he said nothing about it."

"Of course not, because they haven't stepped outside the house yet this morning. But the second they do they will certainly get wind of it."

"Then Miss Morton can easily deny it. She was there. Nothing happened."

"She was there?" Eloisa asked, stepping closer to him and speaking low. "The whole time?"

Rhys hesitated. Not long, but just enough to have Eloisa's eyes narrowing.

"Nothing happened," he said. Then, because it obviously required more emphasis, "Nothing."

"That doesn't matter," Eloisa said. "Everyone will think something happened. Especially when Daniel finds Haverford!"

"What do you mean, finds him?" Rhys said, his body going alert.

"He plans to challenge him to a duel, of course. Family honor—if you recall it's the Gray family's particular peccadillo."

"Mother's taken to bed," Jubilee added. Then, with a

glance at her silliest sister, "We're supposed to be tending to her, aren't we, Delilah?"

Delilah pouted, but let herself be dragged away. But not before calling back to Rhys. "For the Gray who doesn't invite scandal, you are certainly bringing it to the fore this season!"

"She's not wrong," Eloisa said once they left. "Once this gets out . . . there is no way Morton will allow Father any grace. That is your younger sisters' entire futures gone. No seasons for them. And if Daniel has to run to the Continent too, then——"

"Eloisa, this is very important," he said, so intensely that her jaw dropped open, then quickly snapped shut. "Where did Daniel go?"

It took him almost the whole day to find Daniel. He checked the clubs—even though Daniel was not a member, and the only club he belonged to was the Medical Society of London—he thought it possible that one of Daniel's many vague friends might have gotten him in. When that didn't pan out, he began with the gambling houses. Starting with the one where he last found Daniel. Then working his way down the list Ned had created for said last time, even though Ned had admitted his knowledge of places of vice was sadly lacking these days.

Luckily, Daniel was not as au courant as he likely thought he was, because he was in the third place on Ned's not-particularly-fashionable list of halls.

The minute Rhys walked through the door, he felt the change. All eyes fell on him. All conversation muted to a dull whisper. It had been growing all day, this awareness of people's attention. Or rather, people's attention had grown. But there was no doubt about it—the rumor that Haverford began had spread.

Rhys couldn't let that bother him. He'd had notoriety before when he'd attended the queen—he dealt with it simply by ignoring it (and moving to Greenwich) and eventually it faded. He could only hope that this would fade too—but only if he stopped Daniel from doing something utterly boneheaded.

He found him at the faro table, of course. Daniel was nothing if not dedicated in his dissipation, and faro was by far the fastest path for him. If these were normal circumstances, Rhys would worry about whether his mother had advanced Daniel next quarter's allowance already, worry that he was drinking too much and showing physical signs of that vice, and whether he had eaten a vegetable in the past week. But this was not a normal circumstance.

"Daniel," he said, slapping a hand on his brother's shoulder. "Thank God I've found you."

Daniel turned from the table, and the respectable pile of markers in front of him. It seemed for once in his life he was winning. That, or the other players were taking it easy on him, knowing the situation and that his brother's ability to collect on those markers might be hampered in the near future.

"Rhys!" Daniel said, his grin easy, but his eyes strong and sober. Maybe he was playing better on his own terms after all. "There you are! Come have a seat, play with me."

"No, I'm afraid I cannot. And neither should you."

"Oh, but it's my last night before the dawn, you have to do as I request," Daniel said blithely. He raised his glass, and the other men at the table cheered, "Hear, hear!" all but abandoning their cards.

Rhys's blood ran cold. "What's happening at dawn, Daniel?" he asked, already knowing the answer.

"The duel, of course. Haverford wasn't hard to find. Not with all my friends here helping me." Daniel raised his glass again, and this time drained it of its contents before letting out the most obnoxious belch.

The table cheered again. But Rhys wasn't having any of it.

"Call it off," he said, his voice like steel.

"Call it off?" Daniel repeated. "Are you mad?"

"No, I'm the only sane one left," Rhys replied. "It's utter foolishness."

"Someone is saying my brother dishonored a lady, and I intend to hold him to account for it." He looked up at Rhys, and for a moment, he could see his brother's resolve behind the flippant veneer.

"Right. It's being said about *me*. And I'm the one telling you to call it off. I don't need you to defend my honor. Especially not in a duel."

"Maybe I'm not defending your honor," Daniel countered. "Maybe I'm defending hers."

"Hers? Miss Babcock?" Rhys's brow came down. "You've barely met her."

"And I seem to have more of a care for her reputation than you do," he said. "Not to mention Miss Morton's."

Rhys drew up, unable to reply to that.

"Haverford is spreading a rumor about my brother—about a *Gray*—far and wide," Daniel continued. "And you are not the only one who bears the weight of it. Someone had to stand up and force him to retract his statement."

And then he saw it. The absolute certainty in his brother. The unquestioning belief that he was doing what was right in the face of what was wrong. His manhood—his very being—held in the balance of this act.

In calling a lie of something that was at least half true.

Rhys rubbed a hand over his eyes. "Maybe he would retract his statement," he said, trying to find a solution. "Have you asked—"

"Of course I asked." Daniel humphed. "Did you think I just went up to him and slapped his face with a glove and demanded satisfaction? I followed protocol."

Protocol—yes, there were rules for this sort of thing. Never mind that dueling had been waning in fashion since the end of the colonial war. In the Gray household, it was always known that this was how men resolved disputes. And their father had made certain they all knew the rules.

"Who's your second?" Rhys asked.

"My friend Vincent—you remember Vincent? Just down from school for a few weeks, and we met up quite by accident at the opera last night," Daniel said, and pointed to the cherub-faced youth next to him. He was well into his cups, his eyes shining with the anticipation of an eventful day and a half. He would ask Vincent's last name, but he rather wondered if Daniel knew it.

"Vincent." Rhys nodded. "This must be quite the exciting trip to London for you."

"'Tis!" Vincent remarked. "Absolutely cracking!"

"Did you go to Haverford, arrange this meeting?"

"Of course he did," Daniel replied. "And before you ask, yes he asked Haverford to apologize, and was coldly refused."

Rhys glanced at Vincent, who looked as if perhaps he had accidentally skipped a step when meeting with Haverford's second.

"Would you have accepted it if he had?" Rhys mused, but Daniel didn't hear him, or pretended not to.

"Everything will turn out fine," Daniel said. "You'll see."

"I'll talk to Haverford then," Rhys said. "His quarrel is with me."

Vincent piped up. "Haverford is a liar and at odd ends, and everyone knows it. Once Daniel has met him on the field, he'll back away."

"And what if he doesn't?" Rhys asked. "What if he aims his gun at your heart and fires?"

"He won't."

"He might," Rhys said. "And what happens then? What happens when the bullet enters your body? When it rips through your arteries and muscles and—"

"Don't start in on that," Daniel said coldly, drawing himself up in his seat. "I've heard it all before. It won't work on me."

"Vincent hasn't." Rhys moved over to Daniel's new-found friend. "Tell me, Vincent, do you have any idea what to do if someone is gut shot and bleeding out? Just how much time do you have to get him to help before he loses too much blood to survive? Or what about if he slips into unconsciousness? Or—"

"Stop listening to him, Vincent," Daniel said, standing and dragging the now pale-faced young man with him. "He is not going to stop this by scaring you. He's not going to turn us into cowards the way he did the Thorndike twins. Gentlemen," he addressed the table. "Take back your markers—I'm all played out."

As the rest of the table greedily dove for the markers in front of Daniel's seat, Rhys grabbed his brother's arm. "Just . . . just tell me where the duel is taking place," Rhys said, suddenly desperate.

"Not on your life," Daniel said, shaking him off. "Or mine, come to think of it. Come on, Vincent."

"Fine," said Rhys, standing. "Then I'm coming too."

"You're going to be my shadow all night?" Daniel asked.

"And maybe in the next ten hours I'll be able to talk you out of this nonsense."

"And maybe in the next ten hours you'll learn some resolve and stand as a man does," his brother sneered back.

Rhys was about to reply when there was a commotion coming from the other side of the room, the sound of silver clattering to the floor, and a body falling with a thud.

"Miss . . . miss? Can you hear me?" a gentleman was saying, leaning over the form of one of the dealers. "Good God, she's completely slack. Someone help!"

Rhys glanced over, saw the young woman lying prone and pallid under her rouge on the floor. Men stood, gathering around her in equal parts consternation and annoyance. The one closest to her was trying to jar her into consciousness with repeated slaps to the cheek.

Rhys looked back at Daniel, who wore a smirk on his face, but a hard disappointment in his eyes. "Go," he said, nodding toward the girl. "Sounds like she needs a doctor."

"Daniel—" he began, then stopped himself. "Dammit all. I'll find you, you know. I won't let this happen."

But Daniel just scoffed. "Go help the stranger, Rhys. You'll always choose them over your family, won't you?"

Rhys swore under his breath, then stepped away to where the crowd had gathered around the girl. "Clear away—give her air!" he said, parting the onlookers with the authority he commanded in crisis. "And you—stop slapping her."

As he leaned over the girl, and began to administer to her, he glanced back to where he had left his brother.

As expected, Daniel was gone.

IT HAD TAKEN him a day to find Daniel the first time, but it only took him the night to find him again.

He first tried Haverford's lodgings. If nothing else, he would explain the situation to Haverford, and as the slight was against Rhys, and not Daniel, somehow broker a peaceful resolution. But of course, Haverford was not at home. Apparently no one saw the value of an early dinner and a good night's sleep before possibly dying of a gunshot wound. His man was surly and underpaid, so that at least led Rhys via a few pound notes to learn where Haverford had sent messages that evening.

And he recognized one address as the Medical Society of London.

After all, every duel required a doctor on the field, in case of injury.

He took off at a run for Gray's Inn—the long building of offices that housed the Medical Society's two rooms. There, he did not find the letter, or its recipient, but he did find the porter, who told him that Dr. Hill had been in that evening and received a letter.

Rhys knew Dr. Hill only a little, but enough that he felt no compunction pounding on his door in the wee hours of the morning. Unfortunately, he did so approximately ten minutes too late, according to Hill's valet. Luckily, the valet knew exactly where Dr. Hill had gone, as between dressing Hill in his sturdiest boots that morning and taking his order for a hearty breakfast upon his return, Hill had, between sips of a flask of brandy to stay warm, divulged the particular field he was off to.

And so Rhys found himself crossing the northern fields of Regent's Park in the morning mist, searching for his brother. He found him in an open area, just off the edges of a copse of trees. There were five of them. His brother, Haverford, Vincent, Haverford's second, and the doctor—who stood with his back turned to the proceedings.

They were walking away from each other. Stepping out paces. Their pistols raised in front of their faces.

And Rhys looked down on them from the top of a rise, over a hundred yards away.

"Stop!" he yelled. He wished he had a horse. Wished

he had more than his own two feet under him. But he had taken off so quickly that morning he hadn't even thought to borrow one from Ned. He caught hacks to where he needed to go—and the hack he'd taken to Regent's Park couldn't take him off the road and out into the field.

"Stop!" he cried again, waving his hands in the air like a lunatic. He didn't care—he would run right into the middle of the line of fire, if it would stop them. But it was all for naught. Because as he stumbled down the hill, he heard Haverford's second's voice, floating over the morning.

"Ten. . . . Turn and fire!"

The gunshot echoed across the field. One report, followed quickly by a second. And when Rhys finally reached the dueling grounds, it was to discover one man lying on the ground . . . and a shocked Haverford standing over him.

19

*M*argaret had spent all of yesterday in the garden, and she decided today would be no different. She had barely said two words to Phoebe, even though she pressed for details of what had happened in Greenwich. Margaret simply told the barest facts. That the rain had delayed their return, and they put up at a very reputable establishment. She didn't mention the visit to the observatory, or to Rhys's laboratory. Even those parts of the journey, however innocuous and innocent, seemed too personal to share—let alone what happened after Sylvia had gone to bed.

She blushed as her mind leapt to her boldness that night, in the rain, with just the two of them. Most people would not think a young unmarried lady would ever say such things, or even think them. Especially a shy young lady like Margaret.

But Margaret's shyness had never been demure. There had always been a bluntness to it. And that, coupled with her inability to pretend, had her speaking her mind, often to people's consternation.

But Rhys hadn't been shocked by it—or if he had, he

didn't let that shock stop him from hearing what she was saying. Rhys would always hear what she said. And that was one of the reasons she had fallen in love with him.

It was not something she was willing to deny anymore. The word had tumbled through her mind, and the realization had caused her to stop and stand perfectly still for a full five minutes. If Frederick had not come back out with a wheelbarrow full of fresh soil, she would likely still be there.

Of course she was in love with him. She'd imagined herself in love before—with John Turner, and yes, even with Rhys Gray—but those were mere fancies. It did not compare with the gut-deep sense of longing she felt now.

And she had no idea what to do about it.

So she sat with this revelation. She dug with it, planted with it, and was completely unaware of anything anyone might be saying about her and Rhys throughout the day and into the evening. And then she sat with the revelation while she was supposed to be sleeping.

Thus it was somewhat later in the morning than normal when she cut across the dining room on her way to the gardens, unprepared for the sight before her.

"There you are!" Sylvia said, rising from the breakfast table.

"Sylvia?" Margaret said, stopping short. "Whatever are you doing here?"

"Oh, Margaret!" she cried, practically collapsing against her shoulder. "When I heard the news I knew we must talk—so I fibbed and told my father that you and Lady Ashby had invited me over for breakfast this morning. To be frank I fibbed and told Chalmers the same thing so he showed me in here—is her ladyship still abed?"

"Er, no, come to think of it," Margaret replied. "Lord Ashby left quite early this morning to meet with his lawyers"—something about investing in one of Mr. Turner's new mills, she recalled—"and Lady Ashby decided to go with him."

"Good. Good," Sylvia said, nodding with determination. "That is for the best, yes. That we can speak with each other before everyone else descends on us."

The way Sylvia was worrying her hands, it made anxiety creep up Margaret's spine.

"What . . . what do we need to speak about?" she asked.

"About the night at the inn, of course!" Sylvia cried, plopping back into her chair again. "Do you mind if I eat this sausage?" she said suddenly. "I've been up all night deciding what to do, and I haven't eaten a bite since I heard."

As she took a nibble of the sausage, Margaret just stared, trying to collect herself. "Heard? You . . . heard something about the night at the inn?"

"Yes." Sylvia goggled at her. "Didn't you?"

She shook her head.

"Well, then, you're lucky, because I have had just the most horrid evening!" Sylvia cried as she chewed. "My father was out to dinner with a business associate, and he heard it while at the club. He came home immediately to tell me, and to wake up his lawyers, because if it is true he will in no way allow Dr. Gray to continue to court me under such false pretenses and that means that he will have to lay suit to the Gray family for grievous injury and—"

"*Sylvia*," Margaret said, more sternly than either of them knew she was capable. Sylvia's mouth closed immediately. "What were you told? What are people saying?"

"That Dr. Gray ravished you!"

"*What?*" The scrape of the chair as she jolted from her seat punctuated her surprise. "Ravished me?"

"That means that he—"

"I know what 'ravished' means, Sylvia," Margaret said tartly.

"Oh. I didn't know you'd had that kind of education," Sylvia replied, snappish. "But apparently there was a gentleman there who knew Dr. Gray, and claims he saw him and you . . . being inappropriate."

"Well, he's wrong!" Margaret cried. "There was nothing inappropriate."

Not that anyone could have seen, at any rate. The door to their private room had been closed when she had basically propositioned Rhys. And when he had stood, and taken her hand, and . . . had been about to do something when the door opened.

Had someone seen them? Seen how close they had been standing? Seen what was between them, when they were allowed to be themselves?

"Of course nothing happened," Sylvia said, her voice smooth and even. "You were alone with Rhys for no more than a quarter hour. You were in bed with me before the fire had even dimmed. And Dr. Gray is an honorable man. He would never—"

"Of course he would never," Margaret said, and she believed it. Much to her great dismay.

"And you would never either, I know." Sylvia reached forward to take Margaret's hand, but Margaret shied away.

"Margaret," Sylvia said with a chiding smile. "I do not hold you guilty for anything. Come now." Then, her face slowly fell. "Margaret?" she asked. "Did . . . did anything . . ."

The unspoken words were suspended, hanging between them in the air.

"Nothing happened between us," she finally said, trying to sound reassuring. "We are friends."

"Nothing happened," Sylvia repeated slowly. "But something could have. Couldn't it?"

Before Margaret could answer—before she could even

meet her friend's gaze—they were just as fortuitously interrupted as Margaret had been in that inn, as footsteps and shouting approached, and Chalmers burst through the door.

"Oh, Miss Babcock—" a mortified Chalmers said. "Forgive the intrusion, but there seems to be some kerfuffle at—"

"Let me past, you old codger!" A boy of about twelve said as he wedged his body through the space between Chalmers and the doorframe.

A boy with Rhys's sandy hair and dark blue eyes.

"I told you, his lordship is not at home this morning," Chalmers hissed. "You are the most impertinent messenger and I'll have a word with your employer—"

"He's not a messenger," Margaret said. "At least, I don't think so."

"He's not," Sylvia confirmed. "He's Benjamin—Benji—Gray, Dr. Gray's youngest brother. Our families know each other well."

Chalmers eased back, but only slightly.

"Miss Morton," Benji said, not even pausing to give a short bow. "Thank goodness. I have to speak to Lord Ashby, it's . . . it's important."

Sylvia raised an eyebrow. "Benji, the last time you said something was important, you released forty frogs in my father's study." She turned her eyes to Chalmers and explained. "We don't see the younger Grays often, but when we do, they often needle my father for having the gall to live on after having been shot. And Benji is being quite inventive."

"But someone's been shot!"

"Yes, my father," Sylvia replied, and waved her hand to Chalmers. "Miss Babcock and I were in the middle of a private conversation so, if you please . . ."

"Yes, miss," Chalmers replied, and grabbed the scruff of Benji's neck.

"Not your father—my brother!" Benji cried, and both women came to their feet.

"Shot? Dr. Gray?" Sylvia's hand went to her throat.

"Not Rhys. No, he wouldn't—" He wouldn't be so foolish, Margaret prayed. Not after the wars. He would never put himself in that kind of danger.

"Not Rhys—Daniel," Benji said, and wrestled his way free of Chalmers. "He fought a duel this morning over something Rhys did, and no one would tell me, but I have ears, and Rhys found Daniel just as he was shot and brought him back home—but he needs help from Lord Ashby because all the servants have the day off, and—"

"Shot?" Sylvia's voice got weak. She turned an unearthly pale. "Over . . . something Rhys did? Oh no. This is a disaster. There will be such talk . . ."

"No time for that now," Margaret said, cutting off Sylvia with one quick movement. "Chalmers, have two men and Cook sent over to Dr. Gray's residence as soon as they are able. Cook will know how to handle the cleaning and the kitchen to assist Dr. Gray. And the men can help move and carry as needed."

Chalmers gave a swift nod, then stepped away immediately, not bothering to excuse himself, a lapse that circumstance would easily forgive.

"Benji, you stay here and await Lord Ashby," she said. He would no doubt be incredibly underfoot in the Gray household at the moment, and in this regard, at least he would be made to feel useful. "Tell him everything you told us, and what has since transpired. Understood?"

Benji nodded, like a new solider who had just met his commanding officer.

"I must grab my cloak," Margaret said.

"Your cloak?" Sylvia asked, shocked.

"You're right, there's not time for that—besides, it is a very short walk."

"You're going to the Grays'?" Sylvia's eyes widened. "Now?"

"Now is when they need help," Margaret replied, stepping past Benji and out into the hall. "I may not be able to do much, but I can do something. They have no servants. At the very least I can boil water."

She had made it perhaps six steps before she heard Sylvia's light, quick steps behind her. "Then I am coming with you," she said. "I . . . I know how to boil water too!" Then . . . "Or, at the very least, I can figure it out."

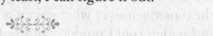

RHYS BURST THROUGH the door to the sitting room, where his mother and two of his three sisters waited impatiently. Never mind that it was an hour of the morning unusual to them all. Never mind that his mother was currently in her flimsiest of robes.

All that mattered was Daniel, currently half slung over Rhys's shoulder and barely holding on to consciousness.

"Move!" Rhys cried, causing all three ladies to jump up off the sofa. He laid his brother down as gently as he could. The groan of pain told him he was not gentle enough.

"Daniel! Daniel!" his mother cried, flurrying her hands. "What has happened?"

"What do you think happened?" Rhys muttered. "He's been shot. He challenged Haverford to a duel."

"Deserved . . ." Daniel said, then his words left him as his eyes became unfocused, staring at the ceiling.

"Shot?" his mother gasped. "Oh heavens, oh God— Daniel how could you, after your father . . . Oh, this is all my fault!" And then she collapsed, weeping onto Delilah's shoulder.

Normally, Rhys would agree that their family penchant for promoting recklessness had certainly played its part. But he knew that this was his doing, more than anyone else's. Short of pulling the trigger himself.

The man who did pull the trigger, Haverford, had fled immediately upon seeing that his aim had been true. He took with him his second in one of the carriages. He also took the doctor, Hill, who had nipped enough brandy to be confused as to who needed his attention. All that left Rhys with was Daniel's second, Vincent, to help him get his brother into the other carriage. Vincent, upon seeing the consequences of what a night of revelry and good times in London could produce, proceeded to vomit out of the window of the carriage on their way there. Rhys didn't care what happened to the lad, and told the carriage driver to take him away.

All that mattered was Daniel.

"Delilah, take Mother upstairs—have someone bring tea," Rhys bit out as he tore his brother's shirt away from the wound. The bullet had entered in the lower ribs, on the left side. He felt underneath his brother. No exit wound. The bullet was still inside. Thankfully, he did not have to worry about the liver. But Rhys prayed it had not hit his lung, else there was little he could do to prevent his brother drowning in his own blood. And his spleen . . . He took the spare fabric he had torn and held it over the wound, trying to staunch the bleeding. The pressure made Daniel grimace.

"Jubilee, go fetch Mrs. Watson—I'll need hot water, piping hot, to clean my instruments. And clean towels, and footmen to help me hold him down and—"

"But no one's here!" Jubilee said. Rhys's eyes whipped

up to hers. For once, his stoic sister looked like a frightened teenager—which is exactly what she was.

"No one's here?"

"Mother said that . . . that there was going to be a scandal and she didn't want anyone talking, so she gave the servants the day."

Rhys did not spare his mother a glance. Her sobbing was answer enough.

"What about Eloisa?" he asked. His eldest sister might be a thorn in his side, but she kept her head on straight—and he dearly needed someone steady to help him.

"She took Rory to see the horses at Tattersalls."

"Damn it all!" he yelled. Which was enough to bring the room to utter silence.

Rhys closed his eyes. Took one breath. Then two. Then turned himself into the doctor who trained on battlefields as gunshots landed at the feet of his tent.

"Jubilee, write a note to Lord Ashby—quickly. Have Benji run it over. This is what I need." He reeled off a list of manpower and supplies that he would require. Jubilee nodded, and ran as fast as her feet would carry her to pen and paper. "Delilah, get Mother out of here. She is in your charge. Understood?"

Delilah, white as a ghost and equally silent, nodded and pulled their whimpering mother away from the room.

Finally, the room was theirs. He heard noises from beyond—his mother's sniffles, Benji's pounding footsteps as he ran out the door—but really, it was just him and Daniel.

"Daniel," he said, still holding the cloth to the wound. "Daniel can you hear me?"

". . . Yes," was the weak reply. "Now I can, thank God."

Rhys's face split into a smile. He was conscious. He made a lame joke. He just might survive . . . if he could make it through what comes next.

"Daniel, can you hold this here?" He put his brother's hand over the cloth. "Just hold it; don't try to put pressure on it."

". . . Think so," Daniel said. Rhys moved his hand away, and Daniel's held steady. Good. Good.

"I have to arrange some things," he said. "But I am right here. I'm not going anywhere."

Rhys stood. There was a long table, a sideboard, just the right size for an operating table. He would take all the bric-a-brac off it, dust it down. Sheets—he needed sheets, to lay over the table, and he needed someone to help him move it to the center of the room, and to move Daniel on top of it . . .

"Rhys," Daniel said, his voice weaker than before. "What's going to happen?"

Rhys paused. He'd given the reassuring speech so many times. The one that started with, "You're going to be fine," and ended with "all will be well, you'll see." He'd even given it to his friend Turner—twice. First, when removing a bullet on the battlefield from his upper thigh, and then years later removing one from his shoulder. But he'd never done it for a family member. For his brother. For someone who looked up at him with eyes he'd known since he was born.

"You're going to be fine," Rhys said, clearing his throat. "But, annoyingly, that bullet did not leave of its own accord, so I'm going to have to fish it out of you. But not to worry, I've done it dozens of times." He took a deep breath. "All will be well. You'll see."

"You said . . . that being shot would make one wish for death."

Rhys stopped, crossed back to his brother.

"I want you to know . . ." Daniel said between hard

breaths. "I'm not wishing for it." He met his eyes. "I do not want to die."

Rhys could see everything in his brother that had filled the eyes of soldiers for centuries. Fear, pain . . . but determination. Some might call it stubbornness. But in Daniel, it was more than that. It was will.

"You won't," Rhys said, fierce. "I won't let you."

Then, before anything else could be said, the door opened, and of all the people in the world, Margaret Babcock burst through.

"Margaret?"

"Lord Ashby and Phoebe are out," she said, breathless. "Cook and some footmen will be right over, but we came immediately. What do you need us to do?"

Rhys locked eyes with Margaret. Her jaw was set. Her stance strong. And at that moment he was so utterly grateful for that strength—because it gave him something to rely upon.

"Oh my," Sylvia said from behind her. Funny, he hadn't even noticed Sylvia was there. "That is a lot of"—she gulped—"blood." She teetered a bit, became pale. "I ah . . . I need . . ."

"Where are your sisters?" Margaret asked quickly.

"Upstairs. Attending my mother."

"Sylvia," Margaret said, abruptly moving to her. "Go and see if Lady Gray needs any assistance, or consoling. She would be ever so grateful of your presence, I'm sure."

Her eyes still on the red splotch across Daniel's shirt, Sylvia nodded and quickly backed out of the room.

The door clicked quietly behind her.

"What do you need?" Margaret asked again.

Rhys met her eyes. He glanced down at Daniel. He had

drifted into unconsciousness and his hand had loosened on the cloth he had been holding to the wound.

"I need you to keep this cloth here, while I move the table."

"Then?"

"Then . . . I cut him open."

$\mathcal{M}$argaret hadn't a clue what she was doing. She only knew that she needed to remain steady. To do everything Rhys required, and not give in to any of those nerves that were threatening her stomach. So she moved quickly around the sofa and knelt beside Daniel Gray, and held the cloth in place. Behind her, she could hear Rhys pushing the table away from the wall and the clatter of the objects that covered its surface as they were tossed aside.

"We need sheets. Clean ones," Rhys said. "Stay there."

He stepped away, and Margaret remained where she was, holding the cloth to Daniel's side. She was alone for a minute, maybe two. Watching the shallow rise and fall of Daniel's breath.

Just keep going, she prayed. *Keep breathing.*

When Rhys returned, it was with a pile of cloth and a leather case she recognized as his medical bag. He came over and looked at his brother and at Margaret's hand on the cloth, and gave a short nod. Then he spread a clean white cloth over the table and sharply tied down the corners so it would not shift.

"Ashby's cook is in the kitchen," he said. "A footman has been sent after Ned, so he'll be here shortly, I'm sure. I wanted another footman here to assist me, but I don't know if the man will have steady enough hands. Do you think you can do it?"

Steady hands? What did he want her to do? Hold instruments? Hold down Daniel while he cut through the skin? Margaret managed to not audibly gulp. But she was strong—a lifetime in a garden had given her durability. And she was strong of mind—she would not be overcome by foolish flutterings or get queasy at the sight of blood. She would do what she always did in her garden—give herself over to the task at hand, and let nothing lead her astray.

She nodded once, a succinct answer to Rhys's question.

"Good," he said. "I'll take his shoulders, you take his feet."

With that order, she let go of the cloth—the bleeding had slowed to a trickle—and moved to Daniel's feet. Together, they lifted the limp body onto the table, setting him down as gently as they could.

Suddenly, a footman entered. He came in with a tray bearing a steaming teapot, a pitcher of cool water, a few bowls, a cake of soap, and a number of candles and candlesticks.

"Over there," Rhys said, nodding to a small side table as he retrieved a fresh cloth to blot the wound again. The footman put the tray down.

"Throw open the curtains," Rhys said. The footman hesitated. "I don't care about prying eyes, I need the light."

The footman pushed back the curtains. Luckily, they appeared to be clean and only minimal dust plumed into the air. Then Rhys turned to Margaret.

"Pour the teapot out into the larger basin," he said as

he worked to completely remove his brother's shirt with as little pain and disturbance as possible.

Once she had, he continued. "Take my medical bag, take the instruments out. Put them into the hot water."

"In their entirety?" she asked.

"Yes. This is as close as I can come to boiling them. Makes them as clean as possible."

She nodded, quickly picking out several small scalpels, pincers, and needle-thin prods, and put them into the basin. A small saw was next. She sent up a silent prayer that he didn't have to use that one.

"Now?" she asked.

"Now light the candles. As many as you can; we need as much light as we can manage."

Margaret nodded to the footman. Together they set out the candlesticks and lit them. Quickly the room became not only bright, but quite warm. Rhys discarded his coat, and nodded at the footman to do the same. Margaret did not wait for permission to roll up her sleeves.

"Now wash your hands, as thoroughly as you can," Rhys ordered.

Margaret did as she was told. Then she moved over to Rhys.

Daniel was shirtless on the table now. He was pale, so pale, and the wound a slash of red in that sea of white. He lay completely inert, only the increasingly slow movements of his chest indicating life.

Wordlessly, she took a cloth from the footman and applied light pressure to the wound. He nodded and moved over to the basin, taking his turn at hand washing.

"Dunno why we have to be so clean," the footman said to Margaret. "Time's a-wastin'."

"It's nothing I've been able to prove," Rhys said, overhearing. His tone was clinical, like he was giving his students a lecture. "But I've noticed that those patients treated with clean hands have fewer fevers and infection thereafter. And if the bullet doesn't kill him, a fever could."

The footman colored, mortified, and said nothing else. Rhys removed the instruments from the water—it was now cool enough that he could reach his hand in without getting scalded—dried them, and brought them over, laying them out on a cloth on the nearby tray.

"Ready?" he said. His voice was steady—not asking, but instructing. As if to say they were about to begin, and thus she had best be ready for it. She gave another short nod in reply.

He peeled back the cloth. Took a scalpel, and placed it to the wound.

Daniel, even unconscious, whimpered at the slightest touch.

"Come and hold his shoulders," he said to the footman. Rhys grabbed a long piece of wood from his kit. "Put this in his mouth," he told Margaret.

When the wood was placed, he put the scalpel to the wound again. This time Daniel whimpered and tensed, but he was being held down, and was weak enough that nothing could happen.

Quickly, but with precision, Rhys made an incision, widening the hole in his brother's side. He sucked in his breath, peering into the inky depths.

"I need more light—and I need this blood mopped up."

Margaret didn't know which to do first, so she did both. With one hand she dabbed at the newly bleeding incision, and with the other she moved a candlestick closer.

"Much better, thank you," Rhys said, his eyes never coming up from the wound.

Silently, they worked together like a pair of hands. He

would ask for something, and she would retrieve it. He poked and prodded with his devices, even with his fingers . . . searching the insides of his brother's body for the bullet. Finally . . .

"There you are," he said with a smile. "It's right up next to the spleen. I think it ricocheted between two ribs and lodged itself there. There are several bone splinters."

"The bullet is in the spleen?" Margaret asked. Over to the side, the footman gulped. He still held Daniel's shoulders as a precaution, but Daniel had stopped making any noise or movement.

"If you are going to lose your breakfast, leave the room," Rhys barked.

"No, sir," the footman said, taking deep breaths to steady himself.

"Good man. And to answer your question, Margaret, it's not in the spleen, but next to it. Lucky thing too. If it had penetrated the organ, well . . . spleens bleed like stink."

The footman visibly retched, but managed to hold it in.

"First things first. The bullet, then the bone shards." He handed Margaret an instrument that looked like a pair of scissors, but with blunt, folded ends. "These are spreaders. Hold them like so. And do not move."

He positioned the blunted ends inside the wound and spread them, giving him room to work. Margaret took them from him and held them as steady as she possibly could.

She held her breath as the pincers went in, but did not close her eyes. When the ball came out, thudding dully on the table next to Rhys, only then did she exhale.

Next he used thinner pincers to bring out things that looked like tiny matchsticks. The shards of bone, dangerously sharp. A half dozen, maybe more. It was painstaking, exacting work. And all the while, she held the spreaders steady. Gave herself over to the task at hand.

Finally, *finally*, Rhys puts the pincers down. "That's the best I can do. You can take those out now."

She lifted the instrument and stretched her hands. They had gone stiff from staying in the same position for so long. Rhys procured a curved needle and thread from his medical kit. He held the needle to the flame of a candle, then threaded it. Once more, he pricked his brother's skin. Daniel did not move.

"Er, if you don't think you'll be needing me . . ." the footman said, his eyes on the thread. "I wouldn't mind getting some air."

"Go," Rhys said, his eyes on his work. "Thank you for your help."

The footman nodded, and then, visibly relieved, stepped away, the door hanging open behind him.

As Rhys finished up the stitches, Margaret took the used instruments at his side and put them back into the basin, staining the water pink. She blew out candles, returned the room to normal. If only she would return to normal too. While she remained calm on the outside, her heart was thudding wildly in her chest; her body, so long held still, nearly shaking with energy.

Once Rhys was finished, they moved Daniel back onto the soft couch cushions, as gently as they could so as to not disturb the sutures.

"Now what?" Margaret asked as Rhys straightened.

"Now—"

Now, apparently, was when Rhys's mother burst through the door.

"How is he?" his mother cried as she came into the room. "We saw the footman leave, and he said it was done. What does he mean by done? Not—"

"No, thankfully," Rhys replied. "But he needs to rest.

Here for as long as he will tolerate, and then we will move him as carefully as we can to his bed."

"He's . . . he's alive, then?" his mother said, weak with relief. "My boy?"

"Yes," Rhys said, his expression turning softer. "He's alive."

His mother collapsed against Rhys's chest. He met Margaret's eyes over the top of her head.

She wanted to touch him. She wanted to reach across the room and take his hand, let him know the power of the strength he had just shown. She wanted . . .

She wanted. That was all. She wanted him.

And the way he was looking at her . . . perhaps he wanted her too.

"Mother," he said, releasing her from his arms. "Stay with him. If he wakes he'll want a friendly face. I'll go upstairs and tell everyone else the good news."

"Yes," his mother sniffed. "Yes, of course." Then she turned to Margaret, as if seeing her for the first time. "Miss Babcock," she said, crossing to her and taking her hand. "We don't know each other very well. But I know you must have been a huge help to my son. Both of them. Thank you, from the bottom of my heart."

Margaret didn't know what to say, so she let the lady envelop her in a wet hug. Only when Rhys spoke was she pried away.

"Mother," he said. "You know what to do?"

"Yes." His mother sniffled one last time, squaring her shoulders. "I have seven children, Rhys. All of you got sick, or bumps and bruises. I've sat vigil at bedsides half my life."

"That's all this is," he said gently as he lowered her into a chair next to the sofa, where Daniel's breath remained steady. "Just another bump and bruise."

"Jubilee and Delilah will be so relieved. And Miss Morton too—she was an angel to me, Rhys. Fetching, carrying, doing everything she could to help. You must know . . . how good she will be for the family."

He merely nodded as he gently closed the door behind them as they emerged into the empty hall. Wordlessly, he took Margaret's hand, and guided her into another room. A small study. Papers lived in neat piles, medical books and drawings scattered over the shelves. His space.

He pulled her in, closed the door behind them.

And took her face in his hands.

She had no time to think. No time to breathe. There was just Rhys, and his mouth on hers.

He held her steady, his fingers gently cupping her neck, his thumbs playing along her jaw as he drank her in. As if she was the water of life and he a beggar dying of thirst. She closed her eyes and let him drink. Let him slake whatever was inside him that was driving him to this madness. And was driving her to this madness too.

She laid her arms against his chest. He let one hand drop to her waist, pulling her against him. Lining her up against him. Chest to chest. Stomach to stomach. Thigh to thigh. She could feel every hard, long inch of him. It was beyond thrilling—it was utterly mesmerizing.

She let her hands feel him, let them explore. His chest. The thin lawn of his shirt. The hard planes of his back. He took the invitation to explore as well. Letting his hands gather the back of her dress, letting them drift lower, to the curve and rise of her bottom, sending sparks of nervous energy up her spine.

She went up on her toes, trying to find a way to take more. He backed her against the door, giving her everything she didn't know to ask for. His mouth opened—hers followed suit, tasting him. He pressed into her, giving and feeling, until they both were panting, lost to time and each other.

"In the inn," he breathed, his forehead against hers, his fingers delicate on the back of her neck. "You asked me what I wanted."

Her eyes drifted open, hazed with lust.

"This is what I want. This is *all* I want."

She took one breath. Two.

"And it's the one damned thing I cannot have."

He released her then, pushing away from the wall violently. Then frustrated, he ran a hand through his close-cropped hair and took a steadying breath. She watched as he resumed the mantle of doctor—professional authority settling across his shoulders, understanding and intelligence on his face. No one would ever guess what his hands—what his mouth—had been doing just moments before.

Except for her. For as he pulled open the door of the study, he gave her one last look. It hid nothing from her. All the want, all the pain, all the weariness was plain to see in his eyes.

And then . . . he was gone.

Leaving Margaret in the study. Not knowing where she should go, what she should do . . . or what on earth had just happened.

21

The next few days were tumbled together for particular households in Grosvenor. First, the Gray household restructured itself entirely around Daniel and his care. After his room had been properly prepared under Rhys's watchful eye, Daniel had been moved up to his own bedroom, where he was tended to by a stream of sisters and maids—the latter of which were quickly called back from their day off, gossip be damned said Lady Ashby.

Of course, the gossip was unending. A duel involving a Gray was enough fuel for society's fires; add to it that there was an actual injury, and well, it was a constant uproar.

In some ways, Rhys was glad of Daniel. Oh, not glad he had gotten shot, of course, but glad to have something that took all his attention and focus. Keeping track of Daniel's heartbeats, checking his wound for signs of infection, and making sure his bodily functions progressed on a normal course made it so the outside world could not enter his thoughts.

Thoughts that would tend to Margaret at a moment's notice, if given the opportunity. And then flooded into guilt, because of her. If he hadn't been so reckless with her at the inn, his brother would not be lying abed now. And if he hadn't kissed her after she had helped him with Daniel—kissed the dickens out of her—his body would not be in unendurable conflict.

One good thing was that at the Gray house, at least, the news of the duel drowned out any other gossip that might have preceded it—namely the rumors about Rhys and Margaret. Haverford showed himself to be rather green when it came to villainy, and turned tail and ran for the Continent. Or possibly America, where he could seek his fortune. Either way, he was not in London to defend his actions, and therefore it was his character that was raked through the mud, and his account of the evening at the inn that was called into question.

This was a relief to the Gray household, as well as to the Mortons. Sylvia's father, who had been red-faced and livid when he learned of the initial rumors, had barely been placated by his daughter's assurances that nothing of the sort had happened. And while they had been undercut by the way she hedged when she said she had gone to bed early, the true difficulty was everyone else knowing about it. So to have a duel fought in her honor (laterally, at least) was cleansing in one respect. Although his feelings on duels were, perhaps, a little less romantic than others.

"Damned glad that it wasn't you, Dr. Gray, who stood on that field," Morton told him, pumping his hand a few days later. "And that you were there to clean up this mess. That seems to be a forte of yours."

He tapped his cane against his thigh, reminding everyone of the scar that was put there, and the man who did the stitching.

"Thankfully Daniel seems to have avoided a fever," Rhys said equitably, allowing his mother to avoid answering. The Mortons had come to the Grays' as a gesture of solidarity, being among the first to call when Lady Gray had again opened up their doors, a few days after the incident, as they had taken to calling it. Enthusiasm for facing the public varied between family members. Delilah was of course front and center and eager to be seen. Jubilee was nowhere to be found—likely happily reading a book to her bedridden and therefore trapped brother. Benji was tasked with entertaining Rory in the gardens. Eloisa was there, but she was unusually silent. Every time Rhys glanced her way, she was watching him. Silently assessing. The only time she looked away was when the door would swing open, admitting a new guest to be received.

And they were flooded with visitors. For a family that had spent the past several years on the gray margins of scandal, and had only recently come to London, an awful lot of people seemed to know their address. And they all watched as Mr. Morton shook Rhys's hand.

And, under his mother's watchful eye, Rhys bowed over Sylvia's.

"Yes, of course," Sylvia murmured sweetly. Now that she was in her father's presence, she was completely demure. "It's wonderful to hear that your brother is recovering."

At that moment, new arrivals sounded at the door. The sitting room—the scene of the very dramatic surgery that had taken place only a few days before—was now host to several of London's more enthusiastic gossips, who had been lining up at the door when official calling hours commenced. As such, Rhys expected to see only vaguely familiar yet incredibly eager faces when the door was opened. Instead, he found himself staring at a potted plant.

"Er, this is for Mr. Gray." Rhys recognized Frederick, Margaret's assistant in Ned's garden. "I'm supposed to give it to—"

"Flower deliveries are in the back," his mother said, stern and yet mortified.

"Yes, but it ain't flowers," Frederick argued. "It's a ficus."

It was a ficus. A very short one, but on its way to becoming a tree. Hearty and simple. The sight of it made Rhys crack a smile.

"Hello, Frederick," he said. "You can give the plant to me."

"It's for your brother—the ill one," Frederick said. "From Lord and Lady Ashby, but really from Miss Babcock. She thought he'd like to see some green while he recovered."

At the sound of Margaret's name, Rhys's heart began to thud. He hadn't spoken to her since their one fleeting moment in the study, after she had been so very steady and capable assisting him. But oh—he'd seen her. Every time he closed his eyes, he'd seen the way her lips looked—those perfect lips, swollen from his kisses. The way the skin at the base of her throat pinked with heat at his touch.

Why hadn't she come herself? Because she knew the melee she would cause, the gossip they would create being seen together? Or . . . because he had told her he could not have her, and she didn't want her heart to break again?

But Frederick was still holding out the ficus, and everyone—all of London, practically—was watching. Gently, Rhys took it.

"Oh, Miss Babcock is so very thoughtful," Sylvia said.

"I agree—a very good sort of girl," his mother replied. "Although—"

"She's a true friend to our family," Eloisa said abruptly, standing up. "Why don't I take that plant up to Daniel? Relieve Jubilee of her duties—and relieve Daniel of Jubilee."

The room tittered good-naturedly as Eloisa came forward and took the plant from Rhys. Their eyes met as she passed.

"Escaping?" he asked under his breath.

"Forcing you to stay," she replied. "And face what's to come. Hold on tight, Rhys—things are about to get sticky."

As Eloisa passed through the doors, she pulled Frederick along with her, who was reciting a litany of plant care that he had no doubt been forced to memorize before leaving Ashby's.

Rhys turned back to Morton, whose jaw was set and his gaze assessing. And, Rhys realized, he was assessing *him*.

Suddenly, Rhys knew the real reason Morton was there. He was taking stock of their situation. Of where his daughter stood in Rhys's estimation. His mother, always shrewder than she played, knew this too, because the next words out of her mouth were designed to force the situation.

"You simply must come to dinner tonight," she said to Morton, putting on her very best smile and flattery. "You and your daughter. Just a cozy family meal. After all, I believe our families will have much to discuss." Then she raised her voice, making sure everyone could overhear. "And celebrate."

A few whispers and smiles behind fans fluttered across the room. Enough so Sylvia turned a very pretty sort of pink, and Rhys flicked his eyes to his mother, who met him steely glare for steely glare.

Anger flared in his chest. His brother was recovering upstairs, and she wanted to bring this up? She wanted him to have to face the circumstances of his life?

He could tell her no. He could embarrass his family and the Mortons in front of those ladies in London who delight in gossip. But he didn't. However, not trusting himself wholly, he decided to not say anything whatsoever.

His agreement turned out to be absolutely unnecessary in any case.

"That would be marvelous!" Morton boomed. "On behalf of myself and my daughter, I accept."

"I imagine that won't be the only thing you'll be accepting," his mother teased.

"Mother!" Rhys snapped, drawing no small number of eyes his way. "Miss Morton, I apologize," he said, turning to Sylvia.

"No, it's quite all right," she barely whispered, her face becoming an even deeper red. There was something about the way the girl was standing, half hiding behind her father, that made Rhys think she was as uncomfortable with the arranging of things as he was.

It was a thought that piqued his curiosity, and gave him a glimmer of hope. Unfortunately, that glimmer was quickly squelched by the way his mother gripped his arm.

"Wonderful," she said, smiling to Morton. "I think it's time we all broke bread together. My son agrees with me." She turned her eyes to him. Uncompromising. "It's time, Rhys."

So that was it. No more waiting, no more feeling the waters. He must take the steps forward that had long been laid out for him—whether he had agreed to them or not.

"Yes, Mother. I suppose it is."

※⁂※

MARGARET HAD SPENT the last few days unable to sleep. First, she was worried about Daniel. Never having seen, had, or performed surgery before, she was naturally curious to know the results of it. Luckily, the belowstairs network of servants crisscrossed Grosvenor, and Molly knew everything, down to the amount of tea the young man had drunk that morning.

"No fever at all, miss," Molly had said. "He's still weak, mind, but he's been able to ask for books and to have the curtain drawn back and the like."

Relief had flooded through Margaret. And also something else—a touch of pride. To think, she had been instrumental in saving someone's life. Although, to be fair, Rhys had done the bulk of the work.

Rhys.

Far more consumingly, her mind tended toward Rhys. About how he had been that morning, seeing him turn from his usual good-natured, go-along self into an authority, issuing commands, putting all his focus and learning into the patient who had lain pale on the table before him. The rush of power that had flooded through her, making her breath catch and her heart quicken, to see him work.

And then there was what came after.

She replayed those moments in her head so many times. Him taking her hand, pulling her wordlessly down the hall. The way those hands had then held her, the way his mouth had . . .

Suffice to say, sleep was not easy in coming.

So she worked in the garden. She didn't want to see anyone—although plenty of people wanted to see her. That same belowstairs network of gossip that kept her informed about Daniel's progress had told the world pretty quickly of her involvement in the matter. So they descended on Ashby's house—luckily Phoebe was able to ply them off onto her husband, claiming the needs of her child. If anyone thought about the overattachment of a parent who had two nurses and a nanny for her child, it was not mentioned. And Lord Ashby was so very gregarious and sociable he deftly fended off any questions about Margaret, Rhys, or bullets.

Once word got out that the Grays would be receiving

callers, Margaret had sent over the plant—a shrub that she knew would be difficult to kill . . . just like Daniel would, she prayed. She sent it over with Frederick, and hoped against her better judgment to have some news of Rhys.

She should have known better.

"Well, Frederick?" she said, practically tackling him when he came back from the delivery. "How was it? How was everything?"

"Fine, miss?" Frederick replied, giving her a look that said he thought she'd had a bit too much coffee that morning. He glanced at Phoebe, who was sitting next to her. They were in the conservatory, which had become as much a sitting room for them as any other. "Mr. Gray is recovering nicely, I'm told. His sister took the plant, put it in his room, by the window, like you said. And they know the precise watering schedule you laid out. I watched her write it down."

"Oh . . . so you didn't see . . . anyone else?"

"Not for too long, miss," Frederick replied. "They all seemed to be planning a celebration."

"A celebration?" Phoebe asked. "Already? I thought Daniel wouldn't be able to see people for several weeks, at least."

"Not for the younger Mr. Gray, my lady. For Dr. Gray. Something about a special dinner with the Mortons. Time for celebrating, is what I managed to overhear."

He moved over to the long table, where Margaret had potted the ficus, and began to arrange the tools to his liking. There was a neglected miniature orange tree that he had acquired from a neighbor who had disposed of it. All it needed was some pruning. Margaret was all set to praise him for his initiative and good eye, but she found her throat had gone dry.

"Special dinner," she repeated. "With the Mortons."

"Talk in the kitchen was that it was for the marriage. Dr. Gray and Miss Morton. Their cook was saying it was about time too. Although she was worrying over what kind of meat she could get at the butchers at this time of day."

"And when is this special dinner supposed to take place, Frederick?" Phoebe asked, not even bothering to be oblique.

"Tonight, my lady," he replied as he began to trim dead leaves. "I expect their kitchen maid will come around soon enough asking to borrow a few hands."

"Of course," Phoebe said, keeping a cool, watchful eye on Margaret. "Frederick, would you go tell Cook about the impending likelihood of said favor being asked? I'm sure she would appreciate the warning."

Margaret felt as if the world had stilled around her. As if the breezes coming in from the open French doors had frozen in midair, the rustling of the leaves had died. But she knew it wasn't true. She knew the birds chirped in the garden beyond. That the little clock she had found in the attic and polished up to sit on the shelf with the gardening books still ticked incessantly.

She was still here. And time had pressed on to its inevitable conclusion.

"Well," Phoebe said, still watching her. "I suppose it is time. Rhys has been putting off his future all summer."

Margaret could only nod.

"I wonder if he thinks it was worthwhile. Delaying the inevitable," Phoebe continued.

Margaret thought over every moment that had happened since she came to London.

All the ones that made her happy featured Rhys. Vauxhall Gardens. Stealing a dance at some party or another. The visit from the Horticultural Society. Greenwich. But then, she realized . . . all the ones that had made her unhappy featured him too. Featured the worry on his face. The way he was torn between her and Sylvia. She had to wonder . . . if she had not come to London, could she have spared him that pain?

But would she have forgone that pleasure?

"I cannot speak for Rhys," Margaret said quietly. "But I would not change it for the world."

Phoebe cocked her head to one side, considering. "I don't think he would either."

She turned then, regarded the room around them.

"Do you know, I have no talent for plants," she said. Margaret smothered a snort. "I know, you're shocked, but I don't," Phoebe said with a cheeky smile. "I like to paint, so I tend to think I have some kind of eye for potential beauty, but I had completely dismissed this room and the garden as nothing. I never saw it for what it could be. But then you came here, and turned it into this."

Margaret followed Phoebe's hand as it waved over the room. The light from the open and clean windows. The height, accentuated by tall plants in the corners and stagger shelves that allowed for smaller pots to be placed in random patterns. The furniture she'd had moved in, and mixed with the workstation and the growing things and curious objects she'd found neglected, and given new life to. It was a room that was as much outdoors as indoors.

And the garden beyond was alive with color and sunlight.

"I wanted to make the place special. To say thank you for your hospitality," Margaret murmured, for once not blushing.

"And you certainly have. I want to live in this room, all summer. But I would have never thought of this. I would have gone through my life not knowing that I could have such a place—if you had not come here. And while I would have been perfectly fine . . . I know my life would have been the poorer without it. Without you."

Margaret met Phoebe's eyes. Phoebe's hand fell over the top of hers. With a squeeze, she rose. "I have found that in all decisions, there is a single moment where things could go in a different direction than intended. And those moments are of the utmost import. They require . . . boldness."

"Boldness?" Margaret asked.

"Yes. Because once they pass, the path not taken can only become regret." With a sigh and a stretch, she turned toward the doors. "I think I'll see what Ned is up to. See if I cannot tempt him into being a gentleman of leisure for one afternoon."

And with that, Phoebe was gone.

Margaret was left alone in the beautiful conservatory with nothing but her roiling thoughts. Tonight, it seemed, would be the night that Rhys would make his engagement to Sylvia Morton official. But until he did . . . Until he did there was still a window. That was what Phoebe had been saying. A window of possibility.

And Margaret, she knew, was the only one who could open that window.

And she would need boldness to do it.

With a sudden flash, she realized just what form that boldness would take. But oh, she thought, blushing hard red, would she be able to do it? Would she ever have that courage? That lack of restraint?

Did she dare?

Yes, she decided. Yes, she could. Because if she asked herself what the worst that could happen would be, it was letting this entire summer fade into regret.

And she could not let that happen.

No matter what.

22

$\mathscr{F}$or what had been billed as a "cozy" family meal, dinner that evening was alarmingly elaborate, even by Lady Constance Gray's standards. When she had been one of society's best-known hostesses, she prided herself on throwing fabulous feasts, with risqué touches and dizzying entertainment.

And while there might not be any of her usual risqué touches (she was fully attired and her famed portrait was tucked away upstairs where no one else would see it), there was an alarming amount of food. And as for entertainment, well . . . Rhys was certain that was up to him to provide.

The entire family was present, minus Daniel, who was still too weak for such an event. Delilah and Jubilee sat to one side, doing their best to entertain the younger Miss Morton, Alice. At twelve, she was actually closest in age to Benji. But Benji had become uncharacteristically red and silent in the presence of Alice, stealing glances at the girl from across the table, and so it was left to Jubilee and Delilah.

Eloisa was sitting at his mother's right hand, always

ready to jump in with smooth conversation when a lull appeared. But there were not many. His mother and Mr. Morton were more than willing to fill the silence with reminisces, whether real or imagined, about the home county.

"And then there was the time that Mr. Stevens—"

"No, my lady, I do believe it was Mr. Robertson who—"

"Oh yes, of course, it was Robertson! And he left that poor dog alone for three days—"

"And when he got back from town, the dog had eaten everything in the larder and thrown it back up again!"

"The village talked of nothing else for six months!" Lady Ashby said on a tear-filled peal of laughter. "Oh, I tell you I longed for London then! Something other than talk of Mr. Robertson's dog!"

"I imagine London is eager to welcome you back, my lady," Sylvia said demurely from Rhys's right side. They had been placed rather prominently at the center of the table. And while it presented a picture to place them together, in truth it did not allow for much private conversation.

Thankfully.

Rhys knew what was expected of him tonight. He was to propose to Sylvia Morton, allowing for his father's return, and for Morton to solidify his standing in genteel society. It would make both their families happy, and presumably himself and Sylvia as well.

He just needed to convince himself to do it.

And to find a way to do so privately.

Because as much as his mother might enjoy a public declaration, Rhys was damned well going to give Sylvia a choice in the matter.

That morning, when his mother had basically said a proposal was forthcoming, Sylvia had turned red and given him a look of complete mortification. And it made him think that perhaps she had some hesitation when it came to marrying him. And while that might have been wishful thinking, even if she *did* welcome an offer, he would not do her the disservice of doing it publicly.

"You look like you've swallowed an eel," Eloisa said in a whisper as another course was laid out in front of them. Rhys was sure the food was impressive, but as he hadn't been able to eat a bite he was unable to vouch for it. Sylvia was distracted on his other side by something her father was saying, thus allowing his sister the chance to needle him without being overheard. "Do your best to not get sick on the table."

"I will try. And I'll thank you to not crow over me at this moment."

She turned to him. "I'm not."

He harrumphed.

"Rhys," she said, and he turned to see honest surprise on her face. "I'm not."

He felt all the righteous indignation he usually reserved for his most callous sister dissipating from his core. And for once, he felt like being honest.

"I never thought it would be like this."

"What do you mean?" she asked.

"I always thought when I married it would be for . . ."

"Are you about to say love?" his sister chided him.

"No," he replied, but his mind swam with *yes*. "I simply never thought it would be so . . . forced."

"Forced," she repeated. "Rhys, it's not forced."

He gave her a look that spoke what he couldn't say at that table, with his mother and sisters and potential wife present.

"It's not," she said. "You have a choice."

"Do I?" he asked. "Did I have a choice when you arranged for Miss Morton to come to Greenwich?"

"What are you talking about?" Eloisa's brow came down. "I had nothing to do with that."

"You're the only one who could have managed Mother to—never mind. Tell me all about this choice I supposedly have."

"It's not supposed," she replied, almost laughing, but then seeing the pain apparent on his face, quickly sobered. "It is not an easy one, granted, and Mother—and I, admittedly—will fight you tooth and nail over it, but you still have a choice."

"You mean where I choose between marrying someone I do not love, and estranging and disappointing my family to marry someone I do?"

It took Rhys a moment to realize what he'd said. But judging by the eyebrow that rose to the sky, Eloisa had heard it immediately.

Then, after a moment, "You're in love with her, then."

It was a statement, not a question.

"I'm going to do my duty by the family, so does it even matter?" he said, sullen and defeated.

Eloisa simply stared at him with wide, unblinking eyes. "God, I hope so."

Rhys didn't know what to make of that. And he would not have time to do so, because Eloisa quickly turned in the opposite direction and said, "I think it's time for us to retire to the sitting room. Don't you agree, Mother?"

"Retire?" their mother admonished. "Eloisa! The treacle tart was just served."

"Yes, but if we take our desserts into the sitting room, it will allow for more conversations. *Private* conversations," she said with a knowing wink to Rhys. A wink Lady Constance Gray did not miss.

"Of course!" she said, rising from the table with a clatter of silver on serving dishes. "Mrs. Watson, be so good as to have the treacle brought to the sitting room. We'll all have a lovely time there, eating our desserts. And, er, Rhys . . . would you mind showing Miss Morton the library before joining us? She was just telling me the other day about a book she would like to borrow."

With scrapes of chairs and a scurry of servants retrieving slices of tart, the whole party began the migration to the sitting room doors. As she passed, Eloisa whispered in his ear.

"Time to make your choice, Rhys. I hope you make the right one."

Rhys blinked after his sister, but she was gone just as quickly as the rest of them. Leaving Rhys staring down into the owlish face of Sylvia Morton, surrounded by hurrying servants.

"Miss Morton," he said, clearing his throat. "Have you seen our family library?"

"I . . . have not," she said tentatively.

"Would you care to?"

". . . Yes, Dr. Gray. Rhys. I believe I would."

A choice. Strange, he had been marching toward this for so long—avoiding it at every turn but knowing it loomed before him—he'd never really thought about *his* choice in the matter.

As he led Sylvia to the library, they passed the doors of the study. That door—on just the other side of it, he and Margaret had spent some of the most thrilling moments of his life. He paused, for less than a second, letting his eyes drift to that door as they walked past.

Then, as they continued down the hall, they passed a small table lain with family trinkets. Including a miniature of his brother Francis. Before he had left university, he had been tall and strapping, the picture of pink-cheeked English health. He had their mother's curls, and goodness knows he had been missed by her. Almost as much as their father.

They reached the library doors and Sylvia came to a stop.

"Oh . . . you know where the library is, then?" he asked.

"I was sent here a few times while you were saving your brother's life," she said. "Your mother kept suggesting things to distract her."

"Did any of them work?" he asked as he guided her toward a set of chairs by the banked fire.

"Not really," she admitted.

"I have not thanked you properly for your kindness to my mother during that time," he said.

"I was pleased to be of help," she said prettily, seating herself in one chair, allowing him to sit as well. "I know that I am not as staunch and eager to get my hands dirty as some, but I like to think I can be helpful in other ways."

"Yes," Rhys said, considering.

"In fact, I think that being a help is about being the kind of person another person can't be. To know to serve tea to guests while someone else carries on the conversation. People can work very well in contrast to each other."

"True," he said.

"Take us, for instance," she continued. "We are not terribly similar. We have different strengths, and different ideas for the future. But together . . . I think we would be splendid."

Rhys blinked twice. "I have to give you credit, Miss Morton," he said. "You certainly chance a boldness that I have not managed."

"You mean by speaking about our future openly?" she asked with an amused sort of smile. "I think at this point, speaking in generalities is a bit of a fiction, don't you?"

He nodded. And, he thought to himself, she had earned

that right. She had been told for years that she was to marry him. She had come here to London, danced with him, waited on him. Why shouldn't she have expectations of him?

"I think we shall rub along together rather well, don't you?"

They would, he realized. He could see it. She would sweep into his life in Greenwich, and organize it. There would be meals on the table and things dusted and callers. She would make him stop working for tea every day. She would encourage him to lecture in London, so she could come and visit friends and shop. She would avoid his laboratory like the plague—likely for fear of the actual plague—but otherwise they would build a very comfortable life.

And it made him so very tired thinking about it.

"Yes, we would rub along together well, Miss Morton. Except . . ."

"Except?" she prompted.

"Except . . . is it enough?"

And once the words were out of his mouth, he felt the rightness of them.

Her smile faltered, just at the edges. "Enough?" she repeated. "I . . . I don't know what you mean . . ."

"I mean, is it enough, Miss Morton? Sylvia. I worry that it's not. Rubbing along together. We both deserve more than that." He shook his head. "And to be forced into this to please our families—it's unfair."

"I don't understand," she said, her eyes falling to her hands. "I thought you liked me."

"I do. I think you a very worthy young lady. But . . . there is more to it than that."

She looked up at him from beneath wet lashes. "What more is there? Speak plainly, I beg you."

Rhys hesitated for a moment, not wanting to inflict any more pain on the girl than he had to. And that was enough time for a knock to sound at the door.

"Excuse me, sir," Chalmers said, sticking his head in. "But this note came for you. I would not have disturbed you, but I was told that it is a medical emergency."

Rhys, half annoyed, half relieved, crossed to the door and took the note from the butler.

"I was told it was an emergency by young Frederick, sir," Chalmers said low, making Rhys's heart quicken.

What could the young gardener-in-training's emergency be? But it only took a glance at the handwriting for Rhys to know that it was not Frederick who needed him.

Dear Rhys—it said, and the sight of his name in her hand made his pulse quicken.

> *This is how it all began, isn't it? We met, and then, not willing to let the conversation stop, wrote each other letters. As if we knew we couldn't be mere acquaintances. And so, what better way to say what I need to say than in a letter?*
>
> *And what I need to say is simple. It's good-bye.*
>
> *You have been my friend for a year now, ever since we began our letters. But it feels like longer than that. It feels like there has always been a part of my life reserved for you. For someone who knows how my mind works, because that's how his mind works, too. Someone who is so familiar, and yet it is our differences that make us curious about one another. What other friend in the world would have gone to the Horticultural Society for me? For what other friend would I have helped tend to his brother?*
>
> *You listen to my petty annoyances, and make me smile. I know the way your brow creases when you're*

listening to your patients, and the way it lifts when you laugh.

We take solace in one another. And we celebrate each other, as only the best of friends do. And as such, I would want to stand by my friend, and celebrate his new life with his bride, but I find that it hurts far too much. Because while I love my friend, I am also in love with my friend.

I love you. I've been in love with you longer than you know. Longer than even I knew. And I cannot separate that from the part of me that is your friend. It's all just one person. Just me.

I try to tell myself it will be easier for you too if I leave. For you and for Sylvia. But I know myself to be much more selfish. So I will head back to Helmsley and try very hard to not feel a pang of regret every time the mail arrives.

Unless . . . . there is a reason for me to stay.

A long time ago, when I was hesitant to step outside of my greenhouse, my mother would challenge me. She would look me in the eye and say, "What's the worst that would happen?" And then, once I told her, she would dare me to do it anyway. By naming the worst thing, it had been robbed of its power.

You have dared me to step outside of my greenhouse with every letter you ever wrote. I've been daring myself every single step of this journey to London. Every single step toward you. And so I dared myself to write this letter.

If you choose to give me a reason to stay, you will find me in the garden.

If you do not, know I will cherish every moment we had. They, and you, will not fade from my memory. And I will think on you fondly, and wish you happy.

All I ask is that you pose yourself this question:
what is the worst that could happen?

Love,
Margaret

The blood rushed through his veins as he read every word, drank in every drop of what she had to say. She had put her heart to paper, and he read it over and over. He wanted to memorize it . . . but he didn't need to. He could have written every word himself.

She loved him, he thought, letting the thrill of it course through him. And he loved her; it was undeniable. And leave it to Margaret Babcock to make him see his choice in the simplest of terms.

What was the worst that would happen? If he did not marry Sylvia Morton, his family would be unhappy. And the difficulties with her family would continue. It would put an end to any hope that things would go back to normal. But . . . that wasn't any different than it had been. The past several years had gone on, and it had become their normal.

But if he did marry Sylvia, and he did not go to Margaret right now . . .

She would leave.

And that is something he would regret for the rest of his life.

"Miss Morton, I am so sorry," he said, quickly folding the letter back up. "But I cannot stay."

She rose, clasping her hands tightly in front of her. "You cannot stay? When we are in the middle of our conversation?" she said, her voice as sharp as her face was pale. "A rather important one, if I may be frank."

Rhys knew he would have to break this girl's heart. He

would have to shatter her expectations. But it was better to have a moment of pain than a lifetime of it.

"Miss Morton," he said as kindly as he could. "There's nothing left to say. Perhaps if circumstances were different, I'm sure we would rub along together very well . . ."

He moved forward, and was surprised to see her give a brave sort of smile as her eyes fell to the note in his hand. Her mouth formed a perfect *O* of understanding.

"Dr. Gray, I understand completely." She wiped at her shining eyes. "You said it yourself, if circumstances were different . . ."

"Yes," he agreed as he walked to the door. "If things were different."

But things were different, he realized as he stepped out into the hall and toward the back of the house. Because for the first time, he was letting go of what everyone else wanted.

For the first time, he was daring to go after what *he* wanted.

He just damn well hoped she was still there.

23

*H*e wasn't coming.

Frederick had come back from delivering the letter almost fifteen minutes ago. And while Margaret had resolved to stay in the garden all night, that resolve fell away almost as soon as she entered the conservatory. Because surely it was not that difficult a decision.

Either Rhys read the note and came to her, or he read the note and laughed and showed it to all his family and Sylvia, who recited it around the dinner table, taking turns doing so in silly voices.

Of course, Rhys would not do the latter. But he might simply throw the letter in the fire, and marry Sylvia and live happily ever after, forgetting everything she had written.

And oh, how her heart hurt just thinking about it.

So she paced the conservatory. Lit a lamp. Then two. Then decided two was one too many and blew one out. Then she saw a bloom that needed pruning and quickly pinched it back. Then she realized she was in danger of getting dirt on her gown if she began to garden.

She sat on the couch. Forced herself to sit. She had dressed very carefully before she handed the letter to Frederick. She had chosen a gown of pink satin that Molly had been begging her for weeks to wear. She said it made her look radiant, and when she had seen herself in the mirror, it shocked her how much she looked like a woman. Not a gangly girl. Not an awkward, lanky, forthright person, but a woman. With length and curves, and skin that asked to be touched.

Where was he? Her heart beat in a strangely sluggish fashion—hard, heavy thumps, as if her body knew something her mind would not allow. Keeping her calm, knowing that she had done her part. The rest was out of her control.

And as the clock ticked into the sixteenth minute, she began to get philosophical about the whole thing.

She had laid it all on the line. Told him boldly that she loved him. Wanted him. She would not simply stand aside without having her say. That took more courage than she had known she had.

And because of that, she thought, she would never be fearful of anything again. Never would she have to dare herself to go into town, or to a dance in Claxby—although she would likely not dance very much. She only enjoyed it with certain partners. But she wouldn't stop herself from doing something because it might be awkward or strange. She wouldn't hesitate.

And when the seventeenth minute passed, she knew there was nothing more to be afraid of. The worst thing had been not only named—it had happened.

Nothing else would ever possibly compare, so why worry about it?

Of course, that didn't stop her from mourning the fact that Rhys was not coming.

She hadn't cried in a long time. Not since her mother passed. But now, as she sat on the edge of the sofa, she could feel the sting of it in her nose. Her breath hitching in her throat. She sniffled, trying to catch it before tears fell.

"I do hope you don't have a cold."

Margaret looked up with a start. There, standing in the French doors, thrown open to the garden, stood Rhys. Moonlight touched his hair and shoulders, making him look as if he had dropped out of heaven. But by the look in his eyes, he was wholly and completely earthbound.

She hiccupped on a smile. Then rose on legs she was surprised to find. "You're here," she said.

"Yes, I am," he breathed as he took two steps into the room toward her. "I . . . I came in through the garden."

"I thought as much," she said, wonder playing with the corners of her mouth.

"Snuck in, actually," he said, a little sheepish. If he had a hat, she had no doubt that he would have been worrying it in his hands. As it was, his eyes remained on hers, earnest. "I did not want to knock on the door and disturb Ned and Phoebe."

"They are abed," she replied, glancing up. Through the French doors, she could see the window to the master's bedroom, overlooking the garden. There was a single light still burning. "Or at least, they retired early. Life with a baby, Phoebe says, means sleeping when it is to be had."

"Yes," Rhys agreed. Then he hesitated a moment before closing the distance between them. "Margaret, I—"

"I wrote you a letter," she blurted out.

He blinked. "I received it. At a rather opportune time too."

He took her hand in his, brought it up to his lips.

"Oh?" she asked, her voice a little shaky as her gaze fell to where his lips pressed against her palm.

"Yes, it was just at the moment I had realized that I love you too."

A strange sensation tingled across her skin. It was as if hope exploded into happiness, one tiny pinprick at a time.

"What about Sylvia?" she asked, fidgeting.

"Oddly, I think she's happy for me. For us."

She let that tingling feeling cascade from the top of her scalp, down her neck and shoulders to her spine, where it settled in the exact spot that Rhys's other hand rested, at the small of her back.

She lifted her face to his, and with all her newfound boldness, closed the distance between them.

Her mouth met his with a blinding need. What started out as sweet quickly turned breathless. Hungry.

His mouth moved from hers to her neck, to the soft lobe of her ear, sending delightful sensations to places on her body surprisingly far away from his kiss.

She brought her arms up, holding fast to his shoulders, strong through the fine wool of his coat. Although the coat itself was annoying. It stood in direct contradiction to the one thing her mind could focus on clearly. One single word. *Closer*.

As one of his hands found its way into her hair, loosening the confection Molly had worked so hard on, her hands worked their way under his coat, seeking heat. Seeking skin.

"Mmph," was the only reply as her cool hands danced lightly against his flat stomach. She had found his shirt buttons and begun prying at them, finding her way to the soft skin she so unreasonably wanted.

But the shock of it had him pulling back.

"M-Margaret," he said between heavy breaths. "Wait. We should . . . possibly this is not the best idea . . ."

"Rhys," she whispered, holding fast to her recently discovered boldness. "What do you want?"

"I want," he said as she kissed the line of his jaw, "far too much."

"Perhaps a better question is ... what do you not want?"

"I ... I don't want to hurt you."

"You won't."

Another kiss, this time on his temple.

"I don't want you to regret anything."

"I won't."

He took a deep breath, took her head in his hands. "And I damned well don't want you to leave London."

Her eyes found his in the close dark. "Then give me a reason to stay."

One eyebrow went up. His hand stilled on her back.

"I dare you."

There was no question of anything anymore. There was no hesitation, no holding back. He pulled her to him, lifting her onto her toes. And suddenly she felt so very small—something she never had been—and protected. Just by the simple act of lifting her feet off the floor. And at the same time, full to bursting, as if the world could not contain her.

His hand found the back of her gown, the laces there. And with the skill of a man trained to use his hands in delicate work, undid them. The cool air hit her back for a mere second before the warmth of his fingers replaced it, sending shivers up her spine.

Shivering partially from his touch, and partially from the fact that she was not wearing any underthings.

A fact that Rhys realized when the dress, now loose on her body, fell to the ground. Leaving her in little more than her shoes and stockings.

His head came up. He let out a long, slow breath. And that one eyebrow went up again.

"Ah ... Molly said that the dress was built to be worn without undergarments," she said, knowing her face was turning as pink as the puddle of satin on the floor. "And that if I did wear a corset or a chemise it would 'ruin the lines,' whatever that means."

"Remind me to thank Molly later." He let his eyes fall from her face to her shoulders. Her breasts. And down, down, down . . .

For the first time that night her boldness failed her, and she gave into the desire to fold her arms over her body.

Ever so gently, he reached up and stopped her.

"You've never been naked in front of anyone before, have you?" he asked.

"No," she admitted. "Have you?"

The corner of his mouth quirked up, but infuriatingly, he did not answer. Instead, he let his hand slide up her arm, soft as silk.

"This is your anterior forearm. It has three muscles in it, two bones, and is perhaps the most gorgeous forearm I've ever seen."

"Really?" Her forehead crinkled.

"Indeed. Perfectly formed. Strong and soft. And this . . ." His hand drifted up to her shoulder, landing on her collarbone. "This is your clavicle, and it is amazingly graceful. And this," his hand drifted to the little hollow at the base of her throat, "is the suprasternal notch. And it is my absolute favorite part of your body."

"It is?" she asked, her voice a squeak.

"Well, so far. Would you like to know why?"

She gave a small nod. And he lowered his mouth to the hollow, and placed featherlight kisses upon it.

She gasped with pleasure, and felt her entire body relax as if drugged. She arched into him, curving herself to meet his annoyingly still-clothed body.

She let her hands again find those shirt buttons. And

again she loosened them, and slipped her fingers inside. And again, he paused.

"What's this called?" she asked, letting her palm slide across the planes of his stomach.

"Those are the abdominal muscles," he said, sucking in a breath.

"And these?" More buttons loosening. More skin exposed.

"Pectoral muscles."

"This?" Her mouth touched his shoulder, and his shirt hit the floor.

"Ah . . . the deltoid."

"You know an awful lot of names."

"Right now I'm shocked I can remember any."

After that, there was no hesitation. He was wearing far more clothes than she was, so she found herself learning several more names for parts of the human body.

The wings of the shoulder: scapula.

The upper thigh: lateral femoris.

And the truly delectable gluteus maximus.

Before they knew it, they were both divested of their clothing and standing in the moonlight of the garden's conservatory.

And the light let Margaret look her fill.

"Well?" he asked, a smile crooking the corner of his mouth, albeit a bit nervously.

"It's so strange."

"Strange?" he asked in a strangled voice.

"Seeing a person without clothes," she said, and watched as relief flooded him. "From here up, I know you. But from here down"—she let her eyes rake over his body—"you're completely new. Completely . . . tempting."

And tempting he was. He was so strong—not bulky, but

his lithe body was honed planes and taut flesh. There was a dusting of golden curls across his chest, flowing in a line down his stomach to his manhood, which stood out, honing toward her like a diving rod. It asked to be touched.

And so, having the curiosity she was born with and the bravery the moonlight granted, she did.

For Rhys, the moment her hand met his hardening flesh, he began to see stars. He hissed out a breath and stepped into her touch. How was it possible she was so beguilingly innocent and still so forthright? So hesitant and so sure? Her body exposed to him had been temptation enough—long, with high small breasts and a tapered waist that fell into the soft rise of her hips. But if she didn't stop what she was doing right now, this night was going to be over before it began.

"I'm sorry," she said, stilling her hand. "Does it hurt?"

"No," he said gruffly, putting half a foot of space between them. "But if I wasn't crazy about you before, I most certainly am now."

"Does this part of the body have a name?" she asked, and he looked down at her. And found her with a teasing half smile on her face.

"It does. And you'll be properly introduced. In a moment," he said. "But right now, come with me."

He held out his hand—and when she took it, he swept her up into his arms, taking her completely by thrilling surprise.

He took her the few steps over to the wide, soft sofa and placed her gently upon it. There were shawls and throws across the sofa, under Margaret. It made a nest, just for the two of them.

He knelt beside the couch, spread her hair across the pillows. Let his hands and eyes roam free.

She squirmed under his attention.

"Rhys . . ." she said as his palm drifted up her leg, to the sensitive spot at the back of her knee.

"Hmmm."

"Lie with me," she asked.

"Not yet," he said, letting his hands slide up her thigh. She forced herself to hold still. "I want to study this fascinating new subject that I—"

"Rhys. I dare you."

A grin spread across his face in the dark.

"Well, when you put it like that."

He swooped over her, lining his body up with hers, giving her his warmth. His knee fell between her thighs, and pressed.

She held fast to that delicious pressure like one born to pleasure.

His mouth found hers again, and this time their tongues darted and danced. She felt that haze, that sweet drugging climb over her body again. Giving it agency, and taking away all her usual awkwardness. She wanted to shift under him, so she did. She wanted to hold him closer, so she did. She wanted to touch him *there* again, and so she did.

He groaned against her mouth. But he didn't stop her this time. Instead, his own hand found its way to the soft patch of curls at the juncture of her thighs. And she practically came undone when his finger slipped inside her.

"So warm," he murmured, his voice a little shaky. *Want*, she realized. He wanted this as much as she, and was holding on with threadbare control. A ball of pride wound its way through her. She smiled against his mouth.

"What?" he asked.

"I just never knew I could do that," she said. "Make a man—make *you*—struggle."

"I've struggled with my need for you every day for the past year."

"For the past year?" she asked.

"Hell yes. Do you think I write three letters a week to just academic correspondents?"

She bit her lip, trying to hide her smile. He kissed where her teeth had just been, bruising, punishing, making her swollen.

His hand began moving against her, cupping her, teasing her. A little spot of flesh at the crown of her womanhood began to throb with want. His deep study of anatomy had been time well spent as he coaxed that little ball into a pulsing need of hot desire.

It became her center, that little spot. All her focus on it. All his. Because as his mouth dusted kisses along her throat, his hand kept playing . . . kept teasing . . . until . . .

"Let go," he whispered in her ear. "I dare you."

Something shattered in the air. Her body became electric, pulsing like lightning, pure energy made of desire realized. She came to him, she came for him. And she clutched him to her, wanting everything he could give.

"Yes, my love. Yes," he whispered in her ear as the last shudders wracked her body.

"What was that?" she asked.

"That was a woman's pleasure," he said. "Believe it or not, some in the medical community think it's a myth, but I think there is fairly conclusive evidence—"

"Well, of course a woman takes pleasure in this," Margaret said, coming up on her elbows, giving him a look of utter bewilderment at his colleagues' closed-mindedness. "If she didn't, there wouldn't be any reason to do it. The future of the human race depends upon it."

He barked out a laugh that echoed across the conservatory. She started, putting her hand across his mouth.

"Ned and Phoebe, remember?" she said.

"Not to mention an entire household of servants," he

replied, nodding. He gave her a gentle kiss, with more restraint than he knew he had. His blood was still pumping wildly, his body was still taut. But he did not want to push her.

He lifted his head. "We should stop," he said with ragged breath. "It's—"

But as he spoke, his body shifted over her. And the hard length of him pressed against her enveloping thigh.

"There's more," she said. It wasn't a question.

"Yes," he said, his eyes dark with need. "But at the moment you are still a maid, and . . ."

"Rhys." Her mouth found his in the dark. Tempting and persuasive. "I dare you," she whispered.

It was all she had to say.

The kisses deepened. Her body arched against his. And that length of him moved up her thigh, finding its way to the slick warmth it craved.

He held back for the briefest of moments. Then, with his lips still on hers, he pressed forward in one quick thrust.

She broke off their kiss, drew back, sucked in her breath. He came up on his elbows, took her face in his hands. Rained kisses down on her temple.

"I'm sorry," he said between kisses. "I knew it would hurt, I should have warned—"

"No," she said, stilling him. "It's all right."

It wasn't pain, per se, she realized. It was . . . fullness. Being stretched to a degree she hadn't known before. Her body, already prepared and pleasured, opened for him, adjusted around him. Took him in.

Slowly, so very slowly, he began to move. Long thrusts that sent frissons through her, that feeling of want building in her again. But this time in a deeper place, the pulses of pleasure coming from her core.

His pace quickened. His body pulling and pumping, holding himself over her. There was no one else in the world now. No other place. There was only here, and Margaret, and their bodies joining. Her legs wrapped around his hips, holding him and driving him deeper with each thrust. Her hands ran across his back. Her lips found his throat. His suprasternal notch, and she licked it.

That sensation in her core built higher and higher, and just as she thought she could not take anymore, everything came apart around her. She let the waves of pleasure—as she knew that's what it was now—crash into her, rolling against her over and over again.

As for Rhys, he held on as long as he could, waiting for Margaret. Waiting for her body to awaken again beneath him. But this time, when she broke, he let himself join her. He pumped into her, his body letting go with all the power it had, sapping him of his strength, and he collapsed against her.

He could feel his heart beating against his own two rhythms, both so fast they sounded like a staccato drum. Slowly, he lifted his head, placed his mouth on hers, kissing her gently. Reverently. Then, with aching tenderness, he rolled to the side.

"Oof," he said involuntarily. "A sofa this size is not made for two people to lie down upon it."

"Shame," Margaret said. "I'm now firmly of the opinion that all sofas should be made to fit two. If not more."

He hid a laugh in the crook of his arm.

"I mean," she said, her eyes wide with shock, "that more than two people should be able to *sit* on a sofa. Not lie down on it. Because otherwise, well, wouldn't it just be a chair?"

He began to laugh again, and she put her hand over her eyes. "Oh God, leave it to me to say something completely stupid and ruin everything."

"What are you talking about?" he said, his brow coming down. "You didn't ruin anything. All you did was once again display that marvelously logical brain. You wouldn't be Margaret without it."

"Really?" she asked.

"Really," he replied, and placed a kiss on her temple.

They lay there in silence for some minutes, letting their bodies calm down, letting the night and the room and the world filter back in.

After a time, Rhys shifted his position ever so slightly.

"Are you leaving?" she asked, drowsy.

"No," he whispered. "But my foot is asleep and I—oof!"

Margaret's eyes jarred open to find Rhys lying on the cold ground, having tumbled off the couch.

"Are you all right?" she said, her head popping up.

"Fine." He winced as he rubbed his backside. "But I fear the couch will no longer accommodate us. Come."

He held out his hand. She took it, sitting up.

"Where are we going?"

"Your room, of course," he said. "I'm not done with you yet, but I'll be damned if we try and wedge ourselves on that couch again. I want a proper bed. And a proper lock."

"A proper lock?" she asked.

"So we can take our time, without fear of being disturbed," he said, leaning down to look her in the eye, one winged brow going up. A temptation. A challenge.

"Grab your clothes," he said, planting a quick kiss on her mouth.

She rose to her feet and followed a short trail of shoes and stockings to the puddle of her gown on the floor. While she began to step into the pink satin, she saw Rhys heading to the door with a pile of clothes in his arms, wearing naught but a smile.

"Rhys!" she exclaimed.

"Yes?" he turned.

"Aren't you going to put your clothes on?"

"Why? I fully intend to take them off again immediately." His eyes raked down her body, and the pink dress she held against it. "And yours."

"You . . . you think to get upstairs to my room when we are both stark naked?" she asked. "Are you mad?"

"Margaret," he said with a mischievous smile. "I dare you."

※ ※ ※

AS RHYS DRIFTED off to sleep sometime in the wee small hours, an exhausted Margaret tucked against his shoulder, he realized he had never known such bliss. He had spent so long being told of his path—and avoiding it—that it was an amazement to create his own. He was in love. He was happy. He was content.

He was content as he snuck out of Ned's house sometime before dawn, after whispering words of love into a sleeping Margaret's ear. That contentment remained as he snuck back into his own quiet house and up the stairs, collapsing into his bed, and lulled him to sleep.

And that contentment lasted until the very moment that he opened the papers in the morning and discovered that he was engaged to Miss Sylvia Morton.

24

The sound of footsteps woke him. Usually he was one of the first people up in the house, so he missed the parade of siblings and attendant servants that made mornings chaotic in the Gray household. It must have been incredibly late in the morning, he realized, if all his sisters were awake.

But then again, he did have an unusually late night.

He stretched and smiled, thinking about it. Thinking about Margaret. About the giddy peace he'd known drifting to sleep in her bed, and the pang of regret he felt because she was not there now.

Although, it was better that she was not present. Other than the awkwardness of their unmarried state (something he planned to rectify as soon as possible), there was the fact that he had to have a very difficult conversation with his mother that morning.

He felt somewhat cowardly for having avoided it until now. And for having left poor Miss Morton to break the news to both their families that a proposal was not forthcoming.

Although, chances are she did not. She could have easily said that he'd had to leave due to a medical emergency—and it would be the truth, as far as she knew. Plus, it would delay an uncomfortable conversation with her father.

So, likely he would be walking downstairs to a parent who still expected him to propose.

And he fully intended to—just not to the woman she would prefer.

Yes, he'd done everything backward, he thought as he buttoned up his shirt and pulled on the boots that had been left out for him. But he intended to rectify it, and hoped to make up for it. Although regarding the latter, he had no idea how.

However, the former was his concern now, so he girded his loins and walked downstairs, fully expecting to find his mother in the sitting room. And she was. But he did not expect to see her surrounded by so many people.

Delilah stood on a footstool, with two dressmakers taking her measurements, while Eloisa supervised and Jubilee read the newspaper beside her. Bolts of fabric were laid out, carpenters and laborers were being directed by Mrs. Watson, who took notes from his mother as she did so.

"No, tell them it has to be a pergola—a beautiful outdoor island. Marble preferred, but granite will do in a pinch."

"Her ladyship says that it must be a pergola—" Mrs. Watson said to the laborers, only to be interrupted again.

"With carved figures for the posts!" his mother exclaimed. "Female figures. If they need a model, I have a picture upstairs that—"

"Mother?" Rhys interrupted, utterly bewildered. "What is all this?"

"Oh, Rhys!" his mother cried, leaping out of her chair and rushing over to him. She embraced him with all the strength she had, which was a surprising amount. "I'm so very happy. And glad you are awake—oh, you can help us with the cake! Cook, excellent, here you are!"

Rhys turned around just in time to avoid jostling Cook as she entered, bearing a tray of small cakes, all in different colors and flavors.

"Where should I place this, my lady?"

"Just over there—oh, Watson, do remind the men that we will need some kind of structure to hang boughs of garland off of—I was thinking a vine of blooms twined with silk." As Mrs. Watson turned to the men to relay those exact instructions, his mother once again spoke to him. "What do you think, Rhys?"

"About . . . what, precisely?"

"About the boughs . . . but also about the cake. Oh, I know it isn't usually the man's decision, but since I have you it would behoove us to cater to your tastes at least a little."

"Mother," he stated firmly, his gaze narrowing. "I have no idea what you are doing."

"She's rather obviously planning a party," Eloisa said, unusually subdued, from her place beside Jubilee. "Even you can see that."

"Yes . . . but what for?"

"For you, silly!" his mother exclaimed. "I know that it is uncommon for the groom's family to arrange the celebration, but as Mrs. Morton is no longer with us, and Mr. Morton is not . . . as familiar with society's ways as we are, I thought there would be no harm in taking the initiative."

"And the best news," Delilah said from her tuffet, "is that now that you are to marry, Mama says I can make my come-out! It's a bit late in the season for a formal debut, but I already have invitations to three parties this week!"

"We are all agog with joy," Jubilee replied, her head not moving from the pages of the *Gazette-Post*.

"You're just mad Mama isn't letting you come out too."

"Yes she is," Jubilee said.

"Mother—" Rhys tried to interject.

"She is?" Delilah started.

"Of course she is. I'm of age too. So I'll be right beside you, ruining your shining moment."

Delilah gasped and rounded on their parent. "Mama, that is not fair!"

"Darling, do be reasonable—"

"Mother!" Rhys ground out, bringing the room to a halt. "Am I to infer that you are planning a *wedding* party?"

"Yes."

"For myself . . . and Sylvia Morton?"

"Well, yes, darling," his mother said with a blissful smile. "Now, as for the cakes—are you a lover of chocolate? I can never remember which of you children disliked it."

Holy hell, his mother was taking this worse than he had expected.

"Mother . . ." he said as gently—but sternly—as possible. "I've decided that there will not be a wedding between myself and Miss Morton."

"Don't be silly, dear," she said as she inspected the tray of cakes. "I know you must be a bit nervous—I was when it came to my wedding too—but don't let a case of cold feet get in the way of everyone's happiness."

Rhys felt as if he were in an insane asylum. "No, Mother. This is not cold feet. There will not be a wedding."

His mother turned to him then and looked at him. Really, truly looked at him for the first time since he walked into the room that morning and the whole world had gone topsy-turvy. "Yes, there will, Rhys. It has been announced."

Something in his body shifted. Some kind of sea change

in his blood. While before, he had been bewildered, and trying to sort everything out . . . now he just felt fire.

"What do you mean, announced?" he said, his voice low and cold.

While his mother blinked and made fluttering noises, Eloisa slowly rose and took the newspaper from Jubilee's hands. Silently, she flipped it to the right page, crossed the room, and handed it to him.

There it was, in stark black and white.

> The Family of Lord and Lady Gray are pleased to announce the engagement of Dr. Rhys Gray to Miss Sylvia Morton, daughter of Mr. and Mrs. James Morton of Sussex. The wedding is to take place at the earliest possible convenience.

It was simple, straightforward. No cluttering details about whom the families were or how the couple had been introduced. It did not mince words, and therefore it brooked no opposition.

"We wish you quite happy," Eloisa said quietly. Rhys looked up, surprised to see her still standing by his side.

"Nerves of this nature are unbecoming on a man," his mother continued blithely. "It's always best to simply buck up and move forward. Now, the wedding should be no later than three weeks from now, don't you agree? I've already written to your father, and once he reads the letter I'm sure he will be on the first packet home and—"

"Mother, *enough!*" The words boomed out of him, rumbling like thunder across the sitting room. "I am not marrying Sylvia Morton, and Father isn't coming back. Ever."

Everyone went still. His mother looked as if he'd reached over and slapped her.

Watson proved her worth as a head of household, because she simply moved to the door and held it open, ushering out every day laborer, carpenter, cook, and dressmaker who littered the room. Leaving only silent, stricken Grays.

"He's not coming back," Rhys repeated, breaking the silence after the door clicked shut. "And he wouldn't, even if I did marry Miss Morton. He or Francis. They're in Italy, living high and not having to face any responsibilities. Why the hell would they come back?"

His mother's lower lip began to tremble, but she kept her head high. "Because . . . because of his family . . . and his wife . . . we need him."

"He's been nonexistent in our lives for years. Why would he think of our needs now? Over his own pleasures?"

"How can you think that way about your own father?" she asked on a sob.

"Because that's how he is, Mother," came a voice from the breakfast room entryway.

"Daniel, you should not be out of bed," Rhys said, unable to keep the doctor at bay, even in this most difficult of circumstances.

"Who can sleep with all this racket? Besides, I was hungry." Daniel was leaning against the doorframe heavily, but he was upright and moving under his own power. He turned his eyes to their mother. "Father thinks that nothing and no one can touch him. And that's what he taught the rest of us." He winced and touched his side. "I'm proof of that."

There was a newfound gravity in Daniel's voice. The sober transition from boy to man. It had only taken being shot for him to grow up.

On the other hand, his mother seemed still to be firmly in denial. "Just because your father refused to let his name be raked through the mud, and fought in a duel . . ."

"He fought that duel because he thinks he's always in the right. He presses his way forward and damned if he'll let anyone or anything stop him," Rhys replied, his voice a bit softer now. "Why on earth would he stay away so long unless it's what he wanted to do?"

Daniel came to stand beside him, leaning heavily on the back of the sofa.

"Rhys is right, Mother. Father isn't coming back, not even if there is a wedding."

For one spare moment, their mother's face fell, and Rhys could see everything. The pain, the anger she'd felt for years. The strength of will it took to keep on believing and working toward something . . . and the knowledge that what Rhys and Daniel said was true.

It made his heart ache. It made him want to wrap his frivolous, fluttering mother in his arms and not let go until she was safe and protected again. It made him furious at himself that he'd hurt her. And furious at his father for making him do it.

But just as quickly as it came, that glimpse into his mother's mind fled, and she stiffened her spine and raised her chin.

"I . . . I think you are being spiteful," she said. "Both of you. And you're just saying this because you're nervous about marrying a girl you don't know. But you will in due time and—"

Rhys threw up his hands. "I know Miss Morton well enough that I know I don't love her."

His mother threw up her hands in a perfect mirror of him. "What does that signify?"

"It signifies greatly when I *am* in love with Margaret Babcock."

His mother blinked. His two youngest sisters gasped— possibly a "really?" escaped from the unaffected Jubilee. But Eloisa . . . Eloisa just smiled.

"Well, if you felt that way about Miss Babcock," his

mother finally said after a few moments, "why did you ask the Morton girl to marry you?"

"That's what I've been saying," Rhys replied. "I *didn't*."

His mother became still as a statue. Except for the single eyebrow—so like his own—that rose in a flying wing of dawning realization.

"You did *not* engage yourself to Miss Morton?"

"No." He shook his head.

"But . . . you disappeared into the study with her, you were gone for some time . . . did you perhaps mislead Miss Morton?"

"In point of fact, I told her that I thought we would not suit," Rhys replied. Then his brow came down. "What did she tell you?"

"Nothing," Eloisa answered, the only one of his three sisters who could be moved beyond mute. "She said you had to leave on some kind of emergency, and that she and her father should likely end the evening. Her face was rather flushed, however, and her eyes were shining."

"Indeed—I commented to Eloisa that I thought she was trying to hide her happiness," his mother continued. "Then I made your excuses—although it was terribly rude of you to go; I can only hope someone was on death's door to pull you away—and they left."

Rhys turned narrowed eyes onto his mother. "And you just decided that there would be an engagement, no matter what, and sent it into the papers?"

She pulled back. "What? No!"

"Are you certain?" he asked. "Really? You're the one who kept saying it was time."

"Really, Rhys," Eloisa answered, exasperated. "The family of the groom does not make that announcement. It's simply not done."

"I rather thought it was you," his mother said imperiously. "I *learned* of the engagement from the papers. I thought you were being your usual recalcitrant self, not telling your family first. I had to run around like a mad-woman this morning, trying to find dress fitters for your sisters for the wedding, and we were thinking of having it done here in London—" She stopped herself when she caught a glimpse of Rhys's expression. "Of course, none of that is here nor there any longer. But it was in the *Gazette-Post,* for goodness' sake—of course I believed it!"

"I suppose this means that Rhys will just have to marry Miss Morton," Delilah said. "Oh well, do you think I should wear the blue silk?"

Rhys was about to say something snide to Delilah. As was, he was certain, Jubilee, Eloisa, and even Daniel. But it was his mother who jumped immediately to his defense.

"Delilah, don't be stupid! Your brother has been greatly wronged in this matter!"

Rhys swelled with pride. He couldn't hide his amazed smile. But Delilah wasn't smiling.

"We have all been greatly wronged! Don't you know what kind of scandal this will cause? To break an engagement that was printed in the papers? Mr. Morton could press charges against Father from afar—and against Rhys for breach of promise!" Delilah said.

"No promise was made."

"The promise was made on your behalf, years ago," his mother said weakly. "At least, the courts could see it that way."

Delilah was right. The words and their implications hung in the room. This false announcement caused all sorts of new trouble for his family, and dug up some of the old.

"It could have come from Mr. Morton," Daniel piped up from his observer's seat, lying on the couch. "He could have announced it, trying to press the issue."

Rhys looked down at the paper in his hands. Read the announcement again.

"But it didn't. The phrasing. It says, 'The family of Lord and Lady Gray are pleased to announce . . .'" he murmured. "The *Gazette-Post* is a reputable publication. They would not have published this without a note signed and sealed by one of us."

A look was shared around the room.

"Well, don't look at me," Delilah said with a sniff. "Even though I cannot come out until the wedding and are you certain you do not wish to marry Sylvia?"

"It wasn't her," Jubilee remarked. "She cannot spell 'at the earliest convenience.'" Delilah stuck her tongue out at Jubilee. "And I don't care who you marry."

"I'm hardly up to writing a letter," Daniel said. "And I haven't seen my signet seal since before the duel."

"You lost your signet seal?" His mother tutted. "Those are irreplaceable!"

"It wasn't any of us," Eloisa said. "Really, Rhys. That just leaves you. Perhaps you sent it last night and forgot."

"Hardly," he said. But his hand went up to his lip. An idea forming in the back of his mind pushed its way to the front.

Eloisa cocked her head to one side. "Oh no? What were you up to?"

He wasn't about to tell his sister his whereabouts the previous evening. Lest he wanted to kill them all with shock. Which previously, he would have thought as possibly nice. But now, all his family (all right, not Delilah, but give her time) was rallying to his side.

"It was not me," Rhys said, chewing over the thought that entered his head. "But there is one other option."

It was Jubilee who broke first.

"Well? Don't leave us in suspense! Who?"

25

"Oh, my darling friend!" Sylvia Morton cried. "How wonderful to see you! And on this happiest of days!"

Sylvia sat in the middle of the smart little drawing room in the house her father had rented for the season. Margaret had not spent much time here—Sylvia usually came to the Ashbys' when they spent time together—but the occasions she had been here, the room had not been quite so over-crowded by hothouse flowers.

"Where are all these from?" Margaret asked, reaching out to a Mediterranean bluebell.

"Of course you would ask about the flowers first!" Sylvia laughed. "They are from people."

"People?"

"Offering their congratulations." Sylvia took Margaret's hand and led her to the sofa. Margaret did her best to not let it shake.

She had woken that morning smiling, with the calm nervousness that was borne from being in love and being loved in return. Her body felt sore, stretched, and sated. Her mind spun with all the marvelous things her day would likely hold—Rhys coming to call. Being in the garden together. Writing to her father and Helen, and then to Leticia, telling them of her joy. She suspected her father would put up a bit of a fuss about not being consulted before his daughter decided to marry someone, but Helen and Leticia would talk him around. She was certain that all the joy bubbling up inside of her was visible, and she would be revealed as an unrepentant wanton with every intention of being wanton again, as soon as possible.

Of course, the wantonness would last only until she and Rhys married. And even though no question had been formally asked, the answer was well known. It surrounded them, bound them together, making them as much one person as any ceremony and paperwork might.

When she'd rung for Molly to help her dress, she was half tempted to ask if she looked as different as she felt. But Molly had been surprisingly grave faced when she came in.

"What is it?" Margaret asked, immediately concerned. "What's wrong? Is it Phoebe—or the baby?"

"No, miss," Molly said, wringing her hands. "I . . . I'm afraid that there is some news. But I don't know if it's my place to tell it. But oh! To think of you hearing it from someone else—especially that Miss Morton, I just can't allow it!"

A sudden thought struck her. Sylvia. While Rhys and Margaret had been declaring their love the night before, Sylvia had been left in the cold. Her evening had likely been one of quiet pain and sadness. And, once her father and family were told, rebuke.

"For heaven's sake, Molly, you must tell me now!" Margaret cried. "Did something happen to Miss Morton?"

"Aye, miss," Molly had barked out a pained laugh. "Yes, something happened to Miss Morton. Went and snared that Dr. Gray in her web somehow!"

At first Margaret didn't know if she'd heard her maid correctly. It took Molly bringing in the newspaper for her to believe that she was telling the truth.

"Lady Ashby is pinch-faced about it, and Lord Ashby ain't happy neither," Molly had said. "When he saw the paper he went around immediately to Dr. Gray's residence, but was told he wasn't at home. How the man could be running errands at a time like this, I'll never understand!"

Rhys wasn't at home. So her first recourse, her immediate reaction to go to him and ask him what on earth was happening, was unavailable to her.

Of course, she could have sat still. She could have waited until Rhys came to her. She could have gone down to the garden and dug a hole in the earth until it was deep enough to bury herself. Because that's what she wanted to do—she wanted to hide and ignore it until it went away.

But this . . . this was not going to go away. It had to be stared directly in the face.

"Molly," she had said, "I need to get dressed. I'm going out."

Molly had nodded firmly and put Margaret in her best day dress, and Margaret braided her own hair. She was not going to go into battle as anyone other than herself. Just . . . herself, wearing her nicest day dress, as trousers were not an option.

She'd come straight to Sylvia's. During the entire carriage ride, she went over in her mind what their conversation would be. There would be questions, on both sides. There would be accusations, recrimination. But somehow, someway, she would discover why that announcement was in the papers.

But now that she sat in the drawing room, surrounded by flowers, she hadn't a clue where to begin.

"You are here to congratulate me as well, I take it?" Sylvia said, beaming. "You see that, Alice, I told you my friends would come and see me."

Margaret realized that Sylvia's little sister, Alice, was hidden among the flowers.

"Friend," Alice replied. "Singular."

"I don't understand," Margaret said. "Who are the flowers from, if not Sylvia's friends?"

"Exactly what I've been saying," Sylvia replied. "Now, Margaret, I have no doubt you are curious as to exactly what happened."

"Yes," Margaret said, "I am."

"Well, it was just so marvelous. We were at dinner with the Grays, and it was a veritable feast. I wish I could describe every course to you, but to be honest, I was far too nervous to have any appetite." Sylvia sighed, looking up at the ceiling, as if reveling in the memory.

"Then," she continued, "Dr. Gray—well, I suppose I should be free to call him Rhys now, at least among close friends—asked me to accompany him to the library. And there, we talked about the future."

"The future," Margaret repeated, trying to keep track of every word, even as her mind reeled.

"Then he took my hand, and we became engaged!" she said.

"And . . . and you told your families and everyone celebrated?"

"No," Alice said from somewhere beyond the lilies. "She didn't tell us anything. Kept it a total secret. Papa didn't know until the first flowers began to arrive."

"I am the happiest of women!" Sylvia cried. "Oh, can you believe that my dear doctor and I are finally to be wed?"

"No," Margaret said slowly. "I cannot."

Her friend's jubilant smile faltered, ever so slightly. "I know, it is amazing."

"Sylvia," she said, "I cannot believe that you and Rhys are to be wed. Ever."

Sylvia's face went cold. "Why not?"

"Because I know he left you last night."

"Oh, that!" She flushed with relief, dismissing it with a wave of her hand. "He had to go attend to an emergency. I suspect being a doctor's wife, I will have to get used to such things."

"He left you last night to come to me."

Sylvia eyed Margaret frankly. Held her gaze for several seconds. Assessing.

"You were the medical emergency?" Alice asked curiously.

"Alice, I think I hear Father calling for you," Sylvia said, never taking her eyes off Margaret.

"No he's not."

"Yes he is. Go and see what he wants. Now."

Alice obeyed with all the grudging hatred of a little sister left out of the juicy parts of the conversation. When the door clicked shut behind her, Sylvia rolled her shoulders back and painted a smile on her face.

"Margaret," she began, reaching out her hand, and putting it over hers, "I think we can agree that this season in London has been a rather whirlwind experience for us both. You have been the greatest of friends to me. I would never have been invited to Almack's if it wasn't for you, or enjoyed so many other teas and parties. And I am glad that you got to experience a bit of London before you go back home to Lincolnshire."

Margaret remained silent. Waited.

"But I know that I am not your only friend. You and

Rhys have been exceedingly close. Closer, I think, than you were before your little trip here."

There was nothing for Margaret to do but nod in agreement.

"Good!" Sylvia replied. "I am happy for you."

"You . . . you are?"

"Yes, of course. I am happy that you have a close friend, and you were able to . . . experience that closeness." Sylvia squeezed Margaret's hand in her lap. "But I think we both know that Rhys needs a certain type of wife. Someone who knows how to run a household, and organize a menu, and will act as his emissary to the public. And obviously, Rhys realized that as well."

Margaret looked at the hand over hers, resting so comfortably in her lap—as if she was in charge and knew what was best. Slowly, Margaret withdrew her hand from underneath Sylvia's.

"I do not wish to cause you any pain," Sylvia replied. "I had hoped that you would attend the wedding as my maid of honor. But now I see that might be unfair to you."

Margaret could not look at Sylvia's face any longer. The way she appeared so smug, so concerned, and so full of pity. Instead she let her eyes drift over to the flowers. Dozens and dozens of bouquets. So many, some looked to be copies of others.

Margaret's brow furrowed. In fact, all the arrangements were very much alike. Same combination of blossom sizes, many had the same color schemes. Judging by the similarity of the arrangements, they were all from the same hothouse.

What were the odds that the flowers all came from the same hothouse?

"I think . . ." Margaret said, "I just realized why you have no friends."

Sylvia's face drew back. Lost all its pretend warmth.

"I know why *I* don't have many friends. I'm hardly conventional. But you . . . you don't have any. It's because you're deceitful."

"Of course I have friends . . . all of these flowers and—"

"You sent them to yourself," Margaret continued. "You don't have any friends. People saw through you. Better than I did, certainly."

"Better than you?" Sylvia said, her voice sharp. "What kind of friends would you have without me? *I* took pity on *you*. You would have stayed in your garden and never gone to any parties or balls or danced with anyone."

"I would have been perfectly happy with that. But you wanted things from me. And that's why you decided to keep me close."

"Things you weren't supposed to have!" Sylvia bit out. "I was supposed to be the one people admired! You're awkward and practically a recluse—you didn't even want to go out in society and you got invitations to *everything*! Of course, if I had blurted out I was rich beyond measure, I'm sure I would have been invited places too."

She crossed her arms over her chest, the jealousy coming off her in waves.

"And *that* is the only reason people copied your style or the Horticultural Society had anything to do with you, I'm sure! Because if it was just you—strange, blunt, tall as a tree—I would have been your *only* friend."

"Not my only friend," Margaret answered calmly. "There is Rhys."

"Rhys." The word came out like the hiss of a snake. "Yes, Rhys is your friend. But he will never be more than that. You may exchange letters from afar about botany and skunk cabbage, but there will never be any more than that."

"You are wrong." Margaret met Sylvia's eyes. "As last night proved. Rhys and I are far more than just friends."

For the briefest moment, the confidence faded from Sylvia's eyes. "Did he make you any promises last night?"

Margaret hesitated. "No."

"That's because he made them to me," Sylvia replied, letting her breath out in a gust of relief. "It doesn't matter what you feel, or what happened between you two." She leaned in, let the menace drench her voice. "It doesn't even matter if I have any friends or not. Rhys put that announcement in the paper—and that means I won."

"I wouldn't be so sure of that," came the voice from the door. Margaret's braid whipped around as her eyes found Rhys, leaning against the open door. Behind him was another man, whom Margaret did not recognize.

"Good morning, Miss Morton. I trust you are well," Rhys said, maintaining civility. "Of course I don't need to say good morning to Miss Babcock—after all, it's been mere hours since we saw each other."

Margaret's eyes widened, but her face split into a grin. Sylvia gaped openmouthed like a fish.

"Dr. Gray!" came another voice behind him. Mr. Morton trundled in from the hall, pushing Rhys and the stranger into the room. Morton switched his cane to his other hand so he could shake Rhys's. He squeezed his hand and pumped his arm like it was a well.

"So pleased to see you this morning. And I cannot tell you how happy you have made my Sylvia and me. Although I had expected you to speak to me before you went to her, but I suppose enough talk has passed between our families, eh?"

Rhys extracted his hand as gently as he could and stretched it. "Mr. Morton, your timing is fortuitous. I was just about to fetch you."

"Want to have that conversation after all, eh? Well, my

permission and blessing are granted, so no worry on that score, but—"

"No, sir. However, I was going to request that you resolve your dispute with my father."

Morton blinked.

"I fully intend to, young man. Just as soon as the vicar says you are man and wife."

"I am afraid the vicar will never say your daughter and I are man and wife. No, you are going to resolve your dispute with him, or I will have your daughter arrested for making a false claim."

Morton's cheerfulness disappeared immediately. "What do you mean?" he growled. "What is this nonsense!"

"Mr. Morton, I am sorry to tell you that I am not going to marry your daughter."

Morton's eyes narrowed. "You goddamned Grays. Is this another one of your tricks? I won't be made a fool of. Me or my daughter!"

"It is not a trick. The facts are that I never proposed to your daughter."

"That's not true!" Sylvia cried, perfect teardrops beginning to fall. "Papa . . ."

"Are you calling my daughter a liar?"

"Interesting question," Rhys said. "Let us ask a person with much more familiarity with your daughter. Margaret?" Margaret's head came up. "Do you think Miss Morton is lying when she says I proposed to her?"

Margaret looked from Sylvia to Mr. Morton to Rhys. "Without a doubt, she is lying."

"You have no say here!" Sylvia cried. "You just want Rhys for yourself!"

"Yes, and I her, but at the moment, that is irrelevant," Rhys said, causing Sylvia to nearly swallow her tongue. "I never proposed to Miss Morton, sir."

"Then what about the paper, eh? How did that little bit get in there?"

"Ah yes," Rhys replied. "And now it is time to introduce you to my guest. Mr. Morton, may I present Mr. Stuart Thorndike? We knew each other in the army, and now he owns and runs the *Gazette-Post*."

Mr. Thorndike gave a neat bow that was not returned by Morton. Instead, Morton came over to shove his purpling face into Thorndike's and snarl.

"Well? Who put the announcement in the paper?"

Thorndike raised a brow and shot a quick look to Rhys, who nodded. "I received a letter late last night, signed Rhys Gray."

"Aha!" Morton boomed out. He went over to his daughter and placed a hand on her shoulder. "I always believed you, my girl. You'll have your place in society, mark my words."

"Ahem." Rhys cleared his throat. "He said it was signed Rhys Gray. However, I did not sign it. Or write it. Or send it."

"Have a fine time proving that, won't you?" Morton rounded on him. "Meanwhile, I'll have charges on your father so fast he'll have to go to America to escape judgment!"

"Actually, it is particularly easy to prove," Rhys said, turning to Thorndike. "You brought the letter with you?"

"Indeed I did," Thorndike said as he produced it from his pocket.

Rhys took it and handed it to Margaret. "Now, Margaret, you and I have exchanged correspondence for quite some time. Tell me, is that my handwriting?"

Margaret only needed to glance at it. "No, it very much isn't." Then she peered closer. "It does look familiar, however."

"Familiar . . . like Miss Morton's handwriting?"

"I confess I do not know Miss Morton's handwriting," Margaret said. "But this . . . this looks like the handwriting of Sir Kingsley."

Rhys's winged brow went up. "Sir Kingsley? From the Horticultural Society?"

"Yes. The letter I received from his office, moving the date of our appointment?" she clarified. "Although, it turned out to be a mistake."

"I don't think it was a mistake." Rhys cocked his head toward Sylvia, who was beginning to squirm uncomfortably. "I think someone wanted to ruin your presentation."

Margaret turned to Sylvia then. "But, why?"

"Goodness knows," Rhys replied. "Jealousy of all the attention you were garnering, one supposes."

"You . . . you cannot prove anything!" Sylvia snapped.

"I can very easily get the Sir Kingsley letter," Margaret supplied. "I still have it. We can compare."

"Still—all that means is the same person who wrote that letter wrote the announcement. And neither was me, I assure you. Maybe it was Rhys!"

Rhys just looked at her like she was pressing her luck, which, Margaret thought with a hidden smile, she very much was.

"Let me see that!" Sylvia, agitated, snatched the announcement letter out of Rhys's hands. "Look, it even has your seal!" she crowed. "You *must* have written them!"

"Interestingly, my brother lost his signet seal just the other day. It was in his room before he fought a duel, and he hasn't seen it since."

"So the talk of a duel with your brother is true, then?" Thorndike asked.

"Yes, and please don't print that in your papers," Rhys asked. "And while we rarely if ever allow guests up to the family rooms, you were up there, Miss Morton, weren't you?"

Sylvia didn't know where to look now, so her eyes darted all around the space, hoping to land on something, anything that would vindicate her, but it was futile.

"You were there, helping my mother as she worried about Daniel. Sent to fetch tea from the kitchens and books from the library and anything else she might need. I would wager that on one of those trips you found your way into Daniel's room."

"That . . . that is so silly." Sylvia gave one last attempt. "Why would I take a signet seal?"

"I can only postulate," Rhys said.

"For this," Margaret said. "For this exactly here. Because before we went to the Ashbys on that day, you and I were discussing the gossip. And you asked me if the rumors about Rhys and me were true. You were worried Rhys was pulling away from you. And you thought you might need to push things along somehow."

"If we were to search your things, Miss Morton, do you think we would find a signet seal?"

Sylvia worried her hands, breathing hard and red with pent-up anger.

"Sylvia," her father said, his hand still on her shoulder— but it was no longer protective. Now that hand clasped her tight, as if trying to pin down a wily fox. "Answer the question."

She pursed her lips and sucked in a huff. "What do you want from me?"

"I want you to tell everyone what happened in the library last night."

All eyes turned to Sylvia. She chewed on her lip. "Fine," she bit out. "Dr. Gray made it clear that he thought we would be a compatible couple—"

"*But*," Rhys added, forcing her onto the correct path.

"But he no longer thought we would suit. He said that if circumstances were different . . . So I thought I would simply make circumstances different, and in time, he would accept his fate."

"Goddammit, Sylvia," Morton bellowed. "Did you really think you wouldn't get caught?"

"By all means, let's ignore the fact that she thought to trap a man into a marriage that he didn't want and instead focus on the bumbling way she did it," Rhys said.

"Rhys," Margaret said gently.

"Yes, of course, my dear," he said immediately. "You are right, that was unkind."

Thorndike swung his gaze between Margaret and Rhys. "Suppose I'll be putting in an announcement for you two soon enough, then."

Margaret turned red, but Rhys was all droll civility. "Of course. I have it written up if you'd like to take it now."

Margaret's eyes went wide. "Are you asking me to marry you?"

Rhys's brow came down. "Did I not do that already? Oh dear, it seems I missed a few steps." Then he walked over to her and kissed her hand. "Hold on for just a few more minutes, and let us finish with this madness, and then we shall proceed down that particular path."

Then he moved over to Morton and Sylvia. Sylvia's face was twisted into a mask of such intense dislike; Margaret had never seen her that way. But she had a feeling it had always been there, just beneath the surface.

"The afternoon edition of the *Gazette-Post* is going to print a retraction," Rhys said. "What you do now determines what that correction will say."

Morton kept his hand on his daughter's shoulder and his eyes on Rhys.

"Either it says that there was a misprint, and it is the paper's fault. Both families jointly say that there is no engagement. Or it says that the act was willfully done by a deceitful Miss Morton, who is facing the law for such scurrilous behavior."

"I imagine," Morton said after a few moments, "that a misprint is more easily explained."

Sylvia looked like she was about to explode, but still, she stewed in silence.

"Excellent," Rhys cried. "And now, you will write to my father, and to my father's lawyers, affirming that you will never pursue charges against him."

"I won't have him crowing over me from across our property lines, make that clear to him."

"Don't worry, I have a feeling he will take his time in coming home. But removing the fear my family lives under will make my mother happy. And let my sisters make their debuts."

Morton set his jaw. "You know, Doctor, out of all the Grays, I never thought ill of you."

"Nor I you," Rhys replied, and extended his hand. "I hope we can keep it that way."

Morton grudgingly took Rhys's hand and gave it one short, hard pump.

"Miss Morton, Mr. Morton," Rhys said as he held his hand out to Margaret. "I think it is time that we bid you good day."

They were halfway out the door when Rhys turned around and said, "Oh, and when you find my brother's seal, he would appreciate having it back, if you don't mind."

As the drawing room door closed behind them, the anguished caterwaul of a thwarted Sylvia Morton rent the air. Followed by the distinctive sound of vases breaking.

"Oh—those poor flowers," Margaret murmured.

"I know it is your nature," Rhys replied. "But perhaps the flowers should not be your first concern at this very moment."

Once they stepped outside, they breathed a deep sigh of relief. Thorndike was close behind them. "I admit, that bit of drama would sell a lot of papers," he said with a wink.

"I trust you'll stick to what was laid out—a misprint, and all that?"

"For the good turn you did my nephews, talking them out of dueling?" Thorndike replied. "I'll let my paper take the blame for as many engagements as you like."

Then he tipped his hat to them both and climbed up into his well-sprung gig. "Give my regards to Ashby when you see him," he said. "Never saw a man with that much luck in my life."

"Oh, that's not true," Rhys said, squeezing Margaret's hand, sending a flood of feeling through her. "You've seen me."

Thorndike grinned as the gig drove off. Leaving Margaret with Rhys, holding hands on the street in front of the Mortons'.

"Now what do we do?" she asked, a little shy for the first time since he'd burst into the drawing room.

"Well, I rode over with Thorndike, so I was rather hoping you had a carriage. Although it's a lovely day, would you rather walk?"

"No, Rhys," she said, smiling as she shook her head. "I mean, what do we do? With each other?"

Rhys blinked twice. "Of course! We suspended our conversation in the middle. Damn it all, this is the second time that I've forgotten to propose to you. I have to warn you, I can be forgetful when I am focused on something."

"Such as proving your innocence?"

"I was thinking more like when I'm mixing chemicals

for a medical treatment, but yes, this morning applies too."

She laughed. And he laughed, and then he pulled her closer.

"I was wondering, Miss Margaret Babcock," he murmured, holding her hand up to his lips, "if perhaps you would like to marry me."

She felt the kiss he placed on her hand all the way down to her belly, where it glowed. "I . . . I have some concerns," she said, biting her lip.

"Did you want me to get on my knee?" he asked, making to lower himself to the cobblestones.

"No, but . . . I worry that we are not suited. Or rather, that we are too suited."

"Too suited?" he asked.

"You say you become forgetful when you are focused on your work. Well, so do I—I can lose whole days, trying to track sunlight across a room or a soil's moisture dispersal." His thumbs began to rub over the back of her hands, making her calm and more nervous all at once. "And Sylvia brought up a good point that you need a wife who can keep your house. I am absolutely atrocious at it. I cannot make a menu to save my life, and I have no idea where the linens are in my father's house, and I've lived there my entire life. You think I would have found them by now. I am afraid I am not very good wife material."

Rhys threw back his head in laughter. Then he came forward and kissed her temple. "Oh, my sweet girl. Is that what worries you? Well, fear not—I earn a good enough living that we can *hire* people to do all the keeping house."

"But you need someone who can go out in society, and can act as your hostess as your career progresses and I—"

"I don't care about any of that. I have no grand ambitions to be the most sought after lecturer in London." He held her face in his hands and pulled her eyes to his. "I have the life I want. Except that there is this space that needs filling."

"Tell me about this space," she said, stepping into his embrace.

"Well, it's tall," he said as he placed a gentle kiss on her jaw. "With a long braid down the back." He gave her hair a gentle tug. "And we understand each other, like only soul mates can."

"Soul mates?" she asked.

"What do you think the best of friends are, if not soul mates?" Then he smiled, and let his forehead drop to hers.

"Will you marry me, my very best of friends?"

She did not need to give an answer—he knew it, like he knew his own heart. But she did anyway.

"Yes, best of friends. Yes."

EPILOGUE

The newspaper retraction was printed, as requested, in that day's afternoon paper. The nature of the retraction made it seem like it was a prank played by a younger sibling of one or the other of the families—and what are twelve-year-olds for, if not to occasionally take the blame? As such, there was no whiff of scandal, not one whisper about it.

News of the engagement of Miss Margaret Babcock and Dr. Rhys Gray was met by surprise by some, glee by others, and ambivalence by the vast majority of London society. There was some outcry that the richest heiress to come to London in years was no longer on the market, but then it was remembered that she was a rather odd thing—and she had not been seen at a party in at least a fortnight—so if she was uninterested in society, they were happy to be uninterested in her.

Sir Barty Babcock was, as expected, affronted that such a betrothal could have taken place without his permission. But he was quickly reminded by Helen and Leticia of all of Dr. Gray's goodness when he'd spent weeks attending to Sir Barty's gout last summer, and therefore he could not find fault with him. Plus, the letter Rhys wrote Sir Barty professing his feelings for Margaret, and his intentions to care for her, so touched the man he was found weeping like a baby over his morning pork.

Ned and Phoebe were elated, of course, and determined to host the grandest affair Rhys and Margaret would allow— which was, in total, twelve people. Margaret's father and Helen Turner made the trip down to London directly after receiving Margaret's letter, added to Rhys's family, Ned, Phoebe, and the vicar. There were actually thirteen people, if one were to count the baby, who slept through the whole fifteen-minute ceremony. Leticia and John did not come down, citing Leticia's condition and John's nervousness over impending fatherhood making him less than reasonable. Leticia wrote Margaret a beautiful six-page letter expressing her happiness. For her part, Margaret was more than happy to forgive the absence, as the wedding was held in Ashby's garden, and Leticia would have just sneezed through the whole thing.

But they saw John and Leticia often enough. Margaret, having responsibilities as her father's heir in Lincolnshire, had rooms converted at Bluestone Manor for Rhys's use as a laboratory. And Rhys gave Margaret a room that opened up to the very small back garden of his house in Greenwich. Also, with the hearty permission from their neighbors, she set about cultivating the overgrown, unused green that their townhouse lined. The offspring of her reblooming China roses flourished in that square.

Next to each other, Margaret and Rhys would study and putter and publish. Margaret became a frequent guest of the Horticultural Society. But as they would not loosen their rules about women being members, those meetings were unofficial, and usually held at Sir Kingsley's London residence.

Margaret would teach him how to dig a proper French drain.

Trips to London became more frequent, as not only had Rhys flourished in his lecturing, but his younger sisters had their come-outs, and they needed proper escort and chaperonage. Lady Gray liked nothing more than giving her son an office, and he was, as always, compliant.

Margaret and Rhys hosted the Ashbys at Bluestone every Christmas, and they and John and Leticia would gather around the fire, telling old stories, making up new ones, or doing nothing much at all.

And as much as they loved each other, Margaret and Rhys wanted their time apart too. But not too long. For as they worked, it was comforting to know that they were divided only by a door. And when one became lonely for the other, usually around teatime, they would write each other notes.

Dear Husband, Margaret's would begin.

Dear Wife, Rhys's would respond.

But always, always with the same signature.

Love,
Your best of friends

ear Reader,

My research for The Dare and the Doctor proved to be rather tricky. Not the doctor part, for I have physicians in my family who also love history and can answer questions about Regency-era bullet wounds. But, unfortunately, I do not have relatives in the horticultural arena. In fact, my personal skill with plants barely qualifies for the "oh yeah, we should water the ficus" level.

Thus I spent a great deal of time learning about the history of the modern rose, and discovered that the Regency and early-Victorian era was (pardon the pun) blooming with growth and change for rosarians. At the time, English and European roses were hearty plants, but their blooms left something to be desired, flowering only once and for a few weeks in the summer. (They were also not the tight-budded, many-petaled flowers we know today—that was another century of cultivation and evolution of roses, so neither here nor there.) Between 1750 and 1830, England began to import roses from the Far East—China roses and tea roses. These were significantly smaller, and since they were bred in a different climate, much more fragile, restricting them to being indoor potted plants. However, they bloomed all season long. The first person to successfully create a hybrid perpetual was a Frenchman named Jean Laffay, who is a towering figure in historical rose circles. I'm afraid I stole his achievement and gave it to Margaret, a few years before he released his hybrid perpetual to the world.

By the way, breeding roses is an incredibly involved process and one, I discovered, I would likely not have the patience for.

Hybrid perpetuals did change the face of the English garden, having the hardiness necessary to make multiblooming roses out-door plants, something to be featured and not just set up along hedgerows. No one would know this better than the Horticultural Society of London. Founded in 1804, the original members (like many societies of the day) were all men, and women were barred from joining—however, they were allowed to come to the public exhibition of their gardens in Kensington and Chiswick. In 1825, the head of the Horticultural Society was Thomas Andrew Knight, but he was far more interested in fruit trees than roses, so I gave his office to the fictional Sir Kingsley.

Today the society is known as the Royal Horticultural Society, and hosts the internationally renowned Chelsea Flower Show.

There is one aspect of research for which I was much better equipped, having actually been to Greenwich. Growing up in a naval family, I was exposed early to the meaning of Greenwich Mean Time and the amazements of the prime meridian. Nowadays, Greenwich feels like it's embedded in the center of Greater London, but at the time it was very much its own small, scientifically minded town, and separated from London proper by some distance. The Royal Observatory, where the prime meridian was founded, still stands, as does the Greenwich Hospital. At the time, it was a home for retired sailors ("hospital" referring to a place of hospitality, not medical care), and now it is a part of the Old Royal Naval College. I admit to not having done proper research three books ago, when I decided Greenwich and Greenwich Hospital were the perfect place for Rhys to set up shop, but I worked a bit of that confusion into the novel, hopefully well enough that you didn't notice.

There was plenty of other research that went into this story, including the layout of Vauxhall and the rules of faro and dueling, as well as just what flowers were in a typical English garden of the period and travel times to and from London. But the heart of The Dare and the Doctor belongs not to the fiddly details but to two friends who found in each other everything they never thought to wish for. And I hope you enjoyed Margaret and Rhys just as much as I enjoyed my time with them.

Happy reading!

Kate Noble

Can't get enough of Kate Noble?
Keep reading for an excerpt from the first novel
in the Winner Takes All series.

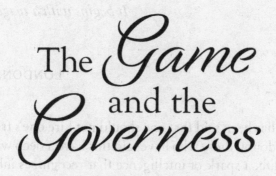

The *Game*
and the
Governess

Available now from

headline
ETERNAL

1

It begins with a wager. . . .

*I*t has been said that one should not hire one's friends.

No doubt, those who have said this have a deep wisdom about life, a spark of intelligence that recognizes inherent truths—or perhaps, simply the experience that proves the veracity of such a statement.

The Earl of Ashby had none of these qualities.

"Determined I was. And luckily, I came of age at the very right moment: I join the army, much to my great-uncle's dismay—but two days later, Napoleon abdicates and is sent to Elba!"

What the Earl of Ashby did have was luck. In abundance. He was lucky at cards. He was lucky with the fairer sex. He was even lucky in his title.

"Of course, at the time, I did not think of it as lucky, although my great-uncle certainly did, I being the only heir to Ashby he could find in the British Empire. At the time I would have believed that the old man had marched to the Continent and locked Boney up himself to thwart me."

It was nothing but luck that had the old Earl of Ashby's son and grandson dying in a tragic accident involving an overly friendly badger, making the nearest living male relative young Edward Granville—or Ned, as he had always been called—the heir to one of the oldest earldoms in the country. It was just such luck that had the old earl swoop in and take little Ned away from the piddling town of Hollyhock and his mother's genteel poverty at the age of twelve, and raise him in the tradition of the aristocracy.

"But then that French smudge manages to weasel his way off the island, and this time, true luck! I actually get to go to war! But the real luck was getting placed in the same regiment as Dr. Gray here. And— Oh, Turner, stop standing back in the shadows, this story is about you too!"

It was luck, and only luck, that found Ned Granville in the right place at the right time to save his friend and commanding officer, Captain John Turner, as well as seventeen others of their regiment on the last battlefield.

"So there we are in the hazy mist of battle on a field in Belgium, of all places—and thank God too, because I was beginning to think war was going to entirely be marching in straight lines and taking Turner's and Gray's money at cards—and suddenly, our flank falls behind a rise and takes a hail of fire from a bunch of Frenchies on top of it.

"So we're pinned down, waiting for the runner with extra ammunition to arrive, when Turner spots the poor runner shot dead on the field a hundred feet away. And Turner, he jumps up before the rest of us can cover him, and runs out into the field. He grabs the ammunition and is halfway back before a bullet rips through the meat of his leg. There he is, lying on the field, and holding our ammunition. But all I see is my friend bleeding out—so of course, I'm the idiot who runs into the fray after him."

His actions that day would earn him commendations

from the Crown for his bravery. They would also earn Ned Granville his nickname.

"It was just luck that none of their bullets hit me. And once I got Turner back behind the line, and the ammunition to our flank so we could hold our position, we beat the enemy back from whence they came. The next morning, Rhys—Dr. Gray here—had patched Turner up enough to have him walking, and he came over, clapped me on the shoulder, and named me Lucky Ned. Been stuck with it—and him!—ever since."

It was from that point on that "Lucky Ned"—and everyone else around him—had to simply accept that luck ruled his life.

And since such luck ruled his life, it could be said that Lucky Ned was, indeed, happy-go-lucky. Why bother with worries, when you had luck? Why heed those warnings about hiring your friends? Bah—so bothersome! It would be far more convenient to have a friend in a position of trust than to worry all the time that the servants would cheat you.

Yes, it might breed resentment.

Yes, that resentment might fester.

But not toward Ned. No, he was too good, too lucky for that.

Thus, Ned Granville, the Earl of Ashby, hired his best friend, John Turner, formerly a Captain of His Majesty's Army, to the exalted post of his secretary.

And he was about to regret it.

They were at a club whose name is not mentioned within earshot of wives and daughters, in their private card room. Well, the earl's private room. And the earl was engaging in that favorite of his activities: telling the tale of his heroism at Waterloo to a room full of jovial cronies.

But as the night wore on, said cronies moved off to

their own vices, and soon only three men remained at the card table: Mr. John Turner, silent and stiff-backed; Dr. Rhys Gray, contemplative and considerate; and the Earl of Ashby, "Lucky Ned," living up to his name.

"*Vingt-et-un!*" Lucky Ned cried, a gleeful smile breaking over his features, turning over an ace.

The two other men at the table groaned as they tossed their useless cards across the baize. But then again, the men should be used to such results by now. After all, they had been losing to Ned at cards for years.

"That's it," Rhys said, pushing himself back from the table. "I will not play anymore. It's foolish to go against someone with that much luck."

"It's not as if I can help it." Ned shrugged. "I was simply dealt a better hand."

"It would be one thing if you shared your luck," Rhys replied, good-naturedly. "But you have always been the sole man left at the table, even when we were playing for scraps of dried beef in camp."

"I take exception to that," Ned replied indignantly. "I do so share my luck. If I recall correctly, Turner here pocketed a number of those beef scraps."

"And little else since," John Turner said enigmatically.

Annoyed, the Earl of Ashby gritted his teeth slightly. But perhaps that was simply in response to his latest hand of cards, which the good doctor was dealing out.

"Besides"—Ned instead turned to Rhys—"you were so busy tending to the wounded that you likely saw little of those games. Even tonight you refuse to play for barely more than dried beef."

"As a man of science, I see little point in games of chance. I have long observed their progress and the only consistent conclusion I come to is that I lose money," Rhys replied with good humor.

"Little point?" Ned cried on a laugh. "The point is that it's *exciting*. You go through life with your observations and your little laboratory in Greenwich and never play for deep stakes. What's the point of that?" He looked over to the stern-mouthed Turner across from him. "What say you, Turner?"

John Turner looked up from his hand. He seemed to consider the statement for a moment, then . . .

"Yes. Sometimes life is made better by a high-stakes gamble. But you have to choose your moment."

"There, Turner agrees with me. A rarity these days, I assure you," Ned replied, settling back into his hand. "Honestly, you are such a stick-in-the-mud of late, Turner, I even thought you might stay home tonight poring over your precious papers—the one night Rhys is in London!"

"If you had chosen to go to any other club, I would have had to," Turner replied, his voice a soft rebuke. "You know the realities as well as I. And I am afraid being a stick-in-the-mud goes with the territory of being a secretary, instead of—"

The silence that fell on the room was broken only by the flipping over of cards, until Rhys, his eyes on his hand, asked in his distracted way, "Instead of what, Turner?"

A dark look passed between the earl and his employee.

"Instead of a man of my own," Turner finished.

The earl visibly rolled his eyes.

"Whatever do you mean?" Rhys inquired. As a doctor, he was permanently curious, yet amazingly oblivious to the tension that was mounting in the dark and smoky room.

"He means his mill," the earl answered for him, taking a loose and familiar tone that might seem odd from a man of the earl's standing, but that was simply how it was with Ashby. With these two men, the wall had come down long ago.

Or so he had assumed.

"He's been whining about it for three weeks now. And if you, Turner, had been a mill owner and not my secretary, you would not have been admitted even here . . . so . . ."

"What about the mill?" Rhys asked, looking to Turner.

"My family's mill has suffered another setback," Turner sighed, but held his posture straight.

"But I thought you had rebuilt after the fire?" Rhys questioned, his blond brow coming down in a scowl.

"I had, but that was just the building, not the equipment. I sank every penny into purchasing new works from America, but last month the ship was lost at sea."

"Oh, Turner, I am so sorry," Rhys began. "Surely you can borrow . . ."

But Turner shook his head. "The banks do not see a mill that has not functioned in five years as a worthwhile investment."

It went unasked about the other possible source of lending; the source that was present in that very room. But a quick look between Turner and the good doctor told Rhys that that avenue was a dead end as well.

"Turner maintains that if he had the ability to save his family mill, he would be far less of a stick-in-the-mud, and more pleasant to be around. But I have to counter that it simply wouldn't be true," Ned intoned as he flipped over an ace.

"You don't think that working to make my family business a success again, making my own name, would make me more of a pleasure to be around?" Turner asked, his dark eyes narrowing.

"Of course not!" Ned said with an easy smile. "If only for the simple fact that you would be working all the time! That makes no man pleasant."

"I work all the time now," Turner replied. "Trust me, running your five estates does not leave me many afternoons free."

"Yes, everything is always *so* important," Ned said dramatically. "All those fields that need dredging require constant updates and letters and all that other nonsense."

Turner's mouth formed a hard line. "Far be it from me to bore you with business matters. After all, I was not a man of learning when I took the position. I spent the first three years untangling the old finances and teaching myself the job."

At the mention of "old finances," Ned visibly tensed.

"Well . . ." Ned tried, judiciously dropping that line of argument. "At least here you are in London. There is more to do and see here, more to stimulate the mind on one block in London than there can be in all of Lincolnshire."

"More for you, perhaps."

"What does that mean?"

"What it means is that the world is different for an earl than it is for his secretary."

"Fellows," Rhys tried, finally reacting to the rising voices of his friends. "Perhaps we should just play cards? I would be willing to wager a whole farthing on this hand."

But they ignored him.

"Don't be so boring, Turner. Nothing worse than being boring," Ned said sternly. Then, with relish, "What you need more than anything else is a woman underneath you. Take your stick out of the mud and put it to better use for a few hours. That'll change your outlook."

"You might be surprised to learn that most women don't throw themselves at a secretary with the same frequency they do at an earl."

"Then *buy* one." Ned showed his (very good) cards to the table, exasperated. "There are more than a few in this house who would be willing to oblige. Mme Delacroix keeps her girls clean. Hell, I'll even pay."

"Thank you, no." Turner smiled ruefully. He tossed his cards into the center of the table as Ned raked up his chips. Lucky Ned had won again. "I prefer my companionship earned, not purchased."

"Which is *never* going to happen as long as you keep that dour face!" Ned took the cards on the table, gathered them up, and began to shuffle. "And by the by, I resent the implication that I am nothing more than my title."

"Now, Ashby, he didn't say that," Rhys began, but Turner strangely kept silent.

"Yes he did. He said that life is different for an earl than it is for a secretary. And while that is true, it implies that any good thing, any bit of luck I may have had in my life, is incumbent upon the fact that I inherited an earldom. And any lack of happiness Turner suffers from is incumbent upon his recent bad luck. Whereas the reverse is true. He is serious and unsmiling, *thus* he has bad luck. With his mill, with women, with life. I am in general of a good nature and I have good luck. It has very little to do with my title. It has to do with who I am. Lucky Ned." A beat passed. "And if I have been too generous with you, *Mr.* Turner, allow me to correct that mistake."

The hand that Ned slammed down on the table echoed throughout the room. Eerily quiet, shamed by the highest-ranking man there, the walls echoed with the rebuke. The earl was, after all, an earl. And Turner was dancing far too close to the line.

"I apologize if my words gave the impression that you owe your happier philosophy to your title and not to your nature," Turner said quietly.

"Good." Ned harrumphed, turning his attention back to

the deal. A knave and a six for himself. An ace for Turner, and a card facedown, which . . .

Turner gave his own set of cards his attention then, and flipped over the king of hearts, earning him a natural. But instead of crying "*Vingt-et-un!*" like his employer, he simply said quietly, "But the title certainly helps."

"Oh, for God's sake!" Ned cried, throwing his cards across the baize.

All eyes in the room fell on the earl.

"Turner. I am not an idiot. I know that there are people in the world who only value me because of my title, and who try to get close to me because of it. That is why I value your friendship—both of you. And why I value the work you do for me, Turner. It's all too important to have someone I can trust in your role. But I thoroughly reject the notion that *all* of my life is shaped by the title. I didn't always have it, you know. Do you think Lady Brimley would have anything to do with me if I was nothing more than a stuffed-shirt jackanape?"

At the mention of the earl's latest entanglement—a married society woman more bored even than Ned, and most willing to find a way to occupy them both—Turner and Rhys cocked up similar eyebrows.

"So you are saying your prowess with women is not dependent on your title either?" Turner ventured calmly.

"Of course it's not!" Ned replied. "In my not insignificant experience—"

At this point, the good doctor must have taken a drink in an ill manner, because he suddenly gave in to a violent cough.

"As I was saying . . ." Ned continued, once Rhys apologized for the interruption. "In my not insignificant experience, when it comes to *women*, who you are is far more important than what you have."

He took in the blank stares of his friends.

"Go ahead, call me romantic." Ned could not hide the sardonic tone in his voice. "But if a woman found me dull, boring, or, God forbid, *dour* like you, I would not last five minutes with them, be I a prince or a . . . a pauper!"

"Well, there is certainly something about your humble charm that must woo them," Rhys tried kindly, his smile forcing an equal one out of Ned.

But Turner was quiet. Considering.

"I promise you, Turner, it is your bad attitude that hinders you—be it with women or bankers. It is my good attitude that brings me good luck. Not the other way around."

"So you are saying you could do it?" Turner asked, his stillness and calm eerie.

"Do what?"

"Get a woman to fall for you, without a title. If instead you were, say, a man of my station."

Ned leaned back smugly, lacing his hands over his flat stomach. "I could do it even if I was *you*. It would be as easy as winning your money at cards. And it would take less time too."

It happened quickly, but it was unmistakable. Turner flashed a smile. His first smile all evening.

"How long do you think it would take?" he asked, his eyes sparks in the dark room.

Ned leaned back in his chair, rubbing his chin in thought. "Usually the ladies start mooning after me within a few days. But since I would be without my title, it could take a week, I suppose, on the outside."

Turner remained perfectly still as he spoke. "I'll give you two."

Rhys's and Ned's heads came up in unison, their surprised looks just as evenly matched. But Rhys caught the knowing look in Turner's eyes, and made one last effort at diplomacy between his two sparring friends.

"Turner—Ned . . ." Rhys tried again, likely hoping the jovial use of Ned's Christian name would snap him out of it, "I am in London so rarely and only for a night this trip. Can we not just play?"

"Oh, but we are playing," Turner replied. "Can't you see? His lordship is challenging me to a wager."

"He is?"

"I am?" Ned asked. "Er, yes. Yes, I am."

"You have just said that you can get a lady to fall for you within a week, even if you are a man of my station. Hell, even if you *are* me, you said."

"So . . ."

"So, we trade places. *You* become *me*. Woo a lady and win her. And I offer you the benefit of two weeks—which should be more than enough by your estimation."

"But . . . what . . . how—" Ned sputtered, before finally finding his bearings again.

And then . . . he laughed.

But he was alone in that outburst. Not even Rhys joined in.

"That's preposterous," Ned finally said. "Not to mention undoable."

"Why not?"

"Well, other than the fact that I *am* the earl, and everyone knows it."

"Everyone in London knows it. No one in Leicestershire does."

"Leicestershire?" Rhys piped up. "What on earth does Leicestershire have to do with this?"

"We go there tomorrow. To see about Ashby's mother's old house in Hollyhock."

"*Hollyhock!*" Ned practically jumped out of his chair. It was safe to say any hand of cards had well been forgotten at this point, as the wager currently on the table was of far greater interest. "Why the hell would I want to go to Hollyhock?"

"Because the town has a business proposal for the property, and the land and building must be evaluated before you decide what to do with it," Turner replied sternly. "I cannot and will not sign for you. That was a rule very strictly laid down by yourself, and with good cause, if you recall."

The trio of heads nodded sagely. The Earl of Ashby did have good reason to be cautious with his larger dealings, and to have someone he trusted in the role of his secretary. And the sale of his mother's house in Hollyhock did qualify as a "larger dealing."

"By why on earth should I go to Hollyhock now? At the height of the season? For heaven's sake, Lady Brimley's ball is next week, I would be persona non grata to her . . . charms, if I should miss it."

"I scheduled the trip for now *because* of Lady Brimley's party," Turner offered. Then, pointedly, "At which she has engaged Mrs. Wellburton to sing."

At the mention of the earl's previous paramour—an actress with a better figure than voice, but an absolutely astonishing imagination—Ned visibly shifted in his seat.

"Yes, well . . . perhaps you are right. Perhaps now is the best time to be out of London. If you catch my meaning."

"We catch your meaning, Ashby," Rhys replied. "As easily as you are going to catch syphilis."

Ned let that statement pass without comment. "Well, what's the proposal about?" Ned asked, before waving the question away. "No, I remember now. Something to do with a hot spring. But, God, *Hollyhock*. Just the name conjures up images of unruly brambled walks and an overabundance of cows. I cannot imagine a more boring way to spend a fortnight. I haven't even been there since I was twelve."

"So there is no reason to expect that anyone would recognize you," Turner replied.

"Well, of course they will recognize me," Ned countered. "I'm me."

"The physical difference between a boy of twelve and a man full grown is roughly the same as for the boy of twelve and the newborn," Rhys interjected, earning him no small look of rebuke from Ned.

"Even if that is so, I look like me, and you look like you," Ned tried, flabbergasted.

"And who is to say we do not look like each other?" Turner shrugged. "We are of a height, and both have brown hair and brown eyes. That is all the people of Hollyhock will remember of a boy long since grown into adulthood. And besides"—Turner leaned in with a smile—"I doubt you would find the trip to Hollyhock boring if I'm you and you are me."

"There is the small issue of your speech," Ned said suddenly. "Your accent is slightly more . . . northern than mine." Which was true; when Ned had been taken from Leicestershire and raised by his great-uncle, any hint of poverty in his accent was smoothed out. Turner, having been born in the rural county of Lincolnshire and raised in trade, had an accent that reflected his lower-class upbringing.

But it appeared he had learned a thing or two in the interim. When he next opened his mouth, Turner spoke with the melodic, cultured tones of a London gentleman.

"I doubt it will be a problem," Turner said—his accent a perfect mimic of Ned's!—with a smile. "But if someone manages to discern our ruse by my speech, I will forfeit, and you will win."

"Gentlemen," Rhys broke in. "This is a remarkably bad idea. I cannot imagine what you could possibly hope to learn from the experiment."

"I shall enlighten you," Turner replied. "If the earl is correct, he will have taught me a valuable lesson about life. If he can, simply through his *natural* good humor, win the heart of a young lady, then there is obviously no reason for me to take the hardness of life so seriously. But if he is wrong . . ."

"I am not wrong," Ned piped up instantly, his eyes going hard, staring at Turner. "But nor am I going to take part in this farce. Why, you want to switch places!"

Rhys exhaled in relief. But Turner still held Ned's gaze. Stared. A dare.

A wager.

"But . . . it could be interesting," Ned mused.

"Oh no," Rhys said into his hands.

"If we could actually pull it off? Why, it could be a lark! A story to tell for years!"

"You do enjoy telling a good story," Turner said with a placid smile.

"And I get to teach you a lesson at the same time. All the better." Then Ned grinned wolfishly. "What are your terms?"

Turner, even if his heart was pounding exceptionally fast, managed to contain any outside appearance of it. "If you are not so fortunate as to win the heart of a female . . ." He took a breath. "Five thousand pounds."

Rhys began coughing again.

"You want me to give you five thousand pounds?" Ned said on a laugh. "Audacious of you."

"You are the one that said life is nothing without the occasional high stakes."

"And you are the one who said one must choose his game carefully. Which it seems you have. Still, such a sum—"

"Is not outside of your abilities." Turner's smile grew cold. "I should know."

"And what if I am right?" Ned leaned forward in his chair, letting his cool voice grow menacing. "What if I win?"

Turner pricked up his eyebrow. "What do you want?"

Ned pretended to think about it for a moment. "The only thing you have. The only thing you care about." Ned watched as Turner's resolve faltered, ever so slightly. "I'll take that family mill off your hands. Free you to a life of better living and less worry." He mused, rubbing the two-days' beard on his chin again. "As it's not functioning, I suppose it's worth a bit less than five thousand, but I'm willing to call that even."

Turner remained still. So still. A stillness he'd learned in battle, perhaps. Then he thrust his hand across the table.

"I accept."

"No! No, this is madness," Rhys declared as he stood. "I will not be a party to it."

"I am afraid you have to be," Turner drawled. "You are not only our witness, but you will have to serve as our judge."

"Judge?" Rhys cried, retaking his seat as he hung his head in his hands.

"Yes—you can be the only person impartial enough to do it." He turned to Ned. "Is that agreeable to you, *my lord*?"

"Yes. That will suit me," Ned answered back sharply, stung by Turner's tone.

"So we are agreed, then? It is a wager?" Turner asked, his hand still in the air, waiting to be shook.

"It is." Ned took Turner's hand and pumped it once, firmly. "Good luck," he wished his old friend. "Out of the two of us, you are the one who will need it."

Secrets...

Lies...

Passion...

Be dazzled by a Kate Noble romance:

'Literally gave me goose bumps – goose bumps that never went away throughout the whole book. This is the kind of deep, touching read that romance fans search for'

Romantic Times

Don't miss Kate Noble's sparkling Winner Takes All books,

available now from Headline Eternal.

headline
ETERNAL